The Rebus and the *Parrot*
Book One

The Bottomless Well
of Time

C R Searle

Cover Design by C R Searle, composited by Ryan Ashcroft,
LoveYourCovers.com

Printed in the UK by TopM. Publishing.

Also by C R Searle

The Rebus and the *Parrot,* Book Two: The Secret of the Château Tollendal

The Rebus and the *Parrot,* Book Three: The Battle of the Stones

The Rebus and the *Parrot,* Book Four: The Children of the Ankh

The Rebus and the *Parrot,* Book Five: The Totem of Tarhuhiawaku

The Rebus and the *Parrot,* Book Six: The Masters of Time

Contents

Prologue 1
List of Characters 5
Chapter 1 13
Chapter 2 31
Chapter 3 58
Chapter 4 113
Chapter 5 123
Chapter 6 146
Chapter 7 156
Chapter 8 173
Chapter 9 180
Chapter 10 196
Chapter 11 205
Chapter 12 215
Chapter 13 220
Chapter 14 230
Chapter 15 245
Chapter 16 261
Chapter 17 281
Chapter 18 306
Chapter 19 316
Chapter 20 342
Chapter 21 358
Chapter 22 377
Chapter 23 390
Chapter 24 401
Chapter 25 411
Chapter 26 429
Chapter 27 440
Chapter 28 461
Chapter 29 476
Brief Historical Notes 481
End Notes 495

Prologue

A far distant beginning

In the fourth month of the Season of Sowing in the year 1336BCE[1] ancient Egypt was plunged into a brief, but bloody war when the army of the Pharaoh Akhenaten, The Sword and Shield of Aten, attacked without warning the Priests of Amun-Ra[2] at their temple stronghold in Thebes[3] and took their vast horde of treasure. A treasure rumoured to be far more than the gold, silver and jewels he took, an engine, machine, or device of some magical sort, he intended to use against the power of the priests. Who hated he had turned against their gods, but most importantly the Lord Seth, who they worshiped, and ruled, instead, in the name of Aten - the sun God.

But no sooner had he then he was betrayed by his once loyal and devoted wife, the fabulously beautiful, Queen Nefertiti and was forced to flee for his life, leaving behind his beloved second wife, Queen Kiya and their only son, Tutankhaten,[4] who we know today by his more familiar name, Tutankhamun.[5] A boy prince barely seven years old when his father left him, who Nefertiti, the mother of his six daughters and an artfully scheming, monstrously cruel and ambitious woman, hated with a murderous passion and planned to kill.

But before he attacked the temple at Thebes Akhenaten met in secret with Queen Kiya and gave her a magic wand disguised as a royal sceptre that would guide her safe to him, no matter where he was gone and no matter how long it took. But only if it was reunited with its twin, a second magic wand, which, disguised as a torque necklace,[6] he had the month before given to her eight-year-old sister, the princess Tefnut.

But Kiya was taken prisoner just hours after this meeting and held captive in a lonely cell in a small, mud brick village on the Giza Plateau until midsummer eve the following year, 1335BCE, when she disappeared from history without trace, never to be seen or heard of again. But no less than her sister, Tefnut, who, after a frantic journey up the River Nile from Edfu[7] into Africa was reportedly killed by the army of the Priests of Amun-Ra, the Drummers who had followed her, though not one of them returned to say they had.

Soon after this, Nefertiti was crowned pharaoh, taking the name, Neferneferuaten, but died in mysterious circumstances just months later, murdered, it was rumoured by the Priests of Amun-Ra she had thought to help with her treachery, leaving her eldest daughter, the princess Meritaten to wonder at the wealth and power that might have been hers had her father not turned against the priests and Tutankhamun, her half-brother, not banished her from Egypt forever, a few short years before his own mysterious disappearance in the Spring of 1327BCE, the year history records he died.

A heart aching, lonely banishment she didn't deserve that nearly three thousand years later found its faintest echo in the last of her royal blood-line, a fourteen-year-old boy and his twin sister born into genteel, if much hated poverty, in Naples, whose hearts thrilled to the stories their mother told them of the wealthy, high-born family they once were, the Meritati, as their name had long ago become.

Twins, who under the patronage of the mysterious Count de Montard were sent from Paris to England in 1796 to meddle, spoil and spy for the French who were once again Britain's mortal enemy in a war that was barely begun. A Britain where a chain of seemingly unrelated and unimportant events was just then beginning to unfold, events, which were to lead a group of newly met boys and girls, no older than they were, into one of the most thrilling, dangerous, and confounding adventures ever told.

One that would take them far beyond the world they had always known to frightening pasts and even more frightening futures in search of a fabulous treasure, the hiding place of which was inscribed on a golden Rebus by the Pharaoh Akhenaten before he died. A picture puzzle of ancient Egyptian hieroglyphs so impossible to read it had long puzzled the secret society of Templar Knights, The Sword, and Shield of Aten, who had found it hidden beneath Jerusalem's Temple Mount in 1128. Guided there, it was said, by a man who had, by the merest chance, found a papyrus scroll in a cave in Qumran,[8] which spoke of it and the treasure it kept secret. The first time in nearly two and a half thousand years anyone knew of its existence. And who, in their desperate bid to keep it safe from the Priests of Amun-Ra, who by some impossible means discovered they had found it, carried it safe from Paris in 1307 only to lose eight of its nine separately hidden pieces by a calamitous betrayal in 1736.

And might yet lose them all if, Lieutenant William 'Billy' Kepple, the newly promoted Captain of HMS Parrot, doesn't first escape the meddling clutches of Pierre Corbeau and his sister Madeleine Beattie, nee Meritati. Who by a chance misfortune have come into possession of a piece of the Rebus, though neither of them know what it is.

List of Characters

The Crew of HMS *Parrot*

Lieutenant, William (Billy) Kepple, newly appointed Captain of HMS *Parrot*

Acting First Lieutenant, Midshipman Samuel (Sam) Robinson

Midshipman, Herbert (Trucky) Spears

Midshipman, Arbuthnot (Butty) Anstruther

Tom (not *her* real name) Dimple

Polly Perkins, servant slave of Hesta Victoria Crookhampton and a girl with the most amazing gift of second sight

Polly's dog, Mister Pitt

Lemmuel (Lemmy) Peter Sharman, a ghost and grandson, though he doesn't know he is, of Johannes de Groot

Pilchard, Lemmy's pet Capuchin monkey

Andrew (Duffy) Duff, Bosun

George (Nipper) Ogden, seaman

Dancer Dyke, seaman

Archie Sparrow, seaman

Alfie Brown, seaman

Peter Owen, gun captain

Joey Warren, loblolly boy

Davey Harper, cooks mate

Marine Sergeant, Finch

Marine Corporal, Penny

Pascal (not his real name), Pierre Corbeau's spy aboard HMS *Parrot*

The Nanochromes of Nogoback

Gabe

Bibi

Raphie

Millie

Evie

Pierre Corbeau and his Gang of Thugs

Pierre Corbeau (Meritati) a French spy and protégé of the Count de Montard

Madeleine Rosa de Meritati/Beattie, Corbeau's twin sister and unhappy, pretend *wife* of Mister Henry Beattie

Jemmy Grub, Corbeau's vicious first lieutenant

Joby Dogget, Grub's trusted friend

Mister Badger, Grub's detested and much put-upon companion

Charlie Begg, Captain of the *Seahorse*

Midshipman, William Kettle, a scheming, traitor in search of the fortune his uncle, Vice Admiral of the Blue Oscar Kettle lost at cards

Emerging Characters

Vice Admiral of the Blue, Oscar Kettle

Lauder Trompe, Admiralty clerk and son of Constantine and Marianne Trompe

Henry Beattie, a distant cousin of Lauder's mother, Marianne Trompe, nee Lamb

Titus Dimple, Tom's much feared uncle and once Purser on Captain John Kepple's, *Cherub,* in 1783

Mister Ho, Titus Dimple's Chinese servant

Louis Barras, who betrayed The Sword and Shield of Aten to Montard in 1736, becoming his servant and creature

Vice Admiral of the Red, Crookhampton of Crookhampton Manor an old fool with a shameful secret of murder and treason

Mrs. Crookhampton, Admiral Crookhampton's daughter in law and daughter of Percy Wicker Selbourn, late of New York

Miss Hesta Victoria Crookhampton, Mrs. Crookhampton's vile, po-faced daughter

Percy Wicker Selbourn, Hesta Victoria's maternal grandfather and crony of Louis Barras

Lieutenant Galbraith, First Lieutenant on Captain John Kepple's, *Cherub*

Lieutenant Redman Crookhampton, Mrs. Crookhampton's missing husband, Admiral Crookhampton's only son and once Third Lieutenant on Captain John Kepple's, *Cherub* in 1783

Captain Bully Drier, late of his Majesties Royal Marines who served with Admiral Kettle, then Commodore Kettle, on board his flagship HMS *Dryad* in 1783, now a famed English detective

Damnable Puzzle, slave on Captain Mooney's, *Celebration of Yorktown*

Smarty Pants, slave on Captain Mooney's, *Celebration of Yorktown* and Damnable's twin brother

Malarkey Postelthwaite, Captain Hamilton's servant on HMS *Surprise*

Benoît, murdered by Louis Barras at Fort Edward (in Book Four: The Children of the Ankh) and the blackmailed cause of Admiral Crookhampton's shame and treason

Lord Dasheart, an aristocrat with powerful

7

friends

Adriana Caetano, the great, great, great, great, great granddaughter of Elizabeth Caetano, a school girl living in the Amazon port of Belém Pará, who in the present-day discovers the secret her family has kept safe for over seven hundred years

Pale Moon in the Morning, an Iroquois Indian princess

Soaring Eagle, Pale Moon in the Morning's grandfather and Shaman of their Beaver Clan

French Marine Cadets, Robert Camus and Allan Deauville, old friends of Billy he met at the siege of Toulon in the autumn of 1793

Incidental Characters

Captain John Kepple, Billy's dad, killed by pirates in the South China Sea in 1783

Mrs. Kepple, Billy's mum

Vice Admiral of the Blue, Oscar Kettle, Captain John Kepple's venal and cowardly squadron commander in the South China Sea in 1783

Lieutenant Hinton, an old friend of Billy's dad and First Lieutenant on board the *Agamemnon,* Billy's first ship

Miss Fry, proprietor, and teacher of the Lymington Dame School

Lady Ceridwen Denbigh, famed author

Reverend Cotton, the Chester Cathedral minister who gave Billy the reference he needed to join the navy in 1793

Doctor Charles of Lymington

Constable Brown of Lymington

Mister Dicks, Lymington's Magistrate

Mister Pyke, landlord of the Blue Posts Inn

Mister Elwyn Jones, Billy's mathematics teacher at the Blue Coat School, Chester

General Prem Rez, leader of the South China Sea pirates

Turzel Begg, Charlie Begg's dad, and until the Battle of Durdle Door saw him accidentally killed, Captain of the *Seahorse*

Albert 'Bloody Bones' Grub, leader of the Langstone Owlers (smugglers, pirates and traitors) and once owner of the *Seahorse*

Clary 'The Cut Throat' Grub, oldest son of Albert and brother of Jemmy

Senor Joes Caetano

Dirk de Groot

Incidental Historical Characters

Henry Adams, Master ship builder of Bucklers Hard

Lord Spencer, First Lord of the Admiralty

Admiral Sir Hyde Parker, Commander-in-Chief of the West Indies station

Commander George Brissac, Captain of HMS *Scourge*

Admiral Sir Peter Parker, Portsmouth's Port Admiral, a friend, but no relation to Sir Hyde Parker

Admiral Hood, Viscount Bridport, Commander in Chief of the Channel Fleet

Admiral Pole

Admiral John Colpoys

Admiral Gardner

Admiral Young

Captain Patton, Portsmouth's Transport Officer

Captain William Bligh, late of HMS *Bounty,* now Captain of HMS *Director*

Fletcher Christian, Captain Bligh's First Lieutenant on the ill-fated *Bounty*

Mister Evan Nepean, Secretary of the Admiralty

Captain Horatio Nelson, late of HMS *Agamemnon*

Mister Joseph King, Captain Nelson's Boatswain

Frank, Captain Nelson's Cook

Mister Fellows, Captain Nelson's Purser

Mister Lisbon, Captain Nelson's Master

Mister Roxburgh, Captain Nelson's Surgeon

Midshipman Josiah Nisbet, a friend of Billy on HMS *Agamemnon* and Captain Nelson's step son

Captain Edward Hamilton, HMS *Surprise*

Captain Edward Pellew, Captain of HMS *Arethusa* in 1795, Billy's second ship and the *Indefatigable* in 1797

Lord Montague of Beaulieu

Mister Jonas Hanway, umbrella maker and founder of the Marine Society in 1756

Colonel William Tate, American rebel

Napoleon Bonaparte, revolutionary General, and Emperor of France

The Duke of Wellington

Louis XVI, King of France

Pope Clement V

General Lazare Hoche

Howard Carter, who discovered Tutankhamun's

supposed tomb in 1922

Lord Carnarvon, Howard Carter's financial sponsor

Lief Ericson, the Viking Chief who discovered America for himself in the summer of 1004

The Drummers – Whose Names We Know

Jean-Léon Montard, Templar Serjeant at arms to Sir Mungo of Denbigh, known to all as the Count de Montard or simply, Montard

Barry O'Brien

Rochester

York

Tostig the Viking

New York Villains

Paul de Groot, owner of the recently sunken *Wasp* and the *Celebration of Yorktown,* son of Louis Barras

Captain Mooney, former Captain of the *Wasp* now the Captain of the *Celebration of Yorktown*

Mister Cripps, Captain Mooney's diminutive first mate

Louis Barras (father of Paul de Groot)

Percy Wicker Selbourn, Mrs Crookhampton's late father

Present-day New York Friends

Ethan

Isaac, Ethan's younger brother

Indie, Ethan, and Isaac's younger sister

Rudy, their friend

The Egyptians

The Pharaoh Akhenaten, Pharaoh of Egypt

Queen Nefertiti, Akhenaten's first and principal wife and reputed to be the most beautiful woman in the ancient world

Queen Kiya, Akhenaten's greatly beloved, second wife, hated enemy of Nefertiti and mother of the Pharaoh Tutankhamun, Akhenaten's only son

Princess Tefnut, Kiya's younger sister

Princess Meritaten, eldest daughter of Queen Nefertiti and ancestor of Pierre and Madeleine Meritati, though they call themselves, Corbeau and Beattie

Raneb, Queen Nefertiti's giant Nubian slave

Sahura, the Chief Priest of the Temple of Khufu and keeper of the sacred oracle.

Anutet, Sahura's son

Chapter 1

Ghosts Of The *Wasp*
And Other Things Past

1796

Our story begins, though it is one of many beginnings it might have claimed, with the building of a 10-gun brig[9] of war at Bucklers Hard that once famous and astonishingly pretty shipyard on the Beaulieu River in Hampshire. A brig her youthful Captain and equally youthful crew would everyday count their blessings it was, because it was a shipyard dominated by the foremost shipwright of his day, the master shipbuilder, Mister Henry Adams,[10] a man unsurpassed in skill and ingenuity.

But though he was, she by all accounts the most difficult vessel[11] he ever built with many a mishap between the laying of her keel and the rigging of her two masts and one so much altered from her original design by the shortage of wood, iron, rope, and canvas almost four years of everyday growing more violent war with France had brought to Britain, when she was finished, she looked nothing like the vessel she was meant to be. She was, in fact, something of an oddity: exceedingly small and cramped by comparison with most other brigs in naval service at the time though she was neatly trimmed and finished in every possible way.

But, with a tendency, Mister Adams observed when first he sailed her to wander in the most alarming way from her course regardless of wind or tide and despite every effort he made to take her where she didn't want to go. Now, as you might suppose there were many attempts to explain this particularly vexing phenomena before she was commissioned into the Kings service. Some said the problem was in her narrow and stunted hull, she was barely 20 feet wide in the beam[12] and just 80 feet long from bow to stern.[13] Others said the fault was in the snug set of her eighteen sails, the spread of her trysail[14] being altogether too big for her mainmast. And still others said it was her shallow draft, she sat just twelve feet in the water and the weight of too many heavy guns she carried. But there were others too, men of darker and more forbidding mood who swore the problem was in her timbers. Timbers which had been salvaged from the wreck of the *Wasp*, an American merchant ship which foundered in puzzling circumstances on the sands of Guernsey's notorious Vazon Bay in the late summer of '95. Timbers, they said with looks of dark dismay, soaked in the blood of her lost crew, men who could not or would not rest until those who now sailed on her had joined them in their watery grave. She was, they said, a *ghost* ship.

To say that this was something of a tall story, a wild exaggeration, is an understatement given the records clearly show that, except for her cabin boy, a cross-eyed lad called, Lemmy and his pet monkey, Pilchard, all the *Wasp's* crew, including two newly purchased Zanzibar slaves, named Smarty Pants and Damnable Puzzle, were rescued and spent a delightfully restful July regaling the locals with stories of their near disaster in the taverns of St Peter Port, before they took passage back to New York. But despite this blatant untruth, the story took hold and in a short time became a legend that no one was inclined to deny.

But ghost ship or no, when she was completed in all her many thousands of precisely fitted parts[15] on Monday, December 12 1796, a gloomy, windswept, snow-blown, bitter cold day that kept most of Bucklers Hard safe indoors beside their cosy, roaring fires, she was named HMS *Parrot* by a very well connected, but decidedly potty old Admiral.[16] Who was encouraged in his rather playful, some said, ridiculously unheroic choice of name for a Kings ship of war by his spoilt and overbearing granddaughter, Hesta Victoria. Who did so for her own silly, giggling, snorting like a pig amusement and dislike of anything to do with his majesties royal navy.

A strange affectation of mind for one so very young - she was only just turned fourteen last October, in those fervently patriotic times, but one that was explained, in only in part, by the resentment and hostility she felt towards their Lords of the Admiralty.[17] Who, she and her mother - a bitter woman whose hateful prejudice it mostly was, steadfastly claimed refused to support her grandfather's elevation to the peerage they both so desperately wanted *themselves*.

But there was another reason for their malicious spite, one that has a far more pressing claim upon our story than the denial of a hoped for minor peerage, hurtful though that probably was, which cut the family Crookhampton to the quick at its every mention – and it was almost every day mentioned. The grievance they claimed was this, that in the closing days of the American War of Independence (Rebellion/Civil War)[18] - a war the British lost with a disgraceful lack of good grace and smart to this day they did, not surprisingly really because they won most of the battles they fought against the American's, who were mostly British, despite they claimed they weren't, her mother's family, who had been New York residents for over a hundred and fifty years, had been robbed of their vast American fortune by the criminal inaction of an English[19] royal navy Captain.

Who, Mrs, Crookhampton claimed with a violently spluttering, red faced indignation, and fanciful disregard for the truth to anyone who would listen to her ceaseless prattling on about it, had refused to rescue them from the mob of New York hooligans – Sons of Liberty they jauntily called themselves, who attacked their farm on Bowery Lane[20] in the late July of 1782, when the war was all, but lost. *'But just stood there,'* she would balefully cry, *and watched them break their way into to our home, the home my father built before I was born and with fifty stout seamen and Marines who might have prevented their dreadful outrage.'*[21] A mob of thieves and blood thirsty cut throats, who first tarred and feathered and then slowly hung Hesta Victoria's late lamented grandfather, Percy Wicker Selbourn – a vile dog, you will later come to know and hate, by the neck from the ancient Mulberry tree that stood in their front garden beside the lane for the turncoat British spy and thieving rogue of a tax collecting brigand they knew him to be. And when that shameful act was done stole every penny they had before burning their house to the ground. A fortune in gold and silver from her late father that would have bought a hundred peerages, even a Dukedom[22] she tearfully claimed. And she was probably right about that.

Little did she concern herself the brave Captain she referred to with such a hateful contempt was fighting a rearguard action that night against a near overwhelming force of American Militia, who were trying to destroy the several British ships and transports anchored in the East River[23] in the safe harbour that was Kep's Bay, so close to the Bowery Lane they could see the tops of their masts across the meadows that separated them by little more than half a mile.[24] An attack he repulsed after many a long hour of bloody fighting earning himself an Admiralty commendation and the command of a frigate[25] he so cherished.

Story has it that when Hesta's mother found her way to England in the early December of that same year she had nothing in her pockets save a few shillings and the crumpled letter her father had given her just moments before he was carried off to his well-deserved end. A blackmailing letter of the most wicked kind she very quickly delivered to the man he named his *creature*, Admiral Crookhampton of Crookhampton Manor.

A letter he was so utterly shocked and appalled to receive he hardly noticed the squint-eyed, gaptoothed, snout-nosed, gloat-faced, wizened little

18

harpy who gave it to him with such a delicious glee he would do all it said. A letter that quite remarkably saw her married to his only son Redman Crookhampton, before the New Year was in, a newly promoted Lieutenant of twenty years so like his father he might have been his twin, who was thankful beyond words to sail to the South China Sea a week later aboard the 36-gun *Cherub*.

A leaky old tub – as most of the navy's ships were then, which quite astonishingly was commanded by the officer she thought the cause of her father's death and her own misfortune, Captain John Kepple, a coincidence so remarkable it is hardly believable, but a coincidence that is so much a part of this amazing story. Who sadly and much to the distress of his wife of two years and yet unborn son, William, who never knew him, but everyday felt his loss, as children often do a parent they have never known, was killed by pirates in the Straits of Malacca that same year.

Of Redman Crookhampton, nothing was ever heard of again, save a single word brought to them in the late October of 1788, almost five years later, by one Titus Dimple, the *Cherub's* Purser.[26] Who claimed without proof, he was still *alive,* the wretched prisoner of General Prem Rez leader of the South China Sea pirates and because he had no proof, was refused the hundred guineas[27] he so shamelessly begged was his just reward.

The same pirates he remarked who had killed Captain Kepple in '83, the same pirates he himself, he whined, had only two years before escaped by the skin of his teeth. A lie they were convinced it was, that flew in the face of the most convincing if desperately alarming story Commodore[28] Oscar Kettle, who commanded the South China Sea squadron[29] then, told on his much-celebrated return to England in the late summer of '85 he was killed beside his Captain in the ship action *he,* Commodore Kettle, had so bravely rescued from certain defeat. Earning a much deserved, the papers roundly said, Rear Admiral's blue flag and a much-prized sword he every day wore at his side to mark his elevated distinction to that greatly esteemed rank.

After the naming ceremony, HMS *Parrot* was sailed against her wishes, as Mister Adams and her temporary crew insisted she was, the ten miles down the slate-grey, white-capped Solent to her anchorage at Spithead Roads. Home to Britain's Channel fleet, where, in the coldest winter in living memory, she was to await the arrival of her new Captain and permanent crew. But not before Hesta Victoria, to the alarm of her mother and the sniggering amusement of the Marine drum and pipe band playing on the muddy foreshore, fell headlong into the ice covered Beaulie River and nearly drowned in a cold that froze her to the marrow. Tripped over, she pathetically moaned, by a *monkey,* no one saw but her, Pilchard as we will later learn.

Now, as was the custom of the navy at this time, the command of such a well found, if contrary vessel, as the *Parrot* truly was, was the gift of their Lords of the Admiralty. Who invariably chose an officer of courageous merit, or, if none could be had, one who at least had the good luck to know an important man. One such important man was none other than the now Vice Admiral of the Blue, Oscar Kettle of South China Sea fame.

A fame that had grown vastly in his constant boasting of a story all, but a few knew to be false, though they would never dare say it was. For he was a pitilessly mean, insatiably greedy, vengefully vile, lying, scheming, bullying tyrant of a nasty old dog, who was now, most remarkably the Assistant Deputy Comptroller of the Navy Board of Appointments. A very powerful and very influential position he every day used to his larcenous advantage. And he, for reasons of wanton favoritism, chose his nephew, because his sister said he must, a cowardly, incompetent, mean spirited, big headed oaf of a Midshipman named, William Kettle, for the job.

But here, Fate, which has a lot to do with this story, intervened to spoil his plans and bestow this much sought after command upon another. It happened like this, late on Christmas eve, when suffering from the effects of too much wine, brandy and port and an overly large dinner at Whites, his London gambling club, where he had lost, as he always did, more than he could possibly afford, more in fact than he had ever lost before, and anxious for his bed and the festivities of the day to follow, Admiral Kettle hastily dictated his nephew's commission to his trusted secretary, Mister Henry Beattie.

Who, distracted by the week long, growing more tedious, griping pains he felt in his stomach, which only yesterday turned into the most smelly, flatulent flux[30] imaginable and the severe head-cold that had dulled his mind to a blunt, painfully fuzzy edge, heard the name Kuttle instead of Kettle. It was a silly mistake to make and one Mister Beattie would have recognised in an instant had he the energy to think more clearly than he just then had, but thinking had become nearly impossible for the poor fellow and on the departure of his master he did what he had never done before, he too, decided to have an early night and delegated the task of completing the commission to his junior clerk.

22

A nervous, impetuous and all too desperate to please thoroughly sad sort of boy by the name of Trompe, the orphaned son, a nephew if you will, of a distant American cousin, so distant he hardly believed she was, who through the muffled echo of his uncle's glug-glug, gurgling like the drains aching belly and coughing, spluttering and barely audible syntax, heard and then recorded in his best hand, which was barely a spidery scribble, the name of Kepple, instead of the mistaken Kuttle. A not improbable mistake I think you will agree, but one that was to bring this story to life?

Sadly, on Christmas afternoon, and much to the surprise of his wife (she wasn't, but that story can wait awhile) of less than a year, a beautiful and exotic young lady thirty years younger than his own forty-four years, Mister Henry Beattie, a delightfully mild mannered man, if a little too fond of himself as so many clever, yet unworldly men are, and a great collector of North American Indian and Middle Eastern artefacts, curios and antiquities, which mostly didn't belong to him, passed away quite suddenly, whilst digging into his brandy dripped Christmas pudding. Which he dearly loved, and the commission so carefully transcribed by his nephew the night before, was delivered to the home of Admiral Kettle by that selfsame trembling, unwashed hand later that merry evening.

23

Trusting in his secretary, the now deceased Mister Beattie, though he didn't yet know he was, and anxious to be rid of the sniveling, grub-faced, oiky little clerk who stood in his parlor like a bundle of wet rags, a scene of poverty that reminded him all to clearly of the great fortune he had so unluckily lost the night before, Admiral Kettle signed both copies of the commission in the dull glow of the candle light that lit that elegant room to a haunt of shadows without the least glance at its gilded word. Though not before he had savagely punched and kicked the poor boy a dozen times about his head and ample buttocks to mind his manners, which the half dazed, weeping fellow begged he would as he was tumbled onto the snow piled a foot high, cobbled street and fell into an icy brown puddle.

Before the day was done the commission was wending its way through the icy, snow heaped streets of London safe aboard the wildly lurching, chain rattling, bugle blowing Falmouth coach to catch the postal cutter[31] - an even smaller boat than a brig, that was even then preparing to leave with the mail for Admiral Sir Hyde Parker, Commander-in-Chief of the West Indies station.

On his return to the Admiralty on Boxing Day morning Admiral Kettle discovered the mistake that had been made in his order and in a fit of apoplectic rage ran the length of the upstairs corridor calling for the misbegotten rat-bag of a counterfeiting clerk whose error he now clutched tightly in his massive fist. A noisy, violent, truly frightening commotion that sent the upstairs porter into a broom cupboard to hide and brought Mister Evan Nepean, Secretary of the Admiralty - an even more important man than ever Kettle was, Lieutenant James Galbraith, his early morning visitor and Lord Dasheart, his youthful prodigy, into the corridor to question the noise, which was growing thunderously and incoherently louder by the second.

Not surprisingly, Trompe ran for cover and watched with mounting, stomach churning terror from the safety of the downstairs privy as the Admiral stormed down the stairs in search of him. But, as luck would have it, or was it Fate again, he tripped over his dress sword, a gift from the City of London all those fourteen years before for ridding the South China Sea of pirates, which of course he lied, he did, and screaming unrepeatable profanities and the words *treason, mutiny,* and *forgery* over-and-over again, fell headlong to the stone flagged hall below. Whereupon, he hit his head with such a resounding crash he splintered his skull in several important places and instantly expired.

Without more ado, Trompe, who was as nimble as a cricket for a boy as round as he was ever tall, when he had a mind to be, leapt from the cover of his hide and retrieved the offending commission from the outstretched, still twitching paw of the now dead Admiral. Though it was a most terrible struggle to pull it free of his deathly tight grasp and not without bending the poor man's thumb until it broke with a sickening snap.

But he did and when he had, placed it securely out of sight in his inside waistcoat pocket. When help arrived just a few seconds later in the shape of the burly Marine Sergeant with a moustache like a yard brush, who everyday stood a threatening guard at the front door and the snow-flaked to a pretty white dusting, hard faced fellow with the cold dark, baleful eyes and a fat, ever sniffing, hairy red nose, who regaled in the name of Captain Bully Drier, the famed English detective and hero of the Battle of Durdle Door,[32] as everyone knew he was, who the Sergeant had just a moment before ushered in through the door for his eight o'clock appointment with the now crumpled corpse, he had managed to compose himself. And to such a degree. his attitude of barely disguised guilt and sick-to-the-stomach relief at his good-fortune, was mistaken for genuine, if hard to believe, concern for the fallen warrior. A picture of loyalty that so touched and impressed Mister Nepean, he marked him out for future promotion. But not so Bully Drier, a man of an altogether different stamp, who thought him a suspicious, slinking, oily cove, worthy of a second; no, a third and very possibly a fourth look.

Sometime later, safe in his attic room overlooking the snow carpeted Horse Guard's parade with the copy of Midshipman Kepple's commission stretched out before him like a strangled cry from the grave – if such a thing is possible, which this story will tell you it most certainly is, he contemplated the events of the morning with a growing sense of bewilderment. Why, he thought, did Admiral Kettle claim so violently the commission was a *forgery*, when he himself had dictated it to Mister Beattie – and Mister Beattie never made a mistake. *Or did he?* He wondered. Acting on a hunch he reached into the massive oak cabinet that stood beside the door and took out a large, well-thumbed ledger, in which was printed, in the most attractive copperplate hand-writing, the names of every Midshipman in the King's Navy and found, without the least surprise, the names of William Kettle, surely a relative of the Admiral and, of course, the name of William Kepple whose name he had written.

Putting two and two together, no easy task for

a boy as slow witted as he was generally thought to be, not least by the uppity Lord Dasheart, who hated the very sight of him with an uncommon passion and daily planned his downfall, Trompe realised that the commission staring up at him from the rickety trestle table he wistfully called a desk, was, in all probability, intended for Mister Midshipman William Kettle and not, as was so clearly written by *him* – he trembled, he had, Mister Midshipman William Kepple, a monstrously silly, truly unforgivable mistake by any judgement that would see him dismissed from his employ and cast out onto the streets of London before the day was done. A thought which made him quiver uncontrollably with fear. And all-the-more so when he stared out of the dirt grimed window and saw Admiral Kettle's prostrate, fast stiffening body placed on a horse drawn cart in the snow swept yard below and Captain Bully Drier stare up at him and with such an accusing look he quickly backed away.

And a mistake, perhaps even treason, some might call it, Lord Dasheart for one most certainly would, he could not admit too or set right without ruining himself in the bargain. *But who could know?* He asked himself as he warmed his half gloved, shivering fingers over the stump of candle that lit his desk a poor light, now poor Mister Beattie was dead of the wasting flux? Who indeed? And in that instant of cowardly self-preservation he made his mind up, he would tell no one and carefully placed the commission he had written into the file marked, *Lieutenant's Qualifying List (West Indies Station) December 1796,* as quickly as he could and farted a huge sigh of relief, which was ever his noisy, not to say, despicable curse in times of fretful anxiety. Though, with a feeling and it was no more than that, he now had in his possession an intelligence that might in some way prove to be the means of his own future advancement, a ridiculously improbable idea that was sadly to be his undoing.

Such was the fiercesome and thoroughly deserved reputation of Admiral Kettle throughout the Navy at this time, absolutely no one, would gainsay a word he said - particularly if they thought him still living and capable of damaging their career. So, when his order reached Admiral Sir Hyde Parker, no one, least of all him, thought to question a commission ordering the thoroughly unremarkable, but decidedly likable and capably promising, Mister Midshipman, William Kepple, only son of Captain John Kepple, late of HMS *Cherub* and a man he knew well and vastly admired from the American Rebellion, to take charge of his Majesties gun-brig, *Parrot*.

After-all, by golly, didn't his namesake and a very dear friend, the inestimable Admiral Sir Peter Parker, Portsmouth's Port Admiral, promote his nephew, George, Lieutenant, at just thirteen and his own son, Christopher, Post Captain at just seventeen - a rank so achingly desired by every Lieutenant in the kings navy it was unthinkable it should be given to one so young.[33] So why not promote Midshipman Kepple, just turned fourteen last February and still four years short of his qualifying examination, Lieutenant and give him a command he would probably sink in a week. Such were the ways of the Admiralty and the men of power and influence who decided these things. As he too decided things!

Chapter 2

Tom Finds *Herself* Where
She Never Thought To Be

Midsummer eve 1335BCE

Tom pressed *herself* to the still surprisingly warm to the touch, black stone face of the obelisk[34] she was crouched beneath. One of two that towered so very high above her head, five yards in front of the massive, stone built gateway they so imposingly framed, she had to bend and stretch her neck until the back of her head almost touched her spine to see their pointed tops. So, high, they were higher by thirty feet or more than the *Parrot's* mainmast, which she knew, from Duffy's daily attempts to teach her the seamanship she didn't want to learn, soared a dizzying eighty feet above her decks and each one four times wider at their base than its own impressive, tree-like stump of rope wrapped, iron bound oak.

A horseshoe shaped gateway, which opened to a bleached white, gently rising, massive causeway, which arrow-straight pierced the pressing crowd of low buildings which hugged its two sides in ghostly dark, forbidding stacks to the very foot of

31

the biggest of the three, snow white, gold capped pyramids which climbed into the moon bright, magenta sky before her. Each one so colossal they almost filled the horizon, so impossibly big she felt crushed by their size to a smallness she had never known before, and she had once travelled to Salisbury with her mother to see the famous cathedral spire. A sight, like this, that made her gasp.

Where was she? She wondered, her eyes following the tall, cyclopean, stone built wall on either side of the gate to their furthest ends three or four hundred yards in each direction, she guessed, it was hard to . *But more importantly, where was Polly? Why wasn't she here, beside her?* She asked, as she turned to search the flower strewn, stone flagged, rectangular courtyard behind her for the least sign of her, or anyone else for that matter. Because the flowers said there must be others nearby? Whose gloved hand she was holding so very tightly in her own, just half a second ago, as the Pod glowed a soft blue, sensuous light and sent them on their way, so tightly she imagined she still did.

A thought that darted her eyes this way and that as her now acutely heightened senses tried to make sense of what she could see and hear in that tremulously still, oddly expectant, inexplicably deserted night. The full moon, stars, and planets so iridescently bright and so impossibly close to the broad curving sweep of the horizon she felt she could reach out and touch them with her fingers. A magical night so colourfully rent with muted shades of red, orange, and yellow it made her gasp the world could be so utterly beautiful. The giant puff-ball of ink-black cloud, which, like a three masted ship under billowing sails floated across the twinkling, finger-like river delta just visible below the steep dropping escarpment to her right. The soft, hypnotic whisper of the leaves in the tiny crop of stunted palm trees that grew on either side of the gateway in such a pretty way, they effortlessly reminded her of the stories she loved to read of Ali Baba and the Forty Thieves, of Aladdin's Wonderful Lamp and The Seven Voyages of Sinbad the Sailor, whose wicked name gave her such a terrifying fright when first she read it. Each one conjuring frights of djinns, ghouls, monsters, grand viziers, sorcerers and magicians, but every time defeated by heroes who were so effortlessly brave or heroines as noble, beautiful and cunningly clever as, Scheherazade and her sister Dunyazade. The faint, musical trickle of water coming from somewhere in the shadows behind her, a fountain she supposed, or a small waterfall, which hid a small habitation beyond the grove of palm trees that grew more densely there. The hoarse croak

33

of frogs, the lowing of contented cows, the persistent bark of a dog, the buzz of insects, the faint, rhythmic beat of a drum, the tuneful tinkle of cymbals and the muffled, sweeping scrape of brushes hard at work.

Commonplace, reassuring sounds that did much to calm her nerves, but not so much she didn't want to run away as fast as her legs would carry her. *But where would she run too and to what purpose?* She asked herself, turning to look again at the causeway and the soaring pyramid it connected, which to her astonished surprise was changed by some extraordinary trick of her eye, or was it the whimsy of colours that so exquisitely framed them, into something truly wondrous. A spear of gigantic proportions that rose without break or blemish from the now strangely magnifying effect of the rounded gateway, which held her eye with such a strange possession, she could not look away, to pierce the full moon behind it at its very heart.

A spear tipped in lustrous gold transformed by that same whimsy of light and shadow into a doorway that seemed to beckon her into another world beyond the moon. A world beyond the magenta sky of stars and planets that was its pretty backcloth. An optical illusion she knew from a hundred country walks that left her eyes dazzled by the bright sun to see what was never there, sticks poked into water bent askew, cartwheels long passed lifted to the sky by her mind's eye to see them spin again, as waterfalls often will when you turn your eye to the muddy bank.[35]

An illusion that held her in such a sublime, almost hypnotic thrall she truly believed she could walk to the centre of heaven if only she dared to take that first step and pass through the gateway that now seemed to beckon her with such a powerful urge; but she didn't dare.[36] But more intriguing than this, the more she looked at it, the more it looked like the ankh cross[37] professor Tollendal had branded onto her arm all those weeks ago, so new it was still quite red and itchy. The proud mark of the secret society she, Billy, Polly and Marie-Ange now served and would serve until their oath sworn duty was done; *The Sword and Shield of Aten.* The shimmering moon, its looped top, the pyramid base, on which it appeared to sit, the horizontal top of the T bar and the causeway its vertical stem.

An illusion instantly and forever lost when through the corner of her eye she saw a flag suddenly flutter on the causeway, one of the many she now saw were hung from thin, gallows-like structures along its two sides, just like the flags and bunting that dressed Lymington High Street from the St. Thomas' church at the top of the hill and with a flourish of colour outside The George to mark its great importance as a Coaching Inn, to the cobbled Quay at the bottom, on May Day. Where the pipe band of soldiers or Militia would play and the children would dance and where, since 1793 French soldiers and Émigrés gathered outside the inn to fish, plot and plan their return to France, though many were hurt the last time they did. The same year the Gendarme Ronsin and his gang brought such misery to professor Tollendal and Marie-Ange.[38]

The same sun bright yellow flags, which draped each side of the gate from the top to the bottom in front of her, which to her surprise, now she looked, hid, though hardly at all, two, ten feet tall, coal-black, ear-pricked, statues of jackal-headed men[39] standing in coffin-like, recessed plinths, twenty feet above her head.

Where was she and where was Polly? She frantically asked herself, again, her eyes turned from their menacing gaze, her warm, moist breath clouding the still tight shut, black tinted, helmeted visor she wore on her head like an upturned glass bowl. Her heart desperately pounding the fear she felt to find herself alone and in a place, she was not meant to be. The terrifying far distant future world Gabe had described to her and Polly in such vivid detail a few hours before in *Nogoback*. Had, only a few minutes ago, sent them there in his particle splitting - and she had no idea what that meant, despite he told them, time travelling Pod, if Billy's precious Tompion was to be believed? Which she knew it was. She sighed, her eyes rested on its re-assuring glass face, its gleaming gold case a comfort in her gloved hand. Sent them there with such a cheerful confidence they would quickly and safely return with his companions; the *Nanochromes*.[40] That extraordinary *race* of super human children he was so very proud to be their leader and who could blame him he was? They could fly without wings, easily replace, or repair every part of their body - they even had spare heads, their own and others, and could even make themselves invisible in the blink of an eye wearing the same special clothes she now wore.

Children, no older than her own twelve years, though many were much younger, who against all the odds had survived the ravages of the mid-twentieth century climate change, which in a few short decades led to the great polar freeze that almost turned the planet upside down and the near mass extinction of humanity in 2084. Surviving for nearly three thousand unimaginably long years in a complex system of subterranean caves and biospheres their long dead ancestors had built for them, until, at long last, the world was re-born anew for them in 4930. But though it was, when they emerged to feel the sun warm on their faces for the first time they discovered many different species of humans had come to colonise and dominate the planet in their absence, but possessing the powers of the animals they now resembled. Humans who were determined to destroy them and because they were, and they could not harm them - though they had the power to do so, decided to leave their lush, subtropical island home forever.

But not to go just anywhere! And there were many habitable places in that new born, physically changed world they might have chosen to live out their lives in peace and each one so far away from the Zebra Men, Lizard Men, Scarab-Beetle Men, Lion Men, Bird Men, Fish Men, Dog Men, and Piranha Men,[41] to name but a few of the monsters who everyday wanted to kill them, they might never be found. No, ignoring that might be the most sensible thing to do? The easiest thing to do? They decided instead, to go back in time, as their ancestors had always planned they would in the two, time travelling Portals they had constructed for just such a purpose. A one-way trip to a world where mankind might begin life anew, Gabe said, and with such a bright, infectious optimism they couldn't disagree. The world of 250000 years ago. A world he named, Nogoback, because they never would go back.

A world no modern human[42] had ever walked upon or left their destructive mark, *or so they thought?* Where they could build a new world never again making the terrible mistakes their ancestors did and by doing so, save the world from the tragedy of 2084. But though he and half their number had escaped in the first Portal, the one Ethan, Isaac and Indie had somehow hitched a ride in and Indie with Billy's Tompion in her pocket she longed to ask her how she did, the rest of their companions were trapped against their will by, of all people, the Count de Montard. An impossibility, but true none-the-less and because it was, she and Polly were determined to know what he was up, too and even more than they wanted to rescue the rest of the Nanochromes - though they wanted to rescue them from harm. Must know before they returned to their world of 1797 and the quest to find the Rebus of Akhenaten they were now embarked upon.

'Nanochromes,' such a delicious word, she whispered it several times, rolling it on her tongue like the home-made toffee she liked to eat, though it was an age since she last had one. The children of *Eve, Gabe* called them, a boast that claimed

they were without human flaw or imperfection, children made of a special type of modified human tissue he called chromosomes and a special material called nano-plastics.[43] Crystalline chemicals and metals so advanced in their tiny engineering you couldn't tell they were.

A fusion of syllables that gave rise to the word, Nanochrome! *Machines,* really, because they mostly were, but more powerful and more durable than the flesh and bone their ancestors of so long ago were made of. Though he looked no different than either she or Polly did, or any child and would grow and age as they would, though it would take a great deal longer – ten thousand years, perhaps to grow to youthful middle age, was his best guess, though it might take longer, his freckled skin and unruly mop of delightful curly, mousy-brown hair every bit as *real* to the touch as their own. But machines most remarkably, he claimed, and she didn't disbelieve him, possessed of *souls,* just like them, she and Poll must rescue in the Pod that split them into a trillion tiny parts.

A machine she knew was there only safe return to the Land of Nogoback, a world every bit as terrifying as the future he had described, perhaps even more terrifying, as they had already braved some of its many hardships; too may, she shivered. A land of giant dinosaurs, an octopus so big it was bigger than any house she had ever seen, swarms of fish or were they lizards that could eat you whole, flying raptors and giant termite-like insects, which really did almost eat them and, of course, the Toba Men who so very nearly killed them and would soon kill Gabe if they didn't get back with the help he needed. A terrifying world, but a world that was their only hope of ever getting back to 1797, to Billy, Duffy, Sam, Trucky Spears, Marie-Ange, Lemmy, Pilchard and all the rest of the *Parrot's* boisterous crew of grubby boys, so full of mischievous larks and comic japes she longed to see them all again. Well most of them, she smiled, thinking she wouldn't care if she never saw, Midshipman Arbuthnot Anstruther, or the red faced, blustering, Sergeant Finch, who barked his orders so loud he hurt her ears - not that he dared bark a word to her, or Dancer Dyke and Nipper Ogden, ever again. All four of them low born scrubs, she would never like, well, not Midshipman Anstruther, whose mother was as rich as could be, as he one day would be.

No, this was neither the Land of Nogoback nor was it the subterranean caves of the Nano-chromes, but somewhere in between! She had somehow *got off* too soon, she now realized, and if she had, then perhaps Polly had, too, *but where was she if not here and what had caused this ca-*

lamity? She asked herself, fearing she might be anywhere and just as frightened as she was?

But just then, as she began to worry herself into a fret, she felt a faint thrum and tickle coming from Kiya's wand, still safely tucked into her belt, and knew with an instinct that was so blindingly obvious, she wondered she hadn't thought of it before, it was *her* wand that had caused this mishap. Had, in its *unfrozen* state, interfered with the working of the *Pod* and brought her here and if it had, then Gabe might know it had and rescue her? It was a slim chance, she thought, her eyes turned again to the three colossal, satin smooth, milk white, gold capped pyramids that rose so majestically into the sky above her she gasped again they did.

A place she now realised, she knew, if not so well as this, had delighted to see so many times before, but not in life, but in one of her Dame School teacher's, Miss Fry's, treasured text books, so treasured only the most senior girls could read it. A slim brown volume she remembered was called, *In the Footsteps of the Crusades, Travels in the Levant[44] and Ancient Egypt,* by Lady Ceridwen Denbigh,[45] which boasted a score of sketches of its ancient wonders, including the pyramids at Giza and the Sphinx squatting so tall on its haunches above the pink granite wall behind her to her far left it was just like the picture in the book, only so much better in *real* life.

So utterly wonderful she gasped. This was Egypt! The Egypt of the pharaohs, Polly's Egypt, if half of what Kiya had blustered in the burning tower was true and she knew it was! *But what was she to do now?* A question barely formed on her lips when she heard a low, tuneful whistle and saw a small, bare chested, bald headed boy aged about nine or ten dressed in a short to the knee, white pleated linen skirt and grass sandals that flopped on his feet pushing a sort of broom in front of him coming out of the shadows directly behind her. Followed soon after by two dozen more equally small boys doing much the same thing in the lazy way boys do their chores, and urged they should, all the harder by a tall, grump of a bald man no better dressed than they were, who whipped them so hard when they stopped she heard it crack on their skin.

But she saw them too late to hide and coming so quickly upon her they surely couldn't help but see her. A strange, barely human creature dressed in a red belted, baggy yellow suit, a pair of red ankle boots, matching gauntlets and with a red and black visored helmet pulled over her face that made her look like a frog on stilts.

'Invisible, make me invisible, please, quickly,'

she whispered in her panic, as Gabe had said she and Polly must, if they should ever need, too. Their suits being made of a special kind of light-absorbing[46] *magic* thread that would hide them if they asked it, and no sooner did she, then she disappeared, but half a second too slow not to be seen.

'What was that?' Asked the first boy, leaning on his broom.

'What was what?' Asked his friend.

'Don't know, something there,' he pointed to the obelisk.

'A djinn most likely,' answered a third boy with a careless authority neither boy thought to dispute, so obvious was his conclusion, their brooms once again bent to sweep the courtyard clear of sand, dirt, and petals. Everyone knew that djinns lived in the temple of Khufu, as they did in the temple of Khafre next to it and the little temple of Menkaure a little further on from that.

'Djinn,' whispered Tom, knowing that one word in all the rest he spoke and guessing he spoke of some sort of ghostly, impish thing. Something, she had a dozen times heard Sal the Arab boy and faithful servant of Sir Mungo, mutter when some minor tragedy, misfortune, or mishap befell him, which was most every day, as far as she could tell, and no surprise in that given his life was a most precarious adventure!

A boy as suspicious as any boy she had ever known in her life, though, truth to tell, she knew hardly any boys at all, Lymington being such a small place. As were his two companions, the impossibly cheerful and never down hearted, Roland and the, oh so very serious, Ned, each so very brave, but so very suspicious.

But who could blame them they were, all three were nearly five hundred years' *dead and buried* when she, Polly and Marie-Ange met them in the forest of Le Petite Ménec, in May. Murdered by those devils, Montard, O'Brien, York, and Rochester on the road to La Rochelle in that first cowardly attack on The Sword and Shield of Aten in 1307. And just days after their companion Templar Knights[47] were almost destroyed to a man by the soldiers of King Philip IV of France and his eager pawn, Pope Clement V, if for an entirely different reason. They were jealous of their money, power and influence in a Christian world that dearly loved them.

And now they were ghosts, though she hardly knew what that word meant anymore, after all the ghostly comings and goings she had witnessed in the last few months. The first, Lemmy and Pilchard, stowaways on the *Parrot* murdered like they were and for the same reason. So Montard, who was once a trusted Templar in the service

45

of Sir Mungo of Denbigh, though never a knight or a squire, as Roland and Ned both were, could steal the Rebus of Akhenaten for the Priests of Amun-Ra, whose great power and magic he used without fear or mercy. And now in the future, she and Polly were a few minutes ago, going, too. Still must and would not return until they knew what he was up too. A very dangerous diversion.

Two parts of which, and there were nine parts in all, as she now all, too well knew, she had held in her own hands, one belonging to Marie-Ange, the other a piece she and Polly had quite amazingly found in Pierre Corbeau's satchel in the Portsmouth's Fountain Inn, never knowing how it got there, but more importantly, who it once belonged too; which they very soon must. Trivets, Billy called them for the simple reason they looked so much like the kitchen trivet his mother used to stand her pots and kettles on and were just as useless, as far as she could see. With not one squiggle of their beautifully inscribed hieroglyphs making the least jot of sense to anyone, not even to professor Tollendal, who had the only translation in the world to read them with. As Billy, now did.

No less, she thought, than the thousands she now saw beautifully etched in row after climbing row into the four sides of the obelisks all the way up to the top, except the one at the very bottom in front of her, the ankh, its closeness strangely comforting; a message of hope.

'*I am a djinn,*' she smiled, they thought she was as the last of their gang, a straggler aged about six with a pot belly, who almost walked into her, swept a cloud of sand, dust, and crushed petals straight into her visored face. So, thick and clinging when she tried to wipe it clean it smeared to a prism of rainbow colours that dazzled her eyes. But to such a peculiar effect for the third time in less than five minutes she experienced yet another illusion, or so she thought, but one quite different from the other two. A smoke-like, ethereal wisp of something rising above the middle pyramid, to her left, which, at first sight, looked like spindrifts of windblown snow, but then, when she looked more closely, looked like the gentle swaying of a curtain. Its rippling, pirouetting folds appearing to stretch from its pointed top to the highest stars and out to the horizon beyond the desert and river delta in a shimmer of primrose yellow and gooseberry green lights.

Lights she realised she had seen before, or something very much like them on that night of dreadful storm and earthquake when Captain Bauda's brave cavalry attacked Billy, Duffy, Ralph, Sal, and Poll, near the Quadrilatére stones[48] and what a scrap that was! The battle of the stones[49]

Sal soon after heroically called it, if only to impress Roland and Ned, they had missed a wonderful fight. A battle that saw Polly bravely climb on top of the Dolmen Stones[50] they hid behind in nothing more than her calico knickers to sing and dance like a loon and too such a frightening effect she stopped Captain Bauda and his men dead in their tracks and just long enough for them to escape. But only as far as the Château where they were soon after caught. Well, not Polly and Sal, who got away only to be attacked in the forest of Le Petit Ménec by the Beasts of Amun-Ra, summoned by O'Brien to find, and kill them, which they almost did.

Lights Billy later said, or was it Sam, she couldn't remember, were the Northern Lights. The aurora borealis, a natural display of mostly red and green lights not normally seen as far south as Brittany's magical Quiberon Peninsula, where they then were, but often seen much further north by sailors in the northern seas.

But it wasn't just one curtain of light, she thrilled to see as she turned on the balls of her feet in an elegant twirl, but nine, each one rotating about the summit of the pyramid in a gently undulating procession and passing her like the paddles on a millwheel fallen on its side, in a seemingly endless wave, the pyramid its hub. A wave she imagined she felt enclose and caress her body, as it did the whole of the Giza pyramid site.

The summit of the pyramid of Khafre[.51] if Lady Denbigh was right, she mused, smiling she probably was, as a wave passed her in a dazzle and she turned to face the next as it came towards her, a luminescence of green and yellow that quite took her breath away so physically present was it. Like the Channel wind when it blew so very fiercely across the pans on Pennington Marshes, where she and her mother often walked before she died, often as far as the castle[.52]

But this was no wind, she realised, seeing it spin in a regular clockwise motion much like a child's wooden top and with the same spinning slant when its motion slowed, as it every now and then did. But nor was it an aurora borealis; a feast of lights caused by the weather. *But if it wasn't, what on earth was it?* She asked herself, running without caution she might be seen to the back of the courtyard to get a better view. Where she quickly and easily climbed the four feet high, smooth plastered wall that was its boundary, her hand rested on the stone gate post that opened to the village of mud brick houses she now easily saw fifty or perhaps sixty yards behind her. Which were clustered in a respectful, if haphazard circle around several much larger buildings of expertly carved stone, where a crowd was gathered beside one of the stoutest buildings, their faces turned from her to peer at some unseen sight, a low, melancholy drum beat and tinkling chime of cymbals calling some sad event. A funeral she guessed, such was its aching lament.

Seeing the sweepers were now half way across the causeway walking in the direction of the pyramid of Khufu and unlikely to return and no one following behind them she turned again to watch the mysterious wave of light pass over her in a puzzlement that grew no less the more she watched them. Several times walking up and down the wall to its furthest end where she found a third enclosure and gate leading to the furthest pyramid on her left, Menkaure, she remembered, her eyes marveling at every tiny detail of their ghostly, writhing forms, but more than this, saw there were other waves reaching into the sky from nearly every point of the compass, some so far away she couldn't see their source, others so near she easily could.

Each wave of light pivoting on some large natural feature of the landscape, a buttress of stone, a high escarpment, a crag-stone hill, or some stone carved monument of some considerable size, but none as large as the three pyramids that appeared to be their centre. And each reaching out to meet its neighbor and so perfectly sequenced in their endless, rhythm they looked like the cogs in a giant clock and some so bafflingly complex in their perfect alignment she hardly knew where one rippling wave began and another ended. And so, filling the sky with their breath-taking meld of colour it looked as if the whole world was set ablaze with a dozen shades of yellow-green fire. A fire shot through with piercing shards of white light that touched the stars above with spear-like pricks.

But impatient to see more than she had, she lifted the dirt streaked visor on her helmet without the least fear she would come to any harm, as Gabe warned her she might. That she could easily breathe in a poisonous gas that would instantly kill her or swallow a gobbet of cosmic dust that would choke her to death. But ignoring he did, slowly lifted it to the top of her helmet and when she had, was astonished to see the pulsating waves of lights had completely disappeared. The sky once again a dark magenta streaked with mellow reds, yellows and oranges and lit by a moon and stars so breathtakingly beautiful she audibly gasped.

But so fiercely humid and so fiercely hot was the midsummer air on her face and with Gabe's caution now returned to frighten her, she quickly closed the visor shut with a snap, her helmet now filled with the most delicious, oily perfume. But not before a man standing unseen in the cultivated copse of sandalwood trees that grew beside the fringe of palm trees that mostly hid the village, saw her face floating five feet above the wall, he every evening passed on his way home and without a head or body to hold it up. A djinn like no other he had encountered and he had seen many. A fright so horribly alarming the poor man ran for his life and with a scream so loud it turned the crowd gathered outside the stoutest building in the village towards her and brought a score of lighted tapirs to those meaner dwellings beside it, as she jumped from the wall to hide in a tight crouch beneath its heavy shadow. Where she stayed for three long minutes, her eyes tight shut, ignoring the sleek black cat that climbed between her legs without the least concern she *wasn't* there, until she was sure she was quite safe.

Shoo Mister cat, she whispered, giving it a gentle shove in its skinny ribs with her gloved hand it ignored with a soft purr. A cat much like professor Tollendal's, Robespierre she realised and a cat just as spoilt and obstinate, a cat she didn't care for, as the wave of light found her once again in its lively thrall.

'What is this?' She asked, standing to see. But no sooner had she than she felt, rather than saw,

the next wave of light tremble as it passed over her head, as if it had stumbled on some unseen obstacle and the next one after that even more powerfully than the last, its spin now deeply angled like a child's fallen hoop. Until in just a few seconds the rhythm was lost in a fast weaving jumble of light and shade that had neither beginning nor end, but moved around her in a serpent-like, shimmering vortex; like slippery eels in a bucket? Poisoned eels by the sickly moan they now made.

But as it did a lattice work, or spider web of hollow translucent triangles began to form above the three pyramids like soap bubbles streaming upwards in the wind, gathering their energy, it seemed so obvious to her, from the chaos of swirling, squirming *living* light that now so engulfed them in the maelstrom of their panic.

Each triangle peeling from their four gleaming white sides like turned pages in a book to form a continuous sock-like structure that spiraled without break into the night sky. Twisting and turning as it did, sometimes so much so, it looped almost to the ground, as if it was under a strain too much to bear. Pulled, she was now certain, by the immediately recognizable constellation of stars that were so perfectly aligned above them it was surely no coincidence they were. That it was planned by someone they should be its destination; but who would do such an amazing thing?

A constellation of stars Billy had a hundred times shown her as he navigated the *Parrot* across the Atlantic Ocean to America, just a few short weeks ago, as much to convince himself he knew where he was going, as it was to convince her he did. Each one now so easily visible she knew they were the constellation of Orion. But most particularly the three stars that were its Belt; the stars Delta Orionis (Mintaka), Epsilon (Alnilam) and Zeta (Alnitak) and in the parallel order that linked Khufu, Khafre, and Menkaure to each of them.

A cats-cradle of bending light that like the draw string on a canvas bag began to pull the rhythm of the waves back together again, but with such a mighty strain she thought it must soon break, did in many parts, tearing like the snagged ladders in her Woollen stockings that took such an age to mend, so much did it resist its every effort, much as a small child might resist its mother, struggling it's want to be free of her control.

It was as if the three large pyramids and their smaller satellite pyramids were deliberately applying an artificial break or damper on the light waves[53] (or were they magnetic waves) that were a natural, if unstable feature of the low escarpment they were built upon, and those other rock formations she had seen both near and far. An instability that was perhaps a daily (or perhaps hourly) feature of these particular stony places for why else would the ancient Egyptians bother to build them, if not to prevent what might every day happen? But what would happen she wondered if the rhythm of the waves gave way to the chaos she earlier saw?[54] Was this the power the Priests of Amun-Ra claimed stolen all those years ago by the Pharaoh Akhenaten, the power to hold the world, the universe in place and the pyramids the engine by which this is achieved? It seemed too much to believe?

But just then, she noticed something odd and very interesting, the lattice frame formed by the pyramid of Menkaure, smaller by far than the other two and noticeably offset to the east to their perfect north south, diagonal alignment, and the three much smaller satellite pyramids that stood parallel to it on its southern side, were acting like a secondary anchor break to the lattice frame so much more strongly formed by the others. As did the very much smaller pyramid on the south-west corner of Khafre and the three equally small pyramids on the eastern side of Khufu, where the boy sweepers had come to a grateful stop, never knowing they were enclosed in its mighty, yet invisible struggle. Something she confirmed when she once again lifted her damp and dirt covered visor from her face, a peep this time and saw again the world was as it was before they swept past her and thought her a djinn.

Each smaller pyramid kinking and tightening the lattice spiral until order was returned, as it now quickly was. But just as it was, Tom felt something irresistibly weird and rather wonderful begin to happen to her, as Gabe said it would, when he launched her and Polly into the future barely ten minutes ago, her body for the briefest moment began to gently expand like an air blown pigs bladder and as it did, break into a trillion shards of rainbow coloured light. Particles of light freed from the quantum gravity that held them together in the universe of empty space that is the stuff of all things, even the hardest diamond, Gabe had patiently explained, particles of light that would instantly collapse to the size of a pin head the *Pod* would then catapult to the future, where in the blink of an eye they would be reassembled in a second, identical *Pod in the second, waiting Portal.* A journey of less than a millionth part of a second he said, if it still worked and he was ninety-nine percent sure it would?[55]

At last, she deep sighed her relief, *he's found me and perhaps dear Polly, too and is sending us back to where we should go.* Or so she hoped, as

56

she was lifted into the sky, her body floating like a puffball on the wind.

Chapter 3

The Bottomless Well Of Time
Speaks To Tom Of Things
She Never Thought To Know

Midsummer eve 1335BCE

Ber hope though she truly did the very
pleasant, dream-like sensation she now
felt, was the beginning of her journey back to the
future and Polly, who she missed, that her being
there on the Giza plateau was no more than a
hitch in Gabe's dangerous plan to rescue the re-
mainder of the Nanochromes from their subterranean prison; it wasn't!

Little knowing it was Kiya's wand still looped
and gently thrumming its magic in her belt that
made her feel the way she did. That her mind was
drifting free of her star stretched body into the bottomless well of time, like a boat cast adrift on an
endless sea. Something Gabe had warned her
might happen. But more than this, she might experience vivid, perhaps even alarming visions of
things long past and perhaps best forgotten.

Which she now did in the most terrifying detail;
the murder of her mother drowned in one of the salt

pans on Pennington Marshes only last December which so broke her heart the pain even now was as fierce as ever it was. Killed, she now saw in the dastardliest way by her uncle Titus Dimple, as she always suspected she was. But helped, she was utterly appalled to see by Captain Bully Drier, who the very next day lied so convincingly to the magistrate, the outrageously self-important and thoroughly insensitive and unkind, Mister Dicks and the toadying fool who was his brainless creature, the lanky, ram-rod straight, buck-toothed, former Corporal of Marines, Constable Brown, she killed herself in a fit of unnatural depression. Something she knew to be untrue, her mother being a woman of practical good sense who knew she had a long life to live and a very young daughter to grow.

And too such a good effect Lymington's newly appointed only last July from Oxford University, where he trained, and now her very much-admired physician, the youthful and robustly healthy doctor Charles was forced to agree, though everyone could see how uncomfortably shrunken into his collar he was beneath Bully Drier's malignant glare. An immensely broad-shouldered man beneath his conker-brown, deep pocketed, fustian[55] jacket, of muscular good height and proud, some would say, swaggeringly proud, military bearing who wore a brace of expensive, Collumbell[57] polished mahogany and silver inlaid, pistols holstered at his broad, leather belted hip.

A dangerous man well named since his youth for his brutally unforgiving ways, which were so perfectly captured in his savage, slope-eyed, hangman's face and heavy lantern jaw, which flexed a constant back and forth chewing twitch, few men could look upon without a visible dread, not least the comically hairy, fat red nose that was its hideous middle. A man who demanded obedience as if by right in the way men do who are born to wealth, power, or social status, trivial though it may be, or if not so well favoured, will use their greater strength or streetwise cunning to have it just the same, knaves, braggarts, and swaggers everyone.

As Miss Fry saw he did and bristled with indignation he commanded the room and all who sat there with such a force, whose pretty flushed cheeks beneath her fur-trimmed, green velvet, winter bonnet blushed to see Dr Charles so ill at ease, as he gave his nervous evidence to the packed court room on that chapped fingers, snow blown, bitterly sad morning. Who adored him as any *aging* spinster turned twenty-four last September would; such a long legged, handsome man. And a man with an income of two hundred pounds a year if his practice should flourish and hers barely a quarter of that when her parlor school was full, which it mostly wasn't, there being so few families of quality in the village to educate a daughter beyond her natural inclination to darn and sew.

Knocked her barely conscious to the frost hard, deep rippled sand with the small, lead weighted cudgel he took from his pocket as she turned from her uncle Titus in an impatient hurry to find the path to the shingle spit that formed the bird clustered sea break beside the Lymington road, barely sixty yards away. And with his eager help dragged her limp and moaning to the nearest pan and held her kicking and squirming beneath the dark cold, salt rimed, ice broken water until she was still and when she was, pushed her into the middle, where the following morning she was horribly found by a passerby, who screamed they had. Screamed until help from the village came.

And with a snigger of triumph when they were finished that brought a pitiless smile to the faces of Jemmy Grub, Joby Dogget and Charlie Begg, the son of Turzel Begg, the once infamous Captain of the *Seahorse,* who was killed at Durdle Door before the Revenue men got him. As they got and hung Albert and Clary Grubb, though it was never the plan they should.

Who stood leaning against the skeleton of a rowing boat deep buried in the sand for half a century to half the height of its broken ribs its bow pressed to the petrified tree[58] that so long grew there she never knew a time it didn't. The moon brightly shimmering on the frost and snow that glazed its pollarded head, trunk and two outstretched branches, the empty boat it moored and the puddles of sand that everywhere surrounded them on that bleak and lonely winter's night.

But then, searching the reason why they should want her mother dead and in such a coldly calculating, hideously callous way, a kinder heart she never knew, would never know again, she saw a second fearful sight rise unbidden from the snake-like writhing mist of green and yellow light that now so completely surrounded her she couldn't see its end; was utterly lost in its timeless thrall.

As she had been once before, she recalled with a shiver of sadness that strained to see what was forming in the gloom before her early last February. When, on a sun bright, cold, and cloudless morning she was suddenly engulfed by a sea fog that came so quickly out of the Channel she didn't see it come, as she fed the donkeys[59] on lower Pennington Common and pondered the lonely future that now stretched before her.

Her darling mother gone and her uncle Titus

now so insistent she must come and live with him, she despaired he did. Despite Miss Fry had given her a home and would let her stay as long as she liked and told him and Mister Dicks she could and with such a brave stamp of her dainty foot, doctor Charles, now her growing more frequent and attentive companion thought her most wonderful. Who, despite she did, or because she did, strutted his half-baked law she must be returned to her family before the month was ended, mid-March at the very latest and all her portable property, too. Or he, damn her uncalled for meddlesome opinion, would know the reason why? Indeed, he would.

A fog so utterly dense she could barely see her poppy-red Woollen, gloved hands in front of her tear stained face or her scuffed black booted feet in the ankle-deep snow that covered the narrow, earth banked lane, she ran along as she hurried home. Her heavy russet-brown winter skirt and fresh washed, white linen pinny hitched to her knees beneath her hooded cloak, as she ran and ran in a blind panic. An avalanche of frightening fog that so completely hid her way, though she knew it so well she could walk it blindfolded, she thought she would never see Lymington's cobbled High Street again! But did, guided by the many sounds that said the world was not gone, but near.

The bray of the donkeys as they impatiently

crowded and pushed the kissing gate she had just a moment before jumped from, as they hungrily searched for the wooden pale of juicy carrots she had left beyond their reach. The cry of the gulls as they circled out of sight above her head, her footfall on the cinder path beside the sea, the crash of the waves on the shore, the clip clop and breathless snort of horses on the cobbles, as she found the quay its dark, wooden sheds rising unseen beside her, the rattle, spin and slip of the iron bound, wooden wheels they pulled, the church bell on the hill, the rhythmic beat of a hammer in the forge, the squeak of a rusty gate, the clank and gurgle of the water pump, the hoot of an owl and the bleating of sheep and lambs in a field nearby. Every one of them a comfort as she hurried on and on.

But there was no such sound now; not one in that yellow green mist! It was as if her mind had been set free of the binding shackles of the world she once knew, but more than this, her own body, too. Always so full of creaks, squeaks, and noisy grumbles she wondered it was. Set free to see everything that ever hurt her. First her mother and now her father killed eight years before, the first dreadful misfortune she knew. A tragic accident everyone said it was and with such a heartfelt sympathy and deep regret it ever happened to such a fine young man, it seemed very likely it was.

But now shown to be the murder it was, no less than the murder of her mother, the blow once again struck by her uncle Titus as they walked one late evening in the New Forest near their home in that blustery autumn of 1788. Where she, not yet turned four and her mother so busy in the kitchen, waited his return with an expectation that longed to see him. The home they had shared as little boys, where they had played on the small holding that was their fathers pride and joy before he died; dead before Titus was two, and in the woods and on the heath, that surrounded it. Fast friends her father said they were until he came home from the South China Sea, four years gone and penniless of the good fortune their father left him and with such an unaccountable evil in his heart.

The dark, low clouds scudding over the tree tops like phantoms as they argued over some matter she couldn't hear, so loud did the wind whistle and whine through trees. Their heavy winter coats pitched to and throw about their white, Woollen stockinged legs in a fury that threatened to carry them off, her father holding tight his tricorn hat with one hand and the scuffed leather satchel he everyday carried to his work, with the other.

Which, in a moment of frustrated fury that would have him obey his brother's angry shouts, her uncle grabbed with such an impatient, violent desire, it burst apart its straps, throwing the heavy estate ledger, books, pens and neat rolled official documents it carried onto the path, where the papers lay a second before the wind scattered them away in such a wild dance they could not be caught, though her father tried.

Important papers belonging to Lord Montagu, whose Land Agent her father was at Beaulieu, she rightly guessed, as she saw him run helter-skelter after them, leaving Titus to empty the satchel to the ground as if he searched for something he suspected was yet hidden in there, his mood as black as the night that hid him. But as her father ran into the gorse and long grass bordering the path to near the forest edge, she saw him fall with a scream of pain that knew he was badly hurt, his foot caught in a rabbit hole. But no sooner did he raise himself to his elbow, his leg so horribly twisted he couldn't move it more than an inch without the most fearful cry of agony, then Titus struck him with a rock so hard he broke his skull.

A murder the same magistrate and the same constable called an accident and no one, not even her mother, to gainsay it wasn't with his leg so broken beneath him and the rock he *fell* so heavily upon, lying at his head his blood still wet upon it and soaked to the ground.

Barely a month later both she and her mother were put from their house of five bedrooms, stables, cobbled yards, outbuildings, orchard and twenty acres of good arable land by Constable Brown and the bailiffs sent by her uncle and Mister Dicks. Whose ownership they had now become by some skullduggery the Court of Chancery[60] would take a thousand pounds and a lifetime of bitter dispute to disprove and with a claim of forged papers her father long owed him money.

An amount her mother could never hope to repay, not even the interest, but he badgered her near every week just the same she must and with many an unwelcome inspection of their little cottage on Captains Row that hoped there was something valuable he might have.

And her father so careful in all his honest dealings with folk his brother never was, not since he was a young man. With more than one voice in Lymington whispering that since his return he had taken up with the Owlers who smuggled their contraband from France into Langston Bay, but not only contraband, but spies too after the war was begun. And worse, traded in guns and slaves and all manner of goods with the Americans who were still our enemy just as much as the French, more so, perhaps because they were mostly British rebels claiming land that was not theirs.

The worst of them all by a mile the notorious

Albert 'Bloody Bones' Grub and his son, Clary 'The Cutthroat', who, until they were hanged last November, owned the *Seahorse,* a black, two masted schooner[61] with a distinctive red strake[62] painted on her side beneath her rails, father and older brother of Jemmy, who tried so hard to kill her and Billy last April on Southsea's mud and bog squelched, Great Morass. Would have, had Polly not seen his plan with her startling gift of second sight; her inner eye as she called it, and why not, it saw far better than her own, did?

A coincidence that surely linked them all in some plot against her parents and perhaps her, too, she must know and prove if she was to avenge their deaths, which she seethed she would when the *Parrot* returned to England, though goodness knows when that would be? But though she searched to see it all explained in the hundred blurred images that one upon one rose before her eyes in a confounding rush. Images of days long past and futures yet come she blinked to get a better look, but hardly saw and even less understood, found herself instead looking at a battle so fiercely fought she gasped with fright it was real.

A well found, three masted, two decked merchant ship, twice and more the size of the little *Parrot* in all its well-trimmed parts, she saw was called the *Potosi* beneath the spill of rope tied nets that clung to the underside of her bowsprit.[63] Which was all about surrounded in the sun that blazed the sea by thirty much smaller, hollow built boats.

Which at first glance looked a bit like the two Indian, bark canoes she had seen pulled up on the gravel shore the day the *Parrot* anchored in New York's Kep's Bay and Billy, Ralph and Duffy went ashore with such a boyish glee, she was so wickedly jealous they did and hatched a plan with Polly and Marie-Ange to do the same and almost ruined their plans. Perhaps she had, she didn't know? She hadn't returned to the *Parrot* that night to know what had happened and regretted she didn't, but dearly hoped they were safe. That they had all got away from the saber-toothed tigers that chased them through the cave of Tarhuhiawaku and hadn't fallen from the cliff or been eaten alive by the raptors that got her and Poll.

'Was that really only last Sunday?' She asked herself, knowing that since she met Gabe, just yesterday, time was a puzzle she would never again understand. The last Sunday she knew before Polly, Ralph and she fell headlong into the Land of Nogoback and the raptors carried them off, though she saw poor Ralph dropped and fall so far, she quickly lost sight of him. Breakfast for

their ravenous chicks as it turned out, a breakfast they only just escaped. Yes, it was! It was Sunday the 4 of June 1797, if that meant anything, now? And she doubted it did. Just a day and a date to remember in a universe that didn't! And with so much happened since then and in just a matter of hours, Billy would never believe her tale.

But these boats were so much bigger than the Indian canoes, were three or four times as big, each one twenty five feet long and five feet wide in the middle and with a single mast twelve feet high that draped a single sail from its single yard.[64] Though not a Lateen sail,[65] she marveled she knew the difference, Duffy would be so proud and Marie-Ange more than a little jealous, but a small square sail, which was loosely tied by a weather bleached rope to the high stern post that curved above a small square of raised, deck, where a large wooden, red painted tiller dipped the placid water with its elegantly slender blade.

Sleek hulled boats of polished, amber-brown teak built for speed and sudden, deadly attack and each one easily able to carry ten or fifteen nimble men on the paddle draped, narrow thwarts[66] that ladder-like held their sides. In the middle of which was a small, red canopied tent a little over four feet high and maybe eight or nine feet long. Living or sleeping quarters, she rightly guessed, from the

70

grass woven mats that littered their decks and the lighted charcoal brazier that stood on a small tripod at their stern-most ends, their canvas or linen tops rolled back on their curved wooden frames to make another use of them now.

To fire a small, ornately carved, long brass cannon, she knew was no bigger than the four, four-pounders[67] the *Parrot* carried on her bow and stern, their muzzles[68] snarled to a gape with the sharp teeth of some vile beast, at the now near stricken, *Potosi.* But not just cannon, but rockets, too, fired from bamboo pots mounted on swinging cradles that streamed their deadly fire in arcs of smoke above the wounded vessel.

Her decks awash with the blood of the score of natives who had fallen from her side to bob like cork buoys in the water below. Her tumble-home[69] dripped in scarlet runnels, her lower main yard fallen in a tangle over her side, her ropes cut and her sails a tatter of rags that spilled the sullen wind through shot ravaged holes. And each boat decorated with streamers of red, gold, and blue and their high prows carved with the head of some fiercesome creature no less horrible than those that decorated the mouths of their little cannon. A fanged snake, a lip-flared, biting lizard, a roaring lion, a fire breathing dragon, or a grinning demon and each painted to such a good effect with a rainbow of vivid colours she almost believed they were real.

But as she feared the *Potosi* would be very soon defeated and her valiant crew killed by the mad rush and desperate scramble of the scores of bare chested, olive-green turbaned natives who still climbed her sides armed with muskets, pistols, axes, spears, knives and swords, a second, three masted vessel suddenly come into view ploughing a dozen native boats to splinters, as she found the *Potosi's* larboard[70] side in a grapple of ropes that in the most seaman-like way held the two of them fast. A frigate she quickly saw was the *Cherub,* Billy's long dead father's, last command, the poor brave man killed in the South China Sea in '83 and Billy not yet born to know him.

And no sooner had it than he led a fifty-strong boarding party of roaring, red coated marines and swashbuckling sailors to her rescue, her larboard guns firing shot after well aimed shot into the mêlée of native boats now trying to get away. The billows of blue-grey smoke they made rising like a choking fog to hide the fight which now pressed both ends of the *Potosi's* upper decks, where knotted groups of breathlessly bloody men fought for their lives with all their might and main and where she saw Billy's father fall mortally wounded at the feet of a desperately frightened young woman, who, though she swaddled a small child in her arms reached out to protect him with her hands, her lap making a pillow for his head. Her husband frightened almost witless by the fight that moved in bloody waves all about him, guarding them as best he could with a pistol he dared not fire; hardly knew how to fire. And wearing a hat now so long out of fashion she had only once seen it's like before and that was on Lauder Trompe's massive head. It was surely his father, so much did he look like him, the same swarthy complexion, the same thick neck, the same hunched shoulders, the same muscular arms, the same squat body, and the same nervous unease. And his brave, defiant mother beside him and surely that was him, a babe in arms; though he looked rather lovely in his pink blanket, so unlike the smelly, fat boy she knew? *'Impossible,'* she murmured.

'To me *Cherubs,'* she heard young Lieutenant Redman Crookhampton bravely shout, his bloody sword in his right hand as he gathered the last of his men beneath the mainmast shrouds[71] for one last mighty charge at the now retreating pirates who were gathered on the forecastle[72] in a cringing huddle, some climbed onto the bowsprit to very near its top, not least their leader who she realised was just about to jump.

A tall, lean, muscular man with a mad gleam in

his one good eye and a brutish curl on his flabby lips, who wore crimson red pantaloons about his legs and a turban of the same rich colour on his head when no other man did, she heard them a dozen times call General Prem Rez. But before he jumped Lieutenant Crookhampton led a whooping charge and with the help of the *Potosi's* Captain, a tall dark haired strikingly handsome Scots fellow of manly bearing called Lauder McDonald and his brave crew and the double blast of grape shot[73] fired with such a devastating, flame spitting roar at the pirates from the *Cherub,* swept them all clean over the sides in a heap of bloody ruin few escaped.

But not before she saw her uncle, Titus jump from the *Cherub's* poopdeck,[74] where he served as the ships Purser,[75] a position bought for him by her father's good wishes with money he could barely afford, onto the *Potosi.* His stealthy advance cloaked by the fog of gunfire that swirled all about him so thick no one saw him climb down a stairwell into the cabins below, from where he emerged barely three minutes later clutching a small, but awkwardly heavy, Rosewood trunk to his chest.

A trunk she knew she had first seen in Portsmouth's Fountain Inn, last April. A trunk she knew was made by the Templar Knights near five hundred years ago to hold a single piece of the Rebus of Akhenaten. A trunk he now carried to his cabin before returning a second time. Only to be thwarted by a smoke grimed, Lieutenant Crookhampton, who sword in hand ordered him back. Little recognizing the murderously determined look on the Purser's face when he did, which turned to a boiling rage when he caught him by his coat tail and spun him around. A lunatic anger that in a fight of barely half a minute tipped them both into the sea, where they were instantly captured and held up to cruel display by the pirates they had defeated, who longing for revenge carried them off.

But as she watched these horrible sights unfold her eyes strayed to the sun blazed horizon ten long miles away where four other ships sailed in a loose and unconcerned formation, their tiny squadron led by the 74-gun, battle ship, HMS *Dryad.* Whose Captain, Commodore Kettle, watched the battle unfold through his telescope, his Captain of Marines, Captain Drier close beside him, the scowl on their faces knowing the *Potosi* was saved and with it, a fortune, lost.

They had betrayed the *Potosi* to General Prem Rez in the Portuguese port of Macau, just the week before with the promise he could keep her cargo, sell her crew and passengers for slaves and they would return to England leaving the South China

Seas for him to raid and plunder and did so for the great treasure of gold he would give them. A scene she saw bargained over a game of dice Commodore Kettle unaccountably won, as he rarely won a game of chance.

How cruel, how utterly mean and cowardly, she thought, as she saw Lieutenant Crookhampton bent to his knees plead for his life some months later before the glittering jewel studded throne of General Prem Rez. His palace an ornate treasure of marble, jade, and ivory as wonderful as any she had imagined in the Arabian Nights. His wrists and ankles manacled with heavy iron chains that scraped his skin to the bone, his near naked body beaten black and blue and wickedly striped by the deep cutting whip they now lashed him with, his face a bloody ruin of snot, spit and blood from the endless blows he endured beneath the shoulder crushing, wood, and iron collar he wore about his aching neck, but yet, still alive, beside the guards who teased and prodded him with their swords.

Carelessly watched as they did by her uncle who stood coolly beside him dressed in a fashionable black tailcoat, trimmed in velvet, a yard of ivory-white, Dupion silk[76] about his neck, black breeches, white silk stockings and silver buckled shoes graced his trim, well fed legs, his powdered, three curled bob wig[77] a dandy's joy upon his head.

'Kill him or keep him for a ransom, Prem, I care not,' he said with a confidence that knew how safe he was as he sipped the ice-cold sherbet he so much enjoyed he boasted he did to poor Redman with a slurp that almost made him cry.

But how? She wondered, as her *mind* found the answer in the asking, seeing him dragged in chains and bloody rags from a foetid prison cell to face the court of General Prem Rez and no better treated than Lieutenant Crookhampton in the weeks since they were landed on the southernmost tip of the Malay Peninsula.[78] But though his life hung in the balance he bargained with a sly and devilish cunning he knew where a great treasure could be had, if he could only retrieve the map that would find it. A map inscribed on a piece of blackened plate he had discovered hidden on the *Potosi* before he was captured and on a second he knew was still hidden in the same place. One of six pieces he wrongly estimated, fashioned like a cut piece of pie that would combine to form a round plate, twice the size of any pastry he had eaten, a plate that would guide them to the treasure. If the story, an unusually drunken, trusting Constantine Trompe had told when they met in Macau was true and he was sure it was. For why else would he and his wife risk their lives a dozen times over to find one piece of the plate hidden in the dangerous mountains of Peru near the ruins of the once great Inca city of Machu Picchu and a second hidden in the fiercely dangerous port of Macau, if it wasn't and with four more to be got? One in Bombay India, their next port of call, one in Massawa in Arabia and two more Constantine fell asleep before he could say where.

Each one fashioned ten thousand years ago, he alone could read, he lied and each one telling a small part of the secret of where the treasure was hidden. A shrewd, wildly impossible guess that knew nothing of the story she now knew by heart; the story professor Tollendal had told them, one that Roland, Ned and Sal better knew than even him. But one remembered in small part by the General, a superstitious man at the best of times, as all men and women of the East are, a story told him by his father before he died of a powerful magician, who came to his court with the same amazing story. A Frenchman he remembered was called the Count de Montard. A coincidence so remarkable he made Titus swear on his life the instant he found all six pieces of this secret map he would send news to him, no matter where his journey took him and no matter how long it did. And threatened him with a knife at his throat that if he didn't, he would send men to find him, no matter where he hid and to make doubly certain he did,

Mister Ho, his faithful servant would travel home with him, *his* servant, or so he thought.

Montard, mused Tom, hearing the General *think* his name as clearly as if he had spoken it aloud and no sooner had he, then to her utter astonishment he rose up from the mist beside her, as if the very thought of him called him to her side. As she now realised it had! As the thought of her mother and father so long dead and so long missed, had just a few moments before called them to her.

A realisation that knew the mist was the veil that separated her everyday waking mind from her sleeping, dreaming mind.[79] Dreams which everyday spoke to her, but in such an imperfect way she hardly knew what they *said*. But knew the pleasures and terrors they could so easily bring and the power they had to make her happy or sad. But more than this, she realised being awake is just a small part of dreaming.

But it wasn't the Montard of recent terrifying memory she now saw, the dark and menacing spectral figure professor Tollendal spoke so earnestly and always so nervously about, who he feared would yet be the ruin of all his plans, no, this was a young man of pleasant, if unremarkable hollow cheeked good looks. Tall, but not as tall as she had imagined him to be, as his reputation demanded he must be, certainly not as tall as Duffy, who was a giant at six feet two inches and perhaps not as tall as Billy, who was five feet nine or ten inches and still growing. A young man of eighteen or nineteen, she rightly guessed and so awkwardly thin beneath the rusted and rent poor man's chainmail armour he wore beneath the rain soaked and mud splattered heavy black cloak and the red crossed, white mantle of the Templers he served, he might be described with some accuracy, as gawky or gangling, but never muscular or robust, as she feared he was.

His long black hair an unruly straggle of greasy-wet, finger twisted threads so long unwashed she guessed it never much was and never more than when he took his Michaelmas[80] bath, as good manners demanded he must. A neglect that gave his sparsely bearded face a corpse-like waxy grime that pimpled his ferret-like face like the pox; perhaps it was the pox?

A face she saw more clearly now in the guttering candle he held in his rain wet, leather gloved hand as he began to descend a narrow, shoulder scraping, spiral stair case from what appeared to be a crypt on the floor above. His scabbarded sword, even though he held it tight to his side, and heavy mud splashed, leather boots tapping a mournful echo on each worn step as he did.

A horribly spooky, mouse run crypt that was lit to a softly flickering yellow light by the two branched, wrought iron candelabra that stood on the narrow, stone plinth beside the still open door he had just come through. Which was everywhere surrounded by a cobweb hung, dust carpeted clutter of carelessly stacked and sometimes fallen coffins. Some of them splintered and broken to reveal a protruding hand, arm, leg, or head, as if the occupants were trying to climb out, their age stretched skin, empty eye sockets and tattered clothes adding to the horror. Beside these ghoulish reminders of the long dead, two, stone-carved sarcophagi[81] of exquisitely ornate design occupied the privileged centre of that ten feet high, massively pillared, intricately vaulted[82] space, protected on all four sides from their unruly companions by fretted wooden screens and holy relics and wherein a cowled dwarf sat, seemingly waiting his return.

His movements on the stairs were slow and nervously tentative, but became all the more cautious - frightened even, when at long last he found the bottom and the stout, wood and iron studded door that now barred his way? The triangular key stone in the lintel of the low Gothic arch above it, deeply carved with the figure of a seated dog, its large, pig-like ears pricked to the least sound, its tail upright, a hieroglyph older than time that spelt a single, dread name, a name he knew well from his father; Seth. A warning to all who came there of the danger that waited within.

A secret place so deep in the bowels of Chartres Cathedral[83] the priests celebrating the Compline Mass[84] as they walked in single file in a prayerful circle around the stone paved labyrinth[85] that for nearly a hundred years had decorated the floor of the nave above, knew nothing of its existence, or those who worshipped there. A worship of the old gods that predated the cathedral by ten thousand years or more and on a site long known for its magic and where a circle of standing stones once stood, a circle known to be the haunt of ghosts and ghouls since before the Romans.[86]

With his hand raised to knock upon the door, Montard took a deep breath, his eyes turned to the stairs behind him and the chink of light he could see in the crypt above and for the briefest moment thought he saw the dwarf watching him. But it was too late to go back, even if he could, too late to escape the meeting that now waited him inside that room and would the dwarf let him, anyway? A meeting long in the making with the mystics and seers who worshiped the old gods, the gods of Egypt, as he and his family had since the days of the First Crusade,[87] whose help he now so desperately wanted, but a meeting he almost didn't keep so busy did his lord and master, Sir Mungo of Denbigh have him attend his duties that night of flight from Paris, whose faithless Serjeant he was.

'Enter,' she heard a stern voice call out to him before his fist struck the door, and, as she did, the door opened to a haunted, torch lit room and a cowled dwarf bid him come in with a curt and impatient wave of his bleached white, skeletal hand. Which, like the hand of the dwarf above who met him at one of the cathedrals little used side doors, barely ten minutes ago, and showed him the hidden trapdoor in the crypt to this unheard-of place, seemed more dead than alive; perhaps was dead? 'Enter,' called the voice, a second time, as his foot faltered on the low step in front of him and then a third time, until, at last, he bravely stepped in and walked towards the roughhewn, stone altar at the far end of the massively pillared, low ceilinged room he now saw in the light of nine, weakly flickering torches. A ceiling so low it seemed to press him to the floor with its overpowering threat. An altar on which a small pyramid of black diorite stone, capped in gold stood.

'What is it you seek, brother?' Asked the cloaked and cowled priest who stood behind the altar, his voice stern and impatient, his hands steepled to his chin, as were the hands of his two companion priests beside him.

'Audience master,' answered Montard, meekly, his eyes sweeping the room from end to end, a room of hidden corners and dark recesses where other brothers, some, he hoped, known to him, waited. But a dungeon-like room decorated on every surface, pillars, walls and ceiling with the most fantastical chalk-white, occult symbols, some he easily recognised, like the pyramids, stars, moons, circles, pentagrams,[88] pentacles[89] and hieroglyphs he saw, but others he didn't. And all of them enclosed singly or in magical clusters in a triangle linked in a web-like pattern of triangles that was strangely hypnotic. Carrying his eyes to some far distant place and seeming to suggest a space and timeless distance far beyond the room there wasn't. And each one pulling his eyes towards the stone statue of the Typhonic Beast[90] that stood behind the priests. A statue he instantly recognised was Seth by its dog-like head and the wooden flail and ankh cross it held in its hands, but so much fiercer than he had ever seen it's like before. Which was framed by the sacred, double enneagon[91] of Egypt, which was carved into the wall behind it. Which, to his astonishment seemed to glow and pulsate, as if lit from the *other* side; was lit from the *other* side.

'With whom do you ask audience, brother?' Came the priests reply, a chorus of whispering voices coming from every dark corner, echoing his grave concern.

'The god of chaos and destruction, the Lord Seth whose great majesty stands before me,' answered Montard, with a shiver that knew the dwarf had come silently up behind him, his deep breathing a deadly threat.

'Then bow your obeisance to your master, Jean-Léon Montard, Templar Serjeant at arms to that fat preening Welshman of the godless *English* shires, Sir Mungo of Denbigh.[92] Bow low before your divine and all powerful master,' bellowed the priest, his voice shrill and trembling, as the dwarf unbidden by anyone, thrashed him to his knees with a thick wooden stick, his hand and the hands of his companion priests pointing to the now more fiercely shimmering, fast pulsating seams of the double enneagon behind them. Which to Tom's utter astonishment began to fill with a dizzying lattice of interlinked triangles, much like those she had just a moment before seen rising above the Giza pyramids to reach into the night sky; to Orion's Belt. Each one spiraling in a worm-like, flexing tube from the sides of the enneagons to their centre, where a third, much smaller enneagon appeared to open to the intensely bright, almost blinding, pulsating light behind it. At first barely a fraction, a glimpse of what was to come, but then, by infinitely slow degree, yet more and more, until she could easily see through aperture into the room beyond.

'And what do you ask of the Lord Seth?' Commanded the priest.

'The power to find what is mine by right of conquest, by the right of my forefather who found it buried hidden on the Temple Mount in Jerusalem in year of the Christian Lord, 1128, when everyone else had given up its search, but, he did, and to the praise of all, was taken from him by those he told, his masters, as they are mine to this day. The Templar Knights whose fall begins this night,[93] whose equal company they refused. The Knighthood he deserved, as I deserve. The Rebus of the heretic Pharaoh, Akhenaten, enemy of the Priests of Amun-Ra and the great treasure of gold, silver and treasure it promises.'

Words barely spoken, when he found himself pulled through the enneagon by a pulse of sun bright orange-white light into a steeply curving, bell-shaped, black-stone chamber, which shimmered in the light that bathed it to its pinched top. Wherein, a circle of nine shaven headed, bare chested, chanting priests dressed in white and purple, starched linen ankle skirts, sat cross legged around a black, mirror bright, polished stone pyramid, strenuously humming a high pitched musical note in such perfect harmony it was barely audible.

Bowing his forehead to the cold stone floor, he trembled as he asked the favour he had so long rehearsed of the priest who now stood so tall above him he dared not look into his face for fear it would be him; Seth. 'I am Sahura, Chief Priest of the Temple Void of Khufu,' said the priest, his right hand rested on the flat, palm-sized, gold medallion he wore on his chest, which was inscribed with the cameo outline of a wing-stretched falcon, clutching in its sharp talons a disk etched with the hieroglyph of Seth, his voiced raised not in anger, but above the chant of his brother priests, 'but more than this I am the Chief Priest of the Priests of Amun-Ra, servant guardians of the mighty Lord Seth, who you and your family have long and faithfully served, god of chaos and destruction, who in his infinite mercy grants you the power to find the Rebus of Akhenaten, as you bid he does, wherever it has been taken and when you have. to return it safe to me, here in the Temple Void of the pyramid Khufu, where it belongs, whence it will be taken to the Temple of Thebes. And when you have you will be rewarded beyond your wildest dreams with gold, silver and jewels too much to count in a hundred long days. But more than this, I will grant you the dread fear and obedience of the men who have for so long ignored, mocked, and abused you with their lowly service? Do you agree, Montard? Do I have your oath you will do all that I ask of you, never asking more than I will give you?'

'Yes, Lord.'

'Then take this blood stone[94] amulet inscribed with the name of our master, I now give to you and wear it about your neck suffering no one to take it from you. Because if they do you will lose and they will gain its magic, which commands the power of the Priests of Amun-Ra to your bidding. Will command the power of space and time to your will, taking you to wherever you ask, as if you were walking through an open door. But have a care Montard and do not abuse my trust in you, or you will suffer the fate of all men who stand against the Priests of Amun-Ra and die a death more terrible than you can imagine; a living hell.'

'Gracious me,' said Tom, as the image of Montard and the priest disappeared in the blink of an eye, 'he is a mortal man like us. A shabby bearded boy barely grown. A mortal man who can be knocked to the floor with a thump or better killed with a knife, if only the amulet is taken from him, which I swear I will if I can get an inch within his scrawny neck, see if I don't,' she vowed.

So, that is how this vile business with Jean-Léon Montard, Templar Serjeant at arms began. A disgruntled young man with a grudge against the Templars he now serves, who believed his family was wronged by them two hundred years before he was born. Were robbed of what they thought was theirs, the Rebus of Akhenaten, which their ancestor found on Jerusalem's Temple Mount but though he did, was refused the knighthood he thought he deserved, was his just reward. So, in a fit of jealous spite he summons up the power of this god, Seth, and the Priests of Amun-Ra, who are his disciples to set it all right, betraying his master Sir Mungo of Denbigh, as he did. Never for one moment realising the Rebus is far more than the treasure map he thinks it is, the key to his fortune, but is the key to a power beyond his understanding, though professor Tollendal is equally sure it isn't. A power beyond any ones understanding, she murmured, as once again her uncle Titus came out of the mist to claim her attention.

But now a year or more after his capture and after months and months of pleading with General Prem Rez to set him free and with money enough, he asked, to help find Constantine Trompe and his wife, Marianne. And so, it was she watched as Titus finally took ship to England with his servant, bodyguard and keeper, the inscrutable Mister Ho. Leaving Redmond to suffer his fate, a slave in the court of General Prem Rez and so utterly alone he despaired he would ever see his father the Admiral again. Though he had long since forgotten his monstrously bossy, not to say ugly American wife and knew nothing of the baby that was his; Hesta Victoria. The first of the many ships he took passage on, on a journey of so many twists, backward turns and contrary winds and tides it was three years before he reached home in the early October of 1787; four long years since he left and without a single penny piece to call his own, so little had the General given him.

Time enough to rethink the rash promise he had made before he left he would find the *six* parts of treasure map. If indeed it was a map, as Constantine Trompe said it was, though his clever wife the following day denied it was. To rethink and then almost forget he ever had. Though Mister Ho was a constant reminder it was something he might one day have to do.

So much so, when he finally landed at Portsmouth dock he had nothing more certain on his mind than to make the fortune he wanted and with his older brother's help or no. And when *no* was the answer, he gave, killed him without a shred of pity or remorse and threw himself in with the Langstone Owlers. But not before he had journeyed to London to see Rear Admiral Oscar Kettle, who rumour had it, had not only stolen Captain Kepple's reputation and just reward in the Straits of Malacca, but also stolen his and Redman's belongings from the *Cherub,* selling all they owned in a charitable auction that was the custom of the days.[95]

And so, it was he stood outside the Admiralty building in the mid November of his return to plead with the Marine sentry on duty to let him in, who on hearing from Admiral Kettle, he mustn't, not ever, sent him packing with a painful boot up his backside and a promise he would shoot him dead if he ever returned.

A sight that made Tom laugh so angry and thoroughly disconsolate did he look as he skirted Horse Guards Parade beside the park[96] in his patched at the sleeves, salt rimed, grey coat and greasy brown, tricorn hat. As rank after rank of red coated soldiers marched in the chill wind that blew in his face to the sound of pipes and drums and the bellow of a fat bellied Sergeant Major with more white stripes on his arm than she could count and turned the corner into a puddle splashed Fludyers Street.[97] Where he met Captain Bully Drier coming the other way and looking so thin, pinched and threadbare he hardly looked the same man who oath swore to the magistrate all those years later, her mother was a suicide best forgotten by everyone.

A meeting that took them into a smart coffee house nearby, where he learned the money raised in the auction of his few belongings had, indeed been stolen by the Admiral, a man who ever had more debts than the money to pay them. But not only this, the purse of fifty guineas he had larcenously embezzled from the crew of the *Cherub* was also gone the same way.

Of the Rosewood trunk and the engraved metal plate he had stolen from Constantine Trompe with such high hopes it would make his fortune, Bully told him, with no great concern it was anything valuable, the Admiral had kept it as a curio until they anchored at Naples on the way home. When, short of funds once again, he sold them, both, trunk, and plate, to an English archaeologist and keen collector of curios and antiquarian objects, who was working for the King of Naples on the newly discovered Roman site at Pompeii. A crafty, learned little man, he vaguely remembered was called, Mister Henry Beattie, who to his knowledge was still grubbing about in dirt, even now.

'So that's how Mister Beattie got his piece of the Rebus, the piece they found in Corbeau's satchel,' gushed Tom, who had long wondered how it got there. 'He bought it from that blackguard, Admiral Kettle, who stole it from my uncle, Titus, who stole it from Lauder's mum and dad. One of two they had in their possession when the *Potosi* was attacked by General Prem Rez and his pirates. Who, her uncle said, found one, somewhere in Peru and the other in China, the Portuguese port of Macau to be precise. But not in New York. And no sooner did she think it, then she saw Lauder Trompe in a new bought suit of clothes and washed as she had never seen him before standing on the fire ravaged, smoke clouded Albany dock, staring at the score of burnt out ships now sunk in the riverside harbour, their blackened masts and yards peeping out of the slate-grey water in a cat's-cradle of twisted fingers. And saw him so close, she easily saw what he was holding in his two hands, a piece of the Rebus of Akhenaten. And there was only one piece in the whole of North America that could be, the piece Johannes de Groot hid after his father was murdered. The piece she, Billy and the crew of the *Parrot* had crossed the Atlantic Ocean to New York to find, the piece apparently hidden in or near the Cave of Tarhuhiawaku in the wilds of the Adirondack Mountains and without the least hope of finding it there, now. 'Crikey,' she exclaimed. But nor did her uncle make any mention of Elizabeth Caetano's piece of the Rebus last seen in Rio de Janeiro's, Mosteiro de Sao Bento[98] in 1736, which was surely their first port of call after the Trompe's left America, empty handed. And if *they* didn't find it, how would they ever hope to find it? She wondered with a despondent sigh that realised it might never be found now. For professor Tollendal distinctly said no word of Elizabeth had been heard in over sixty years; not one that hinted where she might be found in that vast, impenetrable country of endless forests, swamps and rivers that was Brazil.

All of which was vitally important if they were to find the remaining six pieces of the Rebus before Montard or his protégé, but not, she was now quite certain, his friend or his confidante, Corbeau did, whose interest in them was a mystery she had yet to fathom. Two pieces of which were safely hidden aboard the *Parrot;* Mister Beattie's, as she would now forever call that first piece she and Polly found by the merest fluke of chance in Corbeau's satchel, which had a provenance they had yet to discover and of course Marie-Ange's piece. Whose ancestor, Sir Henry le Dantec they did know. And now of course a third piece had been found, Johannes de Groot's, which thankfully Lauder had in his safe keeping, if he could be rescued before he dropped it into the Hudson River as she feared he soon would if he didn't hold onto it more tightly, as the Chinese boy who had just this second come up beside him, urged him he must.

That left six! The piece Marianne and Constantine Trompe had when the *Potosi* escaped the pirates, the three pieces she dared to hope they had eventually found in Bombay, Massawa and somewhere else, a drunken Constantine didn't say. Elizabeth Caetano's missing piece and last, but not least, Sir Mungo of Denbigh's piece, never seen or heard of since 1307, when Montard attacked him on the road to La Rochelle. Information Billy must now urgently have, she sighed, as her uncle and Bully, once again found her attention.

Without funds and thinking Titus might be the answer to his prayers, a man he knew to be as venal as any man he knew, Bully leaned across the coffee table and whispered he was still a slight acquaintance of Admiral Kettle. Who, for a price, he confided, could be pressed upon to sign any letter or document, which passed across his mostly empty desk without a second glance, so drunk was the grumpy old goat for most of everyday. Import and export licenses and tax-free bills of ships laden being of little concern to him, no matter where their cargoes were coming from or going, too. 'Indeed,' said Titus, his interest piqued, as Bully saw it was and because it was, re-marked, as if it was a topic of idle concern to him, he had many times heard both France and America were popular destinations for ships wanting to make a quick and ready profit from the contraband goods that could very easily had by anyone.

And so, their partnership was forged in their sly and mutual poverty, Titus, with his many nefarious contacts in both Lymington and Langstone, finding a ship and a crew, the *Seahorse*, which would every week cross the channel laden with all the contraband they good find and Bully providing the papers from Admiral Kettle that would keep them safe from the Revenue Men, who haunted the south coast every dark night. A criminal smuggling, not to say treasonous enterprise that very soon included Captain Mooney's, *Wasp.* A slaver and gun runner to the rebel colonies that saw them earn enormous profits from their work.

But never more so than when the war with France began in '93, which hatched a plan three years later to rid themselves of a growing ever greedier and demanding, Albert 'Bloody Bones' Grub and his violent son, Clary 'The Cutthroat', legal owners of the *Seahorse,* and have it all for themselves and with Turzel Begg's their Captain. And would have done the same with Captain Mooney, if he hadn't been the wily old fox he was and not so easily tricked from what was his.

And so it was with mounting disbelief Tom saw her uncle and Bully, frequent visitors to Paris, despite the war had grown more earnest and every Channel port on the French coast was blockaded so impossibly tight by the English navy, few, if any, ships got in or out without an Admiralty pass to say they could and the *Seahorse* always had such a pass, signed by Admiral Kettle, sitting with an irascible, Albert and Clary in the crowded Le Café Procop[99] in the Rue des Fossés-Saint-Germain-des-Prés, in the early summer of 1796. A notorious smoke-filled café hung with revolutionary flags and bunting known to be the haunt of every rogue in Paris, where they were talking heatedly of their plan to land the *Seahorses* richest shipment yet, not in Lymington or Langstone, where smuggling was a way of life, but at Lulworth Cove, further along the coast, where few smugglers ever landed their cargo.

A plan they argued back and forth for most of the evening, until, for a greater share of the profit they would both have from this dangerous venture, Albert and Clary agreed and with every assurance they would be safe with papers signed by the Admiral to prove they were. A bargain they sealed with a trip to the Odeon Theatre across the street later that night, where the Comédie-Française[100] was performing, Molière's,[101] *Le Malade des Imaginaire*[102] to a packed house.

Where to her complete and utter astonishment Tom saw Lady Charlotte Desmoulin, Billy's femme fatale, though he red-faced, hotly denied she was, looking more exquisitely beautiful than she had ever seen her before, half hidden behind her Poggi silk fan. A delicate reminder of how artfully feminine she truly was, a present from one of her many admirers she rightly guessed by the way she teasingly displayed it. Her every gesture a subtle hint a hundred watching eyes understood. Not least Pierre Corbeau who watched her with a curious interest from the balcony seat he occupied. 'Mmm,' she exclaimed. 'So, they did know each other, after all! Well, he at least knew her! So, that is why she betrayed them at the river inviting him to the château when she could have sent him away.

And there sitting beside her in a plush red and gold embroidered, winged armchair that almost swallowed him up, was that irritatingly ungrateful little snot, Camille, Albert, Louis St Just. Heir, or so he a hundred times claimed he was, to anyone who would listen to his vain and silly prattle, to the

Duc de Clairvaux and both so much enjoying the show she wondered why they had both lied their way to America when all revolutionary Paris was at their feet that night?

A few weeks later the *Seahorse* anchored off the beach at Durdle Door in the dead of night and shipped her rich cargo ashore until all was nearly done. When to Albert's horrifying surprise a party of Militia Men and red coated Marines ambushed them with a hail of unwarranted musket fire, killing five of their number, whilst taking him and all the rest of his land trapped crew, prisoner; fourteen in all. Including Clary, who briefly escaped to the beach just in time to see, Turzel killed as he called him into the sea, his arms outstretched to help him, as he was never meant to be, and his son, Charlie haul the *Seahorse's* anchor in a wind that carried her safely out to sea, as her uncle and Bully ever intended. And all the time watched by them from the hill above, who later toasted their success in the Flag and Lamb inn in the heart of Lulworth.

Blaggard's, thieves and scoundrels, she fumed to see men so ill-used, smugglers though they were, betrayed by men they thought their friends. How she hated her uncle and Bully for the men they were, but not such fast friends, Bully didn't betray him to Barry O'Brien in the snow-covered garden of the Palais Royal later that year and with Marie-Ange watching them from the street, though she only had eyes for Ralph.

B ut just then, when she thought her waking dream had nothing more to tell her, she turned her face to the warmly inviting glow of the pastel orange sun now slowly rising above the billow of clouds behind her. Its fan-like fingers of darting light reaching out to find her, as she saw Ethan, Isaac and Indie sitting in a conspirator's huddle on a khaki-brown carpet looking at photographs from the spread of newspapers on the floor in front of them.

The same enigmatic series of three photographs that filled the bottom right hand corner of the screen on the new bought for Indie only last Christmas, MacBook Pro, 13-inch: 2.8GHz lap top computer, beneath the frozen face of a young girl. A computer like the dozens she had seen in the Portal, but though she could see it was a truly wonderful machine and with such a lovely shape and showed the date was a future yet to come, it wasn't half as good as any of Gabe's by the look of the funny, hand touch keyboard that made it work. Which sat on the pink-legged, tubular metal desk above them. The same children she had left, barely fifteen minutes ago, still sleeping peacefully in three, of the thousands of glass-domed beds that filled the basement of Gabe's crashed and forever stranded in Nogoback, time travelling Portal; and little knowing how they got there. As they must remain asleep until she got back. Hopefully, in the next hour or two, she groaned looking at Billy's Tompion, the time unmoved since she saw it last.

A bedroom decorated in mix of soft pinks, cornflower blues and sun flower yellows so tastefully composed by Indie's mother it called her in, so inviting did it look and with a view of the slate grey, icy East River through the pink curtained window across to Long Island she barely recognised it; but oddly did. And furnished with a bed so big it was three times the size of the little truckle bed she every night slept in beneath Billy's wooden, coffin-like cot and every night feared the mouse that lived there would nest in her hair, chopped short to her ears like a boy though it was.

Which was covered in a luxuriously thick, Duvet much like the one she and Polly slept under the first and only night they stayed with Gabe in the Portal, but covered with a gorgeous, Disappearing-Nine-Patch-Quilt[103] that was cleverly scalloped at its pink edges, much like the sort she and her mother several times made and sold in Lymington market after her father died; was murdered she corrected herself, her fists balled in anger at what she had seen just a few minutes ago. But with an arrangement of colourful stripes, flowers and plain prints that was so lovely she gasped anything could be so beautiful and with a score of soft, cuddly dolls and animals neatly arranged on the top of it that made her giggle there was any room for her to sleep in it with the heap of four fat pillows that crowded the barley turned spindles of the wooden head board, above which, posters of astonishingly pretty boys looked down on her as she slept.

And speaking about her in a way that clearly knew her. Knew a great deal about her, it would seem? Which, could only mean one thing, she beamed her relief and excitement, they, and all the Nanochromes were released from their year long, medical hibernation, which Gabe said he couldn't, until she and Polly returned with the second Portal and the rest of the Nanochromes they were sent to rescue. A rescue too long delayed by Kiya's wand, which not only brought her here by a magic seemingly far stronger than his, but now appeared to want to take her back to the temple complex of Khufu, so much, did she now begin to feel herself sucked back there. Its tremulous, growing erratic movement now pulling her body back together in a gathering sparkle of light that stretched to infinity.

'See, I told you,' said Indie with a thrill of excitement, lifting a page from *The New York Times* from the floor and placing it beside a page from its rival newspaper of the same day, the *Daily Post* on the end of her bed, each one showing the same series of three small, photographs, 'and here we are again, like I said, on YouTube,' she pointed to her computer, 'and with a message from this girl I told you about, Adriana, who asks us to contact her on Facebook, as soon as ever we can. Like now?' She pleaded. 'Oh, my god, can you believe it, a girl living in Brazil with the same surname as the girl, Tom told us about, when Gabe woke us up in Nogoback, is trying to contact us. The same, girl the Count de Montard tried to kill all those years ago, Elizabeth Caetano and missing without trace since he did.'

'They know about *her,*' gasped Tom, hardly believing they did. 'Did I tell them when I *got* back? *Get* back, I mean.' She smiled, relieved she must have, as she sat on the bed so close to Indie she might have touched her on the cheek. Almost did, as she and her brothers bent to study the three photographs, which appeared to show the three of them standing, crouching, and kneeling, not ten feet from where Kiya was hiding in the graveyard of Wall Street's historic, Trinity Church. Though it was a much-changed church and yard from the one she knew and so crowded by tall buildings it wasn't the same place at all and the streets thick traffic and people hurrying to and thro'.

In the first picture, the crew cut Isaac, is sheepishly grinning into the camera, as if caught momentarily, but delightedly, off guard, by the photographer on the bus, though his pixie face, is blurred by the rainbow dapple of sunshine that washes over him. Ethan is barely in shot and Indie hardly at all. In the second picture, Isaac is still in the centre of the picture, but is now hesitantly waving to the camera, his up raised hand masking most of his still grinning, gap-toothed face, as Indie, now in shot crouches to her knees to look at one of the grave stones that everywhere dot the yard beneath the many shrubs and trees. Ethan, is now a little further into shot, but is barely recognizable to anyone, but those with a close acquaintance with his dimpled chin, shoulder, and right knee.

All very innocent and unremarkable! A tourist shot like so many others that captures something of the west facing profile of that delightfully beautiful city church, through the trees and perhaps a score of its many daily visitors from a bus so obviously travelling north on Trinity Place, until, that is, you see Kiya surreptitiously crouching behind a tree, as if she was hiding from them, or perhaps watching them. A sight that so catches the eye you cannot help, but look at her, so wan and so haunt-ingly beautiful does she look dressed in a blue rib-boned straw bonnet fallen seductively askew on her bob-cut, jet-black hair, a black cloak draped almost to a fall from her near, naked shoulders and high-waisted, pink cotton dress that was sure-ly two hundred years out of fashion; but so pretty.

In the third picture, they are all four gone. Though the several people walking, standing, and stooping beside them in the second photograph are all still in shot and with a caption to say the photographs were taken with a Nikon D300, digital camera, at five second intervals and with a head-line that read, The Ghost of Trinity Church.

'What made you go on YouTube, Indie?' Asked Isaac, his face turned to look at the paused com-puter screen.

'I just knew someone would have uploaded these photographs, like they always do spooky pictures like these. But there were hundreds of them. You wouldn't believe how many creepy pic-tures there are on there, but then I found these and a message from Adriana and it nearly blew my mind, that's when I phoned you, two,' she sighed, pointing to the screen, her voice a breathless ex-citement, 'she wants us to contact her; she does.'

'But you haven't? You've not contacted her yet, have you, Indie?' Asked Ethan, his voice a caution of concern.

'No, but I nearly did,' she moaned, 'but I waited just like you said, I should, until you got home from soccer practice. 'But you can see for yourself, she wants us, too,' she sighed, pointing to her wide eyed, frozen face on the computer screen. 'And when you have, we can go on Facebook and see what she wants,' she said pressing the play button to reveal an attractive young girl of perhaps thirteen or fourteen years of age with a tight braided, coal-black ponytail fallen over her left shoulder almost to her waist, speaking in an accented, but perfect English, fill the screen, talking it seemed, from her bedroom. The blue painted wall and yellow window frame behind her open to the sunny street outside, which thrummed to the sound of cicadas and chirruped to the cry of birds.

'Hi guys, my name is Adriana Caetano, saw your photographs in the local newspaper and then on TV last week, well I almost did,' she laughed at her own joke, her flawless coffee brown face broadening into a wicked grin of soft, full lips and perfect white teeth. 'The Diario do Para in Belém, Brazil where I live, which is the massive sea port on the mouth of the Amazon, but you probably know that anyway and thought you might like to contact me on my Facebook page and tell me how you did it? I know the lady who took it claims you are all ghosts?' She laughed, but its trick photography, isn't it? Like on Candid Camera?[104] So tell me how you did it, 'cos me and my *nine* best friends, yeah, poor me, just *nine* best friends in the whole wide world would love to know how you did it. Our guess, well, *Lizzie's* best guess, is you did it like the fairy girls[105] in England, did theirs all those years before. Fooled everyone, even Kodak and Houdini, who knew a trick or two, so no telling what you can do with a clever digital camera and Photoshop editing to make a picture tell a story of ghosts and mummies?' She laughed, again, but a hesitant laugh that didn't believe they did. 'Did you see the film with Rachel Weisz, isn't she gorgeous and Brendan Fraser, who I adore? We all thought it was fabulous and really funny in parts, but so frightening with all those horrid beetles crawling all over the place and pyramids and stuff. But tell us how you got those fabulous photographs to come out so well, like it was all real? Bet it was easy-peasy-lemon-squeezy when you know how, so let us *nine* know your secret? And I hope it's not just cut-outs?

'That doesn't make much sense,' squirmed Isaac impatiently, who hated to be outdone by his younger sister. 'Why would she think we did it with cut outs like those English fairies were and not Photoshop, and how would we do that anyway, if the photographs were taken by this tourist woman from Brazil from a bus, she's off her head.' He complained, pointing to the three short paragraphs of text beneath the newspaper photographs that explained what she saw that day.

'Yes, it does!' Said Tom. 'If she's a descendent of Elizabeth Caetano and living not in Rio de Janeiro, as we all thought she was, but in a place on the Amazon called Belém and she's trying to tell us something; a secret?

'Yes, it does,' echoed Indie with a shiver that sensed someone was sitting beside her, though her bedroom was as warm as toast on that cold January day. 'She's being cryptic. She doesn't know who we are, but she does know something weird happened in that churchyard last October, she would like to know a lot more about and those few clues she has given us, like, her talking about her *nine* best friends in the whole world. I mean who has precisely *nine* best friends? I don't, do you, two? And she didn't just say it once, did she? She said it three times. Daft unless she's telling us, though not directly, she knows about the *nine!* The nine Templar Knights, Tom told us about, who hid the Rebus of Akhenaten all those hundreds of years ago and six of them still lost when we met her in such an anxious hurry to find her friend, Polly, who should have been with her, but got herself lost!'

'Mmm,' murmured, Ethan.

'And *Lizzie,* well, Lizzie is her way of telling us she's is a descendent of Elizabeth, Lizzie, Caeta-no.

'Maybe,' said Ethan, restarting the YouTube clip.

'Yes, and her reference to *mummies* and *pyramids* and *Rachel Weisz* and *Brendan Fraser,* which is so totally off the wall, is her way of letting us know there is an Egyptian connection to this we should know about, don't you see?'

'Makes sense, I suppose,' said Isaac, reluctantly.

'Yes, I think it does and if I am right and she truly is a descendent of Elizabeth Caetano we must get word to Tom, and soon, before any harm comes to her and Billy.'

'Thank you Indie, thank you so very much,' said Tom, wanting to hug her for being such a caring friend.

'And how do we do that?' Asked Isaac, *he* could be anywhere by now. I mean literally anywhere in the world, the universe or some other dimension of space and time we have never heard of, if there is such a place!'

He's a *she* by the way, Isaac, despite she says she's a boy! Didn't you know? She asked, in that superior way girls do when they know something you don't; the answer to some question or a secret they long to tell, but tease and irritate you all the same they do.

'Really?' Exclaimed Ethan, doubting *he* was.

'Yes, really. She's just pretending she's a boy, but any girl would know that, but then you two only have eyes for Kiya.'

'Yeah, like you don't like her just as much as we do,' growled a faintly blushing, Ethan.

'You didn't answer the question, Indie, how do we find Tom, girl or no girl, when she lives in 1797 and we don't, we live here and now in Kips Bay, New York.'

'Let's Facebook Adriana first, hey, and worry about that later,' she answered, little knowing Ethan knew how.

But just then, as she expertly brought up her Facebook page, Tom felt herself gently pulled from the room by an irresistible force, but not before Indie turned to look at her knowing with a shiver of instinct she was there. But though she did, and Tom longed to stay, she was sucked towards the barely visible pinpoint of light that now pierced the mist in front of her. Her body once again her own and clothed from head to foot in the helmet, gloves, and yellow outfit she had worn since she and Polly climbed into the Pod. But as she felt herself slip through the expanding hole the pinpoint of light had become she turned one last time to look at the giant orange sun behind her floating above a smoke hung, white capped choppy sea, where a terrible battle was being fought by at least forty ships, English, French, and Spanish by their colourful pennants. Many of them already dreadfully scarred, burnt and broken by the deafening cannon fire that now thundered over her head in a terrifying whoosh that sucked the air from her lungs sending great plumes of acrid, yellow smoke into the sky. Their masts, yards, rigging and torn sails fallen violently askew in the maelstrom of battle and where, on one, momentarily crushed beneath the bows of another, she saw a hatless, blood spattered, tearful, red coated drummer boy amongst the carnage of his sinking ship beating his drum as his long dead Sergeant beside him, had ordered he must.

A sight that so held her eye she almost didn't see the *Hirondelle* pass before her, the boy Jord, who she had last seen on the beach at St. Pierre, Quiberon just a few weeks ago, standing in the bows watching her, a length of coiled rope in his hand, his father holding tight the tiller as he brought that drab little Ketch[106] about. And there beside him sat Duffy, his head in his bloody hands and beside him, dear Sam Robinson staring at the wreck of battle. *Odd,* she thought, wondering what battle this was, but no sooner had she, then she saw Billy come out of the wheelhouse his blonde hair askew, the black ribbon of his queue fallen loose, his face, hands, coat, and white waistcoat black with gunpowder. His brow streaked with sweat and blood and furrowed to an aching sorrow to see such a terrible sight of pain and destruction, as he turned to look her way and with a faint smile on his handsome face that somehow knew she was there. Safe, yet, a long way from home, as he now was, the bow of the *Mars, his ship, she knew,* barely visible in the smoke that roared from her guns.

Chapter 4

The Revenge Of The Priests
of Amun-Ra

Midsummer eve 1335BCE

The girl walked without fear across the stone flagged, petal strewn courtyard towards the Temple Complex of Khufu, passing as she did the boys who had swept it clean barely ten minutes before, now formed into two straight lines on either side of her, their shaven heads bowed to the ground in a timid quiet that hoped she and all the priests and soldiers, who guarded her would soon be gone. Its massive, forbidding gateway opening to swallow her beneath its flag fluttered arch, but though it did, she didn't see Tom crouched and hidden in the small grove of three palm trees that grew beside it to her left. Her two gloved hands holding tight to her fast beating heart the wand that had just a moment before pulled her there with such a trembling insistence. But seeing through the corner of her eye, as she passed within six feet of her, a sleek black cat and five of her month-old kittens scramble and play on her feet as she crouched on one knee. Fearful,

113

the growing louder, excited sound they all made would bring one of the sword carrying soldiers to investigate the noise and see one of the kittens had climbed onto to her helmet and two others onto her shoulders, the three of them seemingly floating like bubbles above the ground.

Her bright, turquoise-green eyes fixed instead on the empty, flag draped causeway, which now, so frighteningly stretched before her, its arrow straight, shadow draped path brushing aside the hundreds of rock cut tombs, flat roofed masta-bas[107] and statues which pressed and crowded its sides to the Temple steps of the gleaming white pyramid that was her destination. Which rose into the gleaming, star trailed echoingly silent, blue and crimson red sky in front of her to pierce the moon at its centre with its golden point. The doorway to the underworld, she sighed to the fright of the guards beside her, who followed her gaze know-ing what she saw and what they now did, and the endless life it promised if she could only reach it.

A sight so awesome it made her stop and gasp in wonder the world could be so beautiful and yet so many of her people could be so monstrously cruel and stupid they had no fear of death and the punishment that would be theirs in the after-life to come. Or the better life it promised to those who understood life was an illusion, a test we might

114

be worthy of Aten's love. A thought that stirred her to a shiver when she noticed a single blemish spoil that midsummer night sky, a stark, ominously black cloud drifting towards her on the hot sullen breeze that now stirred the folds on her cloak to a ripple. Its black billowing puffballs, a warning to everyone who saw it and made more threatening by the squawk of the nine, great winged birds that soared, swooped, and danced about it.

'Majesty, we cannot stop here, *they* wait for us,' urged one of the guards beside her, his eyes lifted to the cloud and with the same nervous apprehension it was a portentous omen of bad luck. A pale faced young officer of the lowest rank, who hated the work he now did, his hand gently pressed to the flat of her back in an urging push that found her feet again in a once more effortless stride that quickly found the causeway. Flanked on either side by a heavily armed guard of watchful, nervous soldiers and preceded by a swaying column of bare-chested Priests of Amun-Ra. Who *drummed* a soft, pitiless, hypnotic lament to her coming death; now only a few minutes away.

Barely eighteen years old, but looking so much younger, she wore, as was the royal custom of the time, a jet-black wig over her close shaven head, a sharp edged lustrous bob that fell to her shoulders like a heavy curtain. Her eyes, which secretly searched the shadowy gloom of that late night for the least sign of her hated enemy, were deep set, cold and unfathomable in their look of haughty disregard for the fate *she,* her sister Queen, had sentenced her, too not an hour since. Her nose was exquisitely small. Her cheeks arched, proud, and strangely marked with a neat row of *nine* black dots beneath each eye, the last of which, drew a slanted line from its outer corner towards the gold ringed lobes of her perfect ears, where they ended in a tight-drawn curlicue. Her lips though tense drawn, were full and sensuous. Her teeth snow white. Her chin dimpled and round. Her complexion a sun kissed, radiant olive-brown, giving her oval face a look of timeless, enigmatic innocence. Five feet two inches tall, her long swan-like neck was draped with a spreading necklace of gold, turquoise and priceless, blue lapis lazuli.[108] Her body lithe and well-proportioned under the shift of starched white, pleated linen she wore beneath her gold flecked cloak of red and orange feathers, moved with a natural grace. On her head, she wore her crown of office, a gold band sculpted at the front into the shape of a vulture, poised to strike the writhing cobra it clasped in its uplifted claw. Across her arms, she held a sceptre of fluted ivory, onyx, lapis lazuli and gold, surmounted on one of its ends by a beautifully carved falcons head.

A melody of cymbals and screeching, high pitched flutes announced her arrival at the foot of the great pyramid where the procession, snake-like, climbed a broad, stone stair of nine steps to its landing top. And when it had, turned without stopping before the richly adorned in gold leaf, pillared building that was its magnificent crown, which was etched to its flat roof in hieroglyphs, she knew was Khufu's temple, a Pharaoh who re-vered the old gods as her husband never did, but Seth most of all, whose statue now looked down on her with angry, searching eyes. A few minutes later they reached the north-eastern corner and turned a second time into an empty, stone flagged precinct, where a bamboo scaffold of precarious zigzag steps climbed to near the top of its north face.

'Gracious,' whispered Tom, who had easily fol-lowed them, thinking how dizzying high the steps were to the platform that stood just beneath the base of the gold capstone and with a thatched roof above it that hid the great block of stone recently lifted from its side.

With a sudden hush the high priest and the captain of the guard mounted the first step and de-spite it creaked, groaned, and swayed alarmingly under their combined weight began to climb to the dimly flickering, torch lit landing that was their destination. A journey of several minutes, Tom, following behind at a safe distance hoped would soon end. It didn't and more than once she thought she would fall to her death as the squirm of cats several times tripped her in their impatient want to be with the nice djinn they had found, as none of the others they knew, were. Something the last of the guards saw with a dread fear.

Arriving at the top of the stairs at long last the girl paused for a moment and saw to her horror the smiling, hate-filled, but still very beautiful face of Queen Nefertiti, her sister Queen and her faithful servant, the giant Nubian, Raneb, emerge from the shadows of the landing to stand beneath the taut, rope hung block of stone that would seal her fate forever. A load so heavy the wooden beam that suspended it, no less than the scaffold, groaned beneath its heavy weight and so much she dared hope it would pull the scaffold down before they were done with her.

'You have searched her?' The Queen asked the high priest.

'Yes, majesty,' he answered, bowing his shaven head to the waist of his *white* and *purple,* ankle brushing skirt.

'She conceals no poison in her clothes to hurry her death?'

'No majesty, she has no poison, nor any other means of harm.'

'There is no dagger to empty her veins hidden in the folds of her skirt, or the heavy cloak that warms her?'

'No, there is no dagger, majesty,' he softly answered. 'We searched her carefully before we left the village and the prison that has been her home without visit these many long months. There is no way she can die before her appointed time.'

'You are sure?'

'Yes, majesty, I am sure.'

'Then die, *Kiya,*' she hissed, turning to face the girl, who was now held by her arms by two of the guards. 'Heretic, blasphemer and traitor to all the sacred gods of Egypt, but die slowly, so your torment will still their anger and when you do, know this, your soul will lie entombed in this sacred pyramid, these ancient, timeless *stones,* until the end of days, without hope of resurrection into the afterlife our Lord Osiris, god of death and the underworld, has promised us, *we* his faithful servants. And know this, also *sister,* Akhenaten *our* husband and all those who dared to follow him, The Sword and Shield of Aten, as they so impudently and so proudly call themselves, are dead. Their bodies torn to a thousand pieces by Seth, the god of chaos and destruction, as is your sister,

Tefnut, who you thought had escaped to the Land of Punt[109] last year.'

'YOU LIE,' shrieked Kiya, pulling without the least hope of success to get free of her guards, who now held her all the tighter, so tight they fiercely pinched her arms, knowing that if it was true she was lost and without hope of rescue. 'MY HUSBAND THE PHARAOH AKHENATEN LIVES AND MY SISTER TEFNUT, ALSO. I KNOW THEY DO, AS YOU DO FAITHLESS WIFE OF OUR BE-LOVED HUSBAND, OUR LORD AND MASTER, WHO YOU BETRAYED SO EASILY FOR THE PROMISE OF POWER AND GOLD.'

'I do not lie, Kiya,' soothed Nefertiti. 'Would I dare to kill you and plan the *murder* of your only son, dear sweet, Tutankhamun, if I knew them to be alive? No, they are *dead* as you will be when the food and water I have prepared for you is gone, a month perhaps, more if you are careful not to eat more than you need.'

'But you do not *kill* me, *yet,* Nefertiti,' spat Kiya, as she was roughly pushed into the entrance of the tomb she had carefully prepared for her. 'Nor will you until you are sure *our* lord, the Pharaoh is dead, which he isn't.'

'Mmm, perhaps, but what is this?' She asked, reaching for the sceptre she carried so tightly in her hand.

'It is mine.' she pulled away the little she could, 'I am Queen of Egypt like you until I die or my husband divorces me, Nefertiti,' she calmly answered. 'Which he never will, as you know he won't, loving me more than he ever loved you, the mother of his only son. A son you could never give him, barren wife despite you six times gave him daughters and Meritaten, who you shame, the sweetest of them all. Pharaoh and god of Egypt after him and this,' she sneered, 'is the sceptre of my royal office and neither you nor your guards can take it from me without fear your already blackened souls will perish before they reach the afterlife.'

'Fine words, Kiya, but I care not you think you are still Queen of Egypt and protected by your god, Aten, Seth, the greatest of all god's rules here and Seth has decided you must die, but not yet awhile, I think,' she laughed. 'Take it from her Raneb,' she ordered her faithful slave, 'and throw it from this scaffold as far as your great strength will carry it,' which in the blink of an eye he, did, throwing it further than her eye could follow.

But though it briefly fell to the sandy, stone cluttered wastes beyond the outer wall of the temple precinct, it returned unseen and unheard like a boomerang to find the wand, Tom had only minutes before stuffed inside the top of her suit, though its gentle, growing more insistent, urgent thrumming tickled her so. The two melting into the one as she felt her body crumple into a trillion shards of bright light; her journey to the far distant future of 4930 had begun, again.

'Seal the entrance, Raneb,' ordered Nefertiti, bristling with irritation at Kiya's defiant calm, no less than the smell of her heady perfume, lotus, and jasmine, her own favourite, which seemed to linger, a torment in the air, even when the massive stone closed her lonely tomb forever, 'and *kill* everyone who is witness to this; everyone except Sahura,' she hissed a whisper into his ear, her eyes turned upon the priests who with ropes and pulleys grappled the stone into position.

An order he so eagerly carried out only he and the high priest Sahura survived that awful night of murder to keep the secret of Kiya's fate and he, for barely half the next day. When Nefertiti sent him through the Temple Void of Khufu into the future to capture or kill, Lieutenant William Kepple. Whose face she later that morning saw in the oracle and with a mark upon his arm that told her he was the servant of her enemies, her still *living* husband, The Sword and Shield of Aten.

Chapter 5

The Spithead Mutiny Masks
A *Fateful* Error

6.00am Saturday 11 March 1797

So it was that on a sun-kissed, gloriously blue, impossibly hot Caribbean morning, a bright-eyed and deliriously happy, newly appointed *Lieutenant* William Kepple, said farewell to his much respected and admired Captain and in a uniform only a day before bought. A bemused, but highly impressed Captain Edward Hamilton, who kicked himself he never knew his confident, accomplished, decidedly likeable Midshipman, the son of an old friend and shipmate, was so very well connected. A broad smiling wave that extended to his many envious companions on board the 28-gun frigate HMS, *Surprise* as he gingerly boarded his majesties cutter, *Hawk.* An energetically fast, but leaky old tub that would take him from the very beautiful island of Antigua where he had commanded nothing larger or more demanding than a ships boat crew and a regular sentry duty in the fort on Shirley Heights above the bay, to Portsmouth and his new command, HMS *Par-*

rot.

Intriguingly, because Fate prides itself on the wicked jokes she plays on all of us, he was greeted onboard the *Hawk* by a surly, downright rude, pimple-faced, arrogantly uncouth lump of a great lummox of a boy by the name of *Kettle.* Acting Lieutenant William Kettle. A Midshipman by any other name and not a very good one at that and had you not guessed, the nephew of the very recently deceased and not much missed, Vice Admiral of the Blue, Oscar Kettle, whose brig of war Billy now commanded.

Who had to stifle the boiling anger and jealous envy he felt toward the boy, three months his junior, who had somehow obtained the command he daily wrote his uncle to give him. And who, so his mother had just informed him in the tear stained letter stuffed deep in his salt-stained, double patched pocket, had died leaving a mountain of debt that would see them both in the Marshalsea, the debtors prison in London's Southwark he had many times passed, before the year was out, if nothing could be done to get it back. By which *she* meant, if he could do nothing to get it back. There being no one else who could. And get it back he would, he swore! But first he needed a ship, any ship that could be got and at any price he had to pay; murder, if murder it must be! Even if it meant *murdering the* gloat-faced little scruff of an over-promoted Midshipman who had just come aboard *his Hawk* and stolen *his* cabin, as was his legal right.

With fair winds and kind seas the passage to England took the *Hawk* just five short weeks and with a very sea sick Lieutenant Kepple, she entered Spithead Roads on the afternoon of Easter Sunday, the 16 April, 1797. Just in time for the start of the mutiny of the English Channel fleet that was to entertain their Lords of the Admiralty for the best part of the next six weeks.

This was a crisis indeed, though not the first their Lords of the Admiralty had encountered during that cold and troubled winter of revolutionary war. First, and most seriously, was the aborted landing of a French army in Ireland last December, a shockingly alarming affair that was only prevented by the most fortuitous and terrible storm imaginable that blew the French ships so far out to sea they couldn't get back again.

Second, there was the actual landing of a French army in Wales in February, not that it was a proper army, thank goodness! Rather, it was a clever, if outrageously unchivalrous and *illegal* ruse on the part of the revolutionary French government to ship a bunch of troublesome madmen, criminals, malcontents, and jailbirds to Britain under the command of a half-baked, American revolutionary, by the name of William Tate. A lunatic by any name. Who was, if the truth be known, getting on their nerves, as Americans, much given to their own self-importance, often do, when in the company of Europeans, who they too much forget are the seed of their beginning and the British more than most. But more importantly, they could infiltrate a small group of spies, French and Irish into southern England in preparation for the invasion they were said to be planning later that summer.

However, such was the scale of this newest and most shocking calamity, Vice Admiral Hood, Lord Bridport, the old, nearly retired and not much interested, Commander in Chief of the Channel Fleet, his Admirals, and senior Captains, failed to notice the arrival of the now near sinking, *Hawk* with any interest. Or the young boy, grown a size too short for his new bought navy-blue jacket, white regulation breeches and bicorn hat[110] by the sickness he had endured. Who, later that early evening was carried aboard the smartly anchored, *Parrot* on a canvass stretcher to be greeted by his only crew. A gangly ships boy of moth-ridden, dirty and unkempt appearance, who announced *his* name was Tom; Tom Dimple.

But here our story takes another twist, and one that was to bring the greatest good fortune to Lieutenant William Kepple, because, Tom, for all *his* mock pretensions to the contrary was no boy, but was a *girl* pretending to be a boy and a very passable ships boy she was, too in her odd assortment of grubby naval slops.[111]

Rope-tied at her waist, tar and bilge stained, grey canvas ducks,[112] which fell to a ridiculously funny and very impractical three inches below her knees, a short, salt rimed, navy-blue, nankeen[113] jacket, shrunk in the wash to half its size and several times patched at the elbow with a mismatch of colours no one could deny was a hopeless folly, red and green being someone's favourite mistake, a black silk, loose tied, neckerchief she wore in a triangular pennant at the back of her neck in a very jaunty style, a baggy, blue and grey, hooped woollen jumper the *Parrot's* moths had feasted on for most of the winter, so many holes did it boast in its sleeves and front, which she tucked into her baggy ducks like a draw pulled, puckered purse, knee-length woollen socks of the same drab design, horribly scuffed black leather shoes which once claimed a pair silver, pinchbeck[114] buckles, but now had only one and a tar painted sennet hat[115] that hid her face from anyone's close inspection.

Her once lustrously long black hair cut just that morning with a blunt scissor that left her head itchy and sore all over completed the boyish look she had only last night planned with such an enthusiasm she wondered she hadn't thought of it before. Barely shoulder length now, she doubted her much feared and hated uncle Titus would know her in a small crowd, nor even Miss Fry, her teacher, who she horribly missed. But not so short she couldn't make a neat plait of it with the twist of red ribbon she kept aside from the clothes she came aboard in that gathered it in an untidy bunch at the back of her head much like a terrier's tail. A much favoured hairstyle with sailors of the day, though much longer than hers, that would go unnoticed when the *Parrot* had her crew and even more with the lamp-black, sooty face she now showed the world that gave her a very swarthy look.

Tom, as we will continue to call her for a long time yet had sneaked aboard the *Parrot* the previous evening, hearing, though she was still bereft of any crew, she was to weigh anchor in a day or two for a secret foreign service that would see her gone for a year or two. And she desperately needed to be gone from her uncle who everyday searched for her; but why?

For the keen observer of naval lore and traditions of the day, the fact the *Parrot* had no crew other than the stow-away Tom when Lieutenant William Kepple was carried aboard was a most

128

remarkable state of affairs. Because, all newly commissioned King's ships of the day, regardless of their size, had, as a matter of course, a standing crew of at least four senior Warrant Officers. Reliable men who were appointed to oversee her building and because they did and knew her so very well, formed the core of her new crew.

But, for reasons known only to Captain Philip Patton, Portsmouth's much put-upon just then, Transport Officer,[116] and he was too dumbfounded by their impossible-to-believe fairy tale of ghostly goings-on to tell what he knew to anyone but his wife. Of *things,* scurrying, scraping, moving, banging, breaking, hiding, touching, pushing, tripping, stopping, whispering, hooting, howling, laughing, giggling, and floating in the dead of night. He had reluctantly agreed the *Parrot's* crew of four wide-eyed, glum-faced, pale and trembling jack-tars, Mister Adams vouched were as good as any he had known, could be dispersed throughout the Channel fleet the week before and with nothing said to blacken their good names.

Something Lemmy and Pilchard, the *Parrot's* resident ghosts regretted, having had so much fun at their expense, but not the girl who came aboard yesterday, who ignored them. A very pretty girl until she cut her hair, Lemmy rather liked; liked a lot as it happens.

Not that Captain Patton cared a hoot about the *Parrot,* the ugliest little brig he'd ever seen in all his long naval service, her cowardly crew, or the secret mission she was to be sent upon by the mysterious Lieutenant Galbraith, who had come down from London on Friday with a letter of authority from Mister Nepean, he couldn't ignore. No, he was far too busy just then trying to cope with the mutinous behaviour of the Channel fleet, now grown more dangerous in the last few days than he or anyone thought possible. And if that wasn't problem enough, he had to supervise the arrival of over a thousand exhausted French prisoners of war, the disheveled remnants of Colonel Tate's ragbag army of French and Irish volunteers. All of whom had to be found a suitable prison before the gentlefolk of Portsmouth, Lymington and Langstone could sleep safe in their beds. Who every day complained and wrote to the newspapers they did, the country was awash with spies, smugglers and highway men who had no regard for law or common decency. And, to confound and annoy him even more, his dockyard, Transport Office was to be painted that day with all the bother that would bring and he was moved to a house on the Southsea side of *Wish Street*[117] until it was done. A week at least the foreman said.

It took Lieutenant Kepple three full days to recover from the worst effects of his seasickness, which he blamed, though he was never believed, on a stomach chill he caught the previous winter, when, he rather stupidly drank some brackish water on New York's Long Island, whilst searching for a runaway. A chill that soon turned into a painful, vomiting flux of many week's duration that even now reoccurred. During this time, he was devotedly attended by Tom, who, having nothing better to do, washed and fed the *Parrot's*, impossibly young, but handsome Captain steaming bowls of burgoo. A tasteless, oatmeal porridge so thick and gluey she felt certain she could mortar a small brick wall with it, which she liberally dosed with Blackstrap rum, the only thing she could find to sweeten it and strong enough to curl his tongue to the roof of his mouth and with a gallon of Double-Stingo[118] to wash it down she thought so much better than the spider crawled water she found in a dirty old barrel.

A treatment she thought would quickly settle his gurgling like the drains, windblown, cramped and aching stomach better than anything else she could think of, but though it did, it also made him drunker than he had ever been - he had never been drunk before. Three dozen bottles of which she had most fortuitously found in cupboard in the Midshipman's cockpit. A snugly warm, helpfully out of the way, if dingy little hiding place she had made her own, not far from his own small cabin and very much larger day room, with its lovely, clear glass windows looking out over Portsmouth Roads, she wondered why he didn't sleep in there beside the coke-stove. Even if there was barely any coke or tinder to light it. Or if not in there, then in the wardroom three steps down from that large room on the same deck, where the officers, when they came aboard, would rest, sleep, eat and take their leisure. The rest of that deck being where the crew would make their home forward of the kitchen with its copper boilers and ovens. A low cramped place hung with hammocks and altogether too dark and smelling of new rope, varnish, paint, putty, tar, and bilge[119] enough to make her choke and sneeze for her to explore. And so horribly spooky on the lower decks and particularly when you got up near the rudder with things banging, bumping and groaning in the night so loud she thought the bloomin' place was *haunted*. Not that she cared a jot if it was, she wasn't leaving without the *Parrot* taking her there and certainly not because some daft ghost said she must!

And so, warm, and comfortable was Lieutenant Kepple throughout this time he was loath to leave the deliriously tipsy comfort of his bed, a restful, if precarious wooden cot, much like a hammock, but safer than that precarious canvas perch, which was strung between two narrow beams in the cupboard that was now his cabin, to take his rightful place on the quarterdeck.[120]

But arise he did, though with such a blinding, splitting headache pounding his poor brain to jelly he could barely stand without Tom's helpful, if uncharitable oddly smiling, tittering support. And on a crisp blue Thursday morning alive to the varied sights, sounds and smells of a mutinous fleet at anchor, he read his commission and just for good measure all thirty-seven Articles of War, his protection against all manner of crimes that might be committed at sea, to her.

Having read himself aboard, naval talk for making sure everyone knows who's the boss to a wide eyed, damnably cheeky, smirking into the folded cup of her two hands, unfathomably disbelieving, Tom, Lieutenant Kepple, pondered, with a sudden unease, what he was supposed to do next. Which, to say the least, wasn't immediately apparent to him as he stared across the Spithead anchorage and the score of King's ships that were uneasily anchored there. Portsmouth town to his left, the Isle of White to his right.

But Fate, which had clearly taken a shine to the good-hearted lad, came to his rescue in the form of Mister Midshipman Arbuthnot Anstruther, who, ghost-like and most unexpectedly, announced his arrival in the sweet, melodic voice of the choir boy he once was, from just below the bowsprit, the long wooden pole sticking out from the bows above the figurehead. In this case a bird like apparition painted a slapdash, red, yellow, and green by a *cross-eyed* boy whose job it never was, that looked nothing like the parrot it was meant to be, but rather, a chubby, duck-like creature of dubious plumage with a bent and twisted beak.

A voice barely heard above the raucous squawk of the gulls, which flew overhead in search of the breakfast they longed to have and fretfully moaned they hadn't with complaints that couldn't be mistaken so much of it splashed the deck around Tom's feet, who imagined they blamed her, as she darted and ducked to avoid their well-aimed barrage. The crash of waves on the *Parrot's* black painted hull as the tide rushed into the Roads that bright blue, sunny spring morning. The stretch and groan of her new cut timbers, which longed to be back in the *Wasp* where they belonged, sunk and three months under the sea on a twice a day rising sand bank off Guernsey's Saint Peters Port, so cramped, chaffed and tight were they now. The slap and singing ping of her loose tied ropes against their wooden ties. The tinkle of her brass bell and the scrape of her anchor chains against the sides of the hawsehole.[121] The noise of hammers, saws, pumps, and pulleys on the dockyard. But most of all his pitiful voice was drowned the noisy grumble of the seamen who sat beside him impatient to deliver their unwanted cargo.

'I say there! Hello there! Ship ahoy!' Said the tremulously anxious, growing more nervous boy from somewhere below the waterline in a toffee-nosed, lisping soprano that sounded more like a girl than a boy? '*Parrot* please! Permission to come aboard, if I may, sir?'

Startled from his reverie and suddenly aware of the growing dizziness, not to say awful queasiness he was now experiencing as he gazed upwards at the hypnotically swaying empty yards and rigging of the mainmast[122] and foremast[123] that rose from the deck, like trees, creaking and singing in the odd way they do, high, above his head, by the disembodied voice of Midshipman Anstruther. Lieutenant Kepple forgot himself for a moment, which he was apt to do in moments of high excitement, and with the joy of immediate, if thoughtless action, consigned his nausea and indecision to a half-forgotten memory and sprang into the foremast shrouds like a monkey. Much like the Midshipman he so lately was, and bellowed, with rather more enthusiasm than was altogether becoming for a newly appointed kings officer to the little jolly boat[124] bobbing fifteen feet beneath his feet on the white capped swell of the slate-grey Solent Water, 'deck here, permission to come aboard?'

From below the surly and much put-upon-faces of the boat crew, a very manly bunch of jack-tars, momentarily relieved of their need to mutiny, and their gog-eyed passengers, stared back at a sight they never thought to see. A commissioned officer with his sword at his hip, albeit a cheap and very blunt regulation hanger[125] hallooing from the ratlines of one of his majesties recently commissioned brigs of war, Mister Adams and his two boys surely never built, to answer the lamb-like bleating call of a snotty.[126] But then, in an instant of discomfited realisation that turned his West Indies honey-brown face instantly scarlet, Lieutenant Kepple disappeared from view like the sprite he wished he just then was, to resume a more dignified place on the quarterdeck. And would have done so, had he not tripped himself to a stumble on a coil of rope and fallen flat on his face with a resounding bump beside the mainmast where Tom stood waiting.

'You ok, *Billy?* 'Asked Tom, helping him to his feet using the overly familiar nickname she had a score of times called him without the least remark during his recent drunken confinement. A nickname only his dear, sweet mother and a few close friends ever used.

'Yes, indeed, Tom,' he mumbled, as he picked his flattened bicorn hat from the deck and tripped a second time on a canvas bucket. 'But lend a hand there why don't you. Get the young fellow aboard before he grows himself a beard. Lively now, young 'un, do you hear me. We can't keep him waiting, not if he has my orders in his breast pocket, which I'm sure he does.' And with that, he climbed the steps to the quarterdeck and began to pace back and forth with his hands clasped firmly behind his back.[127] A pose he had often observed Captain Hamilton assume in moments of high drama and indecision, and one that suited his shamefaced mood very well just then.

'Yes, *sir,*' she cried, with mock gravity, her voice a mannish grunt from the back of her throat as she nimbly ran to the starboard entry port to make fast the thoroughly soggy, knotted ropes end that was instantly thrown up to her. And rather more forcibly than she thought quite necessary by the ox-like giant of an ugly boy who was watching her with quiet, thoughtful amusement from below her feet. Which she expertly tied to one of the side rails with a clove hitch, a splendid knot she knew by heart, she had a hundred times tied a dog, a horse, or a donkey to a post with and never one of them to her certain knowledge ever got away. 'All fast here, Billy, she cried, knuckling her fore head as she'd seen it done a hundred times before by the old sailors, who idled their days fishing off Lymington Quay. Her much missed, Hampshire village home for all her twelve years, saluting the ungainly arrival of the Midshipman and his motley crew of sea drenched midgets. Well nine midgets and the giant, who was so much bigger and so much more dangerous looking close-up than he ever was before.

Watching their arrival with an anxiety and self-reproach that puckered his face into an uncharacteristically acid scowl, Billy searched for some clue of understanding to explain the arrival of ten ships boys and one fat, bespectacled Midshipman, who, he doubted had ever seen a day's sea service in his life, on his deck that beautiful April mornings and with all their dunnage.[128] Who unlike his companions who were rigged out in the usual grubby old cast off slops of ducks and shirts, too big or too small to fit their meagre frames and a hundred times patched with every colour of the rainbow, Midshipman Anstruther was dressed in the most elegant of naval fashion. A fashion which somehow contrived to give height to his diminutive stature and shed inches from his portly belly in what can only be described as a blaze of well-tai-

138

lored navy-blue serge, carefully stitched piping, white frilled cotton, black silk, and gleaming brass buttons. Which from the black ribboned, fan-like cockade that dressed his bicorn hat so neatly, which rather eccentrically he wore in what can only be described as the *old style,* that is, from side-to-side, to his gleaming black, gold tasseled boots made his own second-hand clothes look uncommonly mean and wretched by comparison. And wretched they truly were.

Taking a moment to get his bearings and berate the giant for almost knocking him over the side with the mountain of personal baggage he'd just brought aboard, Midshipman Anstruther, finally caught sight of his Captain standing beside the rope wound base of the mainmast and set off to greet him over the narrow expanse of deck that separated them with all the confidence and authority his twelve years, ten days at sea and ten thousand pounds' income per year could muster.

But catching sight of Billy's pinched look of mournful despair and mistaking it for dark disapproval hurried his step and in a fluster of lost confidence and nervous bustle presented himself to the young man, who, he knew from recent experience, could, if he wanted too, make his life aboard the *Parrot* a misery too much to bear. And in truth, Mister Midshipman Anstruther felt he could bear very little misery indeed.

'Midshipman Anstruther reporting sir, late of his Majesties ship, *London,*' he cooed respectfully. 'Vice Admiral Colpoys bids you good day and orders me to repair aboard the *Parrot* and take ship with you without further delay. That is, if you don't mind having me sir?'

'Vice Admiral Colpoys, did you say?' Answered Billy, impressed and rather too sharply for Anstruther, overacting the hard-bitten martinet he was pretending to be.

'Yes,' replied Anstruther wounded by the harsh tone and glacial stare of the handsome young man with the golden pigtail, who stood before him and regretting more than ever the loss of his snug and almost pampered berth aboard the *London.* A 98-gun ship of the line[129] with space enough to lose two dozen well connected Midshipmen for the duration of any voyage. And more than he did the loss of his stepmother of two years, who never much liked him, even before his father died in January. Who, just two weeks ago, waved him a last and hopefully forever, goodbye from the fast closing window of her carriage, momentarily stopped beside the bathing huts on Portsmouth Point, as he took the Port Admiral's barge to his new and never wanted life at sea. A life her companion of two months, a Captain in the local Yeomanry, heartily recommended he would thoroughly enjoy.

'Why are you here?' Asked Billy, shamefully warming to Anstruther's collar tugging, lip-sucking discomfort in a way he would never have believed possible two months ago and conscious of the respectful effect he was having on the gang of ships boys now nervously crowding the maindeck beside the main hatch to catch a first sight of their new Captain. 'And who are all these, these *boys* you have with you?' He sneered contemptuously, as if it was his fault.

'Admiral Colpoys duty, sir,[130] we are sent here to get away from the mutiny.' he pointed to the anchored fleet.

'MUTINY?' Shouted Billy.

'Yes,' squeaked Anstruther, surprised he hadn't heard there was one.

'WHAT MUTINY? WHAT ARE YOU TALKING ABOUT?' He impatiently asked, his eyes searching his face and those of his companions for the lie he thought it was, who each looked away as he did. Except for the giant who nodded he told the truth. A nod as respectful as it was friendly; a boy to trust he realised.

'Yes, mutiny, sir,' replied Anstruther meekly, his courage almost gone, as he took a nervous step backwards and almost tripped over his new sword, an intricately worked, basket hilt of Scottish design, Billy later learned was made by the *John Cater and Sons* of Pall Mall, London. 'Admiral Gardner's squadron refused to put to sea on Sunday and now the whole fleet has gone and mutinied just the same and there is no telling them no different, no matter what he says.'

'Crikey,' said Billy, with unabashed astonishment. 'Mutinied, you say? The whole fleets gone and mutinied?'

'Yes sir,' said Anstruther, confident the intelligence he possessed was of the very greatest interest to this newly arrived Captain and earnestly wishing to say more. To make a good Impression as a young man of his rank should. But, before he could, Billy turned on his heels and walked to the starboard rails to gaze in wonder at the sixteen battleships that were anchored less than a cable[131] distance away from the *Parrot* in line of stern,[132] their sails tight furled and going nowhere.

Mutiny and not for the first time in living memory, he thought. *The infamous and much maligned Captain Bligh's, Bounty had mutinied in the South Pacific in '87 and both the Culloden and the Windsor Castle in '94, the year after he took sea service on the Agamemnon. But no British fleet had mutinied since the civil war of 1642 to 1651. A bit of history he was proud to know, Chester, his home city, being so hot for the King back then. It just did not happen? Could not happen, not with a French invasion daily threatened?*

'Lord Spencer, the First Lord of the Admiralty came down from London on Tuesday, sir, to put an end to it.' Piped Anstruther, ignoring the unwritten rule that no one should speak to a ship's Captain unless first addressed by him. 'He hatched a scheme with Admiral Hood to put before the delegates, the leaders of the mutiny that is, sir, which they are just now considering aboard the *Charlotte*. There, abaft[133] the *Mars*.'

'*Delegates,* you say?' Interrupted Billy, the unfamiliar word rolling on his tongue.

'Yes, a secret council of Warrant Officers and Petty officers, who speak for the men. Steady men who have written their demands to Mister Pitt, the Prime Minister and Parliament.'

'Parliament?' Whispered Billy, hardly believing they would dare and turning on his heels before Anstruther could say more, and he desperately wanted to share all he knew with his Captain, who despite his awful behaviour, looked a decent sort of fellow and not half the villain he imagined he would be from all the tails he had heard aboard the *London* about him being the late and much despised, Admiral Kettle's young protégé. A boy to be cautiously wary of, everyone said.

'BOAT AHOY, *SIR,*' shouted Tom, in a jaunty

and all too friendly fashion from halfway up the foremast shrouds that in its blithe indifference to naval discipline, didn't go unnoticed by the ragged boys standing below her gently swinging feet, who turned their faces in surprise to stare at her. Nor too, by Mister Midshipman Anstruther, who glared at her from the shadow of his oversized hat, a warning he was not an officer to be trifled with by any low born ruffian, such as her.

'Where?' Called Billy, unable to see a thing and reaching for the heavy brass telescope housed in the stout wooden locker beside the mast, he knew by instinct was there.

'Up the front end and over a bit to the left sir, on the Southsea side of things as you're looking at it,' shouted Tom, betraying a total ignorance of the proper naval vernacular. 'Under the back end of that great big boat over there, the one with the painted yellow stripe down her sides, that looks like a sickly chequerboard.'

'LARBOARD, SIR,' shouted the giant, in a deep and measured bass that oozed both confidence and authority. Coming up from under the *Pompée's* stern gallery, about a pistol-shot[134] away now and with a lively breeze behind her that'll close on us in less than a minute.'

'I see her,' answered Billy, with a nod of appreciation that told the giant he was right and much admired he was.

With a look of triumph, the giant winked at Tom in a friendly, but know your place sort of way that made her stiffen with a blushing irritation, so thoroughly cheeky did she think he was, and when he had turned to the entry port to greet the new arrivals. 'LIVELY NOW LADS,' he shouted, taking charge of them as their boat bumped the side with a bang. 'LET'S GET HER FAST.'

Without a second asking this second party of boys climbed the side and gathered on the main-deck beside the hatch in a thoroughly seaman-like and disciplined fashion, their dunnage at their feet. Whilst Tom, not a girl to be trifled with at the best of times and certainly never one to play second fiddle to anyone, least ways a *boy with* no manners climbed to the deck. Little knowing that Billy watched her as she did, wondering if she would fall, so fearfully unsteady did she look as she tripped her way down the stiff tarred ratlines.[135]

Chapter 6

The Strangest Crew
A Captain Ever Took To Sea

10.00am Thursday 20 April 1797

First to climb aboard was a second Mid-shipman, but this time one cast from an altogether different mold from the one who had just come aboard. The now thumb-sucking and sulky, Mister Anstruther, whose rosy-red cheeks, delicate good manner and rich finery betrayed a very privileged background. He was tall for his age, which Billy, sternly watching him from beside the mainmast wrongly guessed was older than his own fourteen years, and he was well built too, in a strong, confident muscular sort of way. Like him, his face was weathered by sun, wind, and salt and his rough, calloused, tar stained hands spoke of years at sea from beneath his grubby pea jacket[136] which was half a size too small for his fast-growing arms; a jacket much like his own.

Ignoring, his fellow passengers, who were still scrambling like a troop of half-starved monkeys up the side of the *Parrot* from an impatient-to-wait, second jolly boat, he walked confidently towards

Billy, pausing only a moment to check the surprise he felt at seeing such a young a boy in charge of so fine a command. Though, he would be loath to admit it to anyone, but a trusted friend, he was glad beyond all reason to leave the cloying, growing more angry and frustrated, week old mutinous *Marlborough* to take ship on this tiny brig; to take ship on anything that floated.

'Midshipman Sam Robinson reporting, sir with twenty assorted ships boys and two lobsterback[137] runts, too short for their muskets from the *Duke, Defiance, Ramilles* and *Glory* and with a letter for you from Captain Patton for your immediate and serious attention.'

'Thank you,' said Billy, liking without hesitation the obviously capable and steady boy who now stood before him, but unable to betray he did to one so *junior*. 'You are most welcome aboard Mister Robinson, but why have you brought so many *boys* with you? Where are all the *seamen?*' He grumbled his face a question.

'I'm not sure, sir,' said Robinson, puzzled, but there seems to be boats picking up from all over the fleet, maybe not all boys, but plenty enough to make no difference. Why just now, I passed Trucky Spears on his way from the *Mars.* Said he was making a last pick up from the *Monarch* before he comes up with us. Should be here any minute now if he hasn't gone and drowned himself, which is more than likely with Trucky.'

'Trucky Spears?' Asked Billy, stamping on any familiarity Midshipman Robinson might have intended by his affectionate remarks.

'Sorry, Midshipman Spears, *sir,'* corrected Robinson, blushing, 'we were together on the *Syren*, *sir,* 32-gun cruising up and down the Mediterranean from January, until November last year searching for the blasted Frogs, who despite we looked, were never there.'

'I see,' said Billy, distracted, and absently stuffing the letter he had just received from Captain Patton into his jacket pocket, quite forgetting its intended urgency. 'But, what can it all mean? Surely Admiral, Lord Bridport doesn't expect me to take ship with a bunch of half-grown ships, *boys*? Does he, Mister Robinson?'

Odd, though it certainly was, even in those far off days, it was never Lord Bridport's intention his newly appointed Captain of HMS *Parrot* would take to sea with a crew of boys, but that was just what was about to happen, albeit under the cloak of a certain self-interested subterfuge that is the way of great men. His orders to his three junior Admirals and their Captains, were clear enough for anyone not wishing to be entirely understood, which is the common way of all men of authority who want to avoid the possibility of any future blame they might have got it wrong. Each ship in the fleet, he ordered, though not in writing, was to give up sufficient seamen and Marines to take immediate duty aboard HMS *Parrot*. That these seamen should consist of all necessary hands to make sail was clearly intended by him, but sadly, though rather fortuitously for this story, ignored by every one of his jealous Captains, who had no intention of giving up their prime hands to another ship and certainly not while they mutinied.

So, it was that by one o'clock on Thursday, 20 April 1797, Lieutenant William Kepple had mustered forty ships boys, one of whom was a girl, twelve Marines and three Midshipmen, none of them a day older than he was and most of them very much younger than he was, on his books. The last being Mister Midshipman Trucky Spears. A tall, spindly youth of thirteen years of age with the haunted look of a Cambridge scholar fallen on hard times, which in some respects he truly was.

They called him Trucky, so Midshipman Robinson, later told him, because of the many times he had kissed the Gunners daughter, which is naval slang for the thrashing young Midshipmen got when they got on the wrong side of a senior officer, which apparently, Trucky frequently did, being a dreamy sort of clever boy. Forced to bend over one of the ships guns, a massive two-piece construction made of a cast iron barrel and a heavy wooden carriage mounted on *trucks*, or wheels, the miscreant is caned until his buttocks bleed or the senior Midshipman's arm gets really tired; which it rarely did. But, being so tall, Trucky invariably took his punishment with his nose pressed hard against the trucks, hence his nickname, *Trucky*.

He was, by all accounts, the son of an impoverished and not altogether competent schoolteacher, under whose misguided tutelage he had managed to grasp, though not entirely master, the rudiments of trigonometry, which is that bit of Euclidean[138] mathematics so necessary for navigation at sea. Some Platonic[139] philosophy, all the rage just then, which had the effect of constantly reducing him to abstract puzzlement, which it invariably does anyone who reads too much of it. Musical scales, which he practiced incessantly and very badly indeed on the old *Stradivarius*[140] violin his mother had given him before she died. And medicine, of which there was very little to know, excepting how to cut and bleed a person until he or she died, but much to get wrong if you dabbled too much in it, which Trucky, when he was in the mood, was apt to do.

'It appears we have no Warrant or Petty Officers, nor any other commissioned officers, but us four, Mister Robinson,' said Billy, as if to confirm his own worst fears, which were growing horrible by the minute as he surveyed the hopeful faces of his meagre command. A dirty, disheveled collection of boys the like of which he had all too often seen aboard a King's ship

'No sir. I mean, yes sir,' said Midshipman Robinson, in his most confident manner. 'But there is time enough yet to see them come aboard before we sail, I think?'

'Yes, indeed there is, Mister Robinson, 'said a heartened Billy, who was ever a confident, resourceful boy. 'There is time enough as you say, but in the meantime, we must do the best we can with the people we have. So, you and *Trucky* ... err mm. I mean Mister Midshipman Spears and Mister Midshipman Anstruther must form them up by watches and see if we have crew enough to work this ship into a half decent company. And for the time being, rate anyone with more than five years' sea service, able, unlikely I know, given their age, but we must make do,' he responded to Mister Robinson's doubtful look, 'but worth a try, don't you think? And the rest ordinary and see if there are any amongst them who could be rated higher? That boy over there,' he pointed to the giant, who was inspecting the *Parrot* with a keen and knowing eye.

'Aye, aye sir.'

'And *you,* Mister Robinson, you will be my second in command until a more senior officer comes aboard, Acting Lieutenant if the thought does not weigh to heavily on your shoulders and with all entitlements. But should a more senior officer come aboard, a Master[141] who can help me with the navigation, you will of course return to your duties as my Senior Midshipman.'

'Yes sir. Thank you, sir,' said Midshipman Robinson, grinning from ear-to-ear to be asked. A chance in a lifetime! A chance to do well! A chance to earn a reputation! And with little chance any officer would come to take his place with the mutiny boiling to a storm on every ship, no matter the Captain was so optimistic.

With his officers and *men* about their duty, Billy walked to the safety and much wanted privacy of his night cabin, rather than his day cabin, which, despite he knew it was silly, overwhelmed him with its grand table, paneling and furniture. And feeling done in and more than a little bit lonely, not to say thoroughly confounded by all that had happened to him since he awoke that morning, read by the guttering stub of candlelight he took from his pocket, as he should have done two hours ago, the letter Sam had given from Captain Patton. Which instructed him most unusually, to proceed as soon as he was able, to the Star and Garter Inn, a well-known hostelry in the town, where he would receive confidential orders and further instructions regarding his stores from a Mister Lauder (pronounced Lorder), Trompe, Admiralty Clerk to Lord Spencer and from there to proceed to the temporary Transport Office in Wish Street arriving at eight o'clock, prompt, where he would receive his secret charts, signal book and the intelligence he alone must know.

'Lord Spencer,' gasped Billy, loud enough to bring Tom, who had been crouched and waiting behind his closed door in the day cabin for just such an eventuality - a call for help, she hoped, she alone might answer.

'Are you all right Billy? Not bad news is it, I hope?' She said.

'No, not bad news, Tom,' replied Billy, absentmindedly. 'Orders, that's all. Orders from the Transport Officer, Captain Patton I am to go as soon as I can to the Star and Garter Inn in town to receive further instructions from some important fellow from the Admiralty. Clerk to Lord Spencer, no less and then *we* are to put to sea, and soon, I think, by the look of it.' And then, without thinking, Billy passed the letter, a quite extraordinary thing for a Captain to do, to Tom, who began to read it as if it was her right to do so.

'Who is this fellow *we* must meet, Billy?' Said Tom, seating herself on a low wooden stool at his side. 'Damn funny name if you ask me. Why would anyone call their infant son, Lauder Trompe?' She asked, pronouncing it, *Louder Trump*. 'It ain't decent or Christian to name an infant in such a vulgar and ridiculous way?'

'Maybe not, Tom, but he's the important fellow *we're* to meet and *we* had best be sharp about it or *we'll* both be on the beach. 'Send Mister Spears to me will you and have Mister Robinson prepare the gig for me.'

'Aye, aye, Captain Billy,' said Tom, dashing off like an excited hare to do his bidding and thinking herself very important indeed. More important than that swaggering giant that's for sure, she beamed she must be.

It was when she had gone, that Billy realised the mistaken intimacy of their conversation. A dereliction of duty that would make him the laughing stock of the fleet should anyone find out and find out they would if he didn't mend his ways and double quick. *A Captain talking to a ship's boy as if they could be any sort of friends? What errant nonsense was that?* He blushed for the second time that day and in the yellow gloom of his cabin resolved he would never entertain *her* again; not ever. That he would immediately put an end to their growing friendship, though in truth, he dearly wished he didn't have, too, so amiable was the scruffy little lad, who had cared for him these last few days.

Chapter 7

Trouble Brews At The Fountain Inn

10.18pm Thursday 20 April 1797

Whilst Billy welcomed his youthful crew, Midshipman Kettle, finding himself suddenly unemployed after the *Hawke* was taken into dry-dock for much needed repairs, was nervously kicking his heels in the shadow of the Fountain Inn.[142] Waiting for news of the new command he had daily written to his uncle Oscar about and now so desperately needed, if he was to pay off all of his debts, as his mother insisted he must. An impossibility as she must know?

Surrounded all around by a boisterous, pushing and shoving crowd of flag waving hicks, oiks, sightseers from the countryside, half-wit-fools, scamps, scallywags, loafers, ragamuffins, schoolboys, apprentices, and drum-thumping, whistle-blowing radicals waving copies of Portsmouth's *Morning Chronicle,* which had the cheek to support the mutiny. Which in barely half a week had crippled the Channel fleet to immobility in a time of war better than the Frogs ever could.

All of them gathered on Portsmouth's Grand

Parade to see what would happen next. Whilst inside, a disgruntled, First Lord of the Admiralty, Lord Spencer, and Admiral Lord Bridport were preparing to leave by the back door, for a meeting with the *delegates* they hoped would bring the mutiny to a rapid end; it wouldn't.

In that intoxicating atmosphere of restless, holiday excitement, bawdy singing, misplaced revolutionary zeal and nervous anticipation, Kettle stole himself to go inside the inn and make immediate representation to Lord Spencer for the commission he felt he justly deserved. But to approach so great a man as he without a letter of introduction from a senior officer, an Admiral at the very least, at such a perilous time of growing ever greater calamity, was a desperate gamble, indeed and one he could ill afford to take now that his beastly uncle was no longer there to salvage any damage it might do to his career, which to date had been less than impressive. Had been ignominious.

But, as luck would have it, or was it Fate again? He spotted a vaguely familiar face pushing her way through the crowd. A squint-eyed, hawk-nosed, pinched-faced, fright of a girl, with a frizz of thin, curly red hair that hung like the fronds of some exotic plant from beneath the gaudy yellow and green turban she wore on her head. The end of which, trailed like a scarf to the hem of her tight

157

fitting, high buttoned, pea green, collared coat, to touch her brightly polished, daffodil yellow, clip-clopping on the cobble stones, shoes.

It was none other than Hesta Victoria, now much recovered from her swim in the Beaulieu River last December. Who with a little dog crushed tight under her arm was beating a passage to the door of the inn with her silk parasol. Followed by her grandfather, the ancient Admiral, a sinister, rather forbidding looking boy, no older than himself and a young servant girl, who was bent almost double under the weight of the polished Rosewood trunk she carried on her poor back,

'HESTA, HESTA VICTORIA,' cried Kettle over the heads of the milling crowd, who, despite he did, gave no room to let him through, such was their contempt for their betters now. And many of them too drunk to move, despite he pushed and shoved they should knocking more than one daft apprentice to the cobbled street. His voice now so bellowing loud he hushed them to a watchful quiet for fifty paces on either side of the Semaphore Station, now climbed by a score of mudlark's and street urchins of every verminous sort. 'Hesta Victoria. It is I, William. William Kettle.'

'WILLIAM?' Cried Hesta Victoria, who knew him only slightly. 'Is it truly you, my dear? Yes, it is I see it now.'

'Yes,' said Kettle, closing in on her party whilst mustering the most endearing smile he could manage. Which, was difficult for someone whose immediate prospects were so grim and with a mouthful of rotting teeth - the curse of all seamen and a spread of crusty, coalescing pimples that stretched and groaned and popped in the most alarming manner with every unnatural pull and grimace he made of his horse like face. But try he did and with a most winning effect.

'WILLIAM,' cried Hesta, with shrill of anticipation genuinely pleased to see her gallant and decidedly handsome friend - the girl was dreadfully short-sighted, not to say a witless fool to boot with no control over her brain or her mouth when over stimulated by events, as she now was. 'Is that really you? Of course, it is. Who else could it be?' She squealed with vain pleasure, as her little dog raised his twitching, strangled head a lazy inch to growl a friendly greeting to him. Which most astonishingly made him stop and shiver with the most pitifully absurd fright, he, sadly, being most unnaturally, not to say, morbidly afraid of the toothsome, hairy creatures since he was nipped on the ankle by one of their kind, when he was a lad.

'William, me boy,' beamed the genial old Admiral, without the least idea who he was, but taking his lead from his granddaughter, who apparently did - who he indulged with an old man's passion if only for the memory of her father, his long dead son Redman, who he everyday missed. 'So, pleased to meet you again and you, grown so very tall and distinguished you damnably handsome young rogue and promoted, too, I see,' he beamed, shaking him warmly by the hand.

'Thank you, sir,' replied a puzzled, but very pleased, Kettle, whose dreams of patronage appeared to be in his grasp. 'I'm so very glad, so very glad indeed, to make your acquaintance, *once* again, sir.'

'Of course, you are, you, young dandy,' answered the old buffer, hugging him affectionately. 'But here, let me introduce you to you my dear friend, Monsieur Pierre Corbeau. A French émigré,[143] escaped last year from the revolution in France, where his family was killed, who we have had the very great pleasure to entertain these last few weeks at Crookhampton Manor.' And turning to the tall, cool-eyed, stern-faced, darkly handsome boy standing beside him, he attempted to make good his promise. 'Monsieur Corbeau, may I introduce you to my very good friend, Mister Midshipman ... err ... Mmm? Oh, dear, me. How silly, I seem to have forgotten your name; though I feel it so close on the tip of my tongue I must soon have it.'

'Midshipman Kettle, sir,' spluttered Kettle, affecting not to be embarrassed by the Admirals vacant rambling after a name he could not know, because they had never met before and he and his granddaughter only once. But knowing he and his late lamented uncle had served together many years before, as young Captains in the war in Canada in 1759. A war that did much good for the reputation of Admiral Oscar Kettle, but not, if he remembered, and he did remember It now, Admiral Crookhampton. Who despite he had many important friends in high places never went to sea again and never a reason given why. A lamentably sad, not to say, very strange and vexing affair and with much talk of his cowardice, dereliction of duty and treachery in New York that was never proved; but mud sticks and it certainly stuck to him?

'Your humble servant, Monsieur,' said Corbeau, bowing an inch to touch the front corner of his jauntily askew, black tricorn hat[144] with his black, leather gloved hand in the merest acknowledgement of his mean and shabby appearance. Which he instantly detested, hating his obvious poverty. Whilst all the while gazing serpent like into his frog-like, bulging, eyes. 'You are here to meet with the Lord Spencer? Am I, right?'

'Sort of, *sir,*' answered Kettle, transfixed by the boys utterly commanding presence, which was like no one he had ever encountered before and him a veteran of five years' brutal naval discipline. Which saw every officer he ever knew, high and low frighten him witless with their threats and so much so, he longed to do the same; would! And better than they ever did. 'If I can affect an interview with him, which I doubt is very likely.'

'Why so?' Asked Corbeau, stepping so close to the boy he almost gagged on the overwhelming smell of garlic that blew from his mouth like the acrid vapors of a ships bilge. A smell made all the worse by the perfume he wore in such an absurd abundance it stung his eyes.

'I suspect he is kept pretty busy with the mutiny, just now, *sir,*' said Kettle, cringing under the boy's cold, reptilian stare, and squirming in his grubby collar for a taste of good clean air. 'Doubt he would have the time for a snotty like me, just arrived, if you know what I mean?'

'*Snotty?*' Asked Corbeau, his faultless, though pleasantly accented English not yet attuned to the intricacies of British naval slang. But before his question could be answered and much to his visible annoyance, he was rudely interrupted by Hesta Victoria, who, in the few short weeks he had known her, had proven herself a headstrong, utterly selfish young woman he daily wanted to beat and strangle with his bare hands.

'Of course, he will have time for you, William. Why ever would he not?' She barked, with the absolute certainty of the empty-headed fool she was. 'And if he doesn't, I'm sure grandfather will make him see he ought. Won't you grandfather?' She hissed, in a tone that made the old man shudder with dread she would somehow make him. As she made him name that delightful little brig he had recently launched and was minded to call the *Pigeon*, after his old command, the *Parrot*. Two birds of quite a different sort, the one sleek, fast, and tirelessly strong, as befits a King's ship, the other not.

'Yes, my dear,' he bleated, the resignation on his face a defeat plain to see.

'That's settled then William, you will see Lord Spence before the day is out or I will know the reason why?' And with that, she took him by the elbow and marched him headlong into the inn in a custodial embrace that brooked no challenge or interference from anyone; not least from him. Hesta Victoria, or so it appeared, had her man, and though Kettle did not know it yet, she meant to hang on to him, come hell or high water.

'Of course, my sweet,' said the Admiral, following her into the warm and spacious, oak-paneled parlor of the inn. Certain, as only the truly insane can be, he could affect the interview she

163

so wanted for her beau. After all, wasn't he newly promoted Vice Admiral of the White, a rank not to be sniffed at, not even by one so high and mighty as Lord Spencer? Even if he hadn't been aboard a King's ship at sea since General Wolfe, no less, retired him from duty for reasons, he fortunately never made clear to the Admiralty before he was killed at the siege of Quebec in the September of 1759. But he remembered with a shudder: *Damn that blackguard Johannes de Groot for the lying, murdering swine he was. Damn him for the murder of Benoît and the traitor he made of him. And damn Percy Wicker Selbourn, who blackmailed him and his son into a marriage that never should have been.*

Oddly, it was the strange custom of the navy of the day, and indeed for many years to come, to continue to promote, in date order, any officer who had reached the giddy rank of Post Captain, which the Admiral had, in the spring of 1758, aged 22, despite they were perhaps the most incompetent officers who ever lived and never went to sea again in a King's ship. And if they lived long enough, as he yet might, could attain the highest rank in the service, Admiral of the Fleet with all the salary and privileges that entailed. But not, as you will recall, the noble title of Baron his step-daughter and granddaughter desperately wanted for him, which she and her mother, had hurried up to town to beg for him that morning, despite the mutiny and all the dangers of revolution that promised.

Once inside Hesta Victoria began to search the grimly determined faces she saw in the fug of blue tobacco smoke that clouded the room for the least sign of naval authority she could find. But seeing no one who matched that tenuous description in the throng of colourfully coated gentlemen, settled herself upon a scruffy young clerk, seated beside the blazing fire with his grey woollen stockings fallen to his ankles like a scruffy schoolboy to reveal legs like a Queen Anne chair; fat and bowed and decidedly hairy and strong. Who was diligently, not to say, nervously laboring over a vast pile of Admiralty papers, which, even then were spilling onto the grey flag-stone floor beside him like autumn leaves caught in a petulant storm.

With a rush of impatience that left the old Admiral, Monsieur Corbeau and their now collapsed little servant at the door, Hesta Victoria catapulted Kettle across the room towards the unfortunate clerk. Who, in a moment of idle distraction was staring out of the cobbled windows into the crowded street, vigorously scratching the inside of his trumpet-like ear a filthy black with the inky end of the stunted, near broken in two, quill pen he held in the fattest hand she had ever seen.

'You,' said Hesta Victoria, poking the clerk in the pit of his well-rounded belly with several rapier-like thrusts of her silken parasol. A delightfully yellow thing, embroidered in a most becoming Chinese motif that almost matched her turbaned hat, coat, and shoes she wore.

'Me?' Said Trompe meekly, standing to attention and tripping a step backwards from her still poised and wickedly sharp parasol in fear and consternation she would stab him again. Upsetting, as he did, his wooden stool with bang and yet still more of his precious papers.

'YES YOU, YOU IDLE, DIRTY LITTLE TWERP,' bellowed Hesta Victoria, in a shrill and sneering contempt of the dwarfish vagabond who stood frozen in terror in his oversized, dozen times patched, grey coat and dun coloured breeches before her, his right hand holding the inky quill like a dagger, so worn and so polished with age it positively shone like a mirror. 'Be so good as to find Lord Spencer and tell him *we* are here.'

'Lord … Lord Spencer, Miss?' Stuttered Trompe, meekly.

'ARE YOU DEAF YOU DONKEY BRAINED FOOL?' Screeched Hesta Victoria, in that especially arch and imperious tone she reserved for anyone of lower rank. Of which, there were rather

166

a lot to enjoy in that long delayed and still rather chilly spring of 1797.

'No, Miss,' said Trompe, anxious not to cause any further offence.

'NO?' Shouted Hesta Victoria, affronted by Trompe's apparent temerity, though pleased by his groveling cowardice, which was a treat better than she expected. 'NO WHAT?'

'No. I mean I'm not deaf,' said Trompe, not only crushed to distraction by the weight of Hesta Victoria's apparently homicidal temper, which threatened to kill him, but by the sudden appearance out of nowhere of a very senior Admiral wearing a gold trimmed bicorn so large it sat on the folded ears of his porcelain fragile, near hairless head like an upturned bowl and a uniform coat so heavily laden with gold braid his epaulets fell to his skinny elbows in a sagging defeat. Followed he was doubly concerned to see by a distinguished looking boy in an ankle scraping black cloak, he pulled tight about his chest in a very continental manner - being a boy who had travelled far and wide and knew such things. Who to his shocked surprise was very cruelly and most insistently pinching the ear of a small, very nearly exhausted servant girl; a foreigner by the dark, but very pretty look of her. Who was struggling with a small piece of canvas covered luggage, a wooden trunk that was so awkwardly heavy on her bent back, it appeared to be stretching her tiny arms near out of their sockets.

'What's your name *boy?'* Asked the Admiral, in the easy way a man used to being obeyed does, a boy of no account.

'Trompe sir, Mister Lauder Trompe, Admiralty clerk to Lord Spencer, who, I'm sure you will know both as a much-esteemed friend and a professional colleague,' he replied, obsequiously and with a bow to his ample, food spilled waist that was a truly groveling flourish. Hopeful his tenuous and very recent link to the great man would win him a moment's reprieve from this uncalled for and very hurtful assault on his much tried upon nerves that afternoon. Nerves shredded to pieces by that lazy nincompoop,[145] Lord Dasheart, a companion clerk, but a very well-connected clerk, whose constant overbearing, truly savage snobbery hourly threatened to be his undoing, so much did that vile dandy hate and want to hurt and shame him.

'Indeed, I do. Now fetch him. Fetch him to me this very instant, d'you hear,' said the Admiral, asserting every inch of authority he could muster over the now thoroughly cowed and quivering boy. 'Fetch him and tell him Vice Admiral of the White, Reginald Crookhampton awaits his pleasure in the parlor. Do it boy. Do it now.'

'He's not here sir,' gulped Trompe, bowing to his waist a second time with a whistling fart and affecting his most earnest manner. 'You have missed him by his coat tails, both he and Lord Bridport left through the back door only moments before to meet with the Port Admiral, Sir Peter Parker at his residence in the dockyard and are not expected back until late this afternoon and even then, they may be delayed with the mutiny.' As he spoke, Corbeau, who had been watching the unhappy boy with a gleefully wicked fascination, gathered several sheets of papers, carelessly strewn about the table and with an indifference to their private and possibly secret nature, settled himself comfortably beside the roaring log fire to read them at his leisure. A cheek of such monumental proportion, the helplessly trapped Trompe felt obliged to ignore him.

But though he did, he several times saw the creepy boy look at him and with such an acid displeasure it made him shiver with nervous fright and with such a familiar look about his face he was at a loss to know where he had seen him before? Never guessing the face, he saw was the image of his twin sister, Madeleine, Mister Henry Beattie's wife, his aunt by marriage, though she refused to admit she was. Who, he would be concerned to know, had several times written to her brother with mention of his name and so unflatteringly did she describe him in those letters, he every time laughed to read them. But now, since Mister Beattie's death and with the loss of the secret papers he every night brought home from the Admiralty and Madeleine so easily copied, when he fell asleep, stunned to a stupor by the draught of opium she gave him, he had need of him. A spy in the making better than the one Lord Dasheart had proved to be.

A boy so enamored with his sister he would do anything for her, but such a rich, spoilt, vainly irresponsible, feckless, idle fool he could not be trusted to keep the secrets that might see him and her hung for the small treason he once or twice did. But thought it a jape that would do no harm if it ever came to light, though Mister Nepean every day warned him and Lauder of the dire, secret importance of the work they did for him; that there were spies everywhere about.

Yes, he would do very nicely, thought Corbeau with a smile, *but how,* he wondered, *was he to trick this boy to the treachery he must do, idiot though he certainly was.*

'The fellow's a fool,' said the Admiral, to the landlord, who had quietly come up

beside him, overdressed to his brown, brightly polished buckled shoes in a crisp white apron that
was twice tied about his upper waist. Who now
looked at Lauder with such a look of contempt in
the creeping, toadying fashion of those who es-
teem their betters. 'Brandy,' demanded the Admiral, his grasp on reality almost exhausted, as sat
down beside Corbeau and called for a table for
luncheon and the best rooms in the house.

However, Hesta Victoria was not so easily put
off as he and when he was gone she quickly re-
newed her attack on the stricken clerk. Demanding that he go immediately to the Port Admiral's
office and fetch Lord Spencer back to meet with
her, 'this very instant do you hear,' she demanded
with an impatient, half-hearted stamp of her foot,
which quite frightened her dog.

'Better we wait, Hesta Victoria, dear,' pleaded
Midshipman Kettle, not wishing to upset the now
thoroughly cowed, flustered and bewildered clerk
any more than she already had. All too aware of
the damage that might yet be done to his perilously
stranded career by her well-meaning, but wantonly
inappropriate demand the First Lord of the Admiralty, Lord Spencer attend upon her as if he had
nothing better to do that morning. 'We've put Mister Trompe to a good deal of trouble when he is
so obviously busy with his work,' he soothed the

shrieking scold, watching Trompe nervously gather up a dozen or more fallen sheaves of paper from the stone flagged floor and quickly and untidily stuff them into the large, leather satchel that sat on the red cushioned armchair beside him. 'And in circumstances over which, I am sure, he has little or no control. Best I think, if we wait a while and should the opportunity arise, speak with Lord Spencer when he returns, which doubtless he very soon will.'

'You think?' Said Hesta Victoria, now thoroughly besotted by the boy and mistaking his anxious groveling to an Admiralty clerk, as a sort of kindness, rather than the professional prudence it really was and with a winning smile to her beau, which she felt certain he now was, she turned on her heals and without a backward glance at the tremulous Trompe joined her grandfather and Corbeau on the ample oak settle beside the fire, where their drinks were already served.

Chapter 8

The Great Hymn Of Aten

Midsummer eve 1335BCE

Kiya watched in silence as the massive stone slid into place, a flooding comet tail of fast fading twinkling, rainbow bright light filling its four side as Tom made her desperate escape, the last face she saw, Raneb's cruelly smiling at her the triumph he felt. 'Dog,' she whispered as she turned, half blinded by the strange light and climbed the nine, steps to the near top of the pyramid where she entered a small square room, softly lit from its low ceiling to its four corners, by the perfect pyramid of multi-coloured light that came from the small hole in its centre.

Rubbing her eyes, she saw the four walls were etched and painted with the familiar, but frightening images of Egypt's many god's: Seth, of course the god of chaos and destruction whose temple this was standing triumphant over the double crowned, green painted Osiris, the good and faithful brother he killed. The father of Horus, whose sacred, ever watchful eye, was elegantly painted on her eyes to protect her from harm. The hawk-headed, Ash, god of the desert; Denwen, the serpent; Hapi, the fat, bearded god of the Nile; the cheetah-headed, Mafdet, goddess of snakes and scorpions; Thoth, the ibis-headed scribe, god of knowledge, Sekmet, the lioness headed goddess of war and many others besides them, all a reminder of the life she had now seemingly left behind forever; the life she loved.

Hurriedly dropping her eyes from the walls and the score of grotesque faces that seemed to look back at her with such a mocking stare, she saw the floor was made of black diorite stone[146] and so perfectly cut, fitted and polished she could see her face in it, but more than this, saw it was deeply etched with the sacred double enneagon of Egypt. The outer part, almost touching the walls, the inner part, describing the rooms centre beneath the apex of light. The two, a perfect symmetry enclosing nine hieroglyphic incantations, spells, and prophecies, at the corners, she couldn't read or understand.

Frustrated she couldn't, that Egypt and the Priests of Amun-Ra possessed so many secrets, she began to search the room more closely and saw it was furnished with a plain wooden armchair, a small desk with a hand mirror and wooden comb neatly set upon it, a bed draped with a canopy of purest white linen and two, small barrel-like boxes, containing perfumes, oils, and cosmetics. Whilst a much larger, third box, containing pens, brushes, a pot of ink, a palette, and two-dozen scrolls of papyrus, stood hard against a wall.

A sight that made her laugh, *they clearly wanted her to write something, but what? A record of her life, so short it had hardly begun? A diary of her death, no one would ever read? A confession of her love for the Pharaoh Akhenaten, who had dared to challenge the power of the Priests of Amun-Ra, to raise the one true God, the Lord Aten above all the rest and who was betrayed in the moment of his victory by his first wife, her sister Queen, Nefertiti and his eldest and most favoured daughter, Meritaten? Or were they merely something to pass the time away? But what time?* She laughed a hollow, pitiful laugh, tears welling in her eyes, her heart an aching stone of now growing fear and despair as she searched the tiny cell for an escape.

Stacked in one of the corners were a dozen lidded clay jars, each as tall as her waist and each one containing something to eat or drink. Ice cold water, wine, beer, honey, dried figs, dates, grapes, fish, dried meat, fresh milk, yoghurt, cheese, and freshly baked bread. Enough, she realised to last a month, if she ate a mouthful every day. Nefertiti truly did intend her to die a pitifully slow death and she would know her sceptre was gone, thrown into the desert beyond the temple wall by Raneb, but not before she had gone mad with fear and loneliness.

In another corner, fabrics of silk, cotton and linen dyed in the richest reds, purples, yellows, and blues draped an upright, open wooden coffin, a coffin cut in the shape of a body, as was the tradition of her high born, privileged class. Her body she saw from the face and silk robed figure painted on the heavy lid beside it. And beside this frightfully mocking, hateful thing was a small wooden boat, perhaps two feet long and two feet high from the top of its single mast to its rounded bottom, it's white, hoisted sail gently fluttering in the faint, warm breeze that somehow found its way into her cell. Its tall prow and stern post a reminder of the hundred boats she everyday saw from her palace window through a fragrance of beautifully coloured flowers, sailing on the Nile below. A reminder of the freedom she had forever lost and the journey she must soon make from this life into death, as is the way of all living things.

And beside this, on a knee-high wood and gold inlaid table beside the stairwell was a collection of thirty, small, stone lidded jars and exquisitely carved shabti statues[147] made of wood, pottery, glass, and precious stone. Hers, she realised, taken from her private apartment, which were placed in a careless disarray, many fallen over in a heap, as she would never have allowed. Worse, two, blue-glass statues, one, the exquisitely carved image of her son Tutankhamun and the other of her sister Tefnut, were fallen on the floor in front of her, as if they had been knocked over by some impatient, hurrying hand, something no servant would have dared to do, when the rest of the room, her prison cell, was dressed to such a morbid perfection. Nor was it! She now saw, seeing in the centre of the table and covered by the clutter, her sceptre, a moment ago ripped from her hand, was miraculously returned. *But how?* She exclaimed, as she bent to pick it up her hand a tremble of excitement, but as she did, saw the six-inch-tall, polished black, diorite stone statue of her husband, was gone. A statue she prized above all the others for its true likeness.

Smiling with relief she was saved and knowing it was her husband's magic that was the reason why, she pulled the wooden chair into the centre of the room beneath the apex of the pyramid light and pulled her feathered cloak about her now visibly shivering shoulders and sat down clutching tight the sceptre, though he every time called it a wand in his urgent, fretful distraction, he had so hurriedly given her on the day he left. The wand he said would carry her safe to him, but only if it was reunited with its twin, the wand he had given her sister, Tefnut, but how, when they were separated by so many thousands of miles?

How could they be reunited? She wondered, as she began to recite, as her husband had asked her, too, the Great Hymn of Aten. A prayer that was always the greatest comfort to them both, as it was to her son, Tutankhamun and her sweet sister, Tefnut, whose service they had dedicated their lives.[148] *You rise beautiful from the horizon on heaven, living Aten, origin of life. You have risen from the horizon; you have filled every land with your beauty. You are fine, great, radiant, lofty over and above every land. Your rays bind the lands to the limit of all you have made, you are the sun.*

Repeating it a second and then a third time and feeling less frightened, now, she wondered again how she and Tefnut might be reunited in their search for the Pharaoh, now a year gone and without word of where he was gone, though the priests searched for him and the treasure he had taken, and as she did, raised her eyes to the apex of the ceiling in contemplation and saw with a shriek of horror the evil Eye of Seth looking down on her. Hidden, until then by the light that had blinded her when she first entered the room, deep carved into the ceiling, its empty, black socket the hole through which it poured like water from a fountain.

'AYEEEEEEEEEE,' she screamed, in the echoing, silence. 'WEDJAT, WEDJAT.[149] LORD ATEN HELP ME, I BEG YOU PLEASE, HELP ME, PLEASE.' She pleaded, as overcome with fear, and anguish she tipped the chair to the floor and ran headlong to the furthest corner of the room, where she crouched like a trapped and wounded animal beneath her cloak. Her hand reached out to her side and almost touching a mark on the wall that had no place there. A mark unlike any Egyptian hieroglyph that would be her final escape tomorrow, but to dangers even more frightening than those she would soon encounter in worlds beyond her imagination. 'HAREISIS. HERU-SA-ASET.'[150] She wailed, as she hid from the light that now seemed to scald her hands and feet like liquid fire. Forgetting he was one of the hundred useless gods she had abandoned for the one true God Aten. But a vengeful god she knew might yet hurt her, despite she had.

Chapter 9

Mister Trompe Tells A Tale Of Mischief
He Never Should Have Told

Midday Thursday 20 April 1796

'Way I help you with your papers Mister
Trompe?' Said, the now fawning Midshipman Kettle, hopeful that he might repair some
of the damage done to his chance of future service
in the King's navy by his impetuous, but rather wonderful friend. Not, you understand, that William Kettle was given to acts of kindness, charity, or fanciful
good will, on the contrary he was a savage, overblown bully worse than his uncle ever was, but he
did have a junior Midshipman's sense of personal
survival. One which recognised that anyone in the
Admiralty's employ, even one so modest and ill attired as Lauder Trompe, might one-day rise in his
career to high office and spike the ambitions of a
junior officer who had done him some meanness
in the past. Spike them in some malicious, mendacious, pay-you-back, sort of way, which he most
certainly would, if he had the chance. Oh, yes indeed he would and with a happy delight.

A drafting, say, to some cold, damp, and leaky

old tub in the Baltic sea; a spell of duty on some prison hulk on a smelly, swampy stretch of the Thames estuary; a mind boringly dull detachment to one of the new-fangled signal stations that were crisscrossing the south coast of England from the Lizard Peninsula to London like a rash; or worse still, a transfer to the Sea Fensibles. A sort of naval home guard made up of shirkers, miscreants, drunks, derelicts, half pay officers, and mad men, from where he knew, there would be no return. No, anything was better than that, even if he had to grovel to this fat little twerp, like he had a hundred times before, but to no avail, the navy hated him.

'Thank you,' said Trompe, surprised and delighted to have found an unexpected ally in the oddly familiar *face* of the Midshipman, who was now bending his heavy, muscular frame to retrieve the last of his papers from the floor. Who thankfully appeared to have some calming influence over the deranged young woman, who had, without any cause, been so beastly rude to him, as he tried so very hard to finish the mountain of paper work that was properly Lord Dasheart's to do before Lord Spencer returned, to find he hadn't.

Not that that silver tongued, lazy-bones of a well-bred, popinjay had done anything, but tease and bully him since they first arrived in Portsmouth and was now off lunching somewhere safe from all concern with his newfound friends. Young blades,[151] idle aristocrats and rich men about town, just like him. A lunch he would be lucky to have, before he hurried off to the dockyard meet the newly promoted Captain of the *Parrot,* Lieutenant Kepple. The young man he had promoted by mistake, but not his really, Mister Beattie's.

'At your service,' said Kettle, relieved to find Mister Trompe so obliging. 'I'm only sorry we have put you to so much inconvenience and at such a worrying time. What with the mutiny and things, I fear you must be most dreadfully busy and overworked, today?'

'Busy, indeed,' answered Trompe, hurrying to push the last of his papers into his over-full, satchel, before Corbeau, who he had several times seen looking at him with a devilish gleam in his eyes, could steal anymore.

'Indeed,' answered, Kettle, their conversation now done.

'Indeed,' echoed, Trompe, quickly shouldering his heavy satchel and, as he did, he reached for his hat on the chair beside him. An astonishingly large and decidedly unfashionable, black Nivernois[152] hat that was once his dear old fathers. But just then, as he turned on the worn-down heels of his hobnailed boots to go, a moment of amiable indecision overtook him. A *fatally* stupid, long remembered moment of indecision, which would cost him very dear in the next few months. Not to say the next few minutes of painfully embarrassed memory. 'Sir,' he nervously stuttered, biting his top lip with his bottom teeth. 'You will forgive my impertinence, but we have not been properly introduced?'

'My apologies, *sir,*' said Kettle. 'My name is Kettle, Midshipman William Kettle, late of his majesties cutter, *Hawk*, just arrived from the West Indies station.'

'Kettle?' Gasped Trompe, catching tight his buttocks for fear they would explode with fright and paling to a sickly shade of greenish grey, as the memory of the demon he had hurried to an early grave sprang into mind like a ghost come to haunt him; which, indeed, it had. 'Err um, deuce. 'Pon my soul, how strange, did you say your name was, *Kettle,* sir?' He squeaked and stammered like the cowardly mouse he was.

'Yes,' said Kettle, surprised, and delighted by Trompe's sudden and quite visible frightening recognition of his most distinguished name. 'Yes indeed, sir. My uncle was Admiral Kettle, Deputy Comptroller of the Navy Board of Appointments. That is, he was, until he died so tragically last Boxing Day. Did you know him at all? Blasted fool went and fell down the stairs.'

'Know him ... err, yes. Yes, I did know him. 'Pon my soul, I very slightly did,' said Trompe, in a strangled choke, trying hard to compose himself and suddenly recognizing in the odious, pimple flushed face of the young man who stood before him with such an arrogant blaze in his cocked-eye, something of the claret red, vicious, malevolent features of the wicked old blighter whose fortunate trip down the Admiralty stairs and sudden death had saved him from an end he every night dreamed would never be. A Tyburn[153] necklace made of hempen rope tied about his traitor's neck. 'I had the pleasure of rendering your uncle one or two small services before he accidentally died last winter. A loss, if I might say, that touched us all most dearly.'

'A loss, indeed,' answered Kettle, reflecting on the fortune that might have been his, had his deranged uncle not gambled it all away in the months before his death. The last of it on Christmas Eve, his dear mother said. Leaving only a mountain of debts, *he* must find a way to pay, or end his days in the prison. It being the quaint, but odd custom of Georgian England to imprison debtors until their debt was paid, even if they had no means of doing so. A fate he would do *anything, absolutely anything* to avoid. Murder even, he recalled, he daily wanted to commit on that forever seasick, Lieutenant William Kepple, who he had grown to hate with an unreasonable passion, during their five weeks at sea together; and him in his cabin. 'He is, sadly missed indeed and no more so, than by my dear mama, his only sister, who cherished him.'

'You were close then, to your uncle I mean? Were you, Mister Kettle?' Asked Trompe, cautiously exploring their relationship, which he felt certain, was rather more distant than the boy would have him believe.

'Quite close,' said Kettle. 'Though, not as close as I had hoped we might have been at the end. Me being his only other kith and kin and ever dutiful and respectful to him, since I was a little boy, despite old, Cromwell,[154] his mastiff bit me to the shin bone when I accidentally stood on his tail and he beat me red-raw with a stick as thick as a Bow Street Runner's[155] cudgel for saying he did. Which wasn't fair, was it?' He grumbled, the memory so terrible, he crumpled to a sickly faint at the sight of any dog, even Hesta's puppy.

'No. Indeed,' said Trompe, thinking the boy would burst into tears, so pained and panicked did he now suddenly look. Was turned all pale and sweaty. 'But, then, things are never what they seem, are they Mister Kettle?'

'No, Mister Trompe,' answered Kettle, gathering himself and trying hard to understand the direction of his growing idle conversation, which seemed a little too familiar for his liking. 'But how could they be when I was so long away from home and him always so busy?'

'But, never-the-less, you had some hope of *preferment,* Mister Kettle? Your uncle being a very senior Vice Admiral?' Asked Trompe, knowing that the answer must be a yes, in a sea service that was almost totally dominated by grace, favour and family appointments.

'Of course, Mister Trompe, who wouldn't hope for better things?' He answered, acknowledging without shame, what they both knew to be true. That rank and patronage were the only certain means to success in those far-off days – as it ever is today! More so than luck, or ability and if you didn't have family rank or patronage, then you must find favour with someone who did and smartly too, if you were to get on in the navy. 'I daily wrote to my uncle for promotion. Anything to get me out of this infernal Midshipman's rig and into clothes more suitable to a gentleman, but mores the pity the drunken old stoat fell down the stairs and died before he could find me a place.'

'Maybe he *didn't,'* answered Trompe, with a reckless abandon of good sense that was dangerously, stupid. Was insane, as only daft people can be and Lauder was daft and lonely for a friend he didn't have. *It was time,* he dimly thought, *to tell what he knew of the Kettle's lost promotion for the reward he dearly hoped to get.*

'What do you mean?' Demanded Kettle, growing weary of the oiky clerk who was making free with his time and good nature and when he was so very anxious to rejoin his newfound friends. Who, at least, promised him the possibility of a hearty lunch and a meeting with Lord Spencer. Or if not him, which he thought most highly unlikely, then one of his Admirals, perhaps, Hood, Gardner, Pole or Colpoys, though any Captain with a ship would do, even Kepple, god forbid.

'Well,' said Trompe, casting a cautious glance over his shoulder in the direction of Admiral Crookhampton and his ill-matched companions, who were distractedly drinking bumpers[156] of brandy and port wine and nibbling at some tasty, cheesy snacks he longed to try. 'I have something here you might be interested in, Mister Kettle,' he whispered, reaching into his jacket pocket to pull out a small dun coloured canvass parcel bound tight with hempen rope and sealed with the Admiralty's mark. 'Do you see this Mister Kettle? Do you see what I have here in my hand?'

'Yes, Mister Trompe. It is as plain as the nose

on your face you have a package of some important sort by the seal I see upon it,' answered Kettle, irritably, growing exhausted by the increasingly familiar clerk with the inky ear and know-it-all, manner, who now dared tease him with his own importance. 'But do not trifle with me, you, damnable saucy rascal,' he warned, once again the bully he was and warming for a fight.

'And what do you think it contains, Mister Kettle?' He tempted and teased, turning the parcel over in his hand.

'I'm sure I don't know Mister Trompe,' answered Kettle. 'But I'm sure you will to tell me, if you think it proper, but in your own time dear boy? In your own time?'

'I certainly will, Mister Kettle. These are orders! Orders from Admiral Lord Bridport for the newly appointed Captain of his majesties brig of war, HMS *Parrot,* now at anchor in the Portsmouth Roads, not a mile distant from where we are standing, Mister Kettle.

'What of it?' Asked Kettle, angrily, knowing who they were for? 'What have orders for the *Parrot* to do with me?

'I think they have everything to do with you, Mister Kettle,' and with that Trompe, stupidly told him his suspicion, he, rather than Lieutenant William Kepple, was the intended recipient of his uncle's benevolent generosity. Though, quite naturally, he omitted to mention the part he had played in that regrettable comedy of *fateful* errors. Suffice to say, the mistake he made in writing the wrong name on the King's commission was laid at the door of the poor unfortunate Mister Beattie, dead these four months. Who, though, blameless was in no position to defend himself against the charge of treason that was its consequence.

'YOU MEAN TO SAY THAT BLITHERING NO ACCOUNT SEA SICK DOG, WILLIAM KEPPLE HAS GONE AND GOT MY COMMAND BY MISTAKE?' Roared Kettle, in a voice so loud it froze the inn to silence and startled Hesta Victoria into so large a swallow of her port wine she exploded into an uncontrollable fit of coughing, spluttering, and snorting so hard she tipped her sleeping puppy onto the floor with a bump that left the poor little fellow thoroughly dazed.

'You know him?' Gasped Trompe, in a sickening whimper, shocked, as only a boy of the most agreeably pacific disposition and quiet forbearance could be by his furious outburst. And genuinely surprised, a story only intended to relieve him of any ill will he may have harbored towards his dead uncle and earn him, he dared to hope, his grateful patronage at some future time, should have produced such a dramatic effect.

'KNOW HIM, I SAILED HALF WAY AROUND THE WORLD WITH THE SMUG LITTLE TOAD AND HIM SEASICK EVERY INCH OF THE BLOOMING WAY IN MY CABIN AND IN MY COMFORTABLE COT DAMN HIS EYES AND ME SLEEPING ON THE COCKPIT FLOOR LIKE A DOG AND YOU'RE TELLING ME THAT SCRAGGY LITTLE RUNT OF A JUMPED-UP SNOTTY HAS, GOD ROT HIS BONES, GONE AND GOT MY *PARROT* WHEN IT SHOULD HAVE BEEN MINE ALL THIS TIME AND ME WITH MORE DEBTS LEFT ME BY MY GREAT TWERP OF AN MISBEGGOTEN UNCLE THAN I CAN EVER HOPE TO REPAY IN TWO LIFETIMES WITHOUT A TON OF PRIZE MONEY TO HELP ME. WHY YOU LYING CHEATING VILLAINOUS LITTLE STINK.' He furiously bellowed, without the least regard for who was listening. And everyone in the Fountain Inn and fifty yards beyond its open door was and with a look of murder, outrage, and desperation on his ugly red, violently twisted face you could not imagine the sight of it.

'Yes. Yes, err, um. 'Pon my soul, I think he probably has,' said Trompe, farting like an off key drunken bugler. Realising the secret he told was a secret he never should have told anyone, least ways not him. Who now stood over him with his fists balled so tight his knuckles cracked, he feared he would hit him and hit him very hard. 'But there's no way to prove he has. As far as their Lords of the Admiralty are concerned, Lieutenant Kepple commands the *Parrot* at the express wish of your late uncle and there is no one, absolutely no one, to say otherwise. It is the law dear sir.'

'I CAN SAY. I CAN SAY OTHERWISE.' Shouted the purple-faced, apoplectic with rage and frustration, Kettle. 'I CAN SAY OTHERWISE AND SO CAN YOU, YOU MAGGOTY LITTLE WORM AND YOU WILL,' he demanded, lifting him from the floor so quick both his dozen times, cobbled boots fell off his feet to reveal socks so full of holes there was nothing left too darn.

'But who would listen to such a fanciful tale of woe?' Purred Corbeau softly, coming up beside them both and hardly daring to believe his good fortune. 'Who would listen to a passed over *snotty* like you, my dear, Kettle, no matter you are the nephew of an Admiral? And who would gainsay the word of so distinguished a man as he, in favour of this half-wit *clerk? There is no proof this Kepple was not your uncle's choice.'*

'*What?*' Spluttered Kettle, horrified to hear him say such a thing, but knowing only too well, how true it was. No one would believe him, not even if he choked the truth out of Trompe, which he very soon would if he didn't choke to death, as it seemed likely he would.

'*What?*' Gulped a wide-eyed, purple faced and choking, loudly farting Trompe, trapped between the two of them in a vice like, tightening grip he couldn't undo.

'No more than I said,' answered Corbeau, who had travelled all the way from Crookhampton Manor that morning to see his sister's *nephew,* who, until a few minutes ago, he had never met, hopeful he might persuade him to his treacherous service by guile, flattery, threat or, if needs must, a modest bribe. But now, most wonderfully his service was delivered up to him free of any obligation, familiarity, or mock display of affection. Mister Lauder Trompe was his minion now and would be until he was done and finished with him.

'BUT WHAT DO YOU MEAN?' Thundered Kettle, no longer master of his own wild emotions and affecting without difficulty the most frightening attitude he could muster before the smug, overblown, too-clever-by-half, *frog,* whose soothing, mellifluous voice was a hypnotic balm. But frightening though he contrived to be, his rage was nothing to the cold and unflappable Corbeau, who smiled contemptuously at the overgrown bully who stood ranting and raving like a child in pain.

'Bluster, complain and threaten all you want, Monsieur Kettle, but if Monsieur Trompe's story is true, and I heard every word *you* said of your wantonly vile, despicably perfidious *treason,* Monsieur Trompe.' He hissed poking him so hard in the ear with his outstretched, manicured finger he made him squeal. 'There is nothing you can do now, but have your revenge another way and like Nemesis[157] the goddess of divine retribution, rise up to strike your enemy down. This undeserving interloper, this shameless imposter, this stealer of your rightful command, this cuckold[158] in your *Parrot's* nest, this Kepple, who swaggers his success whilst you swoon like a kitchen maid over the love she lost to a handsome swain. Is that not so, Mister Trompe? Do I not have it just so?' He triumphed, his voice a harsh, unforgiving whisper as he took the satchel from his limp hand.

'No sir. I mean, yes sir,' bleated Trompe.

'You are, I fear Monsieur Kettle just one more of life's unfortunate losers and in that no better than the men you hope one day to command, the dregs of the gutter. So, swallow your pride and your misspent anger and have your revenge by more certain means than this outrage, which, with the help of Monsieur Trompe, will have you on the quarterdeck of the *Parrot* before noon tomorrow or my name is not Pierre Corbeau.

A promise, for all his preening self-confidence he little knew how to bring about. Though with the help of Admiral Crookhampton, cheerfully eating a vastly heaped plate of roast and mashed potatoes, carrots, peas, roast beef, and gravy, he had reason to hope he soon would. He assured himself with a vanity that acknowledged no equal, brooked no challenge and waited on no one's pleasure, but his own, except, his sister Madeleine, who he dearly loved and longed to see again.

But before he could travel up to London to be with her, he must first help secure the Admiral the peerage he and his family so desperately wanted, the second reason he had made the arduous coach journey to Portsmouth. And when he had, he smiled a delicious smile of satisfaction, he would have four spies in his pocket, where previously he only had two. Lord Dasheart, who had proven himself quite useless in that regard, despite the love he had for his sister, who was not inclined to return his affections. Mister Beattie, who never knew he was. Trompe, an Admiralty Clerk of reckless stupidity, whose papers were already proving a very great interest to him. A half-wit Admiral in the House of Lords, with access to all manner of military intelligence, if only Lord Spencer would agree Crookhampton's elevation and, last, but not least, Kettle. The soon to be Captain of his own ship, HMS *Parrot,* he heard it very loudly called a moment before. Something his patron the Count de Montard would scarce believe was possible in so short a time and better by far than the few copied pages of Admiralty papers he had so far sent to the French revolutionary government in Paris. A man he owed so much! A man whose benefaction had taken him and his sister Madeleine from poverty to promised riches, in a little over a year; he to Paris, she to London.

A thought that reminded him how he got to England, in the first place, smuggled here on the youthful Captain Begg's *Seahorse* which was crewed by the meanest villains he had ever known. Meaner by far than those who roamed the streets of Naples, his home for so many years of wretched poverty and the worst among them Jemmy Grub and his henchman Joby Dogget. Two stout lads who would do anything for a price!

Chapter 10

Tom Finishes A Journey
Two Hours Too Long Delayed

Sometime in 4930

Tom stared out of the glass or was it plastic window of the second Pod, she couldn't remember, which it was, recognizing immediately the room she had so recently left with its computer and screens, switches, dials and levers covering almost every inch of the wall in front of her and the soft blue light that lit them in haunting shadows so restful it soothed her fast beating heart to a still. The identical room to the one Gabe had taken both her and Polly, too, two hours before in the crashed and stranded Portal in Nogoback that was this one's twin. If Billy's Tompion could be trusted to tell the time, which she believed it now could, if time meant anything and she doubted it did, so very strange was its ways!

An unimaginable delay that lost Polly somewhere along the way and left her stranded and in fear of her life in Kiya's Egypt on midsummer eve 1335BCE, until a fraction of a second ago. So soon in fact she could still smell the sweet jasmine and lotus perfume she wore in her helmet and the balmy warmth of that strange, moon bright, lustrously coloured night on her face.

Who, she one day hoped, would be glad of the unseen help she had given her, which almost trapped her in that horrible little room they put her in, so powerful was its alluring magic. Even if it did mean she would side with the Drummers and that bearded lunatic, Tostig the Viking, when they attacked the Château Tollendal. The beginning of a misunderstanding that had yet to end, she realised, knowing that wherever the wand took her, after that, she still wanted to kill Billy and might yet kill him if she didn't get back to 1797, double quick. *Gosh, she sighed, time was a troublesome thing and no mistake and easily changed if tampered with, as she just had,* she grumbled, easing the lever handle on the heavy metal door down half a turn, which opened with a sudden, sucking whoosh of air and so unexpectedly loud it made her jump.

Troublesome, but helpful, too, she had to admit with a faint relief, as she stepped out of the Pod, but only if she could tell Polly, Marie-Ange, and Billy all she now knew about the Rebus of Akhenaten. No longer quite so lost as they all thought it was and Kiya, so hatefully treated by Queen Nefertiti and her guards, it was little wonder she distrusted everyone. But most of all she longed to tell Billy, who, if he hadn't already, must soon embark on a wild goose chase searching for Pale Moon in the Morning and her grandfather Soaring Eagle, thinking they knew, as Polly had dreamed they did, where Johannes de Groot had hidden his piece of the Rebus before, he was killed, in or near the Cave of Tarhuhiawaku. When all the time it was somewhere else and now Lauder had it. If he hadn't dropped it in the Hudson River?

But before she could, she had to find Montard and when she had, take this second Portal back to the Land of Nogoback, which of course, she *had!* If the future she saw just a moment ago was to be believed! Which it was, if Ethan, Isaac, and Indie had been woken from their long sleep and found their way back home? As she saw they had. As only her safe return would allow! And then found Adriana Caetano, Elizabeth Caetano's descendent in their time and were going to speak to her, something Billy would be astonished to learn. But was that a future that might be undone by a thoughtless act or unintended accident? She didn't know and dreaded she would be the cause.

But did she find Montard, here in 4930, as she now must? She didn't see she had. And if she did, did she take his amulet from him? She hoped she had. Given to him, as she saw it was, by Sahura?

His power to roam the universe of space and time in search of the Rebus of Akhenaten, a boy barely older than her and certainly not the monster they thought he was.

It was easy to find her way back to the Portal's control room, even though it meant a climb of two separate stairways, the opening of five very similar, tight shut doors and two right and three left turns along corridors that looked much the same and when she had, soon after found the secret doorway to the basement dormitory where the rest of the Nanochromes slept. And with no sign it was opened or tampered with, which was so very important, she quickly searched the rest of the echoingly quiet *ship* from front to back for any sign of the monsters he thought might be still guarding it, which, for a year now had prevented its escape. Which Gabe assured her was no more than a thought command into one of the many computers that crowded the control room. And Bibi, Gabe's little sister, would promptly do that, when she was woken, as she would, when she got *back.*

Relieved the Portal was empty of everyone, but the Nanochromes, something Gabe said was vitally important, stressing how important it was all *alien* life forms must be left in Eden, where they could do no harm to anyone, but themselves. To live out their own future. The gentle Frog Men, the least of her worries from Gabe's pleasant description of their friendly ways, but not the fiercesome, Scarab, Lion, Dog, Lizard, and Piranha Men, who she feared the most. Monsters as frightening as any fairytale she had ever read.

Though, if the future could be changed, as Gabe and the rest of the Nanochromes intended it would be changed - must be changed, by their new beginning in Nogoback and if the pollution, which caused the earth to freeze and tilt on her axis in 2084 could be avoided, they might never exist, anyway. And if they didn't exist then nor would they. A conundrum that left her speechless, but something he had several times tried to explain to her and Polly without the least success.

But no matter about that she had a job to do, she smiled as her gloved hand found the six-inch-thick, metal jam of the open door to the outside cave and her feet the top of the nine steps that descended to the floor below. Confident now she would find Montard and know his business, because she knew she already had!

But it wasn't a cave as she understood a cave to be, but a cavernous room the size of a cathedral nave constructed, not with towering pillars, arches, and stone walls, but thousands of flat, green nonagon plates, each one perfectly interlocked with its neighbours to make a balloon-like space that made no sound. Descending the ladder her hands holding tight the two metal banisters she was amazed at the huge size of the Portal, which rose above her head with each step she took, almost to the ceiling. Suspended a foot above the floor, it seemed to her, by nothing more than the pulse of thrumming noise she heard, which like a magnet turned against itself, a natural wonder of the world Miss Fry had shown her, kept it up.

But though it did, she easily saw the ankh cross etched like a flag into its bottom surface and so large it could be seen for miles and wondered what it could mean? And because she did, re-membered the object she had, barely half an hour ago, picked up from the table in Kiya's cell to make room for the wand and sceptre she had left for her to find and in her hurry knocked a dozen pieces over. Which now sat on the seat beside her own, in the Pod where she had left it. A scale model of the three pyramids of Giza carved from polished black diorite stone to show all their temple fea-tures in perfect miniature and with an inscription of hieroglyphs at the bottom to say what it was. Something, she now realised was in some singu-lar way of the greatest importance, but not to her, but to Kiya.

The first Portal, when first she saw it, reminded her of a razor shell, a sort of flattish, tubular thing crashed deep into that mountain plateau, Gabe took them too. Wounded by the arrows the Toba Men had shot at him. But that was less than one twentieth, or one thirtieth of what she now saw. A massive dolphin-like, humpbacked shape, which curved from its high middle to its flat ends like a turbot in the sand, where it effortlessly formed a flat lip, two feet wide she could easily stand upon, where the top met the bottom in a seamless join no Lymington black smith could make. Fifty feet high, it was surely sixty yards long and twenty yards wide, it was so very hard to tell.

It was huge and so much bigger than she ever imagined it would be which showed just how much the first Portal was buried into the ground and covered in forest. Buried, but not broken, as she saw it wasn't from the inside, but buried so it could never journey in space and time again, could never come back here!

Like the first it had a blue metallic sheen to its outer surface, but unlike that one, had no scorch marks to mar its perfect finish, to tell the amazing journey it had made, which glistened like a mirror in the soft green light of the cave and twinkled the row of black windows that cut its sides from front to back all around.

It was easy to see the cave was empty of everything, but the second Portal, not a box or barrel littering its surface and had been for some long time by the faint hint of dust, which covered the floor, which she saw occupied half of that vast nine-sided floor space. The bluish-yellow marks beyond the central walkway, so obviously, the place where its twin once stood.

Following her instinct - nosy curiosity Polly would say, reckless foolhardiness, Marie Ange, would remark, being an altogether more sensible girl and French, too, she followed the walkway to its only exit. Which opened through a nine-sided door to a second corridor about nine feet high and nine feet wide, which stretched to a smooth, unbroken curve, sixty or seventy yards from where she stood into a dark unknown she dared not go alone. Fearing, as she knew she must, she might be captured or killed by Montard before she rescued the Nanochromes. Which of course she did, but not yet and perhaps not for a long time to come.

Turning back in a panic she dared not admit she went straightway to the hidden chamber and the sleeping Nanochromes within. Choosing the girl, she saw lying on the first bed, dressed in a white, ankle length, cotton shift to wake, as Gabe instructed her how. No more than the passing of her hand over the glass canopy that covered her and knowing it was Bibi she woke with a yawn and with such an urgent want to be gone from that place she argued without end for an hour they must.

Chapter 11

Corbeau Plots A Murderous Trap

4.00pm Thursday 20 April 1796

Later that afternoon Billy jumped from his gig and climbed the green, slime covered steps of the Sally Port[159] onto Portsmouth's pier, saluting the smartly dressed, red coated Marine guard, as he did. Leaving Midshipman Spears in charge of a painfully disappointed Tom, who, in a most unseaman like manner, pleaded to be allowed to go with him, and a boat crew manned by the biggest, strongest, and toughest boys aboard the *Parrot,* who laughed she did. Including the giant from the *London,* whose name was, Andrew 'Duffy' Duff, newly and very happily promoted, acting ships Boatswain.[160]

With a last concerned look at Tom, who sullenly ignored the thin smile he offered her, he made his way up Broad Street, through the milling crowd of onlookers and noisy revelers, who crowded every vantage on the pier to glimpse and cheer the mutinous fleet, towards the Star and Garter Inn on Portsmouth Point, the haunt of every Lieutenant in the Channel fleet. A place he had never been to before.

Twenty minutes later after trusting his way to an artful guttersnipe, who mischievously thought it was his solemn duty to support the mutiny by confusing a King's officer, and one little older than himself, who took him to the gun wharf,[161] half a long mile out of his way. He found the solid, red brick walls and sagging mullioned windows of his rendezvous and entered its noisy, dark and smoke fugged portals. Too hot and too sweaty with fatigue and consternation he had kept his Admiralty clerk waiting, he feared he would be angry.

Greeted by the intoxicating smells of hops, sizzling bacon, pork sausages, fresh baked bread, steak and kidney pudding, thick onion gravy, custard, and jam tarts, which filled the room to a mouth-watering ecstasy, he was painfully reminded by a sickly gripe in his belly he hadn't eaten a proper meal in weeks. Except the burgoo, Tom had fed him, which tasted like none he'd ever eaten before and he'd eaten plenty.

Nor, had he eaten anything quite so delicious since Christmas day, last, when Malarkey Postelthwaite, Captain Hamilton's servant on the *Surprise,* gave him a plate of turkey dinner with lashings of gravy and cranberry sauce, straight from the Captains groaning, festive table. A champion beast it was too, he remembered, a full twenty pounds and only a day old when it was brought from a farm on the road to Flatbush, half a mile west of Long Island's, Brookland village. A reward, Malarkey, said it was, for some small kindness he had rendered him a few weeks earlier, though what it was, he never did say. A kindness he failed to discover, because Malarkey mysteriously jumped ship the following day and despite he led a small ships party over to New York's Long Island to find him, they never did. A memory so achingly vivid in the inn's deep crowded and raucous bar, where every face now turned to see him come in, so astonishingly young and thin and pale did he look in his best, second-hand, Lieutenant's uniform, it made him suddenly sad and lonely for the many good times he'd had with his old ship mates aboard the *Surprise*.

From a shadowy recess beneath the Star and Garter's heavy oak stairs, which had the advantaged of seeing almost everything in that cavernous room without itself being, too much in view, three pairs of squinted eyes watched him. First among them was Corbeau, his face a mask of studied interest as he measured his *prey*. A measure that saw no reason to fear this nervous young Captain, why should he, he was no more than a school boy? The second, his eyes red with tears, belonged to a now thoroughly downhearted and decidedly agitated, Lauder Trompe, who, as unhappy as he possibly could be in his present villainous company, was trying to disappear into the collar of his home-spun jacket like a hunted rat down a leaf clogged drain. The third pair, dark and hooded, belonged to a heavy set young tough with a shaven head and a broken nose he tapped with the calloused fore-finger of his massive right hand. His name was Jemmy Grub. Who, seeing Billy arrive, winked a signal to Corbeau, which agreed the deal they had earlier made. Then, with a mixture of menace and chilling self-importance that is the mark of all dangerous toughs, he rose from his chair and without a backward glance at his ill-matched companions in crime, shoved and bullied his way through the noisy throng of blue coated, brass buttoned sailors to the street outside. Where he stood for a short while beside the Toll House entrance to the pontoon bridge to Gosport, smoking a short clay pipe that spluttered and sparked with every suck and puff he made. The smile broad on his face his mostly empty pockets would soon jingle with ten guineas, more if it could be had.

As soon as he was gone, Corbeau addressed Trompe in a harsh and commanding whisper. 'You understand what you have to do, Monsieur Trompe; yes?'

'Yes, I think,' he stammered, with a reluctance that begged his release from a contract he knew to be ill conceived, traitorous to Lord Bridport's wishes and dangerous beyond any words he could conjure just then.'

'Remember what I said, as soon as I leave make yourself known to this Lieutenant Kepple. Give him his written orders and then escort him immediately to the dockyard. Remember, take him to the dockyard first and when he has finished his business there, take him directly to the Transport Office, where he is to receive his orders, which for a day or two at least, I am heartily glad to say, is to be found at the far end of Wish Street.[162] Once there, you will make whatever excuse you can and bid him goodbye, but once free of him, you will remain concealed nearby, until Grub and his boys have dealt with him. When he is done, he will give you his charts, signals, and any *other* papers he has in his possession, which you will bring to me at the Fountain Inn without a moments delay. You understand this Monsieur Trompe? You under-stand the plan *we* have *all* agreed? How important it is? Do *you*, Monsieur?'

A bold and dangerous plan for all its many shortcomings, but one transformed into some-thing far more important than the kidnap and mur-der of Captain Kepple, the moment Corbeau read his confidential orders, which Trompe was forced at gun point to give him. Orders which instructed him to sail to France within the week with all possible haste to rescue a party of royalist fugitives stranded on the Quiberon coast near St. Pierre, since before Christmas, one of them, so far unnamed, with information vital to the British government. Information he must prevent them having at all costs he had quickly realised. A coup, if he succeeded that would earn the Count de Montard's highest respect and reward, or so he hoped and believed. Never realising his meddling beyond his brief instructions to spy upon, and hinder the English navy was about to change the course of his life forever and return his ancient family to a battle they long ago fought and lost with the Pharaoh Akhenaten for the wealth and power of the Priests of Amun-Ra.

'Yes, of course,' grumbled Trompe, shuddering to see the fervent look of excitement in Corbeau's eyes, which had the dangerous glaze of a madman. 'But why must I wait around like a Bond Street pickpocket to bring you his charts and signals, when Grub can do the job just as well as me?' He sulkily asked, increasingly concerned for his own safety, and wondering why a recent émigré from France, should want to stir up such a hornet's nest of trouble for the sake of Kettle's promotion. A bullying, pretentious fool of a boy no better, he now sadly realised than his dead uncle.

'Do as we agreed, as I have ordered you must Monsieur Trompe,' growled Corbeau, testily. 'Grub has his own very particular uses, but ferrying secret naval documents into the Fountain Inn under the noses of Lord Spencer, Lord Bridport and every Admiral and Captain in the Channel Fleet, isn't one of them. It is you, in your role of trusted Admiralty clerk who must do that! Remember, it is vital that Kettle has time to study the charts before Admiral Crookhampton presents him to Lord Bridport tomorrow morning as a substitute for the missing Kepple who we will hide away until they realise he has run.'[163]

'But,' interrupted Trompe, trying to glean a way out of the awful situation he and his big mouth had gotten him in and marveling at the peculiar way, the oddly shaped dimple on Corbeau's chin, a sort of thin inverted Y, twisted and contorted with every angry syllable he uttered, so like another, he knew, but who?

'No buts, Monsieur Trompe. If Midshipman Kettle is to obtain the command he so much desires, the one you so wantonly and negligently gave to another, he must not only remind Lord Bridport of his illustrious family pedigree, but also his expert knowledge of that treacherous coast, he himself knows well form '95, Kepple is ordered to sail, too that is second to none. The urgency of this mission will not allow him to seek a replacement officer from within his mutinous fleet and with Crookhampton's influence he will have no option, but to appoint him to the *Parrot* at the earliest opportunity, if she is to sail, as she must, on Saturday's tide. Do you understand the importance of this Trompe?'

'Yes, but isn't there some other way we could settle this wretched matter, after all, who's to say that Kepple isn't the better man and more deserving of the *Parrot* than that thundering great oaf Kettle. Besides, kidnapping and robbing a King's officer in the execution of his duty is a hanging offence, you know? Make no mistake.' Which, indeed it was, but so was treason.

'Do as I order you Monsieur,' he bridled impatiently. 'And if you do, you will be amply rewarded for your efforts, not least by my *silence.* Remember a word in the right place will see you hang for the underhand, spiteful trick you played on Midshipman Kettle's promotion. A mistake our little enterprise tonight will rectify and with no harm done to anyone, least ways you. Except Lieutenant Kepple's pride, which I am sure he will very quickly recover. Don't you agree?'

'Yes, I suppose! But Lieutenant Kepple, he

will not be harmed in any way, Monsieur Corbeau you must most earnestly promise me that, I could not forgive myself if he was?' Bleated Trompe, honestly concerned nothing more serious would happen to him than the knock on the head and temporary imprisonment he was promised would be his only fate. An imprisonment in Lumps Mill on Southsea's Great Morass from where he would emerge in a day or two, a week, at the very most, bruised and badly shaken by his ordeal to find his new-found command and with it his once promising career, had long since sailed away.

'Lieutenant Kepple, will live, but I fear he will have no future in the King's navy after we are done with him,' replied Corbeau, shaking himself free of Trompe's fretful grasp and with a smile more evil than it was kind, left the stricken fellow without the least hope of reprieve.

Watching the creepy French boy go with a mixture of fear and loathing that brought an acid bile to his parched throat, Trompe pondered his threat to expose him to Lord Spencer for an error that was hardly his doing. A threat that would see him sacked from the Admiralty before the day was done, but worse, much worse than this, might even see him hung for the spy Corbeau said he was for letting him read his secret naval papers; which he never did. 'He just took them for himself

213

without asking and kept them for himself though I asked twice he should give them back,' he mumbled. Little realising Lieutenant Kepple had found him and was standing at his side his bicorn hat tucked neatly under his arm and a genial smile on his face.

Chapter 12

Kiya Dreams Of Things Past And A Future Yet To Come

Midsummer eve 1335BCE

Shivering beneath her cloak, Kiya huddled herself in the corner and stared through half shut eyes at the *evil Eye* of Seth. Fashioned with such a dreadful cruelty it was the eye of an animal; a jackal of course, for no human eye could cast a look so dark and baleful as the one that now so hatefully fell on her. A cold, pitiless, heavy-lidded stare that knew no mercy, the black hollow of its empty socket pouring its mocking light into her prison tomb like a poisoned fountain. A mocking, seamless pyramid of light so perfect in its symmetry she could see its sharp edged, rainbow dazzled sides cut the dark as if it was a *real* thing. Something made of glass or polished metal and not the canopy of moonlight it was.

For an age, she looked at it, mesmerized by its hypnotic beauty, its gentle shimmer, its radiant, seemingly dancing colours, until, without the least warning it suddenly and most fortunately vanished leaving the room an impenetrable black.

So, black she couldn't see her hand in front of her face. 'What?' She gasped, blinking, and rubbing her eyes to see again and when she could, rightly guessed it was the ethereal black cloud she saw in the pale night sky before she entered the tomb that had darkened the moon. And knowing it was and it would soon drift away on the warm breeze she leapt to her feet and in a single bound snatched the mirror from the desk and the fallen chair from the floor and climbed up to the ceiling, so low she easily reached it on her tip toe. And when she had, wedged the mirror into the stone cut hollow of the eye and waited for the cloud, so unusual at this time of the year, it had to be a sign, to sail away.

A minute or two later it did and the light returned, but this time a steeply angled shaft of light that flooded the stairwell to the heavy stone that now locked her in.

'Lord, Aten, help me I beseech you do not desert me your faithful servant,' she whispered. 'Give me strength to find my way from this cursed place. Shield me from the evil Eye of Seth who watches me from above. Help me, I beg you, defeat my sister Queen, Nefertiti. Give me *life* forever as my husband promised me before he left and let me find him I beg you.' A prayer she repeated without end until she fell exhausted to the darkened floor, her sceptre clutched tight in her two hands and pressed to her forehead and *dreamed* she fell into a constellation of spiraling stars and soft, billowing, clouds that sucked her through an endless void of crimson light, until, at last, she saw a half-naked girl standing on a giant stone in a vast, never ending field of stones in a thunder and lightning storm of drenching rain, surrounded everywhere about by horsemen and soldiers who were trying to kill her. It was Tefnut, her sister. There could be no doubt, though a Tefnut she had never seen before, so untidy was her hair and the ragged clothes she wore.

Maat[164] *called Tefnut*, in her strong, clear voice, her eyes lifted to the sky. *Come to me, Queen of heaven and smite my enemies, who are all about me. Come to me now sacred mother of the moon and stars and carry me safe home in your arms. I beg you. Hear me my lady, Maat; I am Tefnut, your faithful servant, daughter of Aten; sister in law of the Pharaoh Akhenaten and sister of his true and faithful wife, my beloved sister Kiya. Hear me goddess I am your servant.*

I see you, I hear you, Tefnut, cried Kiya, her voice a lament as the image faded, hot tears welling in her Kohl black eyes to a sting that spilled a stream to her cheeks. *I am coming sweet sister.* But try as she could, she could not see a way. She was lost. It was then she heard a second voice. A girl's voice from so far away she could barely hear the single, unfamiliar word she said; *Tarhuhi-awaku.* Not once, but three times she said it and with the word came the first glimpse of who she was through the early morning mist that surrounded her like wisps of cotton on a gentle wind.

Tefnut, she cried. *Tefnut, is that you? Hear me Tefnut, please; it is me, your sister Kiya who calls you.* But the girl she now saw made no answer, but sat cross-legged beneath a red blanket on a ledge in front of a flower and frond draped cave beside a narrow waterfall, her open hands held wide in prayer on her lap. A waterfall which fell into a shallow stream in a sunlight dappled glade everywhere surrounded by dizzying, snowcapped mountains covered in a canopy of endless trees. A place unlike any place she had seen in her life before and so utterly different from the flat, endless desert wastes of her own beloved, Egypt. An Egypt she longed to see again. *Who are you?* She asked, the girl, without answer. *Tefnut, Tefnut, is that you my love?* She cried, knowing all the time it wasn't, but was someone else, someone whose fate was bound to hers. And as she did, a second figure appeared in her dream, this time it was, Tefnut, but seeming to float above the stream in a translucent light, as she walked, unhurried towards the seated girl.

Tefnut. I see you my love. She called. *I see you as clearly as I did before, but in some other place. Sister I see you. Hear me. I beg you hear me. Come to me,* but she didn't hear nor did she come, but walked towards the girl. Who seeing her dropped her blanket from her shoulders and ran to greet her with a smile of perfect joy on her pretty face and as she did, they both disappeared into a darkness that consumed her dreaming mind with its perfect, utterly silent emptiness.

Chapter 13

Mister Trompe Is Blackmailed
To A Treason He Never Wanted,
But Can Little Avoid

4.10pm Thursday 20 April 1797

'Mister Trompe? Mister Lauder Trompe?'
Asked Billy, not at all sure the downcast young man with the unwashed in days, ink blackened ear, talking to himself and so lost in his own thoughts, he surely didn't realise he was there, was his intended meeting. Though he felt sure he was.

'What?' Answered Trompe, his mind barely grasping the arrival of his appointment, though it was most assuredly him by the ill-fitting, second hand, Lieutenant's uniform he wore! 'Yes. Yes, it is, sir. I am Mister Lauder Trompe, Admiralty clerk to Lord Spencer.' He said, standing to receive his guest with a hand as large and as strong as any Billy had ever gripped. 'You must be Lieutenant Kepple, newly appointed Captain of his majesties gun-brig *Parrot*? Please do sit down, why don't you. I'm delighted to make your acquaintance, I truly am,' He gabbled like a turkey.

'Yes. Yes, I am. And thank you, I will,' answered Billy taking the offered seat beside the nervously blushing clerk and thinking himself very late, indeed to have caused him such distress. 'Have you been waiting long Mister Trompe?' He solicitously asked. 'Captain Patton made no precise mention of the time we should meet this afternoon, but as I am to meet him, at eight o'clock sharp in Wish Street, a goodly walk from here, you will agree, I thought four o'clock would suffice to complete our business and with time to spare,' he fibbed, knowing it was the boy's silly jape that delayed him.

'No, you are not late Lieutenant Kepple. A moment only, if at all, sir,' answered Trompe, quickly taking stock of his companion. Who was not at all like the beastly cad who had turned his well-intentioned, not to say consoling words of comfort so sharply against him. 'Would you care for a drink before we begin, Lieutenant Kepple, I can recommend the brandy, a rather fine French Cognac, if I do say so myself?'

'NO. NO,' said Lieutenant Kepple, more loudly than he intended, observing the half empty bottle of brandy and the three balloon shaped glasses that cluttered the table, one barely touched, his he guessed. Who was still nursing the aching remnants of the fearfully sore hangover that woke him that morning an experience he hoped never to repeat any time soon.

'Well, best we begin then,' answered Trompe, feeling slighted by what he took to be Billy's high-handed refusal of a drink that was only meant to please - he was ever an overly sensitive soul, but never so much, as now, the product, no doubt, of so many wretched, childhood misfortunes. His father murdered and his mother dead these last eighteen months and a life of lonely poverty he daily struggled to overcome without the least help or protection in the world. Not even from his aunt, Mrs Beattie, who hated him with a passion and for no accountable reason he could think, save he was Mister Beattie's nephew and she by law his aunt, though she wouldn't let him say she was, because she was only fifteen and more like a cousin.

Blushing in quiet despair he wondered if the open faced, decidedly handsome young officer seated in front of him, wasn't an altogether stronger and more reliable and resilient fellow than Kettle would have had him and Corbeau believe, from the tales of slovenly sea sickness he told to Hesta Victoria's dizzy delight. Who openly called him a cad, a booby, a bounder, and a monstrous thief to steal his ship from under his nose. A boy without breeding. And if he was, then there was trouble ahead for all of them. Trouble he knew he could well do without. Crestfallen and fearful of the bleak

222

hours to come, he took the package of orders he had stuffed in his jacket pocket and handed them to a boy he liked with an instinct he couldn't begin to explain, but knew he must soon betray. 'You will find your orders are most precise in their instruction, Lieutenant Kepple, as is Lord Bridport's authorization for the secret charts and signals you are to receive from Captain Patton's office later this evening, which is moved to Wish Street, but of course you know that. Also, the stores and provisions you are to have from the dockyard stores and the munitions that will be had from the gun wharf tomorrow.'

'Thank you, Mister Trompe, you are most helpful,' said Billy, gingerly taking the folded package in his hand. The first written orders he had ever received, except his commission. 'But hold on a minute the seal, its broken,' he gasped, in surprise. Placing the still tightly bound package on the table, a demand for an explanation that Trompe could hardly refuse; didn't.

'Indeed, it is, sir,' answered Trompe, his face a picture of puzzled innocence and simple, earnest regret. 'It must have broken in my pocket as I struggled through the crowds that clog the streets so fearfully from here to the Fountain Inn. The rogues being most brutally awkward and ill-mannered, as I passed the Navy Post Office forty minutes before and so rough in their drunken ways I was several times tripped near to a fall.' A not improbable lie that gave no hint of Corbeau's improper reading of its contents earlier that afternoon.

Duped by Trompe's plausible explanation, which reminded him of his own difficulty in finding the Star and Garter and really, quite liking the odd shaped little fellow, whose fat, impressively round, nut-brown head of thick black hair supported the oddest hat he had ever seen. And more than a little embarrassed by his own, unwarranted suspicions, he began to read his orders, which, as he said were precise and to the point.

Requiring him to provision his ship without delay and sail on the afternoon tide on the 22 of April 1797 to the Quiberon Peninsula. A finger of land he recalled from his naval history that had fought two great sea battles near its shores in recent years against the French. One, in 1759 during the Seven Years War[165] when Admiral Sir Edward Hawke sank six of Marshal Conflan's fleet of twenty-one ships of the line in the bay it enclosed, preventing the invasion of England, he planned. The second, just two years ago, when Lord Bridport landed an army of three thousand, five hundred, ill-trained, but well provisioned and well-equipped French émigrés soldiers from England's south coast on her isolated shore. Only to see them beaten into

bloody submission in barely a month by a determined French army commanded by General Lazare Hoche.

A quiet corner of north-west France far from
the revolutionary turmoil of Paris, on the Atlantic
coast between the strategically important Brittany
ports of Lorient and St Nazaire, where he was ordered to land and take into safe custody a party
of French royalist fugitives who would signal their
presence to him at one-hour intervals on the night
of Friday the 28 of April 1997, just six days after he
sailed, he sighed he had so little time, and for two
successive nights after that.

'Gracious me, I have no time to lose, Mister
Trompe,' said Billy, trying to take in the danger
and complexity of the mission he was just given.
Which was not the cruise he had hoped would be
the start of his command, but a mission of the very
greatest secrecy, risk, and importance to the British government. One that would ask all the courage and limited seafaring skills he and his crew of
ships boys, possessed.

Wasting no time, he rose from his seat and
made to say his goodbye, but was unexpectedly stopped by a suddenly animated Trompe. Who
with a great show of kindness placed himself at
Billy's immediate disposal, assuring him that a
great deal of time and energy might be saved if he,

a humble servant of the Admiralty, was to smooth his passage through the bureaucratic intricacies of a dockyard notorious throughout the Channel fleet for its tardiness and bewildering, venal corruption in time of dreadful war.

With this readily agreed, Trompe steered his new-found *friend* - and he truly wished he was, so much did he now like the dashingly earnest young man, through the gathering gloom of that early evening, across the swing bridge that opened the town quay to the Solent, past the gun wharf, the Mill Redoubt and pond, the small armory and up the Common Hard to the gates of the Royal dockyard. Then the biggest industrial complex in the world consisting of a village of fine houses for the use of senior dockyard officials, Admiralty offices, a Royal Naval College, stables, coach-houses, boatyards, a little church, a guardhouse full of Marines, shops, sheds, a foundry, a blacksmith, a surgery, a mortuary and even a fire station.

A necessary precaution against the fires they every day had, many of them not the accidents they would seem, but started by French spies and Irish rebels living in the town. Not to mention the workshops and material stores in which every staple of a King's ship could be had for a price and a Transport Office decked in wooden ladders, precarious scaffolds, ropes and pulleys to its gabled roof, the newly applied paint on its office walls drying through open windows.

A price paid in full by a surprisingly vocal, impatient, and authoritative, Lauder Trompe, who signed every docket he was given with a cheerful disregard for the cost. Who, true to his word brought the not inconsiderable weight of Lord Spencer's power to bear upon the normally irascible and penny-pinching dockyard flunkies who at that late hour were more anxious for their supper than they were to meet the needs of a petty Admiralty clerk and his singular companion. An indecently young-looking Lieutenant, who appeared to wield a power and influence over the First Lord of the Admiralty they felt obliged to support and obey with a flattering if frustrated, obedience.

Such was their success and it was a considerable success, when they emerged from the gun wharf tired and thoroughly exhausted three hours later a drove of dockyard laborers was already loading the many stores they had ordered into the barges tied up in the basin that would be their transport to the *Parrot* the next day. And, if the foreman of this venerable band of men was to be believed, and he appeared to be a man of integrity with a guinea of Billy's pitifully small funds stuffed in his greasy paw, the last of those many items would be delivered well before they sailed.

Arriving at the Transport Office in Wish Street just before eight o'clock, with the sky beginning to blacken and a damp cloying mist creeping up from the sea to chill their bones, Trompe bid his planned farewell and left a contented, if now bone weary and foot sore, Billy, at the lamp lit, porticoed door. Safe in the knowledge, as only the truly innocent can be, he would be safe aboard his little gun brig in time for supper.

Ushered inside by one of the two, red-coated Marine guards, who stood sentry outside, he was greeted in the gloom of the narrow hallway by a sour faced clerk with a grunt of irritable impatience that said he was five minutes late. Who, ignoring his outstretched hand and cheerfully polite hello, immediately led him up the even narrower, barely lit by his modest candlelight, noisily creaking stairs, to an attic room, empty of any furniture, save the wooden table that sat in the middle of the dusty floor. On which a single guttering candle burned a feeble half-light and a rough canvas bag lay open beside a scree of maps, papers, and books.

'Lieutenant Galbraith, sir,' said the servant, introducing Billy to the man, seated and half hidden in the shadows beneath the eves, who watched his arrival with a singular interest. A man by the name of Lieutenant James Galbraith, who you will remember, was visiting Mister Evan Nepean at the Admiralty on the morning Admiral Kettle died, and was truly glad he had, so much did he hate and blame the wretched fellow for the death of his friend, Captain John Kepple, Billy's dad. A man who knew, as only a handful of other great men of consequence, did, that, though the bright faced, but now rather tired looking young man who stood before him had been given his command by a simple mistake, it was a mistake now very much approved by the brave company of men he served - the most secret society of *The Sword and Shield of Aten.* A secret society that would do everything in its worldwide power, small though it was, to protect him on the important mission he was about to send him on.

But not tonight, no that must wait until he had safely rescued the émigrés he was ordered to find, three of them unimportant to the war that raged between Britain and France, or the duty he must undertake, but one of them, Marie-Ange le Dantec, so very important he must rescue her at all cost. Even if the others were left behind. A brave and resourceful little girl, as he now fondly remembered she was, from the summer of 1795 they spent together, when the Quiberon was set ablaze by that ill-judged invasion and her grandfather killed by the treachery of a greedy coward.

Chapter 14

Polly Easily See's Through Tom's Thin Disguise

8.08pm Thursday 20 April 1797

As Lieutenant Galbraith began to speak, his tone severe and precise as only a kings officer could be, never straying from the dark that hid his face, Jemmy Grub, holding fast to Trompe's trembling arm and two of his henchmen watched the house from the dark of a nearby alleyway. Readying their plan to kidnap him when he emerged with a confidence born of a lifetime of artful villainy.

But unbeknown to them all, and fortunate it was, Tom, ever a headstrong and impatient young girl and tired of waiting for Billy to come back to the Sally Port, where the *Parrot's* sea slopped a foot deep, smelly gig, endlessly bobbed up and down and bumped the harbour steps in a tedious, thumping monotony, had long since given Trucky and Duffy the slip. And for several hours now had been searching the town for him and getting thoroughly tired and lost in the bargain.

Twice returning to the Star and Garter Inn only

to find herself shooed away by a fat rolled cook with baking flower on her red flushed, gin soaked face and a rolling pin in her hand she threatened to hit her with. Who cried *he* was a grubby little cove with no good in *his* wicked eye. But ever hopeful she would find him before the town watch or worse still, her uncle, who she knew would *still* be looking for her, found her - a fear too awful to contemplate, she gamely pressed on and on.

Reaching the top, the High Street once again, or was it twice again, she couldn't recall, she now joined a boisterous, flag and banner waving crowd making its noisy way towards the Grand Parade to hear what news there was to be had of the mutiny, but before she got there, found herself suddenly outside the lamp lit, front door of the very grand, Fountain Inn and seeing several senior sea officers go inside, thought she would look to see if Billy was anywhere to be found.

Pushing her way through the crowd, who impatiently elbowed her, this way and that in their hurry to reach the Semaphore Station, where a speaker standing on an upturned box was heatedly talking to the cheering throng, she found the open main door to the wainscoted[166] vestibule and peeped in. But no sooner had she, then she was stopped by the rake-thin, red coated Marine who stood an idle guard there, a tankard of foaming beer in his hand

231

and the stub of a smoking clay pipe clenched tight in his mouth. His face a stern and threatening re-buke no less that the bayoneted rifle he held in the lazy crook of his elbow. Who would let no one in, he declared in a growl, save those on Lord Spen-cer's or Admiral Bridport's most pressing personal business, which he said, with a mockingly sinis-ter laugh, she most definitely wasn't. And with a painful shove in the guts that sent her winded and reeling backwards into the busy street.

But never one to give up she quickly turned the corner of the inn and boldly entered the cob-bled coach yard and after a few confident steps and with a breezy whistle on her lips - and she whistled like a nightingale when the mood took her, happened on a young kitchen maid hopeless-ly trying to fill a large, thin copper jug the size of her leg from the green painted, rust flaked water pump that was stubbornly refusing to give up a single drop of its precious liquid. And seeing she was, took pity on her; and glad she was she did.

'Can I help?' She asked with a smile that beamed she would, taking hold of the noisy, loose fitting at its rusty top, dripping a cold river down her sleeve into the trough, pump handle and cranking it down with as much effort as she could muster, which most fortunately, was more than enough, quickly filled the jug to its brim.

'Thank you, *Miss,*' said the diminutive maid glad to be relieved of a task that had threatened to pull her already stiff and aching arms clean off her very sore shoulders.

'*Miss?*' Cried Tom, more loudly than she intended, her hands pressed to her hips in the stern and reproachful manner of her darling Miss Fry, who was too sweet to frighten anyone, least of all her pupils, who loved her. Shocked and alarmed to be unmasked by so small a person as the ragged girl who now looked at her with an amused, oddly knowing look on her startlingly pretty face and in the hearing, or so she imagined she was, of the three men who were readying a very handsome coach and four horses, who turned to look at her, their faces impatient and tired. 'Did you call me *Miss?*' She whispered in a huff.

'Yes Miss,' said the maid, blowing a wisp of unruly hair from her tired face as she lifted the jug up to her knee and splashed it on her deeply stained, grey pinny.

'Hey, wait a minute,' hissed Tom, in a panic as she turned to go. 'Why did you call me *Miss* when it's plain to everyone who sees with their eyes, I'm a boy, not a girl?'

Surprised and intrigued by Tom's claim to be a boy, when she wasn't, well not any boy she had ever met in the ten long years of her growing more miserable, horribly overworked life. 'Really?' She giggled, setting the jug down on the wet, straw-strewn, grass and moss poked, cobbled yard beside the stone trough.

'Yes,' answered Tom, disconcerted by the quizzical smile on her face as she looked her up and down in the most intrusive way. Her bright brown eyes lingering on every curve of her body, her grubby face, her hands, and her tiny feet to see through her thin disguise.

'Mmm,' murmured the girl, placing her hands firmly on her hips to look Tom full in the face with condescending good humor that quite unnerved her. 'You is a girl like me, Miss,' she declared in a harsh whisper, careful no one in the yard would over-hear her.

'I'm not a girl. I'm not,' seethed Tom, her head bent so close to hers they almost touched.

'You is *Miss.* 'replied the maid airily, her tone more amused and mocking than Tom altogether cared for. 'You is a girl, Miss, though why you is pretendin' you is not, I can't rightly say.' And with a cheeky wink that made Tom's face blush to the bone, turned on her heels and slopping even more water on her pinny, crab-like, made her way towards the kitchen door.

'I'm not a girl,' said Tom, hurrying after her and crossly stamping her right foot on the cobble in a comic gesture of indignation that drew a curious glance from the young ostler, who was steadying a white horse into the shafts of a straw filled, sea-blue, box cart. 'I never was a girl and I never will be a girl, I'm am boy, see?'

'You is a girl, Miss,' said the maid, with a chuckle.

'How do you know I'm a *girl?*' Asked Tom, tartly, giving up any pretense, she wasn't. Hopeful an answer - any answer, would help repair the chink in her ragged camouflage of dirt and soot. A chink so easily spotted by a girl, a head and shoulder shorter than she was, she might very soon be unmasked by someone more important. Billy, Trucky or that watchfully, ever smirking at her, Duffy to name, but three. A boy grown very bossy with his new promotion, who almost caught her by her foot, as she jumped out of the gig.

'I know because I've got the power, Miss,' she answered, tapping the side of her button nose three times with her index finger and almost losing hold of the jug as she did, which banged on the cobble with a splash.

'Power?' Asked Tom, bewildered, 'what *power?'*

'The power, Miss and I've got it and though you might fool everyone else in this yard with your boy's disguise, and you do, never mistake you do,

235

there's no foolin', Polly you is a boy. I've got the special power, you see,' she whispered, tapping her nose three times again, 'And I know you for what you really is,' she gently jabbed her finger into her still sore tummy. 'And you isn't no boy, is you, Miss? And you isn't no servin' girl like me, neither, Miss, with your pretty face and pretty ways. Even, though you has gone and got yourself all done up dirtier than that *shit* splattered little pig over there. No, you is a girl, but why is you pretendin' you's not,' she declared in the vulgar, gutter English she was taught by the sailors who brought her from Africa only last year. A coarseness that kept her safe from prying eyes that every day strangled her tongue to speak the way she should, and easily could. A coarseness that knew she was better born than any one would ever guess, though she had long forgotten where and how and who she was.

'*Quiet,*' hissed Tom, her whispered voice a mixture of amazement and sudden concern she would betray her. 'You won't go telling, will you? You won't tell anybody else what you know about me? You promise you won't?'

'I won't blab on you Miss, 'course I won't,' said *Polly* casting a sly look over her shoulder at the two, red-coated Marines who were just coming out of the kitchen door with one of the scullery maids.

A saucy girl by the common look of her, all ribbons and bows and strawberry painted lips poised for a soldier's furtive kiss. 'You can count on Polly to keep a secret, Miss, even if they beat me with a stick until I'm all black and blue and me eyes pop out me head like a corpse on a gibbet. Even if they rope me up by me ankles and throw me down that there well and drowns me deader than dead in the cold water,' she pointed to the stone walled well standing a yard beyond the pump. 'Even if they pulls out every tooth I've got in me head and throw's them on the floor like dead men's dice. Even if they bury me up to me neck in the ground and twist my ears off me head with a pair of red hot iron pliers. Even if they hang me by the neck until me tongue is all black and swollen.' A dramatic, rendition that was ever her very particular way of telling a story and one that Tom smiled with pleasure to hear as she hadn't smiled in months and knew she had found a friend.

'Hush Poll, I believe you. I believe you?' She said, struggling to keep a straight face as the girl reached down for the jug. 'But don't go just yet? Stop awhile and tell me more about this power? This special power you have to see what others can't?'

'I can't tell you no more than that, Miss,' said Polly, setting down her jug and gently pulling at one of the many short, tightly bound pigtails that stuck out of her head like the spikes on horse chestnut. 'It's somethin' some of us foreign folk from overseas have and somethin' *you* white folk never do, you being most peculiarly stupid in that way. I just see's and knows thin's, Miss. Thin's past, thin's now and thin's yet to be.'

'What sort of thin's? I mean things?' Asked Tom, forgetting her mission to find Billy. Who was now earnestly reading the piece of paper Lieutenant Galbraith had just given him, which contained a password he must remember as well as his own name because no copy of it could be had, so secret was its meaning.

'Thin's Miss,' answered Polly, shyly. 'Just thin's nobody else knows, but me. Some thin's important, some thin's that isn't so important. Like you is a girl pretendin' to be a boy, which ain't very important unless you say it is and if you say it is, well it is and I won't say otherwise, but you had best put some more dirt in your ears, clean ears being most uncommon in a boy.'

'Yes, but can you tell me something I don't know, Poll?' Pleaded an intrigued Tom, her two index fingers now searching her ears. 'Can you tell me what sort of things you see? Can you see anything about me?'

'Yes, I suppose,' she answered, 'if I try hard

like I have nothin' better to do with me time bein'
at me leisure and without a heap of chores to do
before I find me bed.'

'Sorry,' said Tom, seeing again how very tired
she looked, but though she did, saw the look of
determination come into her face. And when it
did, for what seemed an age, she said nothing,
but stared intently into her hazel-brown eyes. As
if she was searching out some deep and impenetrable secret hidden there and just as Tom was
beginning to feel a little bit dizzy and cross-eyed
under her relentlessly hypnotic and quite startling
gaze, she took Tom's two hands in her own and
whispered. 'He's in terrible mortal danger, Miss,
he truly is. That friend of yours, the boy you like.'

'Who is, Poll?' Asked Tom, fascinated.

'The one you call, Billy, Miss. The boy you
came to the Fountain Inn just now, lookin' for. He's
in mortal danger and no mistake,' answered Polly,
biting her lower lip.

'*Billy?*' A name she knew for certain she had
never spoken. 'Do you know him Poll? Billy, I
mean? Do you know where he is? Is he here, inside?' Asked a now thoroughly startled Tom and
with a growing sense of alarm that began to tremble her legs to a wobbly panic.

'I never met him in me whole life, Miss,' answered Polly, with a shrug. 'And no one can get

in there,' she pointed to the two soldiers lolling against the whitewashed wall with the maid, 'exceptin' a kin's officer and not even then without a great palaver about papers and signin' this and signin' that, like you've never seen in your life, Miss. Oh my word no, Miss,' declared Polly, unabashed by the fright she had given Tom.

'Then how do you know he's in danger, Poll?' Asked Tom, impatiently.

'Because I seen it, Miss. I seen him bashed on his poor head with a cudgel as thick as me left leg and carried off like a sack of old spuds on a rickety, squeakin' hand cart by the villains what did it to him. The like of which you don't never want to see in your life, Miss, oh no. Three of them it was that done him in. One terrible big, one small and very fat and one of them just middlin' sort of fellow, but with a black patch on his eye.

'Where Poll? Where have they taken him?' Asked a frantic Tom, unable to hide the concern she felt for him.

'They ain't taken him nowhere yet, Miss.'

'What? You just said? Gracious whatever do you mean, Poll?' Asked Tom, now so thoroughly perplexed she hardly knew what to say. 'You said Billy had been taken off.'

'*Not yet he hasn't,* Miss,' she answered, a reassuring smile creasing her face to a wide grin.

'He ain't been taken anywhere, yet. He's still read-in' the letter he has to learn by heart before he can return to his ship. But you'd best be quick if you want to save him, 'cos its certain sure they is goin' to slit 'is throat from ear-to-ear ....'

'Where Poll?' Interrupted Tom, trying desper-ately to gather her thoughts into some sort of or-der, but feeling she never would, so anxious did she feel. 'Where is he now? Cor blimey Charlie, tell me please?' She begged, so fond had she grown of that sea sick boy.

'They be gettin' ready for him now, Miss, hid-den in the street nearby, but I can't properly say where they is 'cos of the mist, Miss, said Polly, upset her powers had let her down.

'*Mist,* Poll? What mist? What do you mean the *mist?*' She asked, confused and barely able to contain herself.

'The mist, Miss, its rollin' up so thick from the sea, I can't see. But he's close. I'm sure of that. But them nasty blighters is even closer,' answered Polly, as helpfully as she could. But then, with the words barely out of her mouth, she froze to a stop as both Midshipman Kettle and Pierre Corbeau came out of the kitchen into the yard, barely three yards in front of them.

'I have to go now, Miss,' she said, in an urgent whisper, frightened and distracted by their sudden

241

arrival.'

'Who are they Poll?' Asked Tom, her eyes nervously fixed on the two strangers whose arrival had stiffened the two Marines beside the half open kitchen door to a sudden attention, the maid beside them smiling it had. One, an ugly great lump of a slovenly Midshipman in a dirty coat, the other, an extraordinarily handsome boy of fourteen or fifteen, she guessed, whose voluminous black cloak flapped around his body in the thin breeze like the wings of a giant bird; a hawk?

'Them two be friends of me mistress,' whispered Polly, sourly, touching her still sore ear with one hand and gripping the beautifully crafted, strangely exotic necklace she wore about her little neck with the other. 'The queer lookin' cove dressed in black is Monsieur Corbeau. He's a Frenchy who's been stayin' with Miss Hesta Victoria, her mother, who's got the gout in her toe and her grandfather the Admiral, since late last year. A friend of a friend, he says, he is, whose come over from Paris, France to escape the revolution that wants to chop his pretty head off his shoulders. Or so he says. Though I'm certain sure the black-hearted dog is up to some damnable, no-good, mischief with his constant skulkin' and searchin' and rummagin' and nosin' about where his beaky nose don't properly belong when he thinks nobody's lookin', which I is. If you know what I mean, Miss? The other one is Miss Hesta's newfound beau, or so she thinks he is. Mister Midshipman Kettle, he calls himself. A great ugly, spot faced, bad mannered brute of a loud-mouthed booby who's just shipped in from the West Indies with your Captain Billy. But they is nothin' to do with you Miss. But if they sees me lollygaggin' about down here, the Frenchy will tell on me for sure, him bein' a devious, sneaky, sly scoldin' rascal with no scruples about gettin' a poor, orphaned girl like me into more trouble than I can get me self out of and if he does, Miss Hesta will beat me with a stick until I scream or roll over and die, as sure as my name's Polly Perkins. Though it ain't me proper name, but one I was given by the slavers who took me. Though I don't recall when?' And turning on her heels she picked up her now half empty jug and dashed into the kitchen before Tom could say another word.

With Polly gone, Tom took one long last look at the now quietly arguing boys in the yard and shivering with an intuition that knew they were trouble, took to her heels, knowing she must find Billy and very soon. But not before she had gone back to the Sally Port, less than two minutes away and persuaded Duffy to help her. A boy she knew was more than a match for any trouble she might encounter in the minutes to come.

Chapter 15

Tom And Duffy Come To The Rescue

8.18pm Thursday 20 April 1797

It was a surprisingly trusting Trucky Spears who suggested they might find him at the temporary Transport Office, on the corner of Wish Street and Green Lane. Knowing, as only an avid collector of mostly useless information, it was recently moved there on Monday last. A hunch that saw Tom, Duffy and an irritatingly complaining boy called Nipper Ogden come up the mist shrouded Park Lane, just in time to see, Trompe, who none of them knew to be other than the stranger he appeared to be, come suddenly out of the shadows in front of them and with a hurried step that saw him gone in a moment, turn suddenly right into Elm Grove. The eastern spur of the brick sagged cross-road of cramped houses, shops, and alleys they were almost upon.

But seeing nothing suspicious in his behaviour and little believing, Tom's crazy story of kidnap and murder, anyway, Duffy, a level-headed boy was just about to tell him off for the time-wasting fool he thought he was, when, to his surprise, he saw

Trompe return and slink surreptitiously into a darkened alleyway behind the Bush Inn in good sight of the Transport Office. A cubby not twenty feet from the low brick wall they were now crouched behind. An alleyway, he knew, as a Portsmouth boy born and bred, was a shortcut through lower Southsea to the Great Morass. A hideous stretch of marsh that at its southern margins presses the ever-narrowing tail of Southsea Common almost into the sea and wherein, no one, but the foolhardiest would dare too venture after dark.

With his suspicions now a little roused, but in no way roused enough to call for help, after all, Mister Spears had only surrendered to Tom's fantastic tale because he wanted to be rid of him before he excited the rest of his bored and growing mischievous crew of ships boys to run, he pulled Tom and Nipper deeper into the shadows of the wall and watched to see what would happen next, if anything would? Which he doubted.

It was long ten minutes later when Billy emerged from the Transport Office clutching a large, well stuffed canvass bag to his chest so tight it might have been a fortune in gold he carried. By then the evening had darkened too deepest black and the mist had thickened to a cold, damp, swirling fog so close upon them the sudden yellow flicker of light in the top most window of the Transport Office was barely seen, but seen it was by Tom, when the curtain twitched and the anxious face of Lieutenant Galbraith looked down on Billy.

'That's him,' whispered Tom, catching a fleeting glimpse of him in the dull glow of the lamp hung beside the door of the Bush Inn. The corner of his bicorn hat pulled down across his face and his boat cloak wrapped tight around his shoulders and the bag he carried. 'He's coming this way,' she breathed a sigh of relief as he slowly, *ever so slowly* came towards them.

Reassured by the steady, rhythmic tapping sound his studded shoes made as they kicked the cobbled street with every step he took and the barely audible words he seemed to be rehearsing like a poem. *'Who can tell the hiding place of the nine,'* she clearly heard him say, *'who can tell the hiding place of the nine,* he repeated. And with every word coming closer and closer, his heavy, confident footsteps getting louder and louder as he neared the safety of his waiting shipmates.

But then, just as Tom was beginning to think all was well and Polly had imagined Billy's capture that night, - though how she knew his name as only she did, she couldn't begin to say, it being a particular fancy of hers to call him Billy, though never in anyone else's hearing, the sound of his footfall unexpectedly stopped. It was as if he had

247

been plucked bodily from the very ground on which he trod, which, unbeknown to her, is exactly what Jemmy Grub and his two companions had done. They had clubbed poor Billy senseless with a piece of muffled wood and then carried him off with such a lightning speed, only a swirling pool of fog and a menacing silence marked their crime.

'Where's he gone?' Asked Nipper, baffled.

'Damned if I know,' answered Duffy, his voice a whisper that betrayed nothing of the growing concern he felt for his Captain. Who despite his general lack of respect for privileged young officers of his type, he liked. Liked a lot, in fact. Though he would never say he did!

'Maybe he's stopped a moment to get his bearings?' Whispered an equally puzzled Tom, who, though, almost certain of Polly's powers, was hopeful she might have mistaken what she saw for something else.

For what seemed like an age, they listened for any sound that would once again announce his presence, but there was nothing except the barely audible squeak of a distant cart as it hurried along its way.

'Do you hear that?' Asked Tom with a gasp, cupping her ear with her hand to catch every sound it made.

'Hear what?' Asked Duffy, creeping from behind the wall.

'That cart. Poll said he would be, *carried off on a cart by villains the like of which you don't never want to see in your life*,' said Tom, with a whistle of amazement and disbelief, she could have known he would be.

'What? Who?' Asked Duffy,' utterly confused and shaken.

'She got it right. Little Poll, she got it absolutely right,' she answered, astounded by Polly's powers of second sight. 'They've got him on that squeaking cart I can hear and are carrying him off to goodness knows where as we speak. *Quick,* Nipper, get back to the Sally Port and tell, Mister Spears that the Captains been taken and is headed off down that alleyway we saw that other cove just now, disappear into like a rat down a drain. Quick now, you silly lummox of a boy we have not a moment to lose before he's killed.'

But Nipper, confused by Tom's incomprehensible outburst, not to say insulting name-calling and the half-mile run he would have to make, stubbornly stood his ground, convinced that Tom, who he hardly knew and didn't much like, had gone clean off her head.

'Go Nipper. Go as quick as you can,' commanded, Duffy, without a moment's hesitation, knowing now his Captain was in the greatest danger. 'And tell, Dancer Dyke, they're probably headed towards Lumps Mill on the Great Morass. He'll know where I mean. And tell Mister Spears to get his nose out of that damn, silly book of his and meet us there as quick as ever he can and tell him to bring all the hands he can muster. Dancer will show him the way.' An entirely inappropriate demand to make of a senior officer, as you might imagine, and one that Nipper would surely ignore, if he had any sense, which he mostly did. 'Go you damn fool, before I put my foot up your bum and knock your brains clean out of your ducks.'

With Nipper sent on his way, though feeling more than a little peeved by the unkind way he had been spoken too, Tom and Duffy took up the chase. At first, gingerly feeling their way along what was little more than the rough-hewn, puddle-spattered, rubbish-tipped, stone-spiked, weed-snagged, dung-heaped, slime-licked, back lane that meandered in a cock-eyed, higgledy, piggledy sort of fashion between the close packed clutter of sagging houses, shops, sheds, and warehouses that over-hung its dank and murky passageway like a parade of drunken soldiers. Then, as their senses adjusted to its dense, frightening black gloom, more quickly, though not as fast as Tom would have liked to go.

Until, after ten minutes of muscle aching, wind-blown effort they caught their very first glimpse of their quarry, momentarily illuminated in the glow of a torch hanging on the gatepost of the large, country house that marked Portsmouth's eastern margin and the beginning of the fields and meadows that would lead them to the Great Morass beyond the dance of brush and brier choked, grassy dunes just ahead of them.

'Look,' whispered Duffy, pointing to the close packed huddle of figures bent in noisy, grunting exertion over a creaking handcart, now just a short pistol shot away. 'It's them.' But, no sooner were the words out of his mouth than the kidnappers were gone again, swallowed like phantoms in the mist that was thickening with every second stride they took to a dense fog.

'Grove House,' said Tom, reading the name on the gate to the sound of an angry, tethered dog down the cinder path.

'Yes,' answered Duffy, as they followed its gently curving boundary wall down the deep rutted, Grove Road, until it gave way to a thick grown hawthorn hedge that twenty paces further on quite suddenly parted to reveal a sunken track. 'Keep close beside me now, Tom, we almost have them, but we must delay our rescue until we know what we are dealing with.

'Aye, aye,' Duffy, whispered Tom, glad he was in charge and not her.

'Good, lad,' he grinned, firmly patting her shoulder to a sag, 'follow me.'

On and one they went between fields and meadows so dark and wet and so thick with rolling, billowing, fog, they could hardly see their hands in front of their faces. For twenty minutes, they walked, stumbled, scrambled, tripped, and sometimes fell over tracks hardly deserving the name, but never so close upon their quarry they would be heard or seen. Until, at long last Tom heard the steady, rhythmic creaking of a windmill's large sails cut the night with its eerie noise and asked, if it was Lumps Mill they had found. 'No,' Duffy grunted his short reply and said it was another and they had a good long way to go before they did.

The further they walked the lonelier and more desolate the landscape became with just the odd, long-gone-to-bed, thatched cottage or lonely stand of trees or ragged crop of bushes to hide them. A land on which a few sheep grazed a miserable existence in the squelch of mud that now gripped their shoes so tight they often sank to their ankles in its mire. Close by a murder of crow's nesting in the trees high above the Jews burial ground on Lazy Lane, cawed a noisy, frightful warning, Tom, who hated the things, shivered to hear.

'Did you see how many there were, Duffy?' Asked Tom, knowing Polly said there were three, nervously reaching his side, as he came to a crouching stop beneath the tangled cover of the willow hedge that barred their way, but hid them from anything beyond its fringe.

'I counted three of the blighters, Tom,' he whispered, drawing back the half screen of branches that hid them. 'Easy enough odds for you and me to manage on our own until, Mister Spears bring's himself along with the reinforcements we asked him for. That is, if you're game for a fight and I'm figuring you are you being so thick with the Captain when we came aboard?'

'Game enough if you are, Mister Duff, if you know your numbers well enough to count to three before your brain gives up on you.' She answered tartly, sweating like a kitchen maid on a hot summer's day on legs she no longer thought were her own, so cramped and sore were they in shoes and stockings soaked to the skin. And, if the truth be known, not at all sure she was game for anything just then, other than a long lie down with a nice hot cup of Mister Whittard's famous China tea to refresh her flagging spirits.

'I think I know them well enough Tom, though, I'm sure I'm not half so properly schooled in my numbers as you think you are.' He answered with a chuckle and then, before she could think to reply, as he knew she would, if he gave her half a chance, he pulled her to her feet by the collar of her jacket and led her down a soft, rutted track, banked on either side by an arching cloister of rustling beech trees and thick grown hedges that closed about them in a dark and forbidding embrace. He knew from his youthful adventures would lead them in a minute or two, to the brink of the Great Morass and the sea so close beyond it they could hear it even now, surging, crashing, tearing and dragging back and forth on the deep pebbled foreshore.

Reaching its end, they saw the brow of a low hill topped by a gallows tree hung with a man-shaped, metal cage, rise before them and in the faint glimmer of moonlight that lit it, saw the ghostly outline of Grub and his gang, now less than fifteen yards ahead.

Just then, as Tom was steadying herself for what promised to be a painful bruising in the fight to come – though not the first she had endured in the five lonely months since her mother's tragic death, she saw a flash of blue light from somewhere down in the marsh. For a moment, she dared to hope that it was Mister Spears and the boat crew come to save them, but it was not to be.

For when it repeated itself twice more and a voice called a reckless halloo, it was answered with an owl-like hoot of glee from one of the kidnappers. 'What is it?' Asked Tom, knowing very well what it was.

'It's a signal from over by Lumps Mill,' he pointed. 'Their accomplices, I'll be bound,' he answered, seeing the cart begin to lurch its way on again. 'And one we must answer as best we can if the Captain's to be saved. Quick now, as fast as your little legs will carry you! After them and hope Mister Spears is coming to meet us as I told him and with every man jack of the *gig's* crew.'

Without a moment's thought for the deadly dangers that now confronted him, Duffy launched himself at the kidnappers and with an astonishing turn of speed that quite amazed Tom, fell upon them before they knew what hit them. The first to receive a bone-crunching swipe from one of his massive fists was Jemmy Grub. A blow so powerful in its deadly aim it would have done justice to his hero, the unbeatable, Tom Cribb.[167]

Sensing rather than seeing the danger that so suddenly fell upon him, Grub half turned to meet his attacker, but whether he was tired by his exertions, or disorientated by the fog that churned around him like a wraithlike cowl, he was a second too slow to dodge the blow that caught him full in his face and with a cry of rage that was stopped before it was begun, was knocked to the ground as he had never been knocked before.

Without breaking his stride Duffy leapt onto the cart like the nimble topman he was and from his lofty vantage beside the canvas sack he almost stood upon, threw himself onto the two lead boys, their hands gripping tight the shafts as they hurried to get away. Who knowing nothing of Grub's sudden, though, sadly, only *temporary* demise, were still dragging the cart for all they were worth, a very slow crawl that ached to rest and be done with their night's work. Weighing fifteen stone before his breakfast Duffy flattened them both like wheat in a summer gale and as they rolled and cursed and squealed in painful surprise, he took them both by their greasy ponytails and bashed their heads together with such a resounding crash it left them as limp as a bundle of rags.

Arriving a moment later with her fists clenched tight and her face screwed into a vicious, fighting snarl, Tom realised Duffy had not only subdued all the kidnappers, an extraordinary feat, I think you will agree, but somehow lost the handcart in the fog and in it, she was certain, or hoped she was, Billy. Though, there was an outside chance she was mistaken and between them they had assaulted a trio of innocent boys in pursuit of their

256

lawful business. 'Look,' she gasped, in horror, as she saw it tumble, helter-skelter down the rapidly inclining, potholed, path towards the marsh. 'After it, quick, Duffy, before he drowns!'

Running as fast as her legs would carry her, which wasn't very fast, she being a well brought up girl who never had to run faster than a playful skip before, and in ducks that scraped her painfully aching legs red raw, she gave chase. But though she tried with all her might and mane she was too slow to prevent it striking the large rock that stood in its way at the bottom of that gentle hill. Break itself into a dozen shattered pieces and pitch it's still unknown, canvas shrouded contents into a thicket of gorse some considerable distance from where she had come to a slithering, upended stop, the spokes of the nearest wheel turning so fast in her face they quite made her dizzy.

'Damn and blast me for a fool,' shouted Duffy, amazed by the speed, height and distance a body could travel when thrown headlong from a speeding cart brought to a sudden stop by a stone. Well a bloomin' great boulder, really, about a foot high by two feet wide.

'Bloody, bloody, bloody, bloody hell, Duffy.' Cursed Tom, like a trooper, leaping headlong into the mist swirled undergrowth, which unbeknown to her concealed a slimy, smelly old bog beneath its soft and pliant folds.

'Can you see him?' Shouted Duffy, coming to its poisonous edge and careful not to step in and dirty his boots.

'I can't see a blessed thing, Duffy as you can well see I can't,' she complained, now waist deep in a thick brown, sticky soup of foul smelling water. 'He's gone and disappeared and if that fall didn't kill him, which I'm sure it did, this bloody bog will drown him better than the sea he loves, ever will. *Oh. Oh.* Dear gawd love me for a fool Duffy, it looks like I'm going to drown in it too, and me only twelve years old this last birthday. Help me Duffy? Help me please. Or I'm a goner?'

Without any thought for the kidnappers, who were even then shakily and somewhat dreamily rousing themselves from the drubbing he had just given them, Duffy stretched a leg into the bog and finding a foothold grabbed her by her short pony-tail and in a single, glutinous, slurping pull dragged her kicking, squealing, and complaining like the *girl* she was onto the path beside him. Though, it must be said, stinking like a cowpat that had been strained several times through a sweaty old sock, filled with year old moldy cheese and rotten eggs and left to cook in a warm oven for a week.

'Hells breath, Tom, you stink like the choked heads[168] on a first-rate ship of the line, that's got itself stuck in the tropics with a case of the fluxing trots and no mistake,' gasped Duffy, amused by his vile and vividly awful description of her reeking, pongy, smelly state.

'So would you if you'd been up to your neck in that bog, Andrew Duff?' Answered Tom, as coolly as she might, but not so cool as to stop him laughing again at the sight of her.

It was then, in that comic moment of indignation and blessed relief that Grub struck. Coming out of the fog like a demon he smashed Tom to the ground with a vicious blow to the head that knocked her instantly senseless and then, with an agility that was quite astonishing for a boy of his size, a muscle-bound, bull-necked, barrel-chested, bow-legged oaf, he sent Duffy flying with a right upper-cut to his jaw that would have killed a fully-grown camel.

But Duffy was as wily as he was strong and with the practiced ease of the street fighter he had always been, he rolled with the punch and though he felt his teeth rattle like skittles in his bloody mouth, he managed to avoid the worst of that terrible blow. Crouching low and shielding his head with his massive arms he tried to position himself for Grub's next attack, which he knew was no more than a second away, but as he did, he slipped on the wet and muddy path and fell flat on his face into a densely-packed thicket of sedge and marram grass that bubbled to see him come.

Seeing his man was fallen and with a bully's keen eye for a mean advantage, Grub began to kick, stamp and punch and pulverize poor Duffy for all he was worth. Each blow harder than the last, until, at long last, he was sure his man was finished, for no one, he was sure, could stand half such a beating as that.

With Duffy near lifeless at his feet, Grub wiped the blood from his crumpled nose and spat the remnants of a broken front tooth from his mouth into the bog and with a mixture of triumphant glee and bitter contempt, stared at his fallen adversary. 'NO ONE LAYS A FINGER ON JEMMY GRUB AND LIVES TO TELL THE TALE. YOU HEAR ME, BOYS?' He growled, menacingly. And then with a vicious impatience that was his trademark, he shouted. 'BADGER? DOGGET? WHERE THE HELL ARE YOU, YOU SHIFTLESS, IDLE PAIR OF SLACK-ARSED, WEASELY LOAFERS? GET YOUR SELVES HERE, NOW.

Chapter 16

A Desperate Fight
Binds A Closer Friendship

9.30pm Thursday 20 April 1797

'Coming Jemmy boy,' said Dogget, finding Grub's side and staring down at Duffy's lifeless body with a fascination and then, seeing no possible harm could come of it, gave him a hefty poke in the ribs with the belaying pin[169] he held tight in his hand. 'You got him good, then I see, Grub?'

'Yeah, I got the bruiser and that little tyke over there, too,' said Grub, with ill-concealed, boastful pride that didn't know how lucky he was he hadn't met his man another day.'

'Who are they Jemmy?' Asked Badger, a short, fat, mop-headed, do-anything-for-a-farthing,[170] simpleton, who was clearly less welcome at Grub's elbow than Dogget.

'How should I know, you jabbering Bedlam[171] loon?' Answered Grub, viciously, his nose and mouth hurting more than he would admit. But, I can tell you this, *Mister Badger,'* he said, poking him in the chest, 'they ain't no friends of mine and if they ain't no friends of mine, then they ain't no friends of yours! So, if you ain't got nothing better to do than talk your gibberish fetch me a length of rope from that broken cart and tie them up before they both wakes and runs away.

'Aye, aye,' chirped Badger, anxious to do what he could to calm the bullying brute. 'I'll be back in a jiffy and no mistake Jemmy, 'pon my soul I will. You mark my words, I'll be back before you know I've been and gone,' he laughed, and with that he was off into the fog to find the six feet of rope they had brought with them.

'Now, where's that young gentleman gone and got himself, Jem? Well, I'll be blowed, he's nowhere I can see with me one good eye,' whispered Dogget. A pinched faced, ferrety sort of boy with a patch over his left eye from the Battle of Durdle Door, just as Polly earlier said he had, and a livid scar on his forehead that ran down to his upper cheek to mark the swiping sword blow he had received from one of the Militia men who ambushed the crew of the *Seahorse* on the beach. Who, lacking Grub' strength and dreadful brutality made his way in the underworld of crime in which they both lived and the frequent violence they often, did with a low and artful cunning, that even Grub, who admired no one more than himself, had occasion to appreciate. Though he never said he did.

'Damned if I know, Joby,' he answered, perplexed by Billy's disappearance, which hadn't seen him cannon shot into the morass. 'But no matter, he can't have gone very far, least ways not trussed up like a Christmas goose.'

'No. But, we'd best find him quick before the tide turns and Charlie takes off without us, him being fearful nervous of the Riding Officers[172] since that business last year at *Lulworth* when his old da was killed.

'Mmm,' murmured Grub, thoughtfully, lifting his greasy tricorn hat an inch above his brow to rub his battered face with a rag. 'You may be right, but leave him to me. You get yourself down to Lumps Mill and Charlie as quick as ever you can and tell him to hold things up with that boat of his until I tell him otherwise and tell him,' he sniggered. 'We've now got three for the long drop into Davey Jones' locker [173] and not just the one we promised the Frenchy,' he laughed.

As Dogget took himself off down the path rubbing his bruised head and aching, twisted neck, Badger returned with the rope and with Grub's grumbling, impatient help, tied Duffy's arms and legs together so tightly he could hardly breathe, let alone move with any purpose.

'There ain't no more of this,' said Badger fret-

263

fully.

'What?' Replied Grub, with a snarl.

'Rope! There ain't no more of this 'ere rope, Jemmy to tie the other one, him lying over there,' he said, nervously pointing to Tom. Who lay still and quiet on the path, his face twitching and grimacing in anticipation of the punch he thought would be his answer.

'No matter,' said Grub, grabbing the back of her thick leather belt, and hauling her up like a folding chair, until her nose touched her knees in a flop. 'This smelly little runt ain't goin' nowhere in a hurry.' And with a chuckle of delight, he dropped her with a crunch into a puddle where she lay as still and as silent as the corpse she would soon be if she made a sound.

'Now,' he said, wiping his bloody hands on the front of Badgers greasy, ill-fitting, homespun, tailcoat jacket. 'We'd best find our brave young Captain and get him on his way before the town watch or the Militia come pokin' their ugly noses into business that ain't nothing to do with them or their kind. So, get yourself in there, Badger and find him quick, drowned or no.'

'What, in there?' Whined Badger, disgusted by the prospect of getting any closer to the bog than he already had, but too scared of Grub to retreat to safer ground. 'It stinks in there, Jemmy. It stinks really bad! And I've got a cold coming on and me stomach is all a churn with the thought of it. Do I have, too, Jemmy?' He whined. 'Can't we wait until Joby gets back with Charlie?'

'Stinks or no Mister Badger,' said Grub. 'Get yourself in there before I throw you in. I want that gods-own-fool of sailor boy and the *password* the Frenchy, says he has and I wants them both, now. Do ya hear?' And with a vicious kick up the back-side he grabbed him by his coat and threw him into the bog where he sank up to his waist with a noisy, hissing squelch.

'Cripes, Jemmy I can hardly breathe for the smell of it,' he choked and gasped, as he wrig-gled and swam and pulled himself by every tenu-ous hold he could find, deeper and deeper into its slime. Sadly, without the least idea where he was going or much more importantly, how he would get out, if get out he could? 'Can't see nothing, Jem-my. Nothing at all,' he whined.

'Keep looking until you find him, Mister Bad-ger, or I'll fix you so your own sweet mother won't recognise you for the muddle-headed midget you truly are,' answered Grub, sitting himself on the flat of the broken cart to lazily smoke the stub of his broken clay pipe. 'ANY SIGN OF THE LUB-BER?' He called, a moment later, careless his voice had carried to the beach, where in a noisy foaming swell, Trucky and his boat crew were just then landing after a long and arduous pull around the coast that had near exhausted the lot of them

'NO. BUT I'M LOOKIN' THE BEST I CAN, JEMMY,' came the equally loud, if thoroughly disconsolate reply from Badger, who, ignoring Grub's threat, had found a moments safety on an island of dry ground where he lay on his elbow in a squelching, dripping heap.

As he did, Tom opened her big brown eyes and through the film of tears that filled them to their dripping brim, saw Duffy tied up in the most fearsome way beside her. But looking more closely, saw he was conscious and more than that, he was silently working his bonds in a determined effort too free himself. As luck, would have it the sedge and marram grass he'd fallen on had formed a deep, sponge-like cushion beneath his head and because it had, had absorbed much of the force of the beating he had received from Grub and though his body ached from head to toe, he was less badly hurt than he would know. Sensing Tom had woken, Duffy, slowly, and careful not to be seen, half turned his head towards her and seeing her bravely smile she was ok, winked her the biggest wink and smiled her the biggest smile he could muster, something that lifted her heart to see. With the merest nod, he gestured to the hunched and smoking figure of Grub, behind her. Who with his back towards them was idly poking the marsh with a splinter of broken cart. But, just then, as he hoped they might yet escape his evil clutches, he heard voices coming up the path, though still a long way off and saw him yawn a long, cavernous yawn, stretch his arms, and stand to meet them, his smoking pipe stuck contentedly in the corner of his mouth.

Taking her lead from Duffy, who quickly feigned he was still deeply unconscious, Tom closed her eyes and lay as quiet as she could, until Grub, stopping to poke her in the ribs with the splinter he now carried like sword, passed on his way. 'Ouch,' she quietly moaned, hopeful he hadn't heard her and as she did, a voice, soft and low and clear, called out from the mist.

'Are you ok, Bosun?'

'*What?*' Asked Duffy, in a whisper, delighted and surprised to feel the strong firm hand that now gripped his upper arm, 'is that really you, Captain, sir?'

'Yes, Mister Duff. Sorry I couldn't be with you sooner, but I've been a little, tied up if you get my meaning?' He chuckled at his joke. More the young boy he truly was than the newly promoted Captain of a King's ship he was trying so very hard to be. 'But, are you ok?' He asked again, silently pulling at his bonds.

'Aye, Captain, I am,' he whispered in wonder and relief. 'But have a care there are at least four, possibly more of them and as dangerous as ever they were. One of them scrambling about in the marsh looking for you and at least three more of them down the path and heading this way by the sounds of them.'

'Don't worry about them, Mister Duff,' growled Billy, more angry than he was afraid, though he was afraid. 'I'll have you free in a jiffy. But where's, Tom?' He whispered. 'I saw him take a dreadful blow to the head just now from the bullying ruffian who laid into you.'

'I'm over here, Captain,' she answered, re-lieved beyond words to see him so suddenly and most wonderfully alive and in an instant, she found his side. 'We thought you were dead or if not dead, stunned unconscious?' She said, brush-ing a plastered wisp of hair from his slimy, blood-streaked, forehead in a most girlish way, which, most fortunately for her he didn't appear to notice. Though, he did wonder, and not for first time, why he was always so very pleased to see her.

'Thought I was, too,' he answered with a smile and a wink. 'But no time for story telling now, young 'un, let's get Mister Duff free of this rope and get away from here before those blackguards come back to finish us off. As they have every intention of doing, from what little I heard of their dastardly plans.' And though he was more than a little stiff and knocked about by his exertions, he began to work the blade of his sword into the ropes. But being a somewhat blunt, chipped, and rusty old thing, which, had rarely been out of its leather and brass scabbard in the four years he'd had it, he made a pretty poor job of it, to say the least.

'Can't you go any quicker than that, *Captain?*' Chirped Tom, impatiently. Who like many well-bred, clever girls of her strong, willful, intelligent, and dexterous type, thought she could and certainly much faster than any cack-handed boy, which was probably true.

'*No,*' he grunted, as she slid her delightfully long and once perfectly manicured, but now dirty fingers, beneath his.

'Let me help,' she demanded, trying to take hold of his sword.

'I can do it, *Tom,' he* grumbled he could.

'Let me, *Billy,* I can do it faster than you can,' she said, working her hands around the handle of the sword. Don't you ever bother to sharpen this damn thing? It's as blunt as a poker, and no mistake, God's breath, boy.'

'Mind your tongue, Tom you are a King's sailor and you will behave as one or I will know the reason why,' growled Duffy, 'and so you should know, there is no *why* that says you can, not now nor any time soon,' he commanded. Not at all happy with the overly familiar way she was talking to *his* Captain, which, he had observed her doing with shocking surprise on several occasions since he came aboard the *Parrot that morning.* And the Captain not minding she did, but allowing her every license to do so! But no longer! He was the Captain's Bosun and friend or no friend, and Tom was very definitely a *friend,* as only friends who have fought and suffered together, can be, no one speaks to the King's commissioned officer like that and gets away with it. Least of all, a ships *boy and one who didn't appear to know his larboard from his starboard as he had more than once shown he didn't*! 'The Captain will have it done when it's done,' he hissed. 'And no amount of interference from you will make it any quicker. So, leave off your doings, *Tom.'*

But Tom did no such thing. It being her want, as you will very quickly learn, to ignore any request, direction, order, or instruction she didn't agree with, least of all if it came from a *boy,* no matter who he thought he was. And so, with a blind indifference to Duffy's gaze, she bent her long-legged, slipping in the mud, skinny weight to Billy's patient and seemingly tireless efforts to get him free. Until, at long last, the ropes that bound his arms and chest fell loose about his lap.

'Got it,' said Billy, his fingers grappling with Tom's to be the first to unwind the last of the ropes; a feeling that left him wondering how soft they were under the sludge and grime that covered them to her wrist like a glove.

'Got it,' echoed Tom, wanting her share of credit and ready to do battle with anyone who disagreed she did, with a wide-eyed, crinkle-nosed look of grim determination, Billy smiled to see. So impishly strange did *he* look and so unlike any boy *he* ever met before.

'And not a moment too soon,' said Billy, with a sudden frown that wondered how he would ever deal with this vexing and imperturbable *boy,* who was unbowed by any authority he claimed and exerted such a winning influence over him, he could hardly refuse *him.* That try as he might, he could not dislike or reprimand as he ought, but soon must. 'Look, its *them,* they're *come, already,'* he whispered, seeing the same blue light that had earlier called a signal to the kidnappers, slowly coming through the mist towards them.

The first to appear out of the mist that cloaked the Morass like a heavy, crumpled blanket was Charlie Begg. A cadaverous looking cove with a cowardly and worried disposition that creased his brow and curled his petulantly thin lips to a sly and ever watchful mistrust of everyone he met. A boy of fifteen who to the amazement of everyone who knew him, and there were few who did, not least Jemmy Grub and Joby Dogget, was the most daring and naturally accomplished seaman there was and with a magnetic nose for direction like his father Turzel before him had, that never lost his way, no matter it was day or night in storm or in shine.

Who since his untimely death at the hands of the Militia and Revenue Men last year at the battle of Durdle Door, as the *Morning Chronicle,* heroically called that night time ambush and massacre near Lulworth Cove, Titus Dimple and Bully Drier had so cleverly arranged in Paris, had Captained the *Seahorse* for them out of Langstone harbour to France and back every other week. Never realising they had stolen it with false papers from Albert and Clary Grub and killed, though they never intended he should be, his dad. Who was in on the plot up to his greedy neck, reason enough to see his son should have his place.

Next to appear, ghost-like in the mist and fog that hugged him like a writhing serpent came the jaunty figure of Joby Dogget, who, much recovered from his earlier fright and painful thumping, was scything the elbow high grass beside the path with his belaying pin and with such a noisy har-rumphing to say how pleased he was. Last, and a yard or two behind those two came Grub, nursing a growing very sore head and a hatefully savage resentment towards Tom and Duffy he was keen to avenge. And soon would, he laughed.

In a single bound Billy was on his feet and charging down the narrow, puddle spattered path towards them with his sword raised high above his head like an axe and a scream of rage so shrill upon his lips it froze the night into a star-tled silence. Not least the crows perched above the Jews Burying ground, who watched him with a hungry fascination that hoped their dinner had just come. An eye, a juicy piece of brain, a blood-spat-tered inch of kidney, liver, heart or lungs, each a welcome treat on a cold nightlike this.

Seeing him racing towards him covered from head to toe in a porridge-like, black and smelly slime poked with twists of grass, Charlie Begg screamed in terror of his life, dropped his blue glass lantern to the soft ground with a tinkling crash and turned on his heels to run. But fast though he was he was too late by half a second to make good his escape as the downward swipe of Billy's blunt sword caught him a glancing blow just above his right ear, a blow that had it been sharper would have cut it off. 'OUCH,' he howled as he dropped like a stone to the ground in shock and surprise his two hands cupped to his head. 'JEMMY, JEM- MY, OH LORD, JEMMY I'VE BEEN MURDERED. JEMMY, I'VE BEEN KILLED BY THE GHOST OF THE BOG. MUMMY, DADDY,' he whined.

Billy's second swing, a bent to one knee deft and dazzling daisy cutter took Joby Dogget hard on his right shin, but as bad luck would have it, its dull edge caught the solid hem of his tailcoat and did no more damage than tear a rent in his green woollen stocking to match the rest he had. Furious beyond the few spluttering words he could say, Dogget instinctively raised his arm above his head and aimed the club-like handle of his belaying pin at Billy's now fearfully exposed, bare head. But though he did and with every intention of brain- ing the wild-eyed, laughing boy who crouched be- neath him he was suddenly knocked dazed and bleeding to the ground when Billy instantly hit him in the face with the metal guard of his sword.

As he fell in a heap and Charlie Begg squirmed on the path in a riot of pain more imagined than real, Grub took up the fight like the raging bull he was. Punching and kicking for all he was worth at the smelly creature from the bog, who ducked and weaved and jigged and danced in front of him in the fog like a phantom. 'COME HERE, YOU

BUGGER,' he shouted, breathlessly. 'FIGHT LIKE A MAN, WHY DON'T YOU? YOU COCK-SURE LITTLE MINCING DANDY.' By which he meant, as all halfwit thugs and bullies do, lay down your sword, which at least makes us even and let me beat you to a pulp, muscle and size being no unfair advantage to boys like Jemmy Grub.

'Come and get me, you overblown cove,' taunted Billy, rather overtaken by his success and now even more determined to carry the fight to its bitter end, even if the boy in front of him was twice his size and more frightening up close than he would ever dare admit.

'That I will, me young fancy,' answered Grub, cautioned by the steely glint he saw in Billy's piercing blue eyes. Eyes that told him he had a fight on his hands and no mistake. 'But first we'll fix the odds so they're more to my liking.' He gently cooed. 'JOBY. CHARLIE. ON YOUR FEET, YOU PAIR OF UGLY TOADS.' He barked, and in an instant marked only by their bitter, noisy complaints, they were at his side, warily advancing towards Billy in a half circle that threatened to overwhelm him, the winding path offering no immediate escape. Wishing he had a sharper blade to fix their hash, something he would ever remember, Billy slashed and stabbed at the ill-matched trio for all he was worth, but to no good effect, and tiring as he did. On they came like a pack of snapping, snarling, baying wolves until Dogget seeing he now had him in easy range of the stunning blow he planned took a bold, half crouching, rocking step forward.

'Quick Tom,' called Duffy, who was unpicking the last of the knots that bound his ankles together. 'Help the Captain, before they do for him. I'll finish up here and be with you in a second or two. Quick as you can now.'

Needing no second asking and pausing only to pick her target, Tom, head bent to a run, hurled herself past Billy and butted Charlie Begg so hard in his stomach she knocked the wind clean out of him in a sickening whoosh that left him rolling and gasping on the ground like a pricked balloon, squealing his belly hurt.

Seeing his chance Billy stabbed the point of his sword into Dogget's grimly determined face as he made to hit him. But he was quick and mean and clever and in a rush of fear and hate that ignored the outstretched blade slashing at his face, threw himself at Billy's chest with all his might and knocked him to the ground in a flurry of hard punches that left him dizzy.

What little advantage Billy had, and it was little indeed, was gone as he struggled to overcome his attacker with one hand, whilst keeping tight hold

of his sword in the other. A task that almost bested him as over and over they rolled and flipped
in a noisy confusion of butting heads, grabbing
arms and kicking legs that gave no quarter. And
no chance for Grub who danced around them like
a one-legged frog on a red-hot skillet to strike his
killing blow with the splintered stick he now held
like a sword in his upraised arm.

But then, just as he thought he might have his
chance to spear him to the path, Billy and Dogget slithered in a clumsy wrestle, headlong into
the bog and without the least word of protest were
swallowed up in its sticky, black ooze in a single
gulp; lost in mist and mud.

'DAMN,' shouted Grub in disgust, bending to
see where they had gone.

'DAMN, INDEED,' answered Duffy, standing
a yard behind him and with a score to settle that
wouldn't keep.

'You?' Said Grub, slowly turning to face him
with a smug indifference that was a measure of
his mindless bravery. 'So, you think you're ready
to take on Jemmy Grub, do you?'

'Ready enough and more, I should think, you
coward,' answered Duffy, a boy who knew neither
fear nor envy, wishing the hot cramping pain that
was throbbing through his numb hands like liquid
fire would stop just long enough for him to make

a proper fist.

Matching blow for solid blow they stood toe to toe and battered each other like Roman gladiators locked in mortal combat, brutal, give no quarter, combat that could have no end, but the defeat and death of the other.

Well matched for strength and size they fought without regard for the pain they felt, but try as they did, neither could get the upper hand and with time and tide against him, Grub began to realise their night's work and more importantly the reward that was his promise from Corbeau was about to disappear. When, suddenly, Badger, slicked from head to toe in slime, and as round as he was tall, struck, coming, as if from nowhere, he rolled himself head over heels into the back of Duffy's legs and knocked him down.

In a flash, Grub, never one to miss an easy chance, was on him and would have finished him there and then, had it not been for the plucky arrival of Tom. Who seeing Duffy fall ran to his aid and jumping onto Badgers enormously fat, wobbling like a birthday jelly, belly, bounced herself onto Grubs shoulders in a bound and locked her legs tight about his neck in a grip that choked the wind in his throat and with grip on his hair, which pulled his eyes to tears.

Fuming with rage, Grub kicked himself free of

Duffy and in a savage anger began to pitch and throw and buck Tom about like sack of Jersey potatoes, but try as he did, he couldn't shift her; not an inch so firm did she hold on to him. But gallant though she was, and she was as gallant as any sailor Duffy had ever seen in his life, she was no match for his prodigious strength and in a moment of wild and frenzied effort that ignored how close he was to the marsh, threw her in.

And though it was never his intention, threw her right-on top of Billy, who just a moment before had captured Dogget in a wicked, back bending, face in the bog, arm lock that was slowly drowning him in its sickly filth. Crushed and winded by her unexpected arrival, Billy was forced to let him go and needing no better chance than this, Dogget kicked himself free of danger and with a choking, bilious splutter of rage and indignation that said he would have his revenge on him one day, hauled himself clear of that foul bog and ran from a fight he dearly wished he'd never started.

It was then that a great hallooing war cry rang out from deep within the swirling fog and Mister Midshipman Spears was heard to call to anyone who was listening, and he wasn't in the least bit sure anyone was, so little did he believe, Nipper Ogden's sorry tale of kidnap. 'HOLD FAST CAP-TAIN KEPPLE! HOLD FAST WHEREVER YOU

ARE! WE'RE COMING! WE'RE COMING! THE *PARROT'S* ARE COMING! THE *PARROT'S* ARE COMING! WITH ME LADS WITH ME I SAY! *PARROT'S* THIS WAY! THIS WAY I SAY.'

Hearing the fast-coming commotion and knowing the game was up, Grub, who was no stranger to danger and cowardly flight, ran for his life without so much as a backward glance. Leaving Badger and Begg's to save themselves as best they could. Which was ever his way, as his narrow, near impossible escape from Durdle Door last year confirmed it was. Which they did, each fleeing the marsh with all the speed they could muster, Badger so much slower than Begg, but each in a headlong rush of panic that saw them so quickly gone Trucky never saw sight of them.

Half a minute later Dancer Dyke, Nipper Ogden, and the rest of the *Parrot's* boat crew of ships boys arrived like a stampede of squeaking water-hogs to give chase, shouting, and laughing for all they were worth the fun they were having; the best they had ever had. Careless of the danger they faced or who their enemy was, leaving a breathless Trucky to help Duffy to his feet and as soon as he had, saw two, shapeless unrecognizable figures, climb out of the bog, each noisily blaming the other for Dogget's quick escape.

Chapter 17

Billy Tells Tom His Admiralty Papers Are
Stolen And The Terrible Trouble He Is
Now In

7.57am Friday 21 April 1797

Cold washed with sea water under the *Parrot's* hose beneath the forecastle deck, fed to bursting and with four hours sleep to liven his dampened spirits Billy woke with a start and another awful headache to the noise and bustle of the afterguard rushing about on the poopdeck above his cabin. 'My charts, my signal book.' He groaned a mournful sigh of deepest regret and anguish he had lost them, stolen he now knew by his kidnappers last night.

'What's amiss, Billy?' Asked Tom, sleepily, who, having been forcibly evicted from her snug little berth in the Midshipman's cockpit by Mister Midshipman Arbuthnot Anstruther, who had taken a very uncommon dislike to her and less forcibly by Trucky Spears the night before, had slept catlike, curled up beneath Billy's cot on a straw filled palliasse.[174] A most improper thing for her to do, but by her reckoning, the safest place in a ship now crowded with so many noisy, skylarking, un-washed, horrid boys there was nowhere else to go. Nowhere else she felt quite so safe.

'What?' He gasped, with a start of fright, know-ing before he asked, who it was, but at a loss to know why Tom was in his, still dark cabin so early that bright morning. If the bent square of rainbow light from the transom window in his day cabin[175] behind him didn't deceive him, it was early morn-ing. A sea slapped, noisy cabin without windows or light except for the long since gone out, glass lantern that was hung on a black tarred beam above his head and the jail-like bars that opened its cream painted, wooden door to his day room. This being a place to sleep in rather than a private quarter's he could rest too long in.

'It's only me Billy, you were talking in your sleep,' she answered, drawing her thin blanket up to her shoulders and wishing the sound of running feet on the deck above would stop, so much did she ache all over.

'Gracious me, Tom, have you been there all night?' He asked, hanging over the wooden side of his very wobbly cot in a most precarious fashion to confirm it was.

'Yes,' she answered, with a yawn, looking him straight in the eye as only a friend could. 'Midship-man Anstruther chucked me out of the cockpit and

I couldn't find anywhere else to go, so I came here, instead. You don't mind do you, Billy? I shan't be any trouble.'

'No, not if it's only for the one night, I don't, but I will have Duffy find you something more suitable as soon as possible. The galley, perhaps where you'll be nice and warm,' he pointed, a hint she might go before she was seen by the Marine who stood guard beside the quarterdeck door to his day cabin and the boy who had promised to bring him a small breakfast that morning.

'Suppose,' she answered, not in the least impressed by his kindly suggestion, which she intended to ignore.

Mmm,' he murmured, seeing she wasn't and feeling oddly guilty. 'What time is it d'you suppose?' He asked.

'It's early yet Billy, go back to sleep, why don't you,' she yawned, too exhausted to move and settling back on her well stuffed bed to sleep like a deliciously spoilt cat. Glad she had washed and changed her clothes when most of the *Parrot* was asleep last night, but though she had, still looked as dirty as she did yesterday.

But Billy was wide awake and ignoring the bruising stiffness he felt in his arms, legs, back, neck and shoulders - well everywhere that moved, swung himself out of his cot and in crab-like motion beneath the low beams found the tin mug he'd last night left on his sea chest. 'There's no time to lie abed, Tom,' he said, hearing the ships bell strike 8.00am, the end of the four-hour morning watch,[176] 'we've got work to do if the *Parrot* is to sail on tomorrow's tide; as it must. Not least, the mountain of stores and munitions I have just ordered, which will soon arrive and for the rest of the day.'

'Must we? Can't we sleep another hour? I'm sure Mister Robinson and Trucky will get along just fine without us, though I doubt that fat slug of a bullying pig, Anstruther will be much use to anyone. Why I doubt he knows the *Parrot's* front end from its back end.'

'Maybe not, but I'm the Captain, Tom and a Captain must earn the respect of his crew if he is to make his mark with them, which I must,' he said, in a voice that clearly betrayed his unease and wonder at Tom's cheek.

Watching him as he took a drink of the grog[177] the mug contained, she saw with a gasp of affection how tired and very young he looked in the white shirt, white breeches, and untidy white stockings he wore, his hair, though tied in a short pigtail fallen falling loose over his ears. His face yellow bruised about his cheeks and his right eye swollen from the many blows he had received last night. 'Suppose,' she answered.

Ignoring her quizzical look, not to say, her still unwashed face, he crouched his head and shoulders beneath the narrow doorway and stepped out of his night cabin into his sun lit day cabin, six times its size and walked to the polished, mahogany table and six chairs that filled its middle from side to side. A room much like Captain's Hamilton's on the *Surprise,* he saw, where, like him, he had hoped to study his orders and plot his course to the Quiberon, but without his charts and signal book, he couldn't. A place, thankfully, no one would enter without his express invitation.

With a sigh of disappointment, he opened the wardroom door, one of two external doors his cabin possessed, the other being the quarterdeck door on the larboard side and standing on the top of the three steps that gave him access, peeped in and with a relief that wondered how he would ever explain Tom's nocturnal presence in his cabin, saw it was empty, and as he did, heard Lieutenant Robinson's voice loud on the quarterdeck. A cream painted room of six, kennel like, adjacent cabins built into the sides and each one no bigger than his own night cabin and with the same jail-like bars opening the tops of the doors and with a table and chairs running fore and aft down the middle on this, the stern side of the mainmast as it dropped to the keel, two decks below. A room, which at its further end opened through a now closed door onto the galley kitchen and with all the smells it now brought, charcoal smoke and the beef stew, lentils, peas, and dumplings the cook was boiling in great copper pots for dinner. Quickly and expertly combing and tying his hair with his finger he walked to the nearest of the eight sash windows that formed the arc of his stern gallery and looked out at the crowded anchorage and saw the *Pompée's* much larger stern, swinging on her anchor. A luxury beyond luxuries he had never known before, never thought to know for ten or twenty years, and pondered the events of the previous day and the singular problem he now faced.

'Tom, they've taken my charts and if that wasn't enough, they've taken my signal book as well,' he sighed, wondering why he confided in her a secret he hardly dared speak aloud and certainly not to Sam or Trucky.

'Is that bad?' She asked, coming up beside him her hand a comfort on his shoulder and begging a drink with her outstretched hand from the mug he still carried in his tar stained hand that seemed so very natural, he gave it to her without the least objection she did.

'It's bad, Tom,' he groaned. 'The charts *we* could probably replace, though it would be fearfully difficult, but the signal book, well that's another story entirely. And one that will take a deal of explaining to Captain Patton if I am to put it right without his severe reprimand.'

'What's a signal book, Billy?' She asked, wincing at the sharp taste of grog in her throat and wiping her mouth with the sleeve of her jumper to a grimy smudge.

'Mmm, its …'

'Here, drink some more of this,' she interrupted, offering him the mug, much as she had done when he was ill and with a fondness that had grown so much more since then. A sister's fondness for an older brother, she thought, knowing it was a fondness different from anything else she had known and she had never known a brother, but would have liked to have had one. Not to be as alone as she had been since her mother died and no one to care for her, but Miss Fry.

'It's a small book that contains the secret fighting instruction for the Channel fleet, Tom, but more importantly, it contains the secret signals we must use to identify ourselves to any of our own ships, should we chance to meet one, and meet one we will before our cruise is over. And without which they will think us the enemy and blow us out of the water without a second thought.

'How does it work, this signal book?' She

asked, lifting the mug of grog from his hands, to sip the last of it.

'Simple, really Tom, when we meet one of our own ships and if she is bigger than we are, that is to say, Captained by someone senior to me, which her size would generally indicate she is, she will signal us, as is her duty, with, say ….,' he momentarily paused, 'a blue flag hung on one of her mizzenmast yards and a red flag in her mainmast, or some other variation and we, seeing this, would consult the signal book and give her the correct answer. Say a red flag on our foremast and maybe a white flag on our main, or if not, some other unguessable combination of flag, light, pistol, or cannon shot or even a rocket flare, their Lords of the Admiralty in their great wisdom have decided. Without which we will never reach the Quiberon.'

'Is that where we're going?' She asked, without the least knowledge of where it was, though guessing rightly it must be somewhere on the French coast. Though not the Channel coast, which she quite well knew from all the newspaper reports of the war. 'And the papers *we* have lost are the only certain way of getting us there, I suppose?' She asked, knowing it was.

'Yes,' he answered, tucking the long tail of his shirt into his breeches and showing rather more of his muscled leg than was proper for a young lady of refined upbringing to see. 'They are unquestionably the most important papers I have ever had in my possession Tom,' he sighed, reaching for his heavy blue jacket, which, though washed and dried over the galley stove, was still in a thoroughly disagreeable and smelly state. 'We are ordered to rescue a party of royalist fugitives, one of whom, we must protect at all costs, a girl, would you believe, called Marie-Ange le Dantec?' He groaned, thinking of Lieutenant Galbraith's urgent, last command. 'But there will be no rescue unless we have the charts and signals to take us there.'

'Then we'll get some more,' she said, with a confidence that grinned her mouth into a perfect smile of white teeth, Billy was enchanted to see, but one that was completely misplaced. 'We'll go back to the Transport Office and ask for some more. They probably have copies of them lying about all over the place.'

'I wish it was that simple Tom,' he deep groaned a half smile that was more sad than it was amused by her unseaman like remark. 'But if I report them missing, which I am duty bound to do and sooner rather than later - *today,* they being as secret as secret can be, Lieutenant Galbraith or Captain Patton or more likely, Admiral Bridport in this time of mutiny will take the *Parrot* from me and give her to someone else more able than I. And, if that ain't bad enough and it is, I assure you, as bad as bad can be, he will court martial me for being so stupid as to get myself kidnapped and then break me or beach me forever and a day.'[178]

'*Break you?*' She gasped in horror. 'What ever do you mean?'

'Throw me out, Tom. Throw me out of the service and without the least prospect of being taken back. Well, not on the quarterdeck.' He moaned, with an ache in his heart that was almost palpable. Knowing only too well the disgrace of it would be more than his dear mother could bear. After all, it was her, more than anyone else, though the Reverend Cotton's letter of reference had been most wonderfully helpful, who had persuaded Lieutenant Hinton, an old and greatly trusted friend of his late father from the American war and the First Lieutenant on the *Agamemnon* or the *Eggs-and-Bacon* as everyone on board affectionately called her, to take him to sea as a gentleman-volunteer, the most junior of all junior sea officers, though, if the truth be known, hardly an officer at all.

'And beach you? You said Admiral Bridport might beach you? Asked Tom as he turned on his heels and returned to his night cabin.

'Never give me employment at sea again, Tom. Abandon me to my fate on a Lieutenant's half pay until I die,' he wistful sighed, flopping onto his sea chest to tie his black silk neckerchief in a knot and as he did, remembered the day he left his home in Chester for a life at sea.

First boarding the yellow and blue painted, bugle blowing, vastly overcrowded mail coach from the snow covered steps of the Feathers Inn at the top of Bridge Street to travel the three hundred and fifty miles to Chatham in less than a week. First to Birmingham, now the thriving centre of England's industrial revolution, the most important scientific and industrial revolution the world has ever known and then on to London and then, with barely half a day to spare, on to Chatham, where he took ship aboard the *Agamemnon* on the afternoon of Monday 11 February 1793, his tenth birthday, would you believe.

Where, Mister Roxburgh, the ships dour, plain speaking surgeon, thought him very small for his age, but despite he did, never-the-less, thought him passably fit for sea service. After that Mister Fellows, the ships Purser fitted him out with flea trapped, second hand slops enough to turn him from the gaunt faced, former Blue Coat, schoolboy he was, into the seaman he hoped to be. Though at a cost to be deducted from his meagre pay of six pounds per annum, he could ill afford, if he was to eat more than three or four times a week. Which he dearly hoped he would and with enough left over to send his mother a few shillings every quarter, money she never asked, but very much needed.

For the first few weeks he had the good fortune to work with Frank, the Captain's steward and did hardly anything more strenuous than dust and clean his cabin and carry charcoal to the little brazier that was kept burning, day and night, rain, or shine, to keep him warm.

But, as the *Agamemnon* made ready for sea, he lost his privileged berth with the kindly, if somewhat prissy Frank and was transferred, on the Captain's orders, to the care of Mister Joseph King, the ships Bosun, who quickly informed him his life at sea would never be as easy again with a stout rattan cane laid heavy on his back and buttocks, ten times a day and a voice that thundered from one end of the ship to the other.

On Wednesday, the 24 April, almost four years to the day, he reflected, careless Tom was watching his contemplation with a growing irritation, the *Agamemnon* left Chatham and made her way slowly down the river Medway to anchor at the Nore.[179] From there she sailed to Spithead to complete her gun powder stores and then to Gibraltar, his first footfall on a foreign shore, though it was more English than it was Spanish.

His first sea voyage and to his dying shame and hopeless regret he discovered that far from the natural sailor he hoped to be - as his mother said his father was, he was seasick every inch of the way. Which, rather surprisingly, brought him to the affectionate attention of the Captain, a petulantly vain, astonishingly brave, excitable little man - he was barely five feet six inches tall, by the name of Horatio Nelson. Who to his great relief suffered from the very same affliction himself, though no one ever remarked he did. Throughout the summer and autumn of that long year the *Agamemnon* cruised the sun drenched Mediterranean and he began to learn something, though far from everything of his new-found life at sea.

How to loosen and reef[180] the twenty-one sails she carried on her three great, soaring mast and spars, for which, not being the least bit afraid of heights in any weather, he showed a remarkable aptitude. How to lift and lower her six anchors. An amazingly difficult and strenuous task needing almost all the ships five hundred crew, but still so hard it left him exhausted until he found his bed. How to work as a crew of eight stout hands one of the sixty-four guns she carried on her three, gun decks, many of them weighing nearly three tons and if that wasn't work enough for one so very young, as he was then and he felt very young, indeed amongst so many older men and boys. How to lift and haul with rope and tackle every moveable object Mister King or his mate, Mister Adams, could find to move, and between them they found a great quantity of stores, materials, and sundry items to move every day of every week, he sailed on her.

Besides this, he also had his duties as an officer in the making. How to stand his turn on watch, day and night until his eyes were red with pain and his body longed for sleep. How to run errands for every senior officer aboard and everyone, he quickly realised, was more senior than he and bullied him without mercy he was. How to navigate the ship by taking a noon sighting of the sun or, if it was night, by the moon or stars, a task he flustered most horribly when watched by the Master, Mister Lisbon, or his sponsor, Lieutenant Hinton. Who, most naturally took a keen interest in his achingly slow progress. And if he was lucky, how to steer one of the ships boats when she was in port. No easy task when the men he commanded were old enough to be his father and apt, with the raucous good humor that is common to all sailors, to curse, spit, splash and clout him at every opportunity for the damnable silly oaf they said he was.

The thought of which made him smile with happy memories. A smile so delightful innocent,

Tom who hated nothing more than a long silence that ignored her for too long, thought to rouse him with a gentle dig in the ribs. But didn't, as lost in thought, he rested his head in his two hands and closed his eyes as if he was dreaming. He was. A dream that called to mind an incident, which though trivial in every conceivable way, spoke of the triumph he hoped he would know again.

It happened when the *Agamemnon* lay at anchor in the Bay of Toulon, a great naval port on France's Mediterranean coast and then a royalist stronghold under fierce siege by revolutionary forces in the south of France. When he and his friend Midshipman Josiah Nisbet, the Captains step son, three years his senior and a great favourite on board and two French Marine cadets by the names of Allan Deauville and Robert Camus, who they had come to know as friends and allies, decided to walk up to Fort L'Eguillette, the military stronghold overlooking the bay.

Arriving at their destination they noticed a sudden wild confusion erupt near the gates and running to see what was amiss, they saw a wagon had overturned and the twenty, iron hooped wooden kegs of black gunpowder it was carrying into the fort were rolling down the hill towards them in a stampede of frightening leaps and bounds that threatened to kill them and anyone else in their path and all the more should the iron hoops spark a flame and ignite the powder.

As he and his friends scampered to safety, he noticed a young man, standing in the middle of the road distractedly writing something of urgent importance into a small note book, directly in the path of the oncoming avalanche. A wild haired, wild eyed, lean, and haggard fellow of middling height dressed in the simple fashion of the day. A black tricorn hat, a short to the waist, seaman's navy-blue jacket, a white shirt, red stock, calf length red and white striped pantaloons, red woollen stockings and heavy wooden sabots.[181] Ignoring the pleas of his friends, who had found safety in the doorway of a nearby house, he turned and ran to the man and without a word of explanation - there being little time for formal introductions, pushed him headlong into a narrow, but rather deep and disgusting, stagnant ditch, from which he emerged a moment later wet, bedraggled and violently screaming his revenge on his attacker, whoever he was with a wicked, glinting dagger he'd plucked from his belt.

With the last of the barrels passed and safely deposited without explosion in a nearby field of poppies, the young man stopped his blood-curdling tirade of threatened revenge and quickly took stock of the situation and realising the debt he owed his rescuer, pulled him from the ditch, in which he still nervously sat.

Almost as soon as he did, his three companions and a score of well-wishers came up beside him and began patting him so hard on his back he thought his spine would break. For a long moment, the young man looked at him with a keen and discerning eye and then, with Deauville and Camus's helpful translation, made a long and flowery speech in a heavily accented, Corsican French. The bones of which were his heartfelt and undying thanks and the debt of honor, he Napoleon[182] - pronouncing it Nabulione Bonaparte. owed him and would ever remember to repay his courage.

Feeling in his pocket he then produced a small, beautifully engraved silver pocket watch, in fact, it was a British made watch by Thomas Tompion of London.[183] And a very fine and very expensive watch it was, too with its innovative, cylinder escapement, which allowed all its many cogwheels to be arranged horizontally and ingenious balance spring regulator, which made it both flatter and more accurate than most watches of the day. The sort of timepiece every junior navy officer would hope to own one day.

Though Billy several times refuse it, the gift being far too generous for him to accept, Napoleon, as he insisted they must all now call him, would hear none of it and taking only a moment longer to write their names in his little book with a pencil, he licked to a wet point, an ostentation that amused them all, he dismissed them without a second glance and then, with one hand tucked into his jacket and the other behind his back, strode off in the direction of the enemy. As if he owned the place, which he very soon would.

Had they known it, the four friends had just encountered a young man, he was just twenty-four years old then, who was not only destined to be one of the greatest generals the world has ever known, but a revolutionary spy who, when rescued by Billy, was making extremely accurate notes on the forts impressive defenses. Notes, which proved to be crucial in its capture a few months later when he commanded the guns that battered it to bloody submission.

As a foot note to this incident, Deauville and Camus were both captured when Toulon fell, but their lives were unaccountably spared, whilst all the other captured royalist troops and six thousand innocent town folks were promptly executed by the newly promoted Brigadier General who now commanded their city. A General who never forgot a good deed or a kindness he was shown, not least by those two, who with a *vault face* so typical of those dreadful times both surrendered to fate and changed sides. Deauville to die at sea a year later, killed by an English cannon.

By this time, the *Agamemnon* had sailed away and Billy served aboard her with growing confidence and growing reputation until the early spring of that same year, such are the Fates.[184] he was transferred to HMS *Arethusa* a frigate under the command of Sir Edward Pellew, just then leaving the Mediterranean for the West Indies. Once there, he was rated Midshipman by his Captain and transferred, much to his regret, into Captain Hamilton's *Surprise* and though he doubted he would, happily served aboard her, until Admiral Kettle's commission called him home, home where he now faced disgrace and the certain ruin of his career.

'But that isn't fair Billy?' Interrupted Tom, giving him the poke in the ribs she had earlier promised him, which to her relief, roused him from the trance-like dreamy state she thought far too indulgent for a boy so young. Though with a look in his deep blue, rather sad eyes that appeared less than pleased, she had. A troubled look she instantly crushed with a smile and a wink that wrinkled the lamp black that sooted her face and *ears.* 'Those coves attacked you when you were no more than twenty paces from the Transport Office. You hardly had the things in your hands for more than five minutes.'

'Yes,' said Billy, rubbing his ribs, and wondering at the nerve of the *boy* to poke him so hard, but more than this, why it didn't seem to matter, she did. 'But the Admiral won't see it that way. He will see it as a damnable failure I must own up to and be punished for. Whether it was my fault or not, you must understand.'

Here Billy spoke an absolute truth, because the navy of 1797, the first line of Britain's defense against revolutionary France's continued aggression against her. Lived for every success it could find against the rag-bag French government they so despised, which everyday threatened to overwhelm the peace of Europe. And sadly, there were few successes they could boast about with General Lazare Hoche, the hero of the Quiberon two years ago still threatening to invade Ireland, or so they thought and Colonel Tate and his Légion Noire, an American of all people, having the cheek to invade South Wales.[185] An invasion that wondered what the American's were up too? Something the British government planned to find out when they sent an embassy to America in the next few weeks. Such was its fear they might enter the war the ally of France, her oldest friend, and

Spain; a truly horrendous prospect despite they had no navy to speak of.

A plan coincidentally finalized later that day by Lord Spencer, who for reasons best known to himself, but never communicated or recorded by Lauder Trompe, somewhat distracted by recent events as you might imagine, or Lord Dasheart, his other clerk, who was too lazy to take much interest, agreed to send Admiral Crookhampton, of all people to meet with Governor Jay of New York. A man of very great influence and old and respected acquaintance of Lord Spencer, who, though a fervent supporter of the French Revolution, being of French and Dutch extraction himself, was known to be an honorable man who daily worked for peace. Who, despite he had done much to force Britain out of her Colonies in 1783 now wanted very much to trade with her and her growing Empire. But he wasn't to go alone, Lord Dasheart would accompany him. A young man he had grown to greatly admire in these last few days, so different in every way from the lazy little oik, who was his companion.

And because of this military and political turmoil Admiral Bridport would not tolerate a failure that would tarnish his name, no senior officer would! That allowed secret naval documents to be stolen and even more when the fleet was a hot bed of mutinous rebellion no better than it was in France in 1789. Had Corbeau wished it he could not have planned things better than he did; hasty though his simple plan truly was. Billy's goose was well and truly cooked. The *Parrot* would sail without him on tomorrow's tide and with Midshipman Kettle promoted Lieutenant, her new Captain.

'Who was that boy me and Duffy saw outside the Transport Office, last night, Billy?' Asked Tom, seated on the stool beside him with a puzzled frown on her tired and dirty face, which hinted a growing suspicion he was somehow involved in his kidnap and near murder.

'Which boy?' Asked Billy, distractedly fastening his thick leather belt about his waist and feeling the comforting weight of his sword, blunt though it was, hanging at his side almost to the deck.

'The one hanging about outside the Transport Office last night a little while before you came out, a short, fat, nervous cove as best as I could see him wearing a peculiar old hat two sizes too big even for his big head.'

'Gosh, Tom that sounds like, Mister Trompe?' Exclaimed Billy, his face both a surprise and a question as he gingerly slipped his feet into his still horribly damp shoes, 'if only from the description of the hat he was wearing, which was the oddest hat I have ever seen on any one's head in a very long time and no mistake. You remember, I told you he was the Admiralty clerk I was to meet at the Star and Garter Inn, yesterday.'

'Yes, I remember his name, *Louder. Louder Trump,*' she deliberately mispronounced it. Once again feeling the glum irritation, she felt when he left her in the gig by the Sally Port with all those silly boys.

'No, you know his name is Lauder, Tom. Lauder Trompe, I believe he said it was. French, his surname, I mean.'

'French, you say, Billy?' She answered, tartly, convinced he was a traitor as so many French émigrés were.

'Yes, and he helped me so wonderfully with the stores *we* needed yesterday evening I really couldn't have done without him. He was truly marvelous. But he left me a long time before that. Why would he be there?'

'I don't know, Billy? But, as I said, me and Duffy and even that boy Nipper saw this ere Mister Trompe, if it was him and it probably was him with that silly hat on his head, because there can't be two the same as it in all of Portsmouth, slip into the alleyway you were taken down like a footpad with the town watch on his tail.'

'What are you trying to say, Tom?' He patiently asked, turning to the door of his night cabin and

303

a day that would settle, one way or another, the rest of his short and so far, he hoped, promising career, like no other would.

'He's in it,' she said, thumping the ball of her right hand into the flat of her left with an absolute certainty. 'Cor blimey, Charlie, Billy, he's up to his bloomin' neck in treason and treachery, I'm certain he is.'

'You think?' He asked, doubting he was, as went into his day cabin.

'Yes, he's got your charts and signal book for sure the blighter has. He stole them, with the help of those toughs.'

'He did?' He asked.

'Think about it, Billy? Mister Spears and the gig's crew searched the marsh and found nothing more than we three. There was no evidence of your kidnap or who did it and there was no sign of that canvas bag you were carrying when you left the Transport Office. So, it stands to reason them three murdering coves who bundled you off on that cart took it and then gave it to someone else and the only someone else who was there when you were taken was Mister Trompe.'

'But what use are they to him? He's Lord Spencer's confidential clerk and would have a fair copy in his file,' answered Billy, baffled by Tom's wild accusation, which he felt sure were not true.

'Without his help, I would have traipsed around that infernal dockyard until my toes dropped off in search of the stores we needed, instead of that, they are arriving as we speak. Listen,' he urged as something heavy dropped on the deck somewhere above to the sound of Duffy's voice. 'Truly, he could not have been more helpful had he been Lord Spencer himself. No Tom,' he said with pointed emphasis. 'Whatever Mister Trompe was doing in that alleyway last night and there are some thousand-and-one things he might have been doing just then, robbing me of my charts and signal book for some sinister purpose wasn't one of them, I assure you.'

And with that final scold he hoped was the finish of her unwarranted suspicion, he left the calm of his day cabin and a thoroughly perplexed, Tom. Who was quietly turning over in her mind all she had seen and heard the day before, not least of which, was the strange behaviour of the handsome French boy and the grumpy, horse-faced lump of a Midshipman she had observed arguing in the stable yard of the Fountain Inn.

Chapter 18

The Apis Bull Helps Kiya See Her Way

Midsummer morning 1335BCE

'There must be a way out. There must be? My husband the Pharaoh Akhenaten promised there was. Some secret way I have yet to *see*,' whispered Kiya, her voice a desperate scream of near despair, her mind a fog of disappointed confusion as she stared, half blinded, into the stairwell and saw again the massive, tight fitting stone that locked her in, her only way out, or so it now appeared.

"Nefertiti will not dare to kill you or our son, Tutankhamun, whilst I live," he had reassured her that last night they met. "But they will lock you in some secret place until I am killed for the people must never know you live in my name. But no matter they do this *wand* I now give you will set you free. Put your trust in Lord Aten, Kiya and the wand will guide you safe to me no matter where I am gone. If you do, your soul will travel to the stars above to *see* the way. Trust the *wand,* though the way may be long and hard. Trust the wand and the secret it hides will be yours."

306

'*The wand, the wand, the wand,*' she repeated, over and over again, gently turning the sceptre in her hand. Its beautifully carved shaft of ivory, onyx, gold, and lapis lazuli perfectly set between its two, heavy gold ends, it was impossible to see how they were joined together. 'But how can it show me the way?' She asked.

Did I truly dream I saw you my sister, Tefnut call out to our mother in heaven, Maat, from the top of that giant stone, surrounded all about by horsemen and soldiers trying to kill you? Did I a moment later dream I saw a girl in a red blanket seated by a waterfall greet you as if you were a long-lost friend? 'Yes, but why?' She sighed, little realizing how long she had earlier slept, that even now the black sky above was beginning show the dawns pale first light. It was then, her eyes half closed to a squint of near tearful frustration, she saw it. The tiniest possible chink of imperfection between the onyx neck of the sceptre and the falcon-head of Horus it clasped so tightly to its shaft. 'What's this?' She asked, with an instinct that saw her instantly twist and pull it until it came apart in torch like shards of bright blue, blinding light.

Dazzled by the light it was a moment before she realized the sceptre was no more than a cylinder containing a second, half-inch thick, solid gold wand of intricately woven, rope design.[186] With a gasp she saw one end of the wand was carved into the shape of a bull's head that clasped a *sun-disc* between its two curved horns. A disc inscribed with the Eye of Horus enclosed within the sacred double enneagon of Egypt, the other end a ball of bright gold the size of her thumb.

'*Apis,*'[187] she reverently whispered, stroking the disc with the tip of her henna tattooed forefingers and staring into the eye.

As she did, the *sun-disc,* began to shimmer like rippling water on a wind-blown pond and as it did a hazy image appeared of a long, narrow boat with an open, blue canopy at its swollen centre, racing down the River Nile. Its curving prow and massive stern posts almost as tall as the rope rigged single mast it carried at its centre. Where a triangular, blue lateen sail was loosely furled to its steeply angled wooden yard in the still and stifling heat, which roasted her muscular, bare-chested, chanting, oarsmen to an exhaustion that would find no rest until the day was done. And thought it was a part of the Nile she had never seen before, a voice clear in her head told her it was the Land of Punt, a thousand miles south of the pyramid that now so cruelly locked her in.

Searching the boat, she saw it was packed with soldiers, many of them battle wounded and exhausted and knew they were the elite of the Pharaoh Akhenaten's faithful bodyguard by the single tattooed mark they each wore on their bodies. On their sword or shield arms to give them strength, on their legs to carry them swiftly and without fear into battle, on their shaven heads to make them wise and knowing and on the front or back of their torsos to protect them from the strike of a sword, the thrust of a spear, the sting of an arrow or the blow of an axe. Some wore the mark discretely, but others wore them in a blazon of pride that would have all men and all women know who they are. And when she looked more closely she saw the same mark on the sail, which, though it was hard to see, was decorated with the same double enneagon in a circle, enclosing a hieroglyph of the most magical protection, but drawn in brightest gold. A hieroglyph, we would know today as the number three, three times drawn in the shape of a triangle, one 3 above the other two, and separated by a horizontal bar and each three, touching one side of the inner enneagon. The symbol and battle flag of the Pharaoh Akhenaten of Egypt, the sacred Pyramids of Giza, and the infinity of Aten's power and majesty. They were, as she was, oath sworn members of *The Sword and Shield of Aten and knew no fear* in the service of her husband and family.

And all of them watching the two much bigger boats that followed them a mile behind, whose limp-hung, red, and purple banners and constantly beating drums declared they were the soldiers of the Priests of Amun-Rah, the best they had. Who would suffer death before they would end their chase, 'AYEEEEEEE,' she screamed, seeing they were. A scream that appeared to wake the sleeping figure of a girl, Tefnut she now saw it was, who lay curled on a reed mat beneath the blue, fluttering canopy like a lazy cat.

'TEFNUT, TEFNUT,' she called, as the girl sprang to her feet in a single bound to find the distant voice that now called to her so sweetly. Her sister, Kiya, she instantly and joyously knew it was. 'HERE. I AM, HERE, TEFNUT MY SISTER. HERE,' she called, to the mocking echo of her cell now lit by the light of the morning sun, as it climbed higher and higher into the sky and not the silver of the moon it earlier was. But though Tefnut searched the long deck from end to end for the voice that called to her she found nothing but the soothing arms of the Captain of the guard, who told her it was a dream she heard and not her sister.

'Are the *Drummers* still here?' She asked the Captain, who smiled again to hear the perfect name she had long ago given the soldiers of the Priest of Amun-Ra, who followed them, their ceaseless drumming a daily torment to their ears.

'Yes, the *Drummers* are still here, princess,' he answered, pointing they were as he knelt at her side, his broad, calloused hands clasped tight about her thin bare shoulders. Her body so little against his own she could barely look him in the eyes, but did with such a regal majesty he would give his life, and the lives of all his men, to protect her. Her head, as it always was, despite the scorching sun that burnt the bleach-white decks beneath their sandals to an unbearable heat, was draped in a heavy, black, bob cut wig that was crowned at the front with the sacred golden Uraeus[188] of her princely office and intricately woven with a blood-red, thin braided cord that cut and looped it nine times before it fell to the nape of her neck in a single knotted tassel. Her eyes, which stared at him with such a brave hope and trusting heart he would keep her safe from her enemies were painted in the same kohl black, intricate design the Pharaoh and her sister, the true Queen of Egypt, Kiya everyday wore, their special mark of Aten's favor; the Eye of Horus. Her neck, arms and ankles adorned with priceless bands of gold, ivory and lapis lazuli no common child could ever hope to wear and her nine times, fan-pleated, starched white skirt, stitched with threads of gold and silver dazzled his eyes. 'But we will soon reach Atbara and when we do, we will turn into the river that gives that grubby mud brick town I once commanded, its name and give them the slip. But only long enough to put you and some of my most trusted men ashore and then they will be no more.'

'*Ashore?*' She gulped, wide-eyed with fear.

'Yes, my lady, as soon as there are rocks and trees and shrubs enough on the river bank to hide your escape, I will put you ashore.'

'But why?' She begged, holding his hands ever tighter.

'Because we cannot hope to outrun the *Drummers* when we reach the sixth cataract,[189] as we did at the fifth, so, I have decided to fight them one last time, but at a place of my choosing, not theirs. A place I know, a narrow gorge of high, steep sloping escarpments filled with treacherous sandbanks and man-eating crocodiles and when we do, we will kill the *Drummer* to the last man and when we have you will be safe to find the Pharaoh who waits for you without fear they will follow you. You will be safe at last my princess.'

'And what of you and your men, Captain?' She asked, seeing their many tired faces look back at her from behind their oars, but not one of them showing the least fear of the death that was now so close upon them.

'I fear we will die, princess,' he answered.

'Then come with me.'

'I cannot. The River Atbara is swollen with the last of the rains and the current is too strong for my already weakened crew to row against it for more than a few miles. So, we must set a trap for them long enough for you to escape overland to the sea; to Massawa.

'*Massawa?*'

'Yes, Massawa, princess it is a port on the Red Sea coast barely three weeks' journey from where I will land you. A port much used by Arab traders from the Gulf who my men will bribe to take you to the Pharaoh, who even now waits for you and your sister at the secret camp of the Nabataean's at Petra. Once there you will be safe and with your safety will come your sister's freedom for no Queen of Egypt can be held against her will whilst her Pharaoh lives that is the Law of Maat and despite she is Nefertiti she must obey.'

'Will I?' Asked the frightened girl, clutching the heavy torque necklace she wore around her neck tight in her hand, her little thumb stroking the Eye of Horus. Hardly daring to believe she would ever be safe again after the long and dangerous journey she had endured these many weeks. One that began with such high hopes of success seven hundred miles away in Edfu the day the Pharaoh Akhenaten attacked and plundered the Temple of Amun-Ra at Thebes of all its secret treasure. And one which should have ended a few days later, had Queen Nefertiti not so wickedly betrayed them to the Priests of Amun-Ra and sent the *Drummers* after her and her guard.

'Yes, you will, the soldiers who will guard you are the best I have, and each one oath sworn in the name of the Lord Aten not to leave you until the Pharaoh takes you in his arms, which he soon will, if he is still at Petra. But no matter if he isn't, they will find him wherever he is. We are The Sword and Shield of Aten.'

'Thank you, Captain,' she said with a heavy heart. 'I will never forget you or your men, or the great sacrifice of courage you make to see me safe to the Pharaoh. May the Lord Aten father of us all grant your Ka everlasting *life* from the earthly *death* that will soon be yours and may your journey to our heavenly afterlife be a safe one. One that befits the heroes you and your men truly are,' she prayed. Her fingers now curled around the Apis bulls head of her heavy torque necklace, her thumb once again gently caressing the sun-disc and the Eye of Horus that was cut into its centre.

'I thank you princess,' he answered, touched

by her gentle kindness.

'Aeeeeeeh,' whispered Kiya, seeing the *necklace* about her neck was the same as the wand she now held in her hand, as her husband said it was. 'It is the same,' she cried. 'But how does it work?' But there was no answer. The picture in the disc faded to nothing and Tefnut was gone. *How can I make it work?* She wondered, turning the wand this way and that. Little realising it was the Eye of Horus and not the wand itself that would reunite them. Horus, the falcon headed god of the sky, the sun, and the moon. Horus the son of Isis[190] and Osiris. Horus the father of all *time*.

Chapter 19

Tom Sneaks A Ride To The Fountain Inn

4.00pm Friday 21 April 1797

For most of the day Tom kept herself busy helping with the unloading of the great quantity of stores and munitions that were brought aboard the *Parrot* by the score of dockyard lighters and bumboats[191] that swarmed her sides from when she and Billy woke that morning to late afternoon and with much more to come until their work was done. As Lieutenant Galbraith, *who had added more to Billy's list of supplies, now* watching their progress through his telescope from the Semaphore Station had insisted they must, or answer to him. More and better stores of water, food, timber, rope, sail, and munitions than Billy had asked, but would need for a journey far longer than the one he was about to undertake.

Ropes for her miles of rigging, some of which were six inches thick and six hundred feet long and so heavy it took every boy aboard to coil it into her tight-filled holds. Acres of spare sail, wooden spars, planks, panels, and thick, rough cut timber, enough to mend the damage from a dozen storms or battles should the *Parrot* have to brave them. Three dozen oars, six fluted anchors and a brand new and most unexpected sailing boat to add to the two they already had; a sleek pinnace,[192] Billy was sure was a mistake, until he saw Lieutenant Galbraith's signature on the foreman's docket to say it wasn't. And thanked him for his kindness. Coils of red-painted chain for her own great anchors, tools for her newly appointed carpenter, sailmaker, blacksmith, and cook. Plates, jugs, jars, cups, and beakers, enough for every meal they would ever eat. Stiff leather buckets, soft canvas buckets and heavy, clattering wooden buckets. Hammocks and blankets for a hundred boys to make their bed.

Great barrels of finest quality gunpowder, cannon balls and lead shot and so many muskets, pistols, and swords you might think they were going to fight the French navy single handed and for the duration of the war. Sacks of coke and charcoal for her galley stove that coloured his growing tired crew black from head to foot. Tubs of sand for her decks and fire buckets, string tied bales of cloth, wool, calico, cotton, and oil skin to clothe them all in the wettest and the coldest seas. Spikes, nails, brushes, paint, varnish, candles, tar, salt-beef, peas, cabbage, potatoes, suet, sugar, salt, flour, bread, butter, oatmeal, water, beer, wine and spirits in every size and shape of barrel and cask the Coopers art could make. And so very many, Tom could barely count them all, but everyone signed and countersigned they were no more than the dockyard would allow.

And if that wasn't enough to keep her busy, the very last boat to come up beside her that day delivered a veritable feast of food for the Captain's private pantry, something she never knew he had, but was rather glad he did. A hamper of bottled preserves, sauces, herbs, and spices; two-gallon pots of strawberry jam; a small barrel each of pickled ox tongues, onions, cucumbers, and walnuts. A barrel of Spanish limes to stop the scurvy[193] rotting his teeth the colour of night. Three giant cooked hams, too big to be carried by any one boy, save Duffy who carried two for the show of it. Two big cases of China tea and one equally big case of ground Brazil coffee and kettles, pots, and a Wedgewood[194] tea and coffee service to pore them in. Six wheels of Cheddar cheese and four of Red Leicester, four gallons[195] of fresh milk, a twelve-pound barrel of butter, two, hundredweight sacks of brown sugar, two, hundredweight[196] sacks of dried macaroni, two-dozen squawking hens in wooden pens, four honking geese similarly caged, a sleepy-eyed goat and a half-grown pig, meat for the table. For which he was assured no payment was required.

A personal present from the man who continued to watch him with such a proud and thoughtful gleam in his eye from the top of the Semaphore Station, so close to the Fountain Inn he had a good sight of the amiable crowd of loafers and sightseers still gathered there for news of the mutiny, which oddly was looking more dangerous by the hour, and the dozens of stern faced sea officers who traipsed in and out to see Lord Spencer.

The oddest of them all, Admiral Crookhampton and his strange party, who he knew by sad and wilting reputation, who had just received the command of an embassy to New York and a Baronetcy he never truly expected or deserved. But the strangest group of men to go in and very soon out of this fashionable watering hole, were the so-called Delegates, Warrant, and Petty Officers from every ship in the Channel Fleet. Steady and reliable men every one of them who had refused to return to their duty until they had the King's own signed and petitioned pardon in their hands. Something that might take weeks? Did take weeks.

Clack-clack, clack-clack, went the heavy shutters of the semaphore above his head as it sent the coded message he had earlier prepared the seventy-five telegraph miles to the Admiralty building in London, in less than *three* minutes. A message that would tell, all was ready, the *Parrot* would sail on tomorrows afternoon tide.

Throughout this busy time, Tom marveled at the way the *Parrot* had come to life in so short a time; in less than a day. The way Mister Robinson, his first Lieutenant and thrilled to be so named by his Captain, marshalled every hand to the many tasks and duties that were needed to make the little brig ready for sea. And just as busy was Duffy, who ignoring every ache in his tired and battered body drove every boy aboard to work as they had never worked in their lives before and with smiles upon their faces that said how happy they were to be soon gone from England and the mutiny.

Even Mister Arbuthnot Anstruther, stripped to his elegantly monogrammed, billowing shirt on that dull and breezy afternoon was bent to an effort his plump little body had never known before. An effort he constantly moaned in a petulant, lisping twitter that was as peculiar as his want to suck his thumb when he thought no one was looking, he would never, ever recover from.

With lists, receipts, dockets, labels, tickets, and bills of every imaginable kind spilling out of his pockets and a never-ending stream of questions to answer from Sam, Trucky, Duffy and every newly and very happily promoted senior rating, he hardly knew the answer, too, Billy found some thousand-and-one things to keep him busy. And so much so, he hardly spoke a word to Tom all day and when at last she found him alone he sent her away with an icy stare and frosty growl that impatiently said, *'Not now, Tom. Not now, please.'*

Much to the giggling pleasure of Nipper Ogden, who didn't much like her and let her know it, despite Duffy saying how brave she was. But no matter he did, she knew how fretfully worried Billy was by the loss of his precious signal book, something she had resolved to find and knew just where to look and if he didn't care to know, then she wouldn't trouble to tell him.

'You look very thoughtful, Tom,' said Sam, coming up beside her as she sat cross-legged on one of the smaller cannons, her chin resting on her two hands as she pensively stared at Billy, leaning, just then against the little wheel house as he drank a mug of hot, milky tea. The honk of geese and the squawk of hens in their wooden coops so loud beside him it was a wonder he could hear himself think and thinking he clearly was, as he stared wistfully out to sea and the crowded anchorage.

'Do I?' She answered, barely acknowledging his presence, an impudence Mister Anstruther, who was watching her with a maddening irritation was just about to reprimand, when he was stopped by Sam's, upturned hand.

'He's very busy, you know and will be until we sail tomorrow afternoon and no doubt for a long time after that,' he kindly said. Wondering why he felt the need to explain the Captain's duty to her, a ships *boy* and no more. But a boy quite unlike any other boy aboard the *Parrot,* one, who despite he was so dirty, carried himself with a singular disregard for authority, who knew by some unspoken past he was the equal of any officer.

'Who?' She answered, blithely, pretending not to know who he was talking about and with a smile so broad on her upturned face he was quite disarmed by her.

'Mmm,' he sighed, little knowing what to say to the hardly washed since her swim in the marsh last night, still smelly boy, who stoutly ignored he was the *Parrot's* Lieutenant, and who, rather more importantly, shared such a mysterious bond of friendship with the Captain. A friendship he had earlier that day insisted should see her treated with favour until he had decided her proper place. 'The Captain, he has much to do just now, more than you and I can ever imagine, but I'm sure he will find a minute to speak to you soon.'

'No matter,' she answered, her mind made up as she slipped from her perch like a cat. 'But should he ask for me, Mister Robinson, I would be greatly obliged if you would tell him I have a head-ache and have gone below to sleep an hour or two and will call upon him when I am feeling better. Later this evening, if he has a moment of peace to share a bite to eat with me.'

'Yes,' muttered, Sam meekly. Feeling like a dismissed servant as he watched her climb through one of the open hatchways without a backward glance, and once again without the least show of compliment to his now elevated rank. 'Mmm,' he groaned, scratching his head.

'A strange one that, Mister Robinson?' Said Duffy, stopping a moment to wash the sweat from his battered face with a dirty rag.

'He is, Mister Duff.'

'But as brave a boy as I ever did know and I've known plenty tougher than he looks.'

'Likely,' he answered, knowing the very high regard Duffy held her in. A regard he had a dozen times said he would try to repay in every way he could, despite her want to be so damnably familiar with the Captain, who treated her with the affection of an older brother.

And so it was, at four thirty that afternoon with the hands settled down to a very welcome dinner of boiled beef stew, lentils, peas, dumplings and beer and with Billy climbed to the maintop[197] to be alone, Tom quietly and without notice, slipped away. Hitching a ride on a departing bumboat, almost the last one to leave and Captained by an enormously fat lady with a clay pipe clamped in her toothless mouth, she landed at Portsmouth point an hour later and after taking a moment to sip a refreshing glass of ice cold beer at the full to overflowing Ship Tavern, made her way, once again, to the Fountain Inn.

Arriving a little after five-fifty, she found to her surprise the Marine guard, so firm in their refusal to let her in yesterday evening, were now standing a lazy, cheerful, indifferent guard at the crowded front door. But ignoring they did, she once again turned the corner into the coach yard, which she saw was full to bursting with a crowd of folk quite unlike the troublesome idlers of the night before. In fact, they were mostly women and children, the wives, and sweethearts, she supposed of the mutineers, who were cheering the news that Lord Spencer was returning to London tomorrow to get the kings pardon for every man in the fleet. *Their men were to be saved,* they cried with a tremendous halloo. The mutiny was over and there was to be a celebration dinner that very night with all the gentlefolk of Portsmouth invited to attend.

Trusting to good luck and hopeful she would find Polly somewhere within, because it was Polly, she was now intent on finding, she cautiously made her way into the Fountain's vast and noisy kitchen. Unnoticed in the hot and steamy, frantic hurly-burly of cooks, pot-boys, and maids, who were busily making ready the evening banquet. A dinner fit for a King of mushroom soup, roast beef, pork, ham, mutton cutlets à *la jardinièrs*, duck à *la Rouennaise,* the cooks speciality, she heard one of the flustered maids boastfully say, turbot, sole à *la Normande* and lobster rissoles you would die for, said the second cook. Not to mention, a mountain of fresh vegetables, rice, spicy savories, and sweets she longed to taste. But didn't dare as she found an open door to goodness knows where?

A heart beat later she found herself in the guttering half-light of a long and gloomy, dungeon-like corridor, lit by the most miserable glass lanterns she had ever seen and began to slowly, ever-so-slowly, tip-toe towards the chink of light that framed a second door at its furthest end. Reaching it, she paused, pressed her ear to the wood and heard the dull sound of merry chatter and a violin and harpsichord playing in the room behind. Never noticing the narrow, dark rising stairs behind her and the two, orb-like eyes that now looked down at her from the half landing above; it was Polly.

Stealing herself to open the door, her hand

firm on the iron, thumb latch, her heart pounding in her chest so hard she thought it would burst right out, she was suddenly pitched headlong into the Fountain's spacious, but very crowded, fire lit parlor by the brute of a smirking waiter who came up behind her with neither a please you, nor a thank you, she should get out of his way.

Which, to her utter dismay was full to near overflowing into the street with Lord Spencer's distinguished naval party, more gold braided, white breeched and waist coated officers than she had ever seen in her life before. More even than Lymington Quay could boast on a warm, summer, Sunday afternoon. And, if that wasn't enough to make her tremble at the knees, and it very soon did, there was a generous helping of Hampshire's best families gathered there in noisy chatter. Her own dear Miss Fry, included, come up to town for the week end and wearing a very fetching pink gown with an ingenious ruche waist she had made herself that so fitted her slim, rather shapely figure she looked quite lovely and Dr Charles, who stood shyly at her side, his face like hers a blush of red that said how happy they both were.

Red-coated military officers, squinting clergymen, lawyers, bankers, well-to-do shopkeepers, dockyard officials, ruddy faced yeoman-farmers and a host of landed gentry come up to town for the fun of the mutiny they thought such a lark it couldn't be missed. Every one of them decked out in their finest clothes, but so much less than their hoity-toity, snooty wives and their archly preening, mostly unmarried daughters, who stood so airily beside them with their snobby upturned noses and prim, tight-lipped, rouge-red, condescending smiles stuck fast on their faces.

Each one, trying to outdo the other in the latest London fashion, brightly coloured or gaily patterned, daringly low necked, high waisted to their lifted breasts, narrow belted with ribbons, delicately frilled at the hem, short, puffed-sleeved, slim fitting, column dresses of silk, cotton, and richest damask. Which fell to their white daringly exposed, silk stockinged ankles and gorgeously slippered feet in a flurry of excited ripples that positively thrummed the nervous excitement they felt. Rustles, squeaks, and swishes, their perfumes a cocktail of sweet blossom drifting all around them.

Looped on their crooked elbows about their waists they wore richly embroidered shawls so long they fell to the floor in a lazy slump; the longer the better it would seem. On their dressed in ringlets and curls, fabulously bouffant hair they wore an assortment of pretty tiaras, turbans, tiny hats pinned with ostrich feathers, broad brimmed bonnets, caps, and ribbons. And in their gloved hands they held painted fans, which they snapped, flicked, fanned, and fluttered like the feathers of some exotic bird to cool the stifling heat of the hundred candles that lit the room to a yellow glow.

Aware how unkempt and dirty she must look in their elegant company she was surprised and embarrassed to see how close she was to the great Lord Spencer, who was standing barely a yard away from her.

A suave, sophisticated and distinguished looking man of thirty-nine, elegantly dressed for all to see in a powdered wig and queue, a six buttoned, double breasted, bottle green tail coat with fashionably wide lapels and a collar so tall it brushed the back of his head, on which the blue sash and garter of the Most Noble Order of the Garter[198] draped his chest, a dandy's waistcoat of cream and apple green hoops that hugged his belly like an old friend, a white silk shirt and matching green stock, white silk stockings and black, bright polished to a candle-lit gleam, silver buckled shoes.

And if that wasn't enough to set her heart a tremble, as she searched the quick escape she now intended, beside him stood five very senior and very quarrelsome Admirals in blue tail coats trimmed with gold brocade. Admiral Sir Peter Parker, the Port Admiral, who, it was said, would promote anyone's relative or friend for a hundred guineas and to any navy job they wanted, regardless of their age or ability. Seventy-six years of age and as plump and jowly as a well-fed bloodhound and with Midshipman Anstruther's attractive young step-mother fixed tight to his arm and her besotted Captain of Yeomanry, her lover of recent weeks, standing at her heels. Admiral Lord Bridport, the seaman's favourite, white-haired, grizzled, and thoroughly dismayed by the events of this last week, which had left him exhausted. Admiral Sir Alan Gardner, a sadly ugly man with no front teeth to speak of and a great protruding, lantern jaw he worked back and forth like an old dog with a bone he couldn't eat, but sucked and sucked just the same. Admiral Sir Charles Pole, pink faced, blue eyed and genial and beside him, Admiral Sir John Colpoys, morose and spoiling for a fight with someone, anyone at all.

As Fate, would have it and Fate is everywhere in this intriguing story, it was Admiral Colpoys who spotted her first and recognizing her for the sailor she surely was, though a grubby faced one in her near regulation slops.[199] He called out in an explosive rage that hushed the orchestra to an instant silence and saw every eye in the room turn upon him, not least a party of four, oddly assorted characters; seated by the blazing fire they had long since considered their own.

The first, a dark eyed French boy with a look of distracted irritation etched hard on his perfectly chiseled, archly intelligent face, who, if he had spoken just then, would have cursed the names of Grub, Dogget, Badger, Begg, Trompe, Kepple and Kettle in equal measure. The second, a stick thin, ginger haired, po-faced, pouting, frog lipped, buck-toothed young girl, who was squinting through gold, pince-nez spectacles fixed with glass so cobble thick they might have spied the moon on a cloudy night. Who patted the bare belly of the oddly twitching, curled up, sleeping dog on her lap, as if it was a drum. The third, a red-faced, genial old buffer bedecked in his Admiral's uniform, who, to his utter contentment and perfect joy had three hours earlier received the news he most desired in all the world; he was to be elevated to the peerage. That is, if Lord Spencer, should have his way with the King, which he surely would, and more, than this fabulous promotion, he was to be given employment too, for the first time in nearly forty years. A job that would take him back to America, before the month of May was out. Lastly, a thoroughly drunk, decidedly unhappy he wasn't promoted, sour faced, belligerent, Midshipman, who was gamely picking his nose clean of a very large, slug-like bogey with a rather fat, tar stained finger. Each of them, staring hard at poor Tom and nodding their cruel approval at Admiral Colpoys, as they watched the fun begin with the glee that is so often found in bully's, braggarts, and overblown snobby upstarts of every type.

'WHAT THE BLAZES DO YOU THINK YOU ARE DOING SKULKING ABOUT IN HERE, WHERE YOU DON'T BELONG, *BOY?* NOT ONE IDLE, MISERABLE SCRAP OF YOU, YOU SKULKING RASCAL. OUT WITH IT, YOU RAT-BAG SCOUNDREL, YOU RUNT OF A NOGOOD SNIVELLING MUTINOUS DOG?' He raged and fumed like a mad man, in his harsh, Irish brogue, his face a bloated crimson red, his mouth a horror of yellow, black, and broken teeth and livid-pink gums. 'ARE YOU ONE OF THOSE SLINKING, I'M SO BADLY DONE BY, MURDERING COVES COME TO KILL US IN OUR BEDS? OR ONE OF THEIR BLOOMING DELEGATES SO COCK SURE OF THEMSELVES THEY TREAT THEIR OFFICERS, THEIR SOCIAL BETTERS BY RANK AND ANCIENT PRIVILEGE, LIKE THEIR SCHOOLBOY CHUMS WITH THEIR STRUT-TING MANNERS AND WANT OF TEA, CAKE AND SYMPATHY AND THEIR DAMNABLE IM-PERTINCE AND, AND... AND,' he blustered, hardly daring to believe what he was about to say in his forty-one years of service, 'THEIR GROW-ING MORE GREEDY, INFERNAL DEMANDS

FOR WAGES NOT YET PAID, LEAVE LONG OWING, BETTER FOOD THAN WE GIVE'S 'EM ALREADY, MORE BEER AND GROG THAN THE GALLON THEY EVERYDAY GET AND LESS OF THE LASH THEY EVERYDAY DESERVE FOR THEIR CONTEMPT OF THE KING'S LAWFULL AUTHORITY WHEN THEY KNOW DAMN WELL THEIR COUNTRY, OUR COUNTRY IS AT WAR WITH THE FROG.' He screeched, turning to face to his now enthusiastically watching, giddy with excitement audience for the approval he now claimed his own, which they did, with a thunderous hallooing applause that carried to the street outside. 'IS AT WAR BOY WITH THE VILEST CUTHROATS THE WORLD HAS EVER KNOW, WORSE THAN THOSE AMERICAN ITCHYBUM SAVAGES I FOUGHT SO DAMNABLY HARD IN THE LAST WAR, TUFTED IROQUOISE AND YELLLOW AND BLACK PAINTED ABENAKI THE WORST OF THE LOT, WHO WOULD SKIN YOU ALIVE FOR TUPPENCE AND COMING TO ME WITH YOUR SIGNED PETITIONS and PAPERS OF SEAMEN'S AUTHORITY STUFFED IN YOUR POCKESTS TO SAY YOU CAN.' He screamed. A remark that produced a loud guffaw of delighted laughter from around the room as the embarrassment, hurt and misfortune of someone else less fortunate than they, so often does; invariably does!

332

'ARE YOU? OUT WITH IT, NOW YOU WICK-
ED, SNOT-NOSED, LITTLE URCHIN? I KNOW
YOUR TYPE. THRASHED THEM A THOUSAND
TIMES, YOU DAMNABLE, BLACKHEARTED
PIPSQUEAK. WHO ARE YOU, *BOY?* SPEAK UP
I SAY BEFORE I HAVE YOU FLOGGED AROUND
THE FLEET AND THEN A SECOND TIME FOR
GOOD LUCK.'

A not unusual punishment in those far-off days
of yore, but one generally reserved for the most
heinous of crimes imaginable, treason and murder being the most likely contenders. But improbable though his threat was, it was threat enough
to send a murmur of fright and excited anticipation
around that splendid room. Not least amongst the
young ladies, who little used to such talk in the
Assembly Room, found it all so horribly depraved
and unspeakably exhilarating they huddled and
wriggled and giggled and fanned themselves like
windmills to better see this unexpected fun, which
they hoped might soon kill the beastly boy.

But all his bluster and threat was lost on Tom,
who, being such a well brought up young lady from
Lymington and quite sure of herself was ignorant
of such dreadful things and hardly knew why this
crazy old fool with the darkly hooded eyes and
bright red, hairy nose, whose breath, smelt of tobacco, gin, and tooth decay, was being so hurtful

and so rudely impolite to her.

'Tom, sir,' she said, with the respect he didn't show her, knuckling the narrow brim of her Sennet hat in salute and lowering her voice an octave or two in a mimic that passed for the boy she hoped she appeared.

'TOM?' Thundered Colpoys, enjoying the spectacle he was causing. 'TOM WHO? YOU VILLAINOUS TERMITE? OUT WITH IT OR I'LL PULL YOUR EARS OFF ONE BY ONE AND FEED THEM TO ME DOG?' He laughed he was so funny as the crowd moved closer with an intake of breath that was an audible gasp.

'Why, Tom *Dimple,* sir,' she brightly answered, without a moment's hesitation and regretting in an instant she had thoughtlessly revealed her surname for everyone in the room to hear, not least Miss Fry and Dr Charles.

'Dimple, you say?' Mused Bridport, to no one in particular, as he stepped into the semicircle his Admirals now made to ponder the sight of the poor boy, a skinny lad, but really quite tall and straight legged for a Portsmouth guttersnipe.[200] 'Not related to that blackguard Titus Dimple up Beaulieu way are you by any chance, young fellow? Hey? No! Of course, you're not,' he muttered, answering his own question, and winning an approving laugh from the room and a hoot of noisy and most unladylike derision from Hesta Victoria standing on her chair to see the spectacle her hand rested on Corbeau's disapproving shoulder as her dog licked his ear. *After all,* she thought, *how could such a skinny, horribly dirty ragamuffin like her possibly be related to such a well-bred, modestly rich man, as he?*

'Damn lucky for you you're not,' he benevolently whispered, wagging his forefinger playfully in her face. A clever and kindly ruse she quickly realised distracted Admiral Colpoys from his wicked theatricals, 'and that's my best opinion. Because I tell you truly, young man,' he gently poked her in the chest, 'there was never a bigger rogue for legal villainy and artful skullduggery this side of the English Channel than that shameful Purser, Titus damn his black name, Dimple. Am I right gentlemen?' He said, half turning towards his companions, who, with varying degrees of shuffling, nodding, harrumphing and sniggering asides, appeared to approve his sage comments.

But not, Lord Spencer, who watching the display of Tom's humiliation with less amusement than the rest of the room was clearly baffled to know who Admiral Bridport was talking about and said as much with an impatient scowl that better than words asked him to desist.

'And there are rumors about him, too. Even

now young man,' he said, in a conspiratorial undertone that hushed the room from front to back in prying expectation. 'Black rumors of treason and Irish rebellion that I hope a young fellow like you will have no part in?'

'No sir,' answered Tom, with a start that made her dizzy and sick to her empty stomach with surprise, for, most amazingly, the man he spoke about, was indeed her very own uncle. Whose wickedness and double dealing had driven her poor dear, trusting mother, his sister in law, to ruin and an early grave and all for want of a small inheritance he claimed was his. A sentimental bauble no more than that, left to her by her dead father to mark her recent birthday and had she not escaped him, when she did, he would have had.

Gathering her wits, which were now horribly frayed, as you might well imagine were after such an ordeal, she blurted out the first thing that came into her head. Something she had heard one of the *Parrot's* newly arrived boys say, when he came aboard, yesterday. 'Begging your pardon, sir, I'm just come up from Mister Hanway's, like so many us young lads have this last winter, to take ship aboard the *Parrot,* sir.'

'*Hanway's,* you say?' Replied Bridport, with an approving nod of his bony head, which almost slipped his hat and wig from his head, knowing, as every King's Officer did, Mister Jonas Hanway was famous for two things. The first, the making of a great fortune out of the manufacture of umbrellas, a modern contrivance he didn't much approve, preferring his hat and boat cloak in all inclement weather. The second, the founding in 1756 of the Marine Society, a home for destitute boys, which having got them from the streets, slums, foundling homes, prisons, and workhouses of every city, town, and village in England, then trained them for a life at sea, even if they didn't want it. Any number of them now serving aboard his mutinous ships and tolerably well, too, he had to admit. 'Hmm,' he snorted with a beam of contented satisfaction.

'Yes, sir,' answered Tom, shuffling nervously under the relentless gaze of the assembled room, which seemed to have pressed rather close to her in the last few minutes. But no one more than Miss Fry who looked at her with such a thoughtful look on her face from within the press of young ladies, who surrounded her to such a distraction. A look that said, *I know you, but how?*

'What do you want boy?' Asked Colpoys, ignoring his Commander in Chief for the fool he thought he was to let the mutiny get so badly out of hand in the first place. Something he had tried to stop aboard his own ship, HMS *London,* Midshipman Anstruther's old ship, you will recall, with a pistol shot aimed at the head of a mutineer that barely missed the poor man and with a ricochet of a cannon that almost killed another.

Thinking quickly and so very glad of the friendship and confidence, Billy had shown her these last few days, and the tidbits of naval intelligence he had shared in their talks alone, she answered, as any respectable sailor would, 'Captain's duty, sir,' a time-honored phrase that gave her the authority to speak on his behalf, even to an Admiral, 'I've *brung* a message, sir, for Mister Lauder Trompe,' pronouncing it properly, which showed she could, always could, 'Admiralty clerk to Lord Spencer,' she finished with a deferential bow he returned with a gentle nod of his head.

'Trompe? Damned if I know anyone called Trompe?' Grunted Colpoys, now thoroughly bored with the fun he had contrived to have with his innocent victim and eager for the dinner that smelt so delicious on the plates, platters, and gleaming silver tureens an Indian file of heavily laden, grey wigged, white aproned waiters were now steering into the parlor from the kitchen behind her and too such an indecent rush to the tables beside Admiral Crookhampton and his party, the Admirals were soon standing alone. Except for Miss Fry, who, still searching the *boy's* name, took a step forward only to be stopped by Lieutenant Galbraith, who bowed his pleasure to meet her and Dr Charles, who came up beside her.

'Trompe, you say?' Said Lord Spencer, distractedly wondering who Lieutenant Galbraith was talking too, his right hand instinctively touching the secret mark on his left arm. 'What business does the Captain of his majesties gun-brig *Parrot* have with my clerk?'

'Begging your pardon, sir, I don't rightly know,' answered Tom, respectfully. Glad the dark shadow cast over her bruised and soot lack face by the brim of her hat concealed the fear and embarrassment she now felt, not least the fear, a now studiously watching through the corner of her eye, Miss Fry might yet unmask her. Who, had she been a little bolder, would have stepped a yard or two closer, despite the attentive Lieutenant, who spoke such fashionable compliments to her. 'But I was supposed to find him and ask him to come to supper aboard the *Parrot* this very evening, so as Captain Kepple can properly thank him for all the help he's been in getting the *Parrot* ready for sea. 'Cos I heard him say to the first Lieutenant, Mister Robinson, though I knows I shouldn't have been listening, but I couldn't help me self, 'cos I was standing at his elbow when he said it, that if it wasn't for Mister Trompe, he'd have traipsed around that infernal dockyard until his toes had

339

gone and dropped off his feet before he'd have got the stores and munitions he needed for our voyage tomorrow. And that's the truth and no mistake so help me, God sir.'

'Mmm,' mumbled Lord Spencer to his Admiral's. 'I'm glad the young fool has been of help to someone, for I swear I will never understand why Mister Nepean insisted I bring him to Portsmouth. For I tell you truly gentlemen that stupid boy has no more sense than my dog, Colin, and he, poor fellow been dead and buried these last two years at Althorp.[201] And I should know because I shot him,' and with a ribald laugh, he turned to Tom and spoke to her with a kindness that told everyone, her ordeal was over. 'Well, young man you have done your Captain's duty well, but tell him he shan't have my clerk for he comes with me to London tomorrow morning. So, my compliments to Captain …? Remind me boy, what is the name of your Captain?'

'Why, Kepple, sir, Lieutenant William Kepple, late of his Majesties ship, *Surprise,* Captain Edward Hamilton. And no finer Captain ever sailed the seven seas,' beamed Tom.

'Indeed,' said Lord Spencer with a smile that knew exactly who he was, the first he had known that week. 'Well, my compliments to Captain William Kepple and his kindness to my clerk, which I am most appreciative of, you will commend him, but there will be no meeting and no supper for young Mister Trompe tonight or for that matter any other night this week. And tell him, too, I knew his father and have long mourned his loss.' And with that, he turned on his heels and closed, what was for Tom, a most wearying conversation.

Dismissed like the no-account ships boy they thought she was, Tom hurried out of the door before Miss Fry could catch her. As she now clearly intended she would and with a look of recognition in her eyes that dropped her pretty jaw almost to her neck, but was caught in a retreat of Admirals that brought her to a bobbing, respectful stop before she could. But no sooner had Tom taken a step into the dark of that gloomy corridor with its deliciously inviting smells of dinner thick in the air, then a small firm hand took hold of hers and with a whispered hush that silenced any protest she might have thought to make, pulled her up the many times turning, back stairs to the attic above. But not so fast she didn't hear Miss Fry call her name from the bottom, the last time she would hear it for over a year, if a *year* in her coming story meant anything?

Chapter 20

Polly Comes To The Rescue

6.48pm Friday 21 April 1797

'You've come for the papers that was stolen from Captain, Billy last night, Tom,' said Polly, reaching the safety of the closet-sized, attic garret, her fright of a penny-pinching, mistress, winsomely called a bedroom. A windowless, cheerless, cobweb hung, spider and cockroach-crawling in plain sight beside the broken skirting board, flea-pit beneath the sagging, creaking eaves of the Fountain Inn. A damp and dirty hovel without light enough to dress at five in the morning when she woke, except for the stump of melted candle she now lit with a tinder box, heating, or furniture. For no one in their right mind could describe the broken-down truckle bed[202] covered in coarse and dirty sacking she slept on, furniture. 'I knew you would come. I've known all along you would.'

'Did you?' Asked Tom, anxious to know more, but delaying the dozen questions she had on her lips, until she had kissed the little maid on both her cheeks and squeezed her so tight, she wrig-

342

gled and growled with pleasure. 'Oh Poll, what would I do without you?' She whispered. 'You are the strangest, cleverest, most wonderful person I have ever met in my life, you truly are.'

'More wonderful than your Billy, Miss?' Asked Polly, with cheeky good humor that said she knew different.

'Yes,' said Tom, shyly, not at all sure she was telling the truth, because he was quite special. Well, for a boy. 'But where are they? The papers I mean and are you absolutely sure they are Billy's?' She begged.

'Yes, them's Captain Billy's right enough. I heard Miss Hesta say they was when, Mister Trompe fetched them here in a panic last night and gave them to Corbeau. Who has them in his room downstairs now. Though he ain't best pleased Billy got away last night. Oh, no he's been shoutin' a rage ever since he did.'

'Thank goodness, Poll.' Said Tom, with a sigh of relief. 'They are the most important papers you could ever imagine. Secret papers, Billy got from the Transport Office in Wish Street just moments before he was kidnapped and near drowned in the Great Morass by some street toughs. Corbeau's paid toughs by the sound of it and would have, had you not told me their plan. Secret charts and signals more precious than gold,' she cautiously

343

and dramatically whispered in her ear. 'Which are to take the *Parrot* to France tomorrow on the most important and dangerous mission that could be given to a King's officer, without, which he will be ruined forever for there are no others to be had, at any price without him saying he lost them. Even though they were stolen by that treacherous, double-dealing villain, Lauder Trompe. Though goodness knows why he did, the rogue? 'But, you are sure Corbeau has them? Tell me, please? I must have them. I must have them before I leave tonight.

Yes, he does,' He has them locked away safe in his room like I said and Midshipman Kettle in there all afternoon tryin' to learn them and tolerably well when I heard Corbeau testin' him, when I laid the evenin' fire in the grate at four, calling him a genius and me a fool.'

'Cor blimey Charlie, Midshipman Kettle is involved in this?

'Yes, him and Miss Hesta both, they're all in it up to their ears, though I ain't so sure, Mister Trompe, is, him bein' so fearful scared of them and only doin' what Corbeau said he must with a pistol pressed to his head. Who throttled him near dead when he asked for his own papers back, the ones he stole yesterday.'

'But why?' She asked.' Why do they want to

ruin Billy and take the *Parrot* from him when he's only just got it?

It took Polly a minute to recount all she had overheard, which was little more than the bare outline of Billy's kidnap, but remarkably she did add something entirely new and truly astonishing. You will remember how, yesterday, Hesta Victoria almost choked on her port wine when Midshipman Kettle exploded in surprise at the astonishing news of his lost commission. Well, it seems that Hesta Victoria wasn't so much frightened by his noisy outburst, which she found oddly endearing, but rather, the mention of the name, *Kepple*.

You will of course recall Hesta Victoria's mother blamed the loss of their vast American fortune on the royal navy, specifically, the inaction of a frigate Captain, who ignored their pleas for help when the Sons of Liberty were at their door and sailed from New York, leaving her maternal grandfather, Percy Wicker Selbourn, swinging from the Mulberry tree in their front garden.

Well, as you already know, this Captain was none other than Captain John Kepple, late of HMS *Cherub*, Billy's father. Guessing he was, though she couldn't be sure he was, Hesta Victoria instantly and with added spite, transferred the hatred she felt towards him, dead before she was born, to his entirely innocent son. Which, is

345

always the way with hate filled families such as hers. This mental acrobat achieved, she cheerfully and enthusiastically joined forces with her *beau* and Corbeau in the seemingly madcap plan they had hatched together to take the *Parrot* from him.

'Gracious me,' said Tom, truly appalled. 'I can't believe it's true, how can she possibly hate Billy for something his father, did so long ago. If he did, and I doubt he did? But even if it is true, why is Corbeau helping them to ruin Billy's reputation? Ruin him forever? What's in it for him? Why would a French émigré just months escaped from the revolution trouble himself?'

'I don't know, Miss,' answered Polly, her face a picture of puzzlement as she sat on the flaring lip of the red brick, chimney stack in the dim light of the candle. 'Try as I might and I have tried as best I can, I can't get *into* his head like I can with most other folk. His mind is so tight shut there's no tellin' what he might be thinkin', but whatever it is, it ain't goin' to do your Billy no good he has taken so powerfully against him.'

'Well, whatever his reasons, there's no time to lose Poll, we must get those charts and signal book as quick as we can and get them back to the *Parrot* before she sails. Tonight! Can you help me Poll? Can you take me to Corbeau's room this very instant? You must.

346

As Tom and Polly crept down the stairs to the Fountain's upper bedroom corridor, Hesta Victoria was regaling her companions with a story almost too awful to tell. A delicious scandal that had been the idle gossip of the county[203] since before Christmas last. 'It appears,' she said, picking bird-like at her duck à *la Rouennaise* with her two-pronged fork and with a sniffy disdain for the unsavory tale she was about to tell, that curled her nose into a pig like snout, 'Mrs. Dimple, God rest her soul, drowned herself in one of the salt pans on Pennington Marshes last December, when her mind was in such a fevered torment of despair and apprehension, she knew no better than she did. Well, that's what Captain Drier said it was and he should know, him being so famous for his capture of the Langstone smugglers at Durdle Door last year, when she was laid out in doctor Charles's surgery for all of Lymington to see and the magistrate Mister Dicks and Constable Brown, who were there to see justice done, heartily agreed, because it could not be otherwise, and she a widow with a daughter only half grown.'

'A sad business,' said Admiral Crookhampton, a kindly man, barely able to keep his eyes open after the little dinner he had just eaten. 'I knew her late husband, well. A fine, upstanding, God fearing man, indeed he was,' he yawned. 'He was Lord

Montagu's Land Agent before he died a tragic accident, tripped in a rabbit hole and hit his head a resounding blow on a great rock, killed him stone dead and a more decent and honest fellow you never met in your life,' he sighed as Midshipman Kettle cruelly sniggered into his dinner. 'An example to us all, Hesta my dear, bless his soul! Been dead these last nine years! The autumn of 1788 I remember it like it was yesterday, such terrible winds, deuce they were. A fine man,' he reminisced as old men do. 'But no head for business! Left a pile of debts and the upkeep of his family to his younger brother, Titus, whose name I heard Admiral Bridport mention earlier, who inherited all he had. And a more unpleasant, sour fellow there never was. As old Bridport said he was and he should know.'

'What happened to the daughter?' Asked Corbeau, gently caressing his nose with a scented, blue silk handkerchief and peering above the mask it made of his face with a look that was as cold and as unfeeling as ice. He was making polite conversation, as he knew he must.

'Well there's the thing,' said Hesta Victoria, 'she's gone and disappeared, not been seen these last few weeks. Has she grandfather?' But he didn't hear, he had, at long last, succumbed to the heat, exhaustion and noisy excitement of

348

that memorable day and fallen fast asleep. Not that Hesta Victoria noticed or cared he had, as she prattled on and on in her usual, selfishly dotty way. 'And old Titus near demented with worry to find her and searching the county from one end to the other fit to bust his brain a stroke for fear she would come to some terrible end like her poor mother.'

'But what has this to do with us my dear, Hesta,' interrupted Kettle, slurping a spoonful of mushroom soup into his greedy mouth, whilst noisily sucking on a mutton cutlet, à *la jardinières* and with a selfish, petulant look on his face that was the hallmark of his lazy, mean spirited, grubbing character. 'Surely we have more pressing things to discuss just now than her?'

'Such as what?' Asked Corbeau, his manner terse and impatient, who was thoroughly enjoying Hesta Victoria's aimless story, the point of which had entirely escaped him, a minute since, as most of what she said, did.

'It may have escaped your attention, Monsieur Corbeau,' remarked Kettle, hotly. 'But we have less than twenty hours before the *Parrot* ups her bloomin' anchors and sails away to France and I'm no nearer getting my hands on her than I was yesterday afternoon.'

'And your point is?' Asked Corbeau, with sly

condescension.

'My point. My point, sir?' Said Kettle, argumentatively, dropping his spoon into his soup with a noisy clatter, 'Is simply this, we must do something and do it damn quick or the wretched thing will go without me? My ship, do you hear or was last night's enterprise on the Morass a jape to make us laugh? A fiddle-dee-dee of no consequence, but to amuse you, sir?'

'Yes, quick, indeed,' said Hesta Victoria, gripped in a mindless excitement that hardly knew up from down.

'And what is this …. something you propose? Do you have a plan?' Asked Corbeau, knowing him to be as shallow as the bowl of soup he was now aimlessly stirring with his spoon.

'Well …. Err, no, I don't have a plan. But we can't just sit here and do nothing, *can* we?' He blurted in an irritable confusion, his truculence, beginning to wither under Corbeau's menacing stare, which serpent-like, startled him.

'But my *dear* Kettle, we have done so much already, have we not? That fool Grub may have lost us Kepple last night, but we have his charts and more importantly, his precious signal book and without them, neither he nor the *Parrot* are going anywhere soon. Are they? And all we need now, is the password that will introduce him … no

350

you, as the friend those traitors waiting your arrival next week will ask for.'

'So?' Asked Kettle, his eyes crossed in baffled confusion.

'So?' Answered Corbeau. 'We wait.'

'We wait? We wait for what, exactly?' Countered Kettle, as confused by Corbeau's cryptic rambling as he had been by the charts of the Quiberon Bay and the signal book he had been forced to study all that afternoon. But study them he had with a frenzy and though he was loath to admit it, had memorized most of the important features of that treacherous bit of French coast like no other coast he knew. So much so, even Admiral Bridport, who, at Admiral Crookhampton's suggestion, had granted him an interview that afternoon and remembering the obligation all senior officers have for a relative of one of their own exalted number, deceased though his uncle was, had thought to commend him on his knowledge of the many hazards that were its curse and with the promise if Captain Kepple should be taken ill or is otherwise incommoded in any serious way, the *Parrot* would be his and no others. The perilous *Passage de la Teignouse*, the equally dangerous *Passage des Soers,* the *Cardinal Rocks* and even the deadly*, Four Shoal* on the eastern side of the bay, on which, so many ships had been lost, including HMS *Essex* in 1759.

'We wait for Kepple to make his move,' said a confident Corbeau, teasing Kettle's stupidity.

'And which *move* is that, may I ask?'

Reaching for his wine in a glass that twinkled shards of russet flame in the firelight, Corbeau took a long, slow sip before he answered, much to Kettle's impatient irritation. 'Kepple has three options, none of them the least satisfactory. First, he can try to enlist the help of someone, a *friend* shall we say, who might be persuaded to help him replace what he has so carelessly *lost* without Lord Bridport ever knowing he has. Something I doubt he would forgive what with the mutiny smoldering on, as it will for weeks. We have already seen his first unsuccessful attempt at this ploy.'

'You mean the boy? Dimple? He was sent by Kepple to get his Admiralty papers back?' Asked Hesta Victoria, amazed by her own cleverness and smiling once again at the idea Admiral Bridport thought that filthy common ships boy, an orphan, too, by his own admission, could be related to the Hampshire Dimple's. A family of some note, though not altogether her type, and, who, her mother had once taken tea with. Even if by some strange coincidence, they did share the same name. A coincidence her mother would be much amused to hear, when she got home.

'C'est exact,' cried Corbeau, in uncharacteristic French, delighted and astonished by Hesta Victoria's quite remarkable grasp of the situation. 'We all heard the boy, he was sent here to invite Mister Trompe to supper. A *ruse de guerre,* mes amis. A trick, I feel certain it was that was supposed to flatter our Monsieur Trompe into providing copies of what he has *lost.*

'Do you mean he *knows?'* Asked Kettle, taken aback by a possibility that left him cold with dread.

'Knows *what?'* Growled Corbeau.

'That Trompe brought the charts and signal book here, *to us?* That we stole them and left him and his crew near dead in the bargain? He *knows we,* did it?'

'Kepple knows nothing of our involvement in this business, this hasty plot,' answered Corbeau, coldly. 'If he did, he would have come here himself and with a troop of Marines at his side to arrest us for the scheming *traitors* he would say we are. No, he is clutching at straws as you, British say. And he must clutch a little longer before we are finished with him.'

'So, what does he do next?' Asked Hesta Victoria, breathlessly. 'You said he had three options, did you not?'

'Indeed, I did, my dear Hesta,' said Corbeau, eager to impress his naïve and woolly-headed companions with what he *thought* he knew, which, in truth, was little more than they did. 'With Trompe gone back to London with Lord Spencer's party tonight, tomorrow morning at the very latest, there is no possible chance he will get his papers back from him. So, he must …'

'But can we really be sure Lord Spencer will go back to London, the mutiny is not yet finished, far from it, Pierre,' interrupted Hesta Victoria. 'You heard how angry Admiral Colpoys was when he spoke to the boy and he may yet stay until it is, despite he says he won't?'

'Yes, we cannot be sure Trompe will not betray us yet,' said Kettle with a conspiratorial, appreciative smile at Hesta Victoria that wondered she was so clever.

'*Yes,* there is no doubt, I spoke to Lord Dasheart, barely an hour ago and he reassured me *everyone* is most definitely leaving tonight or early tomorrow morning. Lord Spencer to see the King at Windsor on Sunday, the rest, to London from where they will not return, despite they think the mutiny will last another month.'

'*Lord Dasheart,* oh la, such a wonderfully handsome, boy, I do declare he has broken every young girl's heart in Portsmouth since he came, save my own, of course, which is most faithfully promised to another,' she gushed. An exclamation of love quite lost on Kettle who was just then shoveling a heap of gravy washed, mashed potatoes, twice dipped in his mushroom soup, into his cavernous mouth. 'But so delicate, I declare a puff of wind would blow him over.'

'Indeed,' said Corbeau, impatiently, his ice-cold stare of murderous irritation lost on her as her fingers searched across the plate and dish crowded table for Kettle's hand.

'But what if he doesn't go?' She said, defiantly.

'He will.'

'But what if he comes back?'

'He won't.'

'But how can you be sure?'

'I have made it my business, he won't.'

'But how?'

'I have bribed Lord Dasheart, who hates him to ruin his career and better still, he carries a letter to my sister Madeleine in London that will see him sent so far away, he will never return to bother us again, America. I have suggested where he may prosper if the Indians don't kill him,' he smiled they might.

'America,' she softly murmured the tips of her bony fingers now gently stroking the back of Kettle's hairy hand.

'Yes.'

'But why?'

'Because he is a slinking, useless fool of an *untrustworthy* boy, who may yet, by some silly indiscretion, betray us to his masters in his nervous want to make amends for the wrong he has done Lieutenant Kepple, as he almost did last night. Would have had I not threatened him. Said he would speak to Lord Spencer! Though he knows the hangman's noose will be his only reward for his treacherous betrayal of the King's confidential service, as I have warned him it will.'

'But, of course, I remember now, Pierre, Grub told you he almost called a warning to Lieutenant Kepple in the fog.'

'And would have, had Grub not strangled him to a silence, until he was properly seized up by Dogget and Badger.'

'Better had they killed him, don't you think?' Remarked Kettle with a callous indifference Hesta Victoria little noticed, as she twined her fingers in his, his sneering, horse-like, puss filled spotty chin dripping with gravy.

'Better he didn't,' answered Corbeau, coldly.

'But why not, if he is such a great threat to our enterprise?'

'Because, my dear, Kettle,' he seethed his irritation. 'Had Trompe been murdered, Lieutenant Kepple would have gone straight way to Lord Bridport with news of his own kidnap and robbery this morning shouting conspiracy and murder for all to hear and who would gainsay, he lied with a French invasion and an Irish rebellion expected any time soon and a mutiny to find an answer, too, where no answer exists. Intelligence that would have earned him a commendation for the bravery he most certainly showed in escaping their clutches and fresh copies of his stolen papers, to boot. But Trompe wasn't murdered and Kepple didn't go to Lord Bridport, so he has, but two options left. One, he can throw himself on the mercy of Admiral Bridport, in which case he will be ruined by the very loss he must own up, too. Or two, he can sail without them and trust to fate he isn't sunk by his own gallant navy before he ever reaches the French coast.'

'And which one of these two options will he choose?' Asked Kettle, reassured by Corbeau's confident manner.

'He will throw himself on Admiral Bridport's mercy, who will arrest him on the spot for the careless, over promoted nave, he is. What else, can he do?' He answered, with a superiority that was, as we will shortly see, misguided. 'And when he does, my dear Kettle you must be ready to act and quickly if you are to have the *Parrot* for your own, which I intend you will.

Chapter 21

The Bottomless Well Of Time
Opens On A Sun Kissed, Dreamy Sea
To Take The Princess Tefnut Far
From All She Ever Knew

Mid-afternoon late September 1336BCE, the Red Sea

Princess Tefnut sat cross-legged on the tall, four legged, ornately carved wooden transom that dominated the stern quarter of the single masted Arab Dhow, above the mighty tiller. That for three days now had sailed her and her five faithful bodyguards from the Red Sea port of Massawa, towards the Gulf of Aqaba. Still two hundred miles north of where they were, but so close the captain boasted he could smell the dessert wind that blew across the Sinai Peninsula in hot, sandy gusts towards them. Though no wind had blown that long, hot day or the day before and they lay almost becalmed on a sea that was an empty, eerie, almost silent still. Save for the creak of wood and ropes and the musical chant of the twenty oarsmen who rowed them on with cheerful song.

It was little more than six weeks since they turned from the Nile and sailed into the swollen with summer rains, River Atbara and under the cover of darkness, some days later, climbed a gently rising, rocky gorge thick with vegetation to begin their slow march to the sea.

But not before they had watched in fearful fascination their brave Captain set his trap for the *Drummers*, the next morning. Who, confident he couldn't escape them now, had followed him in a constantly drumming procession, knowing the muddy tributary he had foolishly turned into was no escape, but a trap that would soon kill him and all his crew. But most of all the princess Tefnut, whose death they had oath sworn would be her end; child or no child they would kill her.

The place he chose was a sharp, west turning bend in a narrow, echoing gorge of shimmering cliffs too steep to climb, where the river suddenly tapered to a bottle neck, barely twenty yards wide, between the gravel banks that hugged their shrub lined shore. Where a hundred crocodiles, bigger than any she had ever seen, lazed their day in the blistering heat that stung her eyes to tears as she watched in terrified silence the drama that was about to unfold from the heights above, though her guards urged her she shouldn't.

With the Drummers, half a mile behind and

their Captains trap concealed by a low escarpment covered in elephant grass and thorny acacia trees, they saw him quickly turn his boat side on to block the channel, anchor it fast and drop his single mast, as if it was broken in some dreadful underwater collision. Ten minutes later the *Drummers* rounded the bend and with a scream of hideous delight that hardly dared believe their good luck to find him *run aground, began* their attack without the least thought for the ambush it was.

But as they did, the first of a dozen well aimed fire arrows, shot by two of his bravest men from the cover of the river bank struck both their tinder dry sails and set them ablaze. But fearless of the flames that now engulfed them the *Drummers* came on and on, their war drums beating louder and louder their want to kill their enemies, until they drove their sharp pointed bows, deep into the swollen belly of the Captain's boat in a roaring, grinding buckle of splinters that saw her instantly wrecked. And as she was, the crocodiles slipped into the brown river to wait their feast of human flesh.

All day long she watched the glow of fire and listened to the clash of steel, the beat of drums and the baleful screams of wounded and dying men, until, near midnight, the river fell silent. By morning, the only signs of battle they could see were the charred and broken, skeleton remains of the three boats, now fallen awkwardly on their sides on the gravel. But of the hundreds of men who sailed on them the day before, there was no sign, not even the clothes they wore.

A day later, they met some friendly tribesmen, Beja they called themselves, from beneath their thick beards and bleached white turbans, who were watering their camels in the river twenty miles upstream. Who seeing they were Egyptians, the masters of the world, and she a princess, bowed their humble obedience before their swords and guided them to the sea, never asking who they were or why it was they travelled.

Midsummer morning 1335BCE, the Pyramid of Khufu

'Tefnut, my sister, where are you, *now?'* Moaned Kiya, aware of a sudden gentle stirring beneath the cold stone stairs she now sat upon.

A soft, but growing ever louder, high-pitched incantation of echoing sound, which, note by climbing note, in barely a minute, trembled and pulsed to a noise so fiercely loud, coming from deep within the pyramid below her, she had to stop her ears with both her cupped hands to silence its now unbearable, pain. But no sooner had she, then the noise stilled to a barely audible whisper, followed by an intense, expectant thrall and when it had, changed again into a mute beam of pure red light. Which, rose through the sides of the largest of the two enneagons etched into the polished, black stone floor in a foot-high dance, like grass in a gentle wind. And when it had, grew in steady, rhythmic inches into a nine-sided pyramid until it pierced the evil Eye of Seth and with such a force the mirror she had earlier placed there, fell to the floor, and broke into several pieces, as it returned upon itself in a pillar of orange-white light, so bright it blinded her.

A light driven by the glow of the morning sun to an unimaginable intensity it could not be stopped by anything and fell, without her seeing it did, through the sides of the second, smaller enneagon to find the bottom of the pyramid like a knife through melted butter. Fell, as it was planned it should to a secret chamber known only to the priests of the Temple of Khufu and the void it hid. Fell on their command and at great risk to them, as Queen Nefertiti, only an hour woken and in no mood to be disobeyed by anyone after her murderous night's work, demanded their Chief Priest, Sahura, he must and when he did, opened the Temple Void of Khufu to a world yet to come.

Frightened out of all reason by the light, which now filled the tomb in an arrow straight shaft, striking, as it was never intended it should, the ruins of her broken mirror in flint-like sparks that struck the walls in a kaleidoscope of dazzling colours, she ran to the bottom of the stairs and crouched in the darkest corner, the Apis wand held tight in her two hands and once again saw the princess Tefnut in the sun-disc, but saw her through the Eye of Horus, as if it was her own.

But this time sitting cross-legged on the flat wooden transom of an Arab dhow sailing on a tranquil blue sea. Though, when last, she looked, a few minute ago, she was racing down the Nile pursued by the army of the soldiers of the Priests of Amun-Ra; the *Drummers* she called them, a name that suited them well.

Closing her eyes, she calmed herself, as she knew she must, before looking again into the sun-disc and the eye that now moved like her own. 'I see you. I see you my heart, but where are you, my love?' She groaned her frustration. 'How can we be together when you are so far away? Tell me please, my darling, where are you, now? Tell me what am I to do? I really don't know what to do?' She franticly called, her voice an achingly sad lament she could do no more than watch her, as if through a tiny window. But as she did, a chance spark of mirror reflected light struck one of the shabti statues on the gold, inlaid table at the top of the stairs, where, in an instant, it was reflected, in a cat's-cradle of intensely magnified light onto all the others. Until, it struck the statue of her son Tutankhamun and then the statue of her sister Tefnut still lying on the floor in a skitter and when it did, pierced the Sacred Eye from over her bent shoulder and struck the dhow in an explosive sunburst. 'AYEEEE,' she screamed, seeing it was gone and in its place a worm-like, writhing black hole had opened above the now, storm tossed, heaving sea to another time and another place. But no sooner did she, then the light contracted in a second explosive sunburst, which filled the stairs in a vortex that in an instant of disbelief lifted her into a coal black sky so fast it left her breath-less.

Mid-afternoon late September 1009, the Hudson River just north of present day Fort Edward, land of the Iroquois Indian Beaver Clan

'Where am I?' Asked Kiya, finding her-self suddenly and incomprehensibly standing on a narrow shelf of stone in a deep wooded canyon beside a roaring, rock strewn, surging waterfall, crowded everywhere about by fiercely, howling, yellow and black painted, near naked savages wearing only a red loincloth, much as slaves of Egypt did. Who, seeing no more of her than the lucent sheen she now appeared to be, against the wet stone wall behind her, had in their grasp a man of great size, quite unlike themselves, on the opposite bank.

A long haired, heavily bearded, brutish man with a whirl of tattoos on his blood-spattered face, dressed in a coat of iron rings that fell to his knees, who screamed he would kill them all in a tongue she had never heard before, but understood, as if it was her own.

As he did, and violently struggled his desperate want to escape the men who with the greatest physical effort pinioned his arms and kneeling legs, as a Shaman[204] of their tribe with three white eagle feathers fixed like a fan in his tufted, close shaven head and fallen over his left ear to touch his bare shoulder, came up behind him and struck him a mighty blow on the base of his skull with a stone axe and kicked him from the high ledge they stood upon into the narrow river gorge below. Bound hand and foot he sank like a stone in the heavy armour he wore unconscious into the surging, brown torrent and as he did the Indians cried in one terrifying voice, TARHUHIAWAKU, TARHUHIAWAKU, TARHUHIAWAKU. The same word

365

the girl in the red blanket had called out to Tefnut. Their voices becoming a chant that echoed louder and louder through the valley, until it reached the highest mountain.

Though she hardly knew why she did, but knowing by some strange instinct she must, she stepped unseen into the water and seeing him fallen lifeless at the bottom of the river, his face and winged helmet half buried in the pebble and sand, picked him up by some magic she knew not how and in the blink of an eye, set him down in a shallow, flower filled, mountain glade beside a gurgling, pebble filled stream, fringed with tall, grass and a profusion of blue, yellow and red flowers that perfumed the air the sweet aroma of late summer, the same glade, she dared believe, she had seen Tefnut answer the call of the girl. A glade surrounded all around by trees so dense and tall, they climbed one upon the other to the snow-capped, mountain peaks she everywhere now saw.

Mid-afternoon late September 1009, the Adirondack Mountains some miles from Fort Edward

So dense and so tall she again thought it must the fabled Land of Punt? A land her husband had often talked about, the source of the sacred Nile, the life blood of their fertile land, where a man or woman could be lost in half a minute if they left the forest path and where monsters roamed, devouring all, who could not find their way out.

So, dense, and tall she could barely see the cloudless, corn-blue sky above their swaying tops, the sunlight a radiant dapple of haze and shadow on her face, or a finger-like fan that burst the never-ending canopy of vibrant greens in shafts of mote speckled light. Their giant, snaking, bursting roots entwining, folding, braiding, lifting, pulling, and splitting the rich red earth and grey stone that everywhere poked through the dark undergrowth in a thousand sculpted forms. Moss and fern covered mounds, ridges, peaks, terraces, and perilously deep clefts that fell in a lazy calm with the stream she now stood beside to some far-off place, hinting some ancient city lay hidden there.

Crumbling stacks of granite rose like statues from the mountain side straining their want to be free of the trees and sticky vines that held them fast in their timeless embrace, like dancers caught in a music that wouldn't stop, their weathered old faces turned to look at her, as she stared at the man lying beside her; now hungrily gulping the precious air that filled his lungs. Each one as tall as the two great pylons that guarded the gate to

Khufu's Temple, she last night passed beneath, swept clean by the boys, who bowed their heads before her as she passed. And now all of them dead, their throats cut by cruel hands and drained of blood, their bodies fed to the Nile crocodiles, their once lively, quarrelsome, laughing bones crunched and stripped of all their meat in half a minute.

And in the far distance, high above the tree line, bluffs and soaring buttresses of blue-grey stone stabbed the sky and scarred the mountains like fortress walls, where birds swooped and soared on hot thermals. A place like no other she had seen before or would again, she sighed, the world was so beautiful, but so cruel. And forty feet above her head was the same ledge and the same flower and frond draped cave beside a narrow waterfall she saw the girl, she felt certain it was, but now almost hidden in the cleft of a red tree, which grew above the cave. A tree bigger and wider than all those around it nestled into the scooped-out mountain side, its massive, curving roots draped like the legs of a Red Sea octopus around the ledge. Which spilled a waterfall from an unseen pool into the stream she now bent to dip her fingers in, her hand rested on a second, red tree, one of two that formed an archway into the glade over a shallow pond and saw it was marked with symbols she couldn't read, a message or a warning so new it couldn't be very old, perhaps no more than a year or two.

'Who are you?' She asked, dripping water from her cupped hand onto the man's scratched and grizzled face, as he gasped and gulped himself awake, not for one second realizing the terrible mistake she had just made in saving his wicked life. Carried to that place not by the power of her wand, the power of good, the power of her husband Akhenaten, but by the same evil power that gives Montard his strength, the power of Seth and Temple Void of Khufu that in the light that filled her tomb carried her step daughter, the princess Meritaten, the slave Raneb and the son of Sahura, the boy priest Anutet, to this same place earlier that day. Though their stay was brief and very nearly disastrous; would have been had Billy, Duffy and Lemmy not helped Meritaten, escape the Indians who attacked her. A mistake that would confuse her friends with her enemies until this story ends, confounding their every attempt to help her; Ethan, Isaac, and Indie, most of all, but Tom, Marie-Ange, and Polly, too.

'Tostig,' he blurted, cowed by the sight of her strangely painted eyes, her sheening black hair and the rich jewels and regalia she wore no less than the ordeal he had just endured. Which he grinned with a mad man's amazing sense of relief, he had quite astonishingly escaped, though not with the Totem of the Iroquois Indian, Beaver Clan he had several days before stolen, the Totem of Tarhuhiawaku their heathen god.

Which was carved into the image of an old man seated on his haunches, they worshipped like a god, his thin bare legs and small moccasined feet protruding beneath the red blanket he wore over his narrow and stooped shoulders, his two clenched fists rested upright on his bare knees, one holding the pipe of peace in the claw of his gnarled old fingers, the other the tomahawk of war. His face deep wrinkled and expressionless beneath his creased and hooded brow, his white painted eyes staring back at anyone who looked at him with a searching gaze they could not hold, his large bent nose a haughty reminder he was the first Shaman of their tribe and with three white eagle feathers fixed in his shaven, tufted head and fallen to his left shoulder to say he truly was. His lips thin and tight shut, his chin firm, his sunken chest spare, the gaunt spread of his ribs showing he had known hunger and suffering more than any man should.

A totem rumoured to show the way to a great treasure he now longed to have, if the ritual of midsummer was followed. The treasure of his Viking Chief, Lief Erikson, he was certain, who left for home five years ago.

'*Tostig?*' She said, freeing the ropes that bound his hands and feet so tightly she had to cut them free with the knife he wore in his belt, which she hid in her cloak.

'Yes, Tostig, son of Ulfarr, Captain of a hundred spearmen,' he proudly boasted, as he at last found his breath and sat bolt upright beside her his leather booted foot dipped in the pond, his eyes suspiciously fixed on the gold torque wand she carried in her hand, which sparkled in the sun that bathed her face in flickering shadows. 'Vassal lord of Leif Ericson[205] whose lands these are in the name of the Viking brotherhood we both serve,' he boasted yet again, pointing with a sweep of his massive, hairy hand the great mountain range of tall trees that lifted and fell all around them as far as the eye could see. His, eyes for the briefest moment finding the gently sloping meadow beyond the thinning trees, three hundred yards to their left, where nine, bleached white, colourfully painted, Indian tepees sprawled the furthest bank of the stream that cut its middle from top to bottom. A thin smoke from a fire curling into the sky, the litter of dead bodies they hid, still lying where they fell, unseen from that distance. As was the body of the strangely clothed black man who

371

helped him when he fell from his startled horse that morning, Raneb, he heard him called by the *boy* before he died beneath the ledge in front of them, his body concealed in the thicket. Struck a dozen times with axe, knife and spear by the Indians who thought he was, his *friend*, though he had never seen him before, his sandaled foot still visible in a cleft of rock, but only if you knew where to look. As were the broken arrows stuck fast in the trees all around them, evidence of the brief, but bloody battle that raged there that morning. The ambush that killed his men, who he promised he would avenge

'Tostig,' she whispered, and as she did felt a strange, electric tug upon her skin that knew she must go.

'Yes, lady, Tostig a common name among my people.'

'Then take yourself safe from this place, Tostig,' she said kindly, 'to your lord before the savages find you are not murdered as they intended, but remember this, my name is Queen Kiya and sometime soon I will come for you and when I do, remember the life I gave you this day and the debt you now owe me, which you must repay me a hundred fold, for if you don't I will kill you as easily as I saved you from the savages.

'Yes, lady, I will remember it always and oath

swear I will repay this debt in full,' he blurted, as she disappeared, lifted into the sky in a needle point of light that left him trembling with wonder and dread. *The second oath of duty he had sworn to a girl like her in less than four hours,* he hardly believed it was true, *and in this very same place, the place where the Indians captured him, and dragged him off to the slaughter they planned. The first, who called his protection in the name of Queen Nefertiti, who appeared out of nowhere with her servants on the ledge of rock in front of him, which he knew hid a stone carved wall to a cave behind the flowers that draped its front, wearing a dress like no other he had seen before. A dress similar, but not the same as Kiya's, decorated with an intricate fish-scale pattern of gold hexagons with red flowers sewn in their middle, which was trimmed at the neck and ankles with a pattern of red, blue, white and black, inch wide geometric squares. A goddess, he was certain she was, as Queen Kiya was.*

Mid-afternoon late September 1795, the Red Sea

'What was that?' Asked Tefnut, shading her eyes as a fierce bright light enveloped the dhow in a haze that lasted barely a second to peer at the distant ship she now saw in front of them a mile or two away, where no ship was before.

'It is a ship, princess,' called the dhows captain from the deck, the sweat heavy on his brow and bearded cheeks, his voice betraying nothing of the fear he felt to see it suddenly and mysteriously appear, when all before him a moment ago was an empty, welcoming sea.

'Mmm,' wondered, Tefnut, blinking her eyes to see it was a sleek, two masted Arab dhow, much like their own, but three times bigger and with a hooded cruel eye painted on either side of her black bow that made her look frightening. 'Where on earth did that come from, Captain, I never saw it before and I have never taken my eyes from the sea, not for half a second?'

'Nor I, princess,' he replied, making his way to the bows, his body swathed in an iridescent rainbow of electric light, neither Tefnut nor anyone else saw, so much did it cover them all in its fantastically luminous hold.

'Who are they?' Asked Tefnut, now climbed down beside him and screwing her eyes to better see the dhow in the glare of the waning light it seemed to spin and flicker.

'I don't know, princess,' answered one of her guards, seeing the score of armed men who now crowded her starboard rails and who seemed to be working the mouth of a strange iron machine to point at them.

'Are they the *Drummers* come to take us back to Egypt?'

'Maybe,' he cautiously answered, struck by the design of the boat, its marvelously crafted wooden hull, so straight and true, no simple axe could make it. Its towering masts, so smooth and round, its great red, flapping sails, its taut hard rigging, fashioned in a forest of ropes, and its strange markings, the like of which he had never seen before on any sea he had sailed.

'What are they doing?' She asked, wiping her shaved head with a *red* cotton handkerchief as she knelt behind the heavy wooden sides of the dhow to find her wig, which she remembered she had left by the stern post.

'I don't know princess,' he answered, as the deafening roar of cannon and musket fire swept the deck from end to end in a blinding roaring, orange- red flash and killed him before he fell to the broken deck.

Twenty minutes later cruel hard grasping hands pulled her unconscious from the water, *the only one left alive,* she dreamt a hundred times she heard them say. And seeing she was a girl barely half grown and a *slave* already by the soot blackened collar she wore about her neck, threw her into the hold. Where she lay for nearly a month in a nightmare of sleep and waking confusion until they found their longed-for destination; Zanzibar. The richest slave port in the Indian Ocean, where they sold her without bargain to an English sea captain who thought she would make an ornamental house slave for some great London house.

Chapter 22

Corbeau Feels The Hurt
Of A Treasure Lost

8.30pm Friday 21 April 1797

It was just after eight-thirty that evening when Corbeau left the party in the dining room below and went back to his room and discovered to his shock and disbelief the charts and signal book he had stolen from Billy, were gone. Had been taken from the small, Rosewood and iron trunk in which he kept them. A locked trunk and so well crafted by the Templar Knights who made it, it could not be opened without its *only* key. A key he knew with an absolute certainty had never left his pocket and where it still was.

In a fit of near uncontrollable rage, he searched his room from top to bottom like a demon possessed for the least sign or clue to the thief's identity, though he had long guessed, who it was. Throwing the pillows, sheets and covers from his bed in an untidy heap onto the floor beneath the mullioned[206] windows which overlooked the stable yard at the back of the inn. Where, even now, Lord Spencer's magnificent coach was making ready to go, his four big horses harnessed between the jingling shafts, his carriage lamps lit and his great quantity of luggage packed on the footboard at the back, where his servant sat in the dickey box.[207]

But finding nothing, but a twist of frayed and greasy *red* cotton ribbon - the remnants of Tefnut's cotton handkerchief, sank to his knees on the polished oak floor and called out his hate filled revenge on Lieutenant William Kepple and all those who helped him. For who else could have planned such an audacious *crime*, but him and that ungrateful, mop-headed wretch of a servant girl, Polly Perkins, whose ribbon he now held between his elegant fingers and that artful, black faced scoundrel, Tom Dimple. Who had not only taken the charts and signal book, but something else, too? Something far more important than the Admiralty papers Kepple needed if he was to sail tomorrow. An object of intriguing, if incomprehensible design and purpose that was once a small and insignificant part of Mister Beattie's vast collection of objet d'art and antique curios, the Count de Montard had expressed a passing wish to see. In advance of the many other things he had assured Madeleine he could easily auction and sell in Paris later that year. The new revolutionary Republicans being as rich, avaricious and pleasure seeking as the old Royalists once were, as he knew to his heartfelt joy they were. The inventory of which had already caused an excited stir amongst collectors, who had promised a small fortune for what he once had. A fortune the Count had promised would be theirs, if this first curio, a piece of a heavy gold plate, he was charged to send to him, was all they had described it to be.

A happy end to the death he had accidentally brought about by the liberal use of the opium and arsenic[208] that killed him over several long winter weeks, which, sadly was enough to kill a horse - but how was he to know that? Though his sister Madeleine, his unhappy *wife*, thankfully didn't know he had, thought the apothecary's draughts she every night gave him helped him sleep long enough to copy his secret Admiralty documents! Would be horrified to learn he had, even if it was a reckless mistake! Though she hated the penny-pinching, bookish little weasel with a passion, so much did she long to be free of him.

A husband who never was, despite the brilliantly forged papers that bound them so uncomfortably together in matrimony. Papers, which easily fooled the Lincoln's Inn[209] lawyer, who was his executor, enough to give her his cottage in Primrose Hill, his collection, and the little fortune he possessed, without quibble or fee when he died and with a smile on his face that wished her well.

Though they belonged to another more than her, his much put-upon nephew, Lauder Trompe. Just one more reason, he sighed, to be rid of him.

For more than an hour he paced his room in a fury of indecision so great it twisted his perfectly sculpted face to an ugly sea of dark emotions. His thick, black brows, the lustrous arch of his emerald green eyes, creased to a knot of morbid dread that narrowed them to a squint beside his blade-like, flaring nose. His high boned, aristocratic cheeks, lightly browned by the Mediterranean sun - his unwelcome home for so many years, pale and gaunt with the worry the Count should hear of his inexcusable loss; his failure. A failure he could not endure - would not endure, not for a second. His lips, in repose so condescending and so mocking of the world he wanted to dominate and control, drawn to a thin and humorless slash, which spoke better than words the revenge he would have on Captain Kepple. Must have, if he was to return his family to the wealth and power they once, long ago enjoyed!

When at last the sharp edge of his fear and anger was dulled by the headstrong plan he had contrived to get the plate back, he drank a large glass of brandy, washed his face in the basin of water the upstairs maid had laid out for his morn-ing toilet, dressed himself in his cloak and hat, took a loaded pistol from his bedside drawer and with quick and urgent strides left the inn by the backstairs and went in search of Jemmy Grub.

But long before he did, Tom and Polly had reached the relative safety of the still crowded Sally Port, where they sat down together on an iron, rope bound bollard, to catch their breath. 'We did it Poll, we really did,' said Tom, between wheezing breaths of excitement, hardly able to believe the good luck that had so easily given her the charts and the signal book she had set out to find with so many doubts and trepidations.

'Yes, we did, *Miss Tom,*' said Polly, bending to tickle and pet Hesta Victoria's lop eared, brindle, white and black, Staffordshire bull terrier puppy. Which had followed her from the inn with a boisterously cheerful bark, now dancing at her heels his urgent want to be picked up and cuddled. 'And without anyone seeing we did, 'septin' this daft old thin' and you ain't goin' to tell no one, are you *Mister Pitt?*' Well not just then, he wasn't, she sighed, as she picked him up onto her lap and calmed him to a floppy, nuzzling sausage of contented bliss in half a second.

Hardly able to rest longer than the half minute it took to get her breath back and anxious to be gone as quick as ever she could and with many a furtive glance over her shoulders to see if they were followed, Tom stood up. And with Corbeau's heavy, painfully digging in her back, leather satchel, dancing on her back like a camel's wobbly hump, began to walk the length of the pier in search of a boat to take *her* back to the *Parrot.* Which she hardly recognised in the dimming light, but knew she had two masts and a bent beaked parrot for a figurehead under her bowsprit.

Quickly passing the Round Tower, she hurried to find the Quebec Hotel and the stone stairs that dropped to the sea beside it, but there was no boat to take her back to be got there. Moving on through the crowds that surged about her she came to the Star and Garter Inn, the haunt of every Lieutenant in the fleet and so suspicious of her seaman's dress, she ran to find the Toll House on the Point, beside the floating bridge. But seeing nothing there, came hurrying back upon herself, passing Polly as she did, who smiled and waved to see her once again. Reaching the Kings Stairs, twenty yards further on, she hid beside the salt stained wheels of a yellow painted bathing machine, which asked a shilling for a day's hire in letters of faded red, blue, and green. Until she saw, a good-sized sailing dinghy come to the bottom of the weed clogged steps below her feet in a flurry of falling sails and noisy calls and climbed down to hail her skipper. A grumpy old tar with a toothless grin and beard so thick and so long you could hide a good-sized cat in it and in an instant, was offered the passage she needed for a sixpence she didn't yet have.

With her fare agreed, she was just about to step aboard, when she remembered Polly and with a guilty ache that knew the *Parrot* was no place for a little *girl like her*, begged the captain some moments delay to say her goodbye. But as she turned, saw her waiting at the top of the steps with a look of deep suspicion etched hard on her soft, round, delightfully, chubby face. 'I HAVE TO GO NOW POLL,' she loudly called, above the raucous squawk and screech of the gulls, which hovered over her head. 'THE SOONER I HAVE THESE PAPERS SAFE ABOARD THE *PARROT*, THE BETTER. AND THE SOONER YOU'RE SAFE HOME WHERE YOU BELONG, THE BET-TER, TOO,' she mumbled an awkwardly silly fare-well. Which fortunately for Billy and everyone else aboard the *Parrot*, Polly was just about to refuse, as only she could.

'I'm comin' with you, *Miss,* no matter what you say,' she barked, with a look of cold determina-tion in her lustrous black eyes that would accept no refusal from her or anyone else for that matter. 'Me and Mister Pitt is comin' with you, so don't you be saying no different, *Miss Tom.* 'Cos, I ain't listenin' to a word you say, unless it's to say we can. So, make up your mind double damn quick, *Miss Tom*, 'cos I ain't goin' back to Miss, high and mighty, Hesta Victoria so she can whip me black and blue, 'cos she thinks she can and no one to say no different. Oh no. I ain't goin' back to her so help me god, *Miss Tom*. I'm comin' with you. I am. Isn't that right Mister Pitt me dear chap? We two is goin' with you, *Miss Tom*. Oh, yes we are me lovely,' she winked. 'We's goin' with, *Miss Tom* and we ain't never comin' back again, not now and not ever, are we?'

'You *can't,*' said Tom, desperate to stop Polly's playful, but not less threatening use of the word Miss in every sentence, before the boatman or someone else heard her.

'Oh, yes I can,' answered Polly, with a gleeful smile. 'And I will, you see if I don't.' And without more ado she slid past Tom, almost tipping her into the sea, and found her seat in the dinghy beside the Captain.'

An hour later Nipper Ogden and Dancer Dyke were hauling them both through the larboard entry port by the scruff of their necks to the obvious relief of Duffy and the wide-eyed surprise of Trucky Spears, who was the Officer of the Watch that evening and very proud he was, too.

As he stood beside the ram rod straight, red faced and blustering, Marine Sergeant Finch, newly promoted to that rank just an hour ago and enjoying it as nothing else before.

Who looked at them both with a mixture of distaste and disbelief, but Polly most of all, who he thought a most unexpected visitor so late that dark night.

An impish looking *girl* of indecent small size and foreign appearance by the swarthy look of her dark skin, who wore a rag of red ribbon loosely tied in her short curly black hair, a faded, several times patched, blue cotton dress that poked the rest of that dirty rag from a side pocket and a horribly grubby with goodness knows what, grey pinny. Which, like the black, scuffed shoes she wore was two sizes too big for her chubby body. Who, despite he glared at her with a frosty disapproval had the impudence to wink a smirking grin at him, before dropping Mister Pitt onto the newly scrubbed deck, where he arched his leg and watered it.

'Permission to come aboard,' piped Tom, knowing Trucky would not refuse her even if the fat, red faced Sergeant hoped he would. 'And begging your pardon, Mister Spears, but would you be so good as to pay the boatman the six pence he wants for the ride he's given us. Though I think that's exceedingly generous for the short run he's made and twice taking us where we didn't want to go and only finding you because I showed him?'

'Why, yes, Tom,' agreed Trucky, instantly forgetting the officer's dignity he was finding so hard to master, much to the astonishment of Nipper and Dancer, who could hardly believe her cheek. 'I have one here, I think. But, then, maybe not,' he smiled, as he searched his pockets for the silver sixpence he knew was there; jacket, waistcoat and breeches. 'Found it,' he chirped, glad he had amongst all the junk that cluttered them, throwing the boatman his fare the moment he did.

'You'd best come with me, Tom,' said Duffy, with a look at Trucky that politely asked his permission to take them both to the Captain. A look that was answered with a nod and a grimace of foreboding that said: *rather you than me, Mister Duff. Rather you than me.*

'Where have you been, Tom?' Snapped Billy, angrily, his face dark with fatigue and worry at her disappearance. Who, with Lieutenant Robinson at his side was studying the makeshift map of the Channel they had both drawn in the half light of his day cabin. A chart that would, at the very least, get them to Ushant[210] in a day or two, if the wind was fair. And if it did they would hug the French coast until they reached the Quiberon, a few days later, by Friday the 28 he dearly hoped. If his rendezvous was to be kept. A madcap scheme, but the only one he could think of.

Irritated by Billy's angry tone and thinking him an ungrateful little toad for speaking to her so harshly in front of Duffy and Sam, who knew how much she liked him, Tom dropped the satchel she had been carrying on her now painfully stiff and sore back onto his map. 'I have them,' she cried, in a beaming gush of triumph. 'I have them, Captain Kepple, *sir.* Though I must say, I owe poor Mister Trompe an apology for all the nasty things I said about him. Him being so amazingly helpful in getting them out of Corbeau's trunk, where they were hidden and us out of the Fountain Inn, with no one seeing us. But I have them, Captain Kepple, *sir.* I have them so you needn't worry.'

'Have what, Tom?' Asked Billy, exasperated by her mocking respect and feeling she was once again getting the better of him and wondering how that was possible?

'I have your charts and signal book,' she said, opening the heavy satchel in a hurry of excitement that left Billy, Sam, and Duffy speechless with amazement. 'The ones Corbeau and Kettle stole from you, well they didn't, but they got someone else who did.'

'*Who?'* Asked Billy, in a daze of confusion that just then noticed a delightfully grinning, Polly and an oddly twitching, Mister Pitt, peeping at him from behind Duffy's back.

'*Corbeau* and *Kettle,* Midshipman Kettle, who brought you from Antigua last Sunday and Corbeau, who is a French spy, though he pretends he isn't,' she thrilled.

'*What?*'

'We have them here, in this satchel, Billy. Poll and me, oh this is Poll, by the way,' she said, pulling her from behind Duffy. *We* stole them back! Right from under their noses! We stole them back,' she babbled, spilling the satchel onto the table. See, I told you we did.'

'Yes, I see you have,' stuttered Billy, relieved beyond words, though, he tried hard not to show he was, to see his charts and the small, leather bound folio of papers, no more than a half inch thick, which was his Admiralty signal book. Which she flicked open.

'But how?' Asked Billy, astonished by the sudden, miraculous change in his misfortune and working hard to keep the utter and complete delight he felt for her from creasing his face into the broadest grin imaginable. A grin that he knew would do much to undermine the severe ticking off he planned to give her when they were next alone, if they were ever alone, again?

Without more ado, Tom, who had guessed

something of her fate from the perplexed look of grateful thanks and indecision on Billy's face, told her amazing tale. How she had gone back to the Fountain Inn. How she was confronted by Lord Spencer's party, which drew an audible gasp of awe and disbelief from Sam and Duffy, who couldn't believe she had spoken to the great man, let alone Admiral Colpoys and Admiral Lord Bridport. How she and Polly, had broken into Corbeau's room, a French émigré escaped from Paris, or so he claimed he was, but in truth was the spy she earlier said he was, who had by some ruse attached himself to Admiral Crookhampton's household late last year, but more important than this, how he had blackmailed Mister Trompe to help him, who had come to their aid in the nick of time.

Chapter 23

Lauder Trompe Finds The Key
To A Secret Treasure

7.14pm Friday 21 April 1797

Entering Corbeau's room on the second floor, Tom and Polly quickly found the polished Rosewood trunk, Polly said was the hiding place for Billy's charts and signal book and set about opening it. But despite their many attempts using a hairgrip, a quill a pen, an elegant brass shoehorn, a devilishly sharp paper knife and a pewter pot they bashed it with until its handle broke clean off, they couldn't budge the lid, or open the lock a fraction, which appeared to be the most cunning mechanical device ever invented by man to keep a body out.

Exhausted by their efforts and thoroughly disheartened by their failure and thinking Corbeau would soon return and catch them there, they had all, but given up. When the door opened with an eerie, heart stopping creak and Mister Trompe, slowly tiptoed into the room with a lighted stub of candle held, outstretched in his trembling hand, the strange shadows it cast moving like phantoms on the whitewashed walls.

It was a moment before he saw them seated, cross-legged on the curved lid of Corbeau's trunk in an eyes-closed cuddle of frozen panic, caught like statues in the searching, yellow glow of his guttering flame. But when he did, such was his spine-chilling shock, he blew it out with a squeal of desperate fright and when he had, farted, a noisy, never-ending fart of panic.

'*What?*' He gasped, pretending he hadn't, though he still did. The light of their own candle on the floor beside the bed, illuminating the strangest buttock-clenching dance they had ever seen, as he tried, without audible success, to still his bowels. A dance that brought such a fit of giggles from them both they fell on the floor beside him with an exaggerated bump.

'*It's you?*' Gasped Polly with a wicked grimace.

'Yes, it's me, Lauder,' he meekly chirped, stepping back to the still open door.

'What are you doin' in here, fartin' like an old donkey to frighten good folk in their sleep, you, vulgar boy?'

'Don't know,' he replied, reaching for the round brass handle.

'*Stop,*' she barked, seeing him pull the door an inch wider open. 'Don't you dare run away from me I've not finished with you yet, not by a long chalk, no I ain't. Now shut that door and quietly now. Good. Now come here and tell me what it is you are doin' creepin' about in Monsieur Corbeau's private room. And don't you dare tell a fib, 'cos I'll know it if you do, won't I Tom?'

'Yes,' said Tom, amazed at the nerve of the girl.

'I've come for me papers,' he mumbled.

'What papers?'

'Secret papers, Miss. The ones Monsieur Corbeau took from me yesterday and then again this morning and never bothering to ask me if he could and now he won't give them back, no matter I've told him three times he must before I go back to London with Lord Spencer, tonight,' he babbled. Hot tears of morbid fear and aching frustration streaming down his puckered face.

'Admiralty papers?' Asked Tom, rightly guessing they were.

'Yes. Have you seen them?'

'No,' she answered, perplexed.

'I was working on them yesterday morning in the parlor, as Lord Dasheart said I must, though it was his work I did and he stole them. Came up beside me and took them from me bag like they belonged to him, which they don't. And if I don't get them back, Mister Nepean will be ever so angry with me, what with Lord Dasheart telling Lord

Spencer what a damnable fool I am and him a lazy dog of a stuck-up boy, no better than me.

'*Oh,* those papers,' said Tom, realising they were some others and not Billy's.

'You won't tell on me, Miss, will you?'

'Maybe. Maybe not,' growled Polly, an evil grin stretched across her face.

'*Maybe?*' He wailed, collapsing into the chair beside the thick-curtained four poster bed in a second pitiful sob.

'Polly, you ought to be ashamed of yourself, now look what you've gone and done to the poor boy, you, *bad* little girl.'

It took the better part of three minutes and their best, soothing, cooing, calming, comforting words to convince him they wouldn't report him to Lord Spencer and have him arrested by the Watch for *treason* and hung in Newgate prison before the year was out. 'You won't ever tell on me, Miss,' he blurted, at long last.

'No,' said Tom, who, to her surprise had grown rather fond of the boy in the few minutes she had known him, as she knew Billy liked him. A boy who was neither the thief, the liar, or the traitorous scoundrel she thought he was. Was just a much put upon timid boy.

'Oh, thank you. Oh, thank you. Thank you so very much. But can I go now,' he farted again, 'before I am missed?'

'Haven't you forgotten something, Mister Trompe? Not least your manners?' Asked Tom, holding her nose with two, pincer-like fingers, making more of the smell than there really was.'

'Forgotten? Forgotten what?'

'Your papers, you, silly goose?'

'Papers? Oh of course. But I don't know where they are and I fear there is no time to look for them now, Lord Dasheart or Lord Spencer will call for me soon.'

'Could they be in here, perhaps?' She asked with a sly cunning that made Polly smile to see it so artfully done. 'Seems the sort of place *he* might have put them, don't you think? It being as stronger as some banker's safe.'

'Yes,' he answered, kneeling beside her, and stroking the lid of the trunk with a hint of *recognition* that would have to wait another week before he knew the reason why. 'Yes, I'm sure they might be. But where's the key?'

'In Corbeau's pocket, where it always is,' answered Polly. 'But maybe you could open it, Mister Trompe? You bein' an Admiralty clerk and so very strong and so very clever in such matters?' She asked.

'No,' said Trompe, unhappily, testing the lid for any sign of movement, but none-the-less, very pleased by Polly's flattering confidence in his meagre abilities.

'Maybe we could try *another* key?' Suggested Tom without the least idea where such a key might be had, having searched the room thoroughly. Or if it could be had, why it should fit a lock made by a secret society of Templar Knights almost five hundred years ago. But here, we must remember, Tom was exercising the logic of *girls*, which as all boys know, is unfathomable to anyone but themselves and then, never explainable to anyone, but another girl of the same mind. 'We might be lucky, you never know, it could happen?'

'It's an idea,' said Trompe, enthusiastically, reaching into his pocket and bringing out a heavy metal ring about four inches in diameter on which was hung a dozen keys of every imaginable shape and size. Each one the property of Lord Spencer. Keys to the mountain of luggage the wily old aristocratic thought necessary for a week away from his home in London and which, as they eagerly contemplated the prospect of success, was just then being lifted onto his coach in the yard below. 'We could try one of these?' And they did. But they were either too big or too small or if they fitted, failed to make the least impression on that ancient lock. 'It's no use, I must go without them,' he fumed, scratching his head under his moth-eaten, bob-wig. 'Though, what Mister Nepean will say when I get back and he finds his papers are missing, as he surely will, I dare not say?' With that, Trompe, who was near exhausted with fatigue and nervous worry collapsed onto the polished wooden floor and with his legs loosely crossed like a Buddha and with his head held between his surprisingly large hands began to rock himself back and forth in a heaving weep of sad and pathetic, gulping sobs.

'You have no other key, Mister Trompe? One of your own? The key to your house, maybe?' Asked Tom, her face a picture of encouraging smiles, who having embarked upon an idea was not about to give up on it just yet.

'Only this one,' he gulped, his spread right hand rested on his chest. 'But it won't fit. I'm certain it won't.'

'Give it to me,' she demanded, her impatiently dancing, right hand outstretched to take it from him.

Reaching into his shirt he pulled out the heavy iron key he wore on a chain around his neck, which was about eight inches long and shaped like an ankh cross. And so, blackened and scratched with age the letters etched on its shaft, cross bar and crowning loop could hardly be read, though he had never bothered to try.

'Let me see it, Mister Trompe?' She exclaimed, desperate to try anything. 'It can't hurt to try, now can it?'

'Suppose not,' he said, without the least enthusiasm.

Wasting no time, Tom quickly inserted the key into the lock and with a twist and a click that saw no resistance, sprang the lid wide open. *'Gracious me,'* she exclaimed, truly surprised to see it had. 'Cor blimey Charlie, we've done it. Lord love a duck; we've gone and opened it. I can't believe it. I can't believe it, Poll. We've opened the deuced thing with Lauder's key.'

'Yes, *we* have,' said Polly, amazed by their inexplicable good fortune, but with a deepening sense of mystery that quickened her heart to an excited, but fearful thrill. 'But if we don't get out of here soon Corbeau will catch us for certain and then we'll be for it.'

In a scramble of excited hands, Tom and Polly raised the lid and rummaged beneath the neatly packed layers of expensive clothes that filled the top, two expensive shirts, two black, silk stocks and some underclothes, yet unworn, beneath which a single book by someone called Voltaire, called *Candide - a very pretty name,* Tom, thought rested on Trompe's missing papers and a leather satchel in which Billy's charts and signal book had been untidily stuffed. 'Are these what you're looking for, Mister Trompe?' Asked Tom, passing the several pages of Admiralty headed paper to him.

'Oh yes. Yes, indeed,' he answered, with a delirious sense of relief as he took them in his excited hands. 'Yes, that's most of them? But there are one or two of them still missing. But no matter, I can make a fair copy of those when I return to London and no one will know I did. Goodness,' he sighed, folding them deep into his pocket. 'You can't know how much this means to me. That fiend Corbeau has frightened blackmailed and bullied me like you wouldn't believe possible.'

'Enough to help him steal these from Lieutenant Kepple?' Asked Tom, lifting the roll of charts and signal book from the bag and demanding an answer with a gaze that cut him to the quick, so sharp was the set of her face.

'Yes,' he answered, sheepishly. 'Though I never wanted, too, you must believe me? I never wanted too,' he sobbed into his hands, snot dribbling onto his chin. 'They made me do it. Told me they would tell Lord Spencer on me. Get me *hung*. Please tell him I never meant' any harm, I liked him from when I first saw him.'

'Did you plan to kill him, too?'

'NO. THAT WAS NEVER *MY* PLAN,' he wailed, with a sincerity that was hard to deny. And with that, he told them everything he knew about the affair. 'They threatened to expose me you see, said they would see me hanged at Tyburn, if I didn't help them, like I was a common highwayman or something. What could I do? I was trapped. I had to do it, don't you see?'

'I don't know,' said Tom, alarmed, and saddened by his story of Billy's fraudulent promotion and now anxious to escape the danger she knew was so near at hand, as quick as ever she could. 'Well, as you say, Mister Trompe you can't change what is done without exposing yourself to a charge of fraud, but you can make amends for the trouble you have caused Lieutenant Kepple. More trouble than you ever imagined and say nothing of what you know of this night's work to anyone. Do you understand me, Mister Trompe? No one must hear of this. This must be our secret. And no one, but no one must know about the mistake you made in his commission.' *Not even Billy*, she whispered to herself. A whisper, though barely a murmur, Polly answered with a nod she agreed.

'I won't, I truly won't. Lieutenant Kepple is a better *man* by far than that villainous rascal Midshipman Kettle will ever be and I will never tell a soul his commission was a mistake. Though a good mistake, I think?'

'Yes, the best mistake you ever made in your

life, but one that will get us all in a deal of trouble unless you can get us out of this inn before we are discovered. A discovery barely a minute away as Corbeau left his gloating companions to find a little peace in his cozy room.

Chapter 24

The *Parrot* Puts To Sea

10.45pm Friday 21 April 1797

'So there you have it, Captain Kepple, *sir,*' said Tom, respectfully. Without Mister Trompe's remarkable assistance those blackguards Corbeau, Kettle and Hesta Victoria would have gotten away with it. Would have murdered you, robbed you of the *Parrot* and ruined him in the bargain for want of their wicked greed and jealous envy.

'This is an outrage, we must send word to Lord Bridport immediately,' said Sam, who astonished by Tom's tale of conspiracy, theft, treason, and near murder could barely control his rising anger and indignation.

'And say what, Mister Robinson?' Asked Billy, coldly. 'What proof do we have of this? The word of a *common* ship's boy,' a damnably low remark that made Tom blaze and blush with anger, true though it seemingly was, 'and a serving maid escaped from her lawful mistress, against that of a French gentleman who is the honored guest of a senior British Admiral. I think he would laugh us out of the room. I think the whole fleet would laugh at us. No,' he barked, with a biting of irritation. 'We say nothing of this to anyone. We sail tomorrow as we are ordered to do and have planned this last hour or more, Mister Robinson and we will put this wicked business behind us for the moment.'

'But?' Blurted Sam, biting his tongue in protest.

'No *buts,* Mister Robinson. That is my last word. Do you understand me? Do you all understand me? What is passed is passed. We will sail tomorrow and settle their hash another day, the lot of them.' And with that he dismissed them all with a wave of his hand.

If Tom had expected Billy's thanks and she did, none was forthcoming, either that night or the following morning. A harshness that surprised both Sam and Duffy, who, though confounded by her amazing story, thought she and Polly deserved them.

And so, it was, on Saturday 22 April 1797, just six days from their rendezvous at St. Pierre, Quiberon and with the wind freshening from the north-east and the tide rising in a flood about her now deep laden hull, HMS *Parrot* hoisted her sails and upped her two anchors and with a grace observed by more than one prying eye on land and on sea, not least Lieutenant Galbraith, who remarked how fine she looked, made her way through Spithead's densely crowded anchorage. Which on that fateful afternoon was not only home to Admiral Bridport's idle, though now, not so mutinous fleet, but a host of other ships, which, though, they had no part in that dangerous uprising, still weeks away from a peaceful end, were obstacles a plenty for Billy to overcome before he found the open sea.

Merchantmen of every shape and size, press tenders, carrying men around the fleet, sheer hulks,[211] their massive cranes lifting high into the sky, store ships, guard ships and prison hulks full to overflowing, with French prisoners. The largest of which, was the *Royal George* in which a thoroughly disgruntled Colonel Tate watched the *Parrot* sail away through iron bars too strong to break. Where an Irish lad by the name of Barry O'Brien, beamed a wicked smile as he saw her heel in the wind and read again the note Corbeau had sent him that very morning. A note that promised his easy escape later that night if he would carry a secret dispatch to his sister, Mrs. Madeleine Beattie of Primrose Hill, London concerning the plan he and Captain Bully Drier had discussed one cold winters morning in Paris almost five months before. The plan to rid him of his partner, Mister Titus Dimple forever, a plan that would reunite him with a *friend* who had long waited his return, General Prem Rez.

As well as these large and thank goodness, mostly stationary vessels, there were others, too, he had to avoid. Fast running cutters, ferries, slow moving barges, deep filled bumboats, lighters, wherry's, luggers and dinghies of every type. All of them plying their trade between the anchored fleet and every one of them vying for what little sea room there was to be had between Portsmouth and the Isle of Wight. Every bit of which, Billy desperately needed for his own as the little *Parrot* began to show a quite surprising turn of speed.

But, if these weren't obstacle enough for him to worry about, as he cautiously inched the *Parrot* on her way, there was also the notorious wreck of the *Royal George* to find and avoid, if he could. Whose mainmast poked a hazardous, hard-to-see in the glinting afternoon sunlight, ten feet above the choppy surface of a slate grey Solent and without bell or buoy to mark it was there. Little wonder then every idle hand[212] aboard was keeping watch from every vantage point they could find to see them safe from harm.

To make matters worse the wind was contrarily blowing the *wrong* way for the quick and easy sail he planned and he had to make a series of clever dogleg maneuvers into the wind, beating and tacking, as sailors call it. First travelling east by south towards the perilous rocks and shallows of Selsey Bill, clearly marked on his precious charts, but so very hard to see from the quarterdeck, as the *Parrot* pitched and rolled and lurched in the gathering, white capped swell and then, when that was done, turning west-by-south, back towards the Isle of Wight. Repeating the process, a second and then a third time until he found enough sea to make a last and final turn into the Channel, four hundred miles from their destination.

It was a difficult and complex piece of sailing that tested Billy's skill to the very limit and in its success, would have surprised and delighted Mister Adams and his men at Bucklers Hard, who you will remember thought her haunted by the drowned crew of the *Wasp,* she was mostly made from. Which indeed she was!

'WELL DONE, MISTER ROBINSON. WELL DONE MISTER DUFF. WELL DONE EVERYBODY,' shouted Billy in a barely contained exhilaration that washed the worry and pain of the last few days, not to say the last few nervous hours clean from his mind and lifted the spirits of his over stretched and anxious to please crew, to a rousing cheer of madcap delight. They had done it. Well they had cleared the Isle of Wight and with no major mishap to blight their record. No mean feat for a novice crew of boys and a novice Captain. 'Now let's get her topmasts, topgallants and royals[213] up and let's make all the sail we can for Brittany.'

As they did, a sleek, two masted, black painted, schooner with a distinctive red strake marking her sides beneath her rails slipped effortlessly into the *Parrot's* wake, less than a mile behind them and took up the chase. At her helm was Charlie Begg transformed by wind and tide from the simpering, dithering coward he was on the Great Morass into the expert seaman he most surprisingly was.

Beside him and never the sailor his smuggler father and brother were, was the bad-tempered, brooding shape of Jemmy Grub, who with his battered tricorn hat tied flat on his head with a scruffy old scarf, was trying without success to button his wildly flapping, tail coat in a wind and spray he already despised.

Nearby and just as uncomfortable, as he was, on that slanting deck was the sad faced figure of Joby Dogget, who with one hand wrapped tight around the mainmasts shrouds and the other around his mouth was doing his best to ignore the gut retching seasickness he felt. As he watched the almost prostrate figure of Mister Badger, collapsed near unconscious over the starboard rails.

Who, still nursing a bruised and sore belly was heaving the last of his breakfast into the sea, most of which came quickly back in a windblown shower of sea mixed spray to speckle him and the rapidly fading Dogget in a plume of boiled beef, red cabbage, black beans, bread, gravy, and potatoes.

'WELL DONE, MISTER BEGG. WE HAVE THEM NOW. WE HAVE THEM CLEAR AS DAY,' shouted Corbeau from the bows. 'BUT KEEP YOUR DISTANCE. THEY MUST NOT SEE WHO WE ARE OR EVER SUSPECT WE ARE FOLLOWING THEM TO FRANCE.'

'Aye, aye,' Monsieur,' answered Begg, pleased by Corbeau's complimentary words and hoping that this little venture, dangerous though it was, would reap an even greater reward from the mysterious Frenchy than the small bag of silver he already had in his pocket.

'PASS ME THE TELESCOPE, KETTLE.' snapped Corbeau, with the high-handed, infuriating authority he so despised. 'Let me see again this *boy* who has made such a fool of *you*.' A wounding remark, as he knew it was that not only ignored his own more recent failure, but the Midshipman's obviously vicious mood. Handing him the telescope with a scowl of resentment, he retreated to the stern and in brooding silence that challenged any of the *Seahorse's* crew of gallows bait to approach him uninvited, watched as the *Parrot* drove herself on under wispy white, blue skies and billowing grey canvass towards her far-off destination.

'Damn their eyes,' he whispered, remembering how Corbeau had woken him at his lodgings in the Blue Posts Inn with the news of the robbery. News that only spoke of the charts and signal book the thieves had taken, something he never thought possible, when he had spoken so scornfully of what Kepple could and couldn't do, the night before. News that sent him into a fury of uncontrollable rage to think their clever scheme to get the *Parrot* back was so easily undone by that boy, Tom Dimple. A rage the like of which the landlord, Mister Pyke, a man of strong Methodist convictions, had never seen before and wouldn't, he said with a bluster of pious indignation, tolerate for a second longer. Even if he was a friend of Admiral Crookhampton, soon to be elevated to the peerage, if all the talk was true and newly appointed, envoy to the Governor of New York, Mister John Jay to bargain a better trade for both their nations. Evicted from the inn by a potman of prodigious muscular size and savage disposition he found himself homeless, penniless and without the least prospect of a command of his own until the mutiny was finished, he recklessly agreed to

Corbeau's plan of swift revenge and taken ship with him aboard the *Seahorse.*

Revenge, he dearly hoped would settle Lieutenant William Kepple's hash once and for all, because he had grown to despise that artfully clever boy better even than Hesta, did, who hated him with a passion. Now on her way to Crookhampton Manor to make ready her grandfather's journey to America in a week or two.

Ignoring Kettle's frosty silence, Corbeau raised the heavy brass telescope to his eye and sweeping the *Parrot's* larboard side from end to end for any sign of Lieutenant William Kepple, brought her stern gallery into full view and saw with a shock that visibly stiffened him, Tom, and Polly, precariously seated on the rails beneath the trysail boom, waving at who knows what?

'DAMN THEM,' he shouted, so loud it froze the *Seahorse's* crew of thugs, scruffs and waifs into a moment's inaction that almost spilled the breeze from her sails and had her in *irons*[214] as she tacked into the wind. And reaching into his pocket brought out the twist of red ribbon he had found in his room last night. A ribbon he knew perfectly well, matched those that were now gaily streaming from Polly's hair, she twisted into neat curls. 'THERE YOU ARE. THERE YOU ARE,' he bellowed, in bitter rage. 'YOU THIEVING PAIR

OF ROGUES. DO NOT THINK YOU HAVE ES-
CAPED ME. I WILL HAVE YOU YET. AND WHEN
I DO YOU WILL KNOW THE PAIN OF CROSS-
ING ME.'

Chapter 25

Billy, Tom And Polly Find
The First Piece Of The Rebus,
Of Akhenaten But Never Knew They Did

2.14pm Saturday 22 April 1797

'He's here, Tom,' said Polly, with such a sudden and uncontrollable shiver it sent Mister Pitt into a whimpering, tremulous panic at her feet. 'Corbeau. He's somewhere close upon us, I know he is.'

'Where?' She asked, turning her head this way and that to see where he could be and seeing nothing more alarming than the cliffs on St Catherine's Point, the southernmost tip of the Isle of White, a half a mile distant on their starboard side. 'I can't see anything but that black ship that's crossing over our wake, back there.'

'I don't know, Tom. I felt him, if only for a second. Felt him callin' to us. Cursin' us somethin' awful like he knows it was us who took them charts and signals.'

'You think?'

'Yes, he knows it was me and you who took them thin's from his trunk, but there's somethin'

411

else, Tom. Somethin' else made him madder than a scorpion that's gone and stung his own self. Somethin' more important even than them papers. Somethin' else we took by mistake, somethin' that was in that satchel you brung aboard with everythin' else, his book, maybe?'

'Not that book, surely?' Asked Tom, feeling the bruise on the small of her back chafe on the stern post and remembering, as if it was a dream, the sharp edge of something hard and heavy poking her as she ran from the Fountain Inn. *But what was it? And why hadn't she thought to look for it before now, when she had the chance last night. Nerves or excitement,* she supposed.

'I don't know, Tom, but we'd best find out, because I think we is in a heap more trouble than we rightly know.' And then, as if each had read the others mind, they turned to look at, Billy, who was standing behind the mainmast, his head turned skywards as he watched the fore and main topgallant sails sheeted home by a lively and very capable crew of topmen. A yard behind him stood a beaming, Sam Robinson, a brass-speaking trumpet wedged firmly to his mouth as he shouted a quick succession of orders to his, *men.*

By long standing tradition he had organized the crew into two watches of near equal numbers. Each watch was then divided into an afterguard, the boys whose job it was to work the sails, guns and anchors at the stern, the forecastle men, who had charge of the sails, guns, and anchors at the bows, the topmen, the biggest, strongest, bravest, and most agile of all boys aboard, whose job it was to set and reef the highest of the *Parrot's* ten main and foremast sails and lastly, the Marines, all twelve of them. Who stripped to their white shirts pulled on every rope and line he ordered them, too until the sweat ran down their faces.

Of these, Billy knew the names of only five, Duffy, of course, the strongest and most capable boy aboard by a mile and so well suited to his role as ships Boatswain he might have been born to it. Dancer Dyke and Nipper Ogden, who had led the charge on the marsh, who now struggled to hold the *Parrot's* heavy steering wheel as the wind took her sails in an exhilarating charge of speed. Archie Sparrow, one of four new boys who'd come aboard from the *Duke* barely an hour before they sailed and a good hand who had already made himself useful, knowing his way around the *Parrot* almost as well as Duffy.

Tom, of course, who he owed so much and who he had yet to thank for *his* daring courage and surprising enterprise the night before. Tom, who he liked and trusted more than anyone else aboard, but who was the most maddening, undisciplined, and unseaman-like *boy* he had ever met in his four years of service and who didn't seem to know *his* proper place and took so many liberties with him, he hardly knew what to do. Tom, who with *his* newfound friend, Polly, a mystery in herself, he had made his servants, though neither seemed keen to wait on him as they must.

For the next three days, the *Parrot* made her way slowly down the Channel and by late Tuesday afternoon was seventy miles south west of the Lizard[215] when, Billy ordered a change of course towards the coast of Ushant and the turn south when they had that would carry them to the Quiberon Peninsula, still two hundred miles away. Where, with a fair wind they would arrive on Friday night and be gone before the next morning.

As he had done for the last three days Billy paced the deck relentlessly and watched with growing satisfaction the workings of his small, but very handy brig. Which to his delight sailed in a very lively way fast outpacing the dozen bigger ships that followed her down the Channel, fat bellied merchantmen their yards crowded with billowing sails, bound for Ireland, the Azores, and North America, he guessed? Fishing smacks[216] off to Newfoundland's Grand Banks, the richest fishing grounds in the world and a haven for all the cod he had ever eaten, their decks crowded with small boats, their red ochre sails a colourful contrast to the grey that surrounded them. A smoke blackened whaler her course set for the South Pacific, the oily smell of her vile trade a stain on the wind that blew steady on her bow. A postal packet just out of Falmouth and the black ship with the red strake which had followed them out of Portsmouth Roads sailing a mile or two behind her, her course as steady as their own.

Never very far from his side throughout this time was either Sam or Trucky, both of whom had proven themselves to be hard-working, efficient, and capable young officers, though Sam was by far the more practical sailor of the two, with a keen eye for the naval discipline Trucky's gentle, free-thinking spirit lacked. 'What speed are we making, Mister Robinson?' Asked Billy, as he stared at the distant squall of rain, which was falling in a thick black curtain, ten miles off their larboard bow and wondered once again, if the good luck that had been theirs in the relative calm of the Channel would last much longer than this? It wouldn't.

4.00pm Tuesday 25 April 1797

'CAST THE LOG, MISTER DUFF,' shouted Sam, an order he instantly obeyed,

415

which would measure the speed and distance the *Parrot* had travelled since last it was done an hour ago. To do this he threw a long length of rope, knotted at intervals of 47 feet and 3 inches and weighted by a wooden *log*[217] over the stern, letting it run out in the *Parrot's* creamy wake for 30 seconds. As it did he counted the number of knots that were paid out and when he was done, shouted in a deep, resonant voice that was heard all over the brig, not least by Tom and Polly who were searching the decks below for Mister Pitt, who had been strangely missing, again, for most of the afternoon. 'Seven knots, Mister Robinson.' By which he meant, seven knots of speed, which for practical purposes also calculated the distance travelled, as seven nautical miles. A speed and distance Billy every evening dutifully entered in the ships *logbook,* his daily record of the *Parrot's* progress.

'Seven knots,' repeated Sam to Billy, it being the tradition of the sea to ignore what everyone aboard, including he, had already heard, and tell him again as if he hadn't.

'Thank you, Mister Robinson,' answered Billy, who much too his own surprise and growing confidence, rather enjoyed this daft formality. So much so, he had sternly barred Tom from both his day and night cabins unless she was doing something useful, like sweeping them clean, or making his bed, or doing his washing, or fetching him a meal, or something to drink, which she never did. Whilst he ignored her every attempt to meet him alone, something she thought silly, mean and stupid, particularly as she so much wanted to talk to him about Polly's dark and, as yet, unproven suspicion, Corbeau was following them.

But there was something else, too, she wanted to tell him, she thought, as she scrambled on her hands and knees after Mister Pitt over the damp and smelly cable that almost filled the Orlop[218] to the ceiling above her head, *the strange things some of the crew, particularly the younger boys, had told her and Poll.* Things stolen from their dunnage, a keepsake, a penny whistle, a bone handled clasp knife, a pair of winter Woollen gloves, a favourite jumper, a pair of new ducks, a piece of scrimshaw,[219] a battered old tinder box, ribbons for their hair, which most of them grew down to their waists and fastened and oiled in braided pigtails every Sunday afternoon, except for, Duffy and the Marines, who wore a short queue like the officers, did. Hatches, latches, lids, and doors creaking open or banging shut when no one was there. Not even Ginger, Blackie, and Snowy the *Parrot's* three viciously feral cats, grown since kittens at Bucklers Hard to fend for themselves.

Who prowled her decks and dark places like Bengal tigers hunting the rats and mice that swarmed the *Parrot's* holds like a plague of African locusts. So many, every boy aboard had a cruel bite on a finger, hand, leg, foot, or toe to say there were, which Trucky dressed with his very own mixture of vinegar, salt, rum, honey, and Bog Moss.[220] Or things tipped or fallen in plain sight of those who saw it happen, and a dozen boys said they often did, from tables, lockers, and shelves. Things so well stowed they couldn't move on their own, not even when the *Parrot* pitched and rolled on a big wave, as she now often did. Things curiously gone from where they ought to be, were everyday kept, one moment in their proper place, as Duffy insisted they must be, the next gone, where it couldn't be found without a long search and sometimes not even then. Everyday things no one could want like an old paint brush dripped in red paint, a canvas fire bucket full of sand, a holystone,[221] a hammer, a spike, a chisel, a sailmakers mallet, needles and thread, knives, forks, spoons, cups and at least three wooden plate left to soak overnight in a wash bucket. The feeling of dreadful, shivering coldness some of them felt pass over them like a winter chill, when they were alone in the dark, mostly near the stern, they all said, and now so often they rarely went below the *Parrot's* sun bright upper decks unless they were ordered, too, and then never without a friend to hold their hand or a light to show the way in corridors so dark they couldn't see. And when they did, the candles, tapers, and glass lanterns they carried in their outstretched trembling hands, which burnt a warm and comforting yellow glow in the inky black dark in front of their frightened faces, were often mysteriously blown out without the least breeze of air to blame, except for the draft they often felt on their necks, as something unseen hurried past them, laughing fit to bust their ribs as they did. Whispering and squeaking voices heard behind doors, screens, and walls and no one there when they dared to look, which they mostly didn't. Footsteps and banging in the night on the poopdeck and ghostly moaning heard in the main top[222] above the wheelhouse and the sounds of something squeaking and chattering like a monkey coming from the locker next to the rudder. But equally vexing was Mister Pitt's inexplicably odd behaviour, which started, they all said, when Polly dropped him on the deck of their little brig last Friday night, where he instantly dribbled a flood of warm wee onto Trucky's new washed deck, like he knew with a certainty there was something there, he couldn't see, but sensed better than they did, it was *real*. A sense of something dark and unnatural that from

419

early morning until late at night sent him running this way and that in search of whatever it was. Scratching and ferreting in a hundred dark corners only to find a rat or mouse was hidden there, which he expertly killed and left where it lay. Supper for one of the boy's he had grown so fond of. Every one of them better by far than Hesta Victoria and Monsieur Corbeau, who often thrashed him with a stick.

Or, if he wasn't searching, he was often seen standing like a statue for minutes on end, furiously sniffing the source of some smell known only to him through the myriad other smells that perfumed the brig. Paint, varnish, turpentine, tallow, tar, salt, bilge, wood-smoke from the galley chimney, dinner cooking in the vats and ovens, which so warmed the deck they slept upon, unwashed human sweat, tobacco, which most of the boys smoked, new-cut, sap leaked wood and the tangy poo and wee from the farm animals that now occupied a corner enclosure on the maindeck, to name, but a few of them. But despite he did, suddenly scampering off with optimistically pricked ears and a determinedly pointed tail like a beagle after a fox he came no closer to finding the culprit.

But worse by far was his constant twitching, whimpering, whining and frightened barking at something invisible, something ghostly they all said, that was surely teasing him to a fine distraction from some safe place and so close, he a hundred times tried to bite it, did once, if the yelp of pain they heard was real.

But Billy was far too busy and far too important now to listen to anything she or Polly had to say on that or any subject concerning the *Parrot*. And never when he was exercising his crew in some shipboard task, not least, the firing of one of her ten, four pounder cannons, which he dearly loved to do. He being such a boy and boys as every girl knows, like nothing better than to make a noise and the louder the noise the better, and cannons make a very loud noise, indeed. Something he did every afternoon, now, though Polly found it a fright she couldn't bear, often freezing on the spot when it began, the look on her face seeming to remember the hint of something long forgotten; a drumbeat, she once remarked.

Each of the guns requiring eight of the biggest boys to work them properly and in a strict sequence of hard to learn tasks that would allow no mistake and which to his constant disappointment they had yet to master without blunder, mishap, or minor injury, in less than nine minutes and twenty-two seconds on his precious Tompion watch. Which he delighted to say, kept wonderful time. A terribly slow time he knew could be bettered by any French vessel afloat, should they ever meet one, and it seemed likely they soon would.

He was also much taken with his small troop of Marines, commanded by the newly promoted Sergeant Finch. A roly-poly, insufferably pompous, stiff, and proper sort of blustering fellow, whose belly was so big, his brass buckled, polished, black leather belt could barely contain it's want to burst out of his impeccably white trousers. A boy whose constant bellowing and forever stamping about the deck in his big black, hob-nailed boots, which Billy allowed, made his bony face redder than the bright red coat he wore. Who was helped in every military task he could contrive by a tall, skinny, long-limbed, good natured Corporal by the name of Penny, who four times a day marched his *men* up and down the deck and whenever Billy said he could, would let them fire their muskets and pistols in puffs of grey-black smoke that smudged their faces and stung their eyes until they cried tears of joy.

But as dusk turned to blackest night and the rain earlier seen began to fall in a blinding downpour that splashed the decks to a slippy, treacherous wet, Billy left his post for only the second time that day for his long-promised supper of cold ham, boiled eggs freshly laid from his chickens that morning, bread, and jam. And with Sam calling the course change he had just ordered went to his cramped night cabin and found to his surprise and po-faced, grunting delight, Tom and Polly sitting cross-legged on the floor behind the door, waiting for him. Both eating the last of three hard boiled eggs, ham, and bread they had brought with them and trying to restrain the fretfully whimpering Mister Pitt, who was hiding beneath his cot.

'What are you two doing here, Tom?' He gruffly asked, wondering if they were eating his supper and wouldn't have been surprised if they were, seeing his private sea chest was open and the leather satchel he had put in there, last night was on the deck between them. A rooting about in his things that was overly familiar, even for a servant. Though obviously not so gruff, it appeared, to stop the winsome smile that blushed her cheeks beneath the muck that hid her face.

'Sorry, Billy,' she answered, careless of her familiarity. 'But it's very important we talk to you, now. It's about this satchel, there's something inside you must see. Something we took by mistake from Corbeau's trunk; look.'

'What?' He asked, hearing the gentle rebuke in her voice, as he took his dripping hat and soaking wet jacket off and sat on the stool in front of her with a yawn.

'This?'

'What is it?' He asked, taking the heavy, flat piece of metal from her grubby outstretched hands to examine it more closely in the dim glow of the candle that lit his cabin hardly at all. It was the colour of dull brass, a sort of orange-brown overlaid with dirt and grease and was shaped, like a cut piece of pie or cheese and was about an inch thick. The curving arc was about nine and a half inches long and the length of each long side was about twelve inches, perhaps a little less, he judged against the span of his outstretched index finger and thumb, and narrowed to a blunted end that might have been half an inch across its flat surface, forming a space in the centre of the final assembly for something to stand upon it. An octagonal space, he rightly concluded after a little thought.

Because, if he remembered anything, Mister Elwyn Jones, his mathematics teacher at the Blue Coat School, Chester[223] - a Welshman, ever taught him about the Euclidian[224] geometry, and it was less than he ought to have remembered, it being so important to spherical navigation, the piece he now held in his hand was one of *eight* interlinked pieces. Which when fitted together would form a substantial and very heavy circular plate at least twenty-four inches in diameter.

He was even more convinced of this when he

examined more closely the jigsaw-like connec-
tions[225] that protruded and indented its two long
sides in a symmetry that surely invited the fit of
a second and a third piece in a sequence that
would finally produce the circular plate he imagined it was, but a small part. On the one side were
two circular tabs, one, an inch and a half below its
curved end, the other, an inch and a half above
its flat end and each one about three quarters of
an inch in diameter. On the other side were two
circular holes of the same size each awaiting the
fit of the tabs of the next piece, a fit that would be
perfect, he imagined, by the exquisite design he
now saw on its top surface. Which was inscribed
from top to bottom with nine radiating lines of al-
ternately long and short lengths, each rising from
the centre of the plate like the rays of the sun and
each one terminating half an inch or an inch from
the arc of the curved end with what looked like tiny
hands holding a small looped cross of a type he
had never seen before.

This upper face was also divided from top to
bottom into three, unequal parts by two horizontal
lines, set three inches apart, one and a half inches
beneath the arc and intersected by the sun burst
of radiating lines. But both lines were angled near
the left-hand edge to form what he deduced was
the beginning of two, equivalent lines on the next

piece of the plate, when fitted together. The corners of two nine sided enneagons by the angle of their corners, which were approximately 140 degrees by his rough seaman's calculation, which would be seen in the round when the plate was complete in all its parts. Calculations he twice every day easily made when navigating the *Parrot*.

Odd, he thought, tracing the lines to the corners with his finger, the plate would have been more symmetrical - prettier, even had they described two octagons parallel with the flat end and the space it hinted, when the eight pieces were fitted together. A space that was almost certainly intended for a ninth piece, a statue he fancied that further locked the pieces together? Between these two horizontal lines and in the space below it was a pattern of marks he knew were Egyptian hieroglyphs something his mother had shown him on a painting of the great pyramids of Giza, which for years hung in the window of Mister Hunter's map shop at the top of Werburgh's Lane.[226] Hieroglyphs no one had yet deciphered, so Mister Hunter once said, but very pretty all the same with their pictures of birds, insects, rabbits or were they hares, snakes, boats, plants, feathers and squiggles.

On the underside of the plate were three small pedestals each cast in the shape of a bird or serpents clawed foot holding a sphere inscribed with an elaborately drawn eye enclosed in the same double enneagon, he concluded, was part of the pattern on the top of the plate. Two of them, an inch below the curved end and one, an inch above the flat end. A pattern, or was it the frame of a pattern, of some significance to the owner? Though the age of the plate suggested he was long dead? Pedestals which when he placed them on the deck raised the piece an inch and a half above it and when he had saw it was an object of great beauty crafted by gifted hands. But why?

'Extraordinary,' said Billy, testing its weight in both his hands, a treasure, which, did he but know it, was about to lead him and his crew on an adventure that would test their courage and resolve to the very limits of their endurance and, which would find no end in the rescue of the French fugitives who were even now waiting patiently for him. 'I can't say that I have ever seen anything like it before, what is it, Tom?' He asked.

'We don't know do we Poll?' Said Tom.

'No, Tom,' she answered, looking him straight in the eyes, eyes so blue and so kind, even in the feeble yellow light, she wondered why she hadn't done so before. And saw him look at her with the same boyish delight, no wonder Tom loved him and wanted to be with him.

'Mmm, it looks a bit like the trivet my mother uses to stand her kettles on in the kitchen, though hers was never as heavy as this, nor as grand, I'm sure, it must way a half a stone at least,' he said, turning it back and forth in his hands with a smile that gently mocked their earnest expressions. 'Is it important, do you think?'

'We think it is,' Tom said in a conspiratorial whisper, quickly telling him of Polly's amazing gift of second sight, her ability to see the future and much else besides and how it had saved *him* on that fateful night and how she now suspected Corbeau was following them in the black ship that by day and by night followed them. Not in pursuit of the *Parrot*, but the piece of plate he held in his hand. 'Oh, and by the way, Billy,' she said with a grin when she finished her gushing tale, 'the *Parrot* is haunted by a ghost. Two, Polly suspects and one of them a little monkey, ain't that right Mister Pitt?' She laughed, taking him into her arms.

26

Tales Of Ghosts
And Other Strange Things

9.30pm Tuesday 25 April 1797

The heavy knock on his door so soon after he had left the deck took Billy by surprise, but thankfully gave him the moment's distraction he needed before responding to Tom's amazing, if improbable story. A story he thought a *childish* fancy. Corbeau following them and ghosts, whatever next? He smiled.

'Enter,' called Billy, abruptly, seeing it was the wet and bedraggled figure of Sam, through the bars of his door.

'Sorry to bother you, sir,' said Sam, cautiously leaning through the quarter open door, which, for them moment concealed Tom and Polly in its shadow. Though not their empty wooden plates of egg shells and bread crumbs, though his food was untouched on the long table in his day cabin, beside his maps. Which were weighted down by his nautical almanac, his sextant, his brass dividers and his brass and wood parallel rule. 'But *she's* not answering *her* helm and I can't make the course you ordered a moment ago. It is deuced strange, but the helm is stuck fast and neither Archie Sparrow, Mister Duff, Nipper or Dancer can shift it an inch to the starboard or larboard.'

'What's that you say, Sam?' Asked Billy, idly scratching his head and slipping the knot of thin black ribbon that tied his hair into a short, but fashionable queue at the nape of his neck, to let it to fall stiff and wet about his head and shoulders in a ragged curtain of gold.

'The helms stuck fast, sir and try as we might we can't move it, not an inch,' he lamented, feeling it a personal failure they couldn't. 'And our heading is still west and not, as you ordered south by west,' a course leading them deeper into the great Atlantic Ocean.

'Have you checked the rudder cables?' Asked Billy, distractedly combing the wet draggle of hair that had fallen over his furrowed brow with his long, hard worn fingers in a half-hearted, weary motion that tried to make sense of this new emergency. One far more serious than Tom's tale of ghosts and French skullduggery. 'Nothing fouled or come adrift, do you think?'

'No.'

'Pintles, gudgeons[227] and chains secure and moving freely?'

'Yes, Mister Duff and Dancer Dyke were down

there not a moment ago and every thing's just as it should be, which is no more than you'd expect in a brig not four months built, and built so well by Mister Adams.'

'Maybe she's fouled somewhere below the waterline, Sam? A piece of flotsam[228] or jetsam[229] caught between the rudder and hull to jam her fast, I've known it happen?' He replied, unaware his familiar use of Sam's abbreviated Christian name had done much to relieve the nervous anxiety he justly felt. Who, had he but known it, had genuinely feared to bring him news of this strange and possibly ruinous event.

'Could be? Though it seems unlikely,' he boldly answered.

'Mmm, maybe? But have Mister Duff check it anyway and report to me as soon as he has,' he briskly ordered.

'Aye, aye, sir,' he answered, knowing now someone was hiding behind the door, Tom, and Polly, he guessed and wondered, not for the first time, what understanding bound them in the intimacy, secrecy and conspiracy they shared. Which was much remarked upon by the crew, though not Duffy, who simply spoke of the debt the Captain owed Tom and Polly. A debt he repaid in the kindness he showed them.

'Odd,' said Billy, to no one in particular, keen to

eat his meagre supper before he returned to his duties.

'It'll be that bloomin' ghost, Captain Billy, gawd save and protect us from his mischievous doin's, which ain't properly natural. Not even for a ghost, which *he* most definitely is and ought to know better for all doesn't.' Said Polly, in a soft, melodic tone that in its certainty sounded so much older and wiser than the nine or possibly ten years she might have claimed, had anyone asked her. Which no one did, she being a slave[230] brought from Africa's Zanzibar last year and sold in the East London slave market near Shoreditch for five pounds and seven shillings and of no importance to anyone, but herself, so Hesta Victoria, everyday said with a spiteful sneer of contempt. An interruption, Billy realised, were the first words he had heard her speak since she came aboard.

'A ghost?' Asked Billy, transfixed by the willfully determined girl, half his size, who now stood before him with her hands clasped tight on her hips. A girl, he now saw, of singular and dignified bearing despite her shabby appearance, who wore an *age* blackened, metal slave collar of exquisite rope-like design about her gracefully long, delightfully pretty neck. Which proclaimed, in a stylish, antique flourish for all to see on the small round brass disc that was fixed to it, she was the Property of Miss Hesta

Victoria Crookhampton of Crookhampton Manor in the County of Hampshire, there to be returned if she is found to be escaped.

But what Billy took to be a slave collar, hating it with all his heart, was the twin of the wand Kiya now held to her heart as she sat sobbing on the steps of her cell in the pyramid of Khufu. The dream-like adventure of just a moment ago, when she saved the Viking Tostig from the Leopard Men, as she now called them, gone, as if it never was. Was just that, a dream.

A necklace which looped about her neck to bring its two ends flush beneath her dimpled chin. An exquisitely carved bulls head with a sun-disc inscribed with the sacred double enneagon of Egypt enclosing the Eye of Horus, clasped between its two curved horns and a rounded boss, but both so dirty with *age their pattern was gone*. A torque, which despite Hesta Victoria's best attempts to get it off, could not be undone by her, nor anyone else who tried, including the blacksmith in Crookhampton village, who tried until he cursed with rage he couldn't, even with his biggest hammer.

'Yes, Captain Billy. There's a ghost in this 'ere *Parrot*. Not a bad ghost like you sometimes get, a ghoul or a demon or a nasty djinn, but a mischievous one just the same, who's been makin' himself a thorough goin' nuisance and a damnable pest

433

to everyone aboard the *Parrot* since when we left Portsmouth last Saturday afternoon,' blurted Polly. 'And when Tom told Mister clever clogs, aren't I so very posh, Midshipman Anstruther, about him and his monkey, thinkin' he was a gentleman we could trust with such an important intelligence, which he ain't, I can tell you plain he ain't. Him bein' a low quarrelsome scrub of a toffee-nosed cove, who thinks he's a damn sight better than the both of us are, he called *him* a villainous little liar and a no good meddlesome upstart, instead. And worse still,' she railed, her voice an excited squeal of disbelief, 'said he would get *him* two dozen lashes with the cat-o-nine-tails, a whip that ought never to be used by God fearin' folk on human creatures and well laid on by Mister Duff, who has arms like a bloomin' gorilla. Which I once saw in an iron cage on Pemba[231] by the way, so I know what I'm talkin' about. And whip *him* so bloomin' hard it will make *him* squeal like a pig and all washed down with a bucket of brine to make it sting all the more, which is cruelty piled upon cruelty. Like *he* was stung by a thousand wasps or bit by a million bitin' ants, if *he* should dare to even think of spreading such a foul and vicious lie about so's to frighten the young uns, which we did, anyway them knowin' more about him better than us. Ain't that the truth I'm tellin' him *Mister,* Tom?'

434

'Yes,' said Tom, mesmerized by Polly's colourful tale, and gazing in a sort of raptured awe at, Billy as he effortlessly tied his hair back into a queue and more pleased than she could possibly say, Polly had not betrayed her, by any thoughtless slip of her busy tongue.

'Gosh,' said Billy with a smile, pulling his still wet coat about his shoulders and as he did, winked at Sam.

'Its true Billy, really,' beamed Tom, eager to tell all she knew of the strange goings on that had haunted the *Parrot* since they sailed. How Davey Harper, a simple lad, who would never tell a lie to anyone was tripped over in the bread room and had a sack of flour poured over his head and shoulders by something small he never saw on the shelf above him. But imagined it was an imp, elf, or sprite? And how, when he had recovered his wits, he followed a trail of tiny feet, smaller than any child could make, from the bread room door to the locked and bolted spirit room, just across the passageway and then, quite remarkably, he groaned, disappeared clean out of sight without a backward step to say where he had gone.

How Alfie Brown a tough, well made, easy going dockside Londoner you wouldn't want to cross unless you had a large shovel to protect yourself with and one of Duffy's best and most trusted hands, had been testing the water level in the main hold, as he was told he must by Mister Robinson, when he was pitched head over heels into the foot deep, smelly pool by a hard kick in the bum by no one, he said, who could have been there without his knowing he was.

How Peter Owen, one of the gun captains, a stout and hearty lad with a shock of red hair, he twisted into a python thick plait, two feet long, had been locked in the gunpowder room and tormented by a lighted candle, which hovered and danced above his head until his nerves were near wrecked by the worry of the thunderous explosion it might cause, if it was dropped. And a hundred times begged and squealed whoever had it, he must stop. And how he had been left there, sobbing like a baby, until his mates had come and found him in a state of desperate panic almost two hours later and too late by half an hour for his tea.

How Joey Warren, one of the loblolly boys[232] had been ferreting about in a cupboard in a locker beside the rudder when a hand had reached into the pocket of his ducks and stole his clasp knife, the second that was took, and how, when he chased the thief he'd disappeared through a bulkhead[233] in a wisp of smoke.

And if that wasn't enough, and it was more than enough to convince Tom, Polly, and most of

436

the crew the *Parrot* was haunted, there was the constant half sighting of a lonely, lost and shabby figure of a little boy walking the forecastle deck in the dead of night, who when he was approached or called, too, would vanish, as if he were never there, though he definitely was.

'But there could be any number of reasons to explain what those boys saw or thought they saw, Tom. A trick of the light, shadows maybe, the whistling of the wind through the masts and yards or just the usual larks, mischief and japes you get from *young* boys far away from their natural home and inclination to behave better than they now do?' Answered Billy, confounded by Tom and Polly's stories of the supernatural and unsure of what he might do to resolve *their* worries.'

'No there, ain't. There's only one reason for them thin's happenin', as all them little boys said they did and the stealin' of their personal thin's from their dunnage as well, which they didn't, and it weren't no jape or silly lark that was the cause of it, it was the ghost. And you can cut me tongue out of me head and nail it wrigglin' to the mainmast like a maggot on a hook, if you think I'm lyin' to you, because no matter you say different, Captain Billy, it was all done by the ghost. Two ghosts to be precise and one of them a monkey. Yes, you can look at me like that,' she smarted, he was gently smiling at her, 'but this here's a haunted ship and no bloomin' mistake it is. A ghost ship, as was whispered in Portsmouth dock by the sailors who said they brought her up from Bucklers Hard in the ice and snow last January. 'Cos, I heard them laughin' they were glad to be done with her and each found another berth by Captain Patton, the Transport Officer. Though I could see in their rum soaked, stiff grinnin' faces they was still scared of what they saw on the *Parrot* and nothin' is goin' to be right in her until we smoke that little rascal out of his hidin' place! 'Cos, he is hidin' down there,' she pointed to the deck, her pretty face a mask of grim determination.

'And how will *we* do that?' Asked Billy, the smile grown broader on his face as he pulled his still dripping hat onto his head and turned to the door and Sam, still standing there, the grin equally wide on his face.

'You leave that to me and Mister Tom, Captain Billy. We'll catch that blighter or my names not Polly Perkins. We'll have him caught by his heels before he knows he's done gone and been caught. You mark my words we'll have him for sure. You bet we will, no doubt.'

'I don't know, Polly. Let me think on it a while. I don't want the crew, particularly the younger boys spooked more than they already are,' he answered

438

and then, wanting to put all thoughts of Corbeau, the *trivet* and talk of ghosts from his mind and get back to working his ship, as he knew he must, he left them with a hurried goodbye to ponder what he could do next.

27

The Ghost Hunt

Noon Thursday 27 April 1797

By midday on Thursday, Billy had tried everything he could think of to alter the *Parrot's* wayward course. He had even hung Nipper Ogden and Dancer Dyke over the stern transom with a rope tied fast to their ankles to check the rudder was free, but despite he did, his every effort to turn her south towards the Quiberon Peninsula met with failure. And the *Parrot* to his confounded amazement ploughed on and on through ever mounting, foam whipped, white-capped seas towards the storm threatened black of the far horizon. At a loss to know what to do, he had, just fifteen minutes before reluctantly agreed to Tom and Polly's remorselessly pestering plan they should immediately start their ghost hunt. A ghost hunt, too long delayed they both impatiently scolded both him and Sam, as girls do when they think they are right and everyone else is wrong.

The story of which had swept the *Parrot* from stem to stern to so enthrall her tired and bewildered crew into a delicious fright of anticipation, every one of them now stood on her slanting decks or hung in her shrouds to watch the fun begin. The two of them eagerly leading their five, glum faced, lightly armed escorts, Duffy, Dancer, Nipper, Sergeant Finch, and Corporal Penny down the for'ard maindeck hatch to the gun deck below. Watched by their grim faced, restless, Captain and his three disbelieving officers beside the wheelhouse, where Archie Sparrow leant on the still unmoving wheel, his eyes searching the sea for the black ship that still followed them, the only one who did, now a speck on the distant horizon. Though no one was more disbelieving and angry than Midshipman Anstruther, who hated Tom and Polly with a passion, so jealous was he of the Captains friendship and favour. Every other entry way to the decks below guarded by a red coated Marine with a musket and orders to shoot anything that came out, but them.

No sooner had they reached the gun deck and Alfie Brown and Peter Own had dropped the grated hatch cover over them, and a freckle-faced Marine guard, who barely fitted his uniform was placed beside it, then they were hurrying down a second ladder towards the Midshipman's cockpit beneath Billy's day cabin, where Midshipman Anstruther and Midshipman Spears had their cramped, though very cozy sleeping quarters.

'This way,' shouted Tom, hurrying down a third impossibly steep ladder, which in dark as black as night, despite the lantern she held, took them first to the Orlop deck and then to the hold beneath that - the bottom of the *Parrot*. Where their search would properly begin amongst the great barrels of water that were stacked in its cavernous space on two, deck-like shelves that fitted against the curving hull between ribs of wood three feet thick. Enough to carry them to America and back, which now seemed likely, she, groaned, as she climbed to the top of one of the two coke piles that spilled from the two wooden hoppers between the main and foremast into the foul pool of water that filled the hold's centre a foot deep. Despite the noisily sucking, chain driven bilge pumps worked day and night to stop it. Quickly checking they weren't hiding in the damp and smelly dark, *which they weren't*. Polly said, with a certainty no one dared deny, Tom hurried them back the way they had come, reluctantly followed by Duffy, Dancer, Nipper, Sergeant Finch, and Corporal Penny, each with a cocked and loaded pistol held tight in their hand. Though pistol and shot had never killed a ghost to Polly's certain knowledge. Clambering over the soggy wet, rat, mice and cockroach run cables in the Orlop until they found the latch locked door to the chimney wide passageway that

442

climbed a dozen steps to the dripping wet, slime covered locker beneath the Midshipman's cockpit that housed the ropes, greased chains, pulleys, pintles and gudgeons that once turned the rudder to Billy's confident command. The most likely place they both agreed to find their ghosts and even more when they found Joey Warren's clasp knife on the deck. And in preparation for this dramatic climax, Polly had, only the day before, mashed, boiled and fermented a special mix of alcohol, roots, herbs, spices, poo, wee and dried bones, and animal bits, into what can only be described as a thick, green, lumpy, gooey, slimy soup of steaming, frothing, bubbling, burping awfulness. A vile concoction that smelt so bad it choked and gagged everyone aboard the *Parrot* into a fit of helpless coughing until it was cooled. Which took most of yesterday evening, when she dried it in the *Parrots* biggest oven and watched it rise like a soufflé into a football sized, rock-hard lump of something indescribable, Nipper and Dancer, much to their annoyance, pounded into half a sack of soft, fine powder that smoked a smelly, luminous green haze.

'Ready, Tom?' Asked Polly, her face flickering in the dim, yellow glow of the lantern she held above her head.

'Ready,' said Tom, so excited she could hardly

breathe.

'Ready,' said Duffy, in his usual fear-naught sort of way, which did little to reassure Nipper and Dancer, who scrunch faced and gog-eyed with fear behind him, stared at her in silent trepidation, hoping above hope, no ghost of any sort would appear out of the woodwork.

With a nod to Sergeant Finch, who looked back at her with a blazing indignation, she began to hop and skip and flap her arms in a dance-like caper in the narrow locker, Nipper thought was reminiscent of the Morris men he had once seen at a country fair and Dancer, a chicken with its head cut off. And no sooner had she begun, then she began to chant a rhyme in a language none of them understood, though every vowel, consonant, syllable and word of it was perfectly said. As Tom heard they were, who didn't yet know the pretense her common talk was; a pretense that couldn't last. Which echoed in that small wet space so shrill and so loud it seemed to creep beneath their skin and into their bones like a freezing winter cold. Though Duffy, who had sailed into Pembroke Dock only last year, thought it must be Welsh, or at least a strangled version of it, such was the gibberish those short-legged folk talked.[234] And would have said it was, had she not suddenly shrieked a terrifying, throat warbling ululation that made him and

444

everyone else jump near out of their skin in desperate fright and surprise. And when she had, and the locker was a deathly, water dripped, echoing quiet, she reached into the sack of powder and sprinkled a handful onto the puddle wet deck, where it rose in a luminous green mist to fill the half lit dark in a choking smoke, almost too thick to see through. Filling every nook, seam, and cranny in that tight space to the roof and bathing the stout cables and chains that worked the mighty rudder in an acrid, choking pall that oozed through the planking to the decks above. A smelly green smoke that rose into the sky above the *Parrot,* as if she was on fire, a sight Corbeau watched from the *Seahorse* in a thrall of expectant fear and fascination.

'Well?' Demanded Sergeant Finch.

'Shush,' said Polly, touching her index finger to her pouting lips to emphasize the urgency of her firm *command.*

'*Shush?* Did you say *shush,* young lady?' He blurted without answer. 'Did she say *shush,* Corporal Penny? Tell me? Did she tell me to shush?' Spluttered a now beetroot-red Sergeant Finch, near speechless with surprise and outrage she had dared to speak to him in such a disrespectful way. And her no more than an escaped slave, as all the *Parrot* knew she was. But cautioned not to

445

say any more than he had by the dark, forbidding look of menace that now clouded Duffy's face to an ugly, warning sneer.

'She did,' whispered Corporal Penny, taller by half a foot than everyone else. 'She most definitely did say, *shush.* No mistaking it. For certain she said *shush,* Sergeant Finch and I do most humbly apologize, she did.'

'Mmm,' murmured Finch, his manner stern and hostile, but utterly frustrated by Duffy's burly and not to be underestimated, ominously intimidating presence.

'*Shush,*' said Polly, once again, as she cupped her ear and listened intently to the fretful sounds of timbers creaking, ropes squeaking, drips dripping, sea slopping and chains grinding in a thrall of expectation that fixed every eye upon her. '*He's* here. That rascally little rogue of a no-good djinn is, *here,*' she announced, with such a certainty, Nipper, and Dancer, still hiding in a shivering crouch behind Duffy, almost wet themselves with fright. 'LETS BE HAVIN' YOU. YOU VILLAINOUS DJINN.' She commanded, in a loud and imperious voice that rather impressed them all, not least Sergeant Finch, who despite himself, just then felt a cold shiver of dread race down his buckling spine. 'LET'S BE HAVIN' YOU. COME OUT YOU NASTY DJINN BEFORE I GIVES YOU A DOUBLE

DOSE OF THIS 'ERE BOGGY STUFF ENOUGH TO MAKE YOU SICKER THAN A DOG WITH WRIGGLY WORMS.'

As if to answer her threat there came a sudden, howling and snapping sound, like a branch breaking in a thunderous gale, followed by a violent, roaring and rush as the ropes, blocks and chains that held the rudder fast, fell loose and the *Parrot* lurched into the wind like a drunken sailor out for a stroll on legs that wouldn't carry him where he wanted to go. And then, though no one, but Polly saw it, a stream of green smoke slipped beneath the closed door behind them with a soft howl of painful irritation that rattled its hinges.

'SHE ANSWERS THE HELM,' bellowed Archie Sparrow, from the maindeck, as he struggled to hold the *Parrot's* wheel before help arrived. 'WE ARE COMING ABOUT. SHE ANSWERS CAPTAIN.' A welcome call that brought a rousing cheer from her still watching crew, who one by one ran to their stations.

'Get more sail on her, Mister Robinson. Every scrap of canvass you can find, courses, topsails, topgallants, royals, and skysails[235] if she will have them and make your course east by south. Lively now. Rouse yourselves you lazy lubbers,' he laughed, 'we've work to do.' Called a recklessly excited and jubilant Billy with an enthusiasm his crew found infectious.

'Is that it?' Asked a disappointed, bent to the knee Corporal Penny, steadying himself against the locker wall as the *Parrot*, so long drifting help-lessly into the Atlantic Ocean, shuddered and healed on her new course in a booming crash of foam and spray that jinked them all from side to side like dice in a rattling cup.

'No! We ain't got him yet,' said a disappoint-ed Polly. 'He's gone and got away under the door whilst you weren't lookin'. So, we'd best get on our toes and nab him quick before he finds his way back here to work his mischief again on this 'ere rudder,' she pointed to its grinding hinges. 'Cos I'm certain sure he will.'

'I don't know about that, Poll,' answered Duffy, thoughtfully rubbing his chin. 'Seems to me we did what we came down here to do. Though, what it was we did, I can't rightly say? But whatever it was, its done and we'd all best be about our duties before Mister Robinson comes down here looking for us. What do you say, Sergeant Finch, are we finished here?'

'We are, Mister Duff,' answered the Sergeant, touching the brim of his black shako[236] with his porky finger and puffing out his red-coated chest in a blaze of silver buttons so hard, his chalk white cross belts threw a cloud of misty white dust into the air in front of him. 'There's been enough of this 'ere time wasting malarkey chasing after ghosts that I knew was never down here in the first place, so we'd best be off and damn quick about it, if you don't mind me saying, Mister Duff.'

'But we can't go now, Duffy, groaned Tom, with her usual impatience and familiarity. 'We haven't got him. He could be anywhere down here. Isn't that right, Poll?'

'That's right, Mister Tom,' answered Polly, tapping the side of her button nose with her Index finger in a knowing sort of way.

'Maybe?' Said Duffy, cautiously. 'And then, maybe not?

'What do you mean, Andrew Duffy Duff?' Scolded Tom, spoiling for a fight with a boy she knew would never hurt her, not for the world, as girls so often do, having an instinct for that sort of thing, no boy ever does!

'I don't mean anything, Tom,' answered Duffy, lamely, ignoring the iron hard stares of disapproval that creased the faces of Sergeant Finch and Corporal Penny into a pucker of disbelief. Who, knowing his fiercesome, well-earned reputation for discipline, could not for one second understand why he put up with her cheeky, know-it-all ways. 'Only, whatever caused the rudder to foul, and it could have been anything, I grant you that, it's gone and we haven't the time to go searching for a ghost that may or may not be here.

'Hmm,' answered Tom, huffily, eyeing the bruised and battered face of Duffy with a grateful affection she found hard to conceal. 'Well, you can do what you want Mister Andrew Duff, but me and Poll are staying here until we have that bogyman in the bag, as the Captain said we could. Ain't that right Poll? We are?'

'We are, Mister Tom, we ain't goin' nowhere, just yet.'

Seeing there was nothing more he could say or do, Duffy pulled the creaking wooden door open and with a warning grimace that silenced their smirking, questioning faces, ordered Nipper, Dancer, Sergeant Finch, and Corporal Penny to follow him back the way they came.

'What now Poll?' Asked Tom, excitedly when they were once again alone in the Orlop.

'We go after him, Tom, that's what we do.' She answered with a gleeful chuckle. And they did, deck by deck, once again, spreading the green powder throughout the *Parrot* until an hour later they arrived at a tiny storeroom no bigger than a closet that housed the stump of the bowsprit, at the furthest point of the bows.

'He's in there, Tom,' said Polly, in a dry, hoarse whisper.

'Do you think he is?' Asked Tom, who despite her faith in Polly and her extraordinary powers of seeing what wasn't there, had grown daunted and dispirited by their lack of success. Not to mention, achingly cramped and uncomfortable by their journey through the damp and rat infested confines of the *Parrot's* below decks, decks never more than five feet high and very often much less than even that; and oh, so very dark.

'Yes, 'cos he ain't got anywhere else to go, now, Tom or we would have seen him transmogrified by the effluvia into the shape of his past life, him, and his monkey.

'You think?'

'Yes,' she answered, pointing to the small, latch closed door, which barred their way with an outstretched finger, now coloured a vibrant, luminous green by its immersion in a powder now almost gone after their long and so far, luckless search. 'Open it Tom, but very slowly now we don't want him getting away.'

Crawling inside on hands and knees they fixed their yellow flickering lantern to the beam above the massive, iron bound heel of the bowsprit that split the room in two and in the dancing, shadowy gloom of that thin light surveyed the tiny, narrowing to a point, space for the least sign of the ghost, Polly felt certain was there. But it was empty from deck too ceiling, except for the heap of stolen things the ghost had taken and the lengths of coiled rope, paint pots, paint brushes, rolls of canvass, barrels and boxes that had been stored there in a clutter since they left Portsmouth.

'Blast and bloomin' damnation,' cursed Tom, seating herself on an upturned canvas bucket. 'What do we do now?'

'We gives him the last dose of this 'ere powder and wait and see what he does,' answered Polly, who had lost none of her zest for the chase and who was sure she had the ghosts trapped and very nearly in her grasp. Slowly opening the bag, she scattered the last of the powder and watched as its luminous green vapors filled the room to a dusty, choking, misty dark gloom.

'AAAAAH, OUCH, OOOOH, OUCH, AAAAAH, OOOH, ATISHOO, ATISHOOO, AAAAAAAAAAAH, ATISHOOOOOOO, ATISHOOOOOOO, STOP IT. STOP IT NOW YOU EVIL MAD WITCH. STOP IT BEFORE YOU KILLS ME AND PILCHARD MORE DEAD THAN WE ALREADY ARE YOU NASTY TOAD,' screamed an unseen voice, in pain and terror of its *life*.'

'Gracious, it's him. You've got him, Poll,' blurted Tom in disbelief she had. 'He's here. I can hear him squawking like a baby. I really can hear him. Can you hear him, Poll? Can you?' She jabbered her excitement.

'Yes,' she answered, peering into the mist for the least sign of her prey, of which, she had to admit, there wasn't the least trace just then. 'But we ain't quite got him yet. Maybe he needs a bit more of this 'ere stuff to get him in the mood to show his face to us.'

'NOOOO, NOOOOO,' shouted the voice, defiantly from the shadows.

'Oh yes,' whispered Polly, reaching into the bag once again and threatening the unseen presence with a fistful of her lethal concoction as it dripped from her fingers.

'NOOOO, PLEASE, DON'T DO IT, YOU NASTY TURNIP FACED LITTLE RUNT OF A NO-GOOD DONKEY BRAINED WITCH, YOU'RE PULLING ME INSIDE OUT THROUGH ME OWN BACKSIDE.' Shouted the voice, in a strong and, if they cared to admit it, rather pleasant American accent, though it peeled with fright and frustrated anger. 'I'M NOT GOING NOWHERE, 'TILL I GET'S HOME. SO, YOU CAN LUMP IT WITH ALL THE REST OF 'EM.' And with a pitiful sob, the voice began to cry. 'I'm going back home to New York to see me dear old mammy who I miss more than anything in the whole world, that's why

453

I fixed the bloomin' rudder so it wouldn't go no-where else, but where I want it too and you and nobody else ain't going to stop me, not ever, no know how. So, leave me be, why don't you? I just want to go home.'

'Not 'till you, show's yourself you good for nothing, bogyman,' said Polly, firmly, spilling a snuff-sized pinch of the powder onto deck with a tiny gush of smoke.

'AAAH, AAAH, OUCH, OOOH, STOP IT, YOUR HURTING ME AGAIN YOU MEAN LITTLE PIG. I AIN'T NEVER DONE YOU NO HURT YOU FAT DOG.' Shouted the voice, as it slowly materi-alized into the shimmering, wispy shape of tearful, cross-eyed boy with a chattering little monkey sit-ting on his shoulder, no more than two feet in front of their two faces.

'Cor blimey Charlie,' exclaimed Tom, gawping intently, not to say incredulously, at the miserable, waif like creature, bare foot and perfectly dressed as any respectable sailor should be, in blue striped ducks pulled tight at his waist with a twist of string and a brown canvas shirt that hung down to his knees like a skirt, made almost perfectly visible by the layer of smoking green powder that dust-ed him from the top of his mop-haired head to his wriggling dirty toes. Which were blacker than the shoes she wore on her feet. 'Who the Dickens are

you, little man? And where did you come from?'
She asked, more sternly than she intended.

'Lemmy, Miss. Me names Lemmy. Short for
Lemmuel. Lemmuel Peter Sharman to be precise.
Lemmuel Peter after me grand pappy, Lemmuel
Peter Costard, who fought the British in the war
of '75 and got himself killed for his bother and
Sharman after me mum's pappy, because she
liked the name better than Costard, though she
dearly loved me pappy, Cedric. Who, was killed
by the French in the French-Indian war of 1758
in the Adirondack Mountains near Fort Edward,
when she was a baby.' Said the boy, in a garrulous
stutter. Vigorously rubbing the tears from his dark
rimmed, red eyes with his right hand, whilst pulling
his pet monkey onto his chest in a fond and gentle
embrace with the other, which so calmed the little
fellow he instantly fell asleep.' And this 'ere's Pilchard, me bestest friend in the whole wide world,
since Captain Mooney drowned us both to death
when he wrecked the *Wasp* in '95, so Mister Paul
could get the insurance money from her.'

'Mister Paul?' Asked Tom, hardly understanding a word the little fellow said, but fascinated just
the same.

'Yes, Mister Paul. It was him who owned the
Wasp, the ship this mostly was before she was the
Parrot. He lives in New York same as me and Pil-

chard, did and that's where we want to go, if you'll let us, please?' He pleaded, but got no reply. 'He has a big warehouse on the East River and lives like a bloomin' toff off the profits he makes from smugglin' and blackbirdin'.[237] All frills, flounce, frippery, and furbelow, as me mother says, who cleans for him on the Broadway, just down from Corre's new hotel, where his pappy built a big red house after he made his fortune, when he came *back* from the Indian war. It was him, Mister Paul, that is, who told Captain Mooney to run the *Wasp* aground, so he could get his hands on of insurance money. Well that's what I heard Mister Cripps the mate, say, when I was listening at the door when I shouldn't have been. He said he needed the money, Mister Paul that is, to buy another ship, not being quite so rich as he makes himself out to be, though everyone back home thinks he is. But someone saw me with me ear pinned against the keyhole and when it was dark he and Mister Cripps threw me and Pilchard into the sea know- ing we couldn't swim a stroke and all tied up by our hands and feet with rope as well to make dou- ble sure he got us good and dead. Which wasn't legal and proper, now was it *Miss*?'

'WHAT DID YOU SAY?' Shouted Tom, 'DID I HEAR YOU CALL ME, *MISS, A SECOND TIME*? DID I?'

'Oh dear.' said Polly, with a smirk that told Lemmy he was in trouble.

'Yeeees, *Miss.*' answered Lemmy warily. Shocked by her fierce reaction to a truth that he knew only too well and backing himself into a narrow space just below the bowsprit.

'I AIN'T NO *MISS*. YOU MISBEGOTTEN LITTLE RUNT OF A MANGY OLD DOG,' she hollered in a most unladylike fit of uncontrollable rage that threatened to burst her head in two, so fearfully angry was she, now.

'No *Miss.*' Said Lemmy, with an appealing look at Polly that earned him a smile and a wink that told him, more than words could say, she was his friend, even though he knew her to be a witch or a sorceress, like they had up Salem[238] way a hundred years ago, and boiled and killed them all in a big iron pot because they were. For what else could she be? This strange girl with a look so deep and knowing in her coal-black eyes he could barely take his squint eyes off her for a second, who had so easily tricked him from his secret hide like fox out of a hedge and who he dearly hoped would save him from Tom, who looked as if she were about to strangle him with her bare hands.

'How do you know I'm a *girl?*' Asked Tom.

"Cos, you are, Miss. Err, I mean *Mister.*' He apologized, pointing a dirty, nail-bit-to-the-quick, finger at her moth-eaten jumper. 'I saw you sneak aboard just after I scared the *Parrot's* old crew ashore and in such a panic they hardly had time to pack their things and good riddance to them all I say, for being such blubbering cowards. And you were dressed as a girl in a pretty white cotton dress with blue and yellow flowers on it. Iris's and buttercups, I think they were and tied at the waist with a pretty blue ribbon and with slippers on your feet to match and a shawl and a bonnet and your hair all done up so nice in a bun with wisps and pretty curls by your ears. You looked lovely, *Miss*. But then you went and cut it all off into the mess it now Is and dirtied your face with lamp black and soot and got yourself dressed in the slops you found in the cockpit, where they was left, when you heard the Captain come aboard. And hid your clothes in that big old carpet bag you keep hidden in the back of the shot-locker[239] in the hold by the foot of the foremast where no one will find it.'

'I see?' Said Tom, in a whisper, knowing he spoke the truth and wistfully remembering what a lovely dress it was. The last dress her mother bought her before she died from the dressmaker on Lymington High Street and how everyone said how pretty she was.

'Yes,' said Lemmy, seeing the shadow of that awful sadness cross her lovely face, and only he

458

knew how lovely she really was, when she was washed and dressed as a young lady ought to be in her finery. 'I knew you was a girl and that's why I didn't try to scare you when there was just you and the Captain aboard and him so ill with a fever you had to undress him down to his Long Johns[240] to wash him like he was a baby. You are a *girl*, Mister. Aren't you?'

'Of course, I'm a *girl,* you, daft coot.' She whispered in a malevolent hiss of frustration and scrunched her eyes tight to stop her tears. 'But no one else does, except, Poll here, and she's sworn not to tell.'

'Why?' Asked Lemmy, shuffling an inch forward and lifting Pilchard to his shoulder as he did in a sleepy flop.

"Cos I like it that way, you ninny. It's a secret and one I want kept until I'm good and ready to say otherwise, do you understand me, you little green twerp.' She threatened with a frosty scowl that made him edge his way back the way he had come. 'Did you hear what I said? You, cheeky little ape? It's a big secret.'

'I won't tell on you *Mister,'* he promised, a knowing grin creeping across his thin and freckled face. A face that, though utterly care worn, frightened and sad, was a simple, honest, and friendly, face. 'If you don't tell on me and Pilchard, that is?' He cautioned her with a toothy smile. And with that, he reached out his hand in a gesture of friendship she couldn't refuse, though there was nothing to hold, but a wisp of green smoke.

'Agreed,' said Tom and Polly, in a rush of excitement. Amazed and thrilled they had found him and by the friendship, intrigue, and adventure, he now promised.

28

A Dreadful Storm Hatches
A Bold But Tricky Plan

2.00pm Thursday 27 April 1797

As Tom, Polly and Lemmy, agreed their secret bargain with a handshake, a fretful Corbeau, watched the *Parrot* through the spray speckled glass of his telescope from the bow of *Seahorse* and pondered his next move. Which was no longer clear to him, so certain had he been his simple plan to follow her to France and capture her when Billy went ashore to rescue the émigrés would serve him well. 'Mon dieu,' he whispered, at a loss to explain why she was sailing west, ever deeper into the Atlantic Ocean, on a course that was leading her further and further away from the Quiberon Peninsula and because she was, was convinced it was a ruse de guerre, a clever stratagem by her Captain to rid himself of any ship that might be following him - as many did. And fearing it was, had, an hour ago, when he saw the green smoke, ordered Charlie Begg to turn the *Seahorse* towards the French coast, knowing she must soon turn south, or miss her secret rendezvous.

461

'She's turned, as I said she would, Monsieur, clear as day. It was just a trick to shake us off,' said Charlie, with a grin of satisfaction, as he watched the *Parrot* jig and roll on a sea that was beginning to bubble and boil in a fit of temper. 'Course east by south and set fair for the Quiberon, if I'm not mistaken. Shall I bring her about now, Monsieur and find her stern, again?'

'NO,' bellowed Corbeau, more than ever persuaded his adversary was more formidable than he had previously imagined him to be. An adversary with courage and guile to escape from Grub, Dogget and Badger in the Great Morass, to retrieve his stolen papers from the Fountain Inn, under his very nose, and with them, the Count's antique curio, which was surely a mistake, but one he must quickly set right or answer why? And now, stifle the plans of an enemy who thought to follow him to his secret destination with a display of expert seamanship, both Kettle and Begg's thought impossible in one so young and inexperienced and with a flourish of billowing green smoke, which like a sea fog, hid the *Parrot* for a full twenty minutes. 'Stay on your present course, Mister Begg, we'll wait until its dark tonight before we turn behind her. There's no point in rousing Kepple's suspicions more than we have? We'll see her well enough when *Pascal* signals us tonight as we planned he would, should we be parted.' With that, he closed his telescope with a snap and pondered an evening sky and rising swell that seemed, even to his landsman's eye, so much darker and forbidding than it ought to be after so fair a day. And a wind that was beginning to blow in violent gusts about his flapping cloak.

Yes, Corbeau had put one of his own people aboard the *Parrot*, a daring and resourceful French boy, who spoke the most perfectly accented English you could ever hope to hear. An émigré spy like him, who came over with Colonel Tate, whose task it was to retrieve the curio Tom and Polly had stolen from him and, if possible, discover the password that would betray the waiting fugitives to him. Because he knew from Lauder Trompe there was a password that would make Captain Kepple and no one else, known to them.

'Winds freshening from the north, Captain. Looks like we are in for a bit of a blow,' said Sam, with remarkable understatement, as the *Parrot* alarmingly pitched, healed and rolled in a wind suddenly changed from the welcome Channel breeze they had enjoyed these past five days, into something that was fast rising into a storm-tossed gale of truly hazardous proportions. A hurricane.

'You think, Sam?' Answered Billy, with a wry smile that knew he spoke the truth, that tried to ignore the copper coloured sky and the ink-black mantle of low, densely tumbling clouds now darkening the heavens to blackest night all about him and a rising sea that signaled the storm he feared was now only minutes away. 'BATTEN DOWN THE HATCHES, SAM AND GET THE TOPGAL-LANTS AND ROYALS OFF HER.'

'AYE, AYE, CAPTAIN, shouted Sam, whose brass trumpeted command, a moment later sent the topmen of the watch aloft to take in her gallants and royals and whose quick and lively ascent of the rigging was dramatically illuminated in the twisting forks of lightning that dashed from the sky in a mighty boom of thunder. A thunder so loud it clapped the storm was come.

Letting go the side rails for a moment as he struggled into his tarpaulin jacket and sou'wester hat, Billy was almost pitched headlong onto the sea-washed deck by a violent shift in the force and direction of the wind, which heaved the *Parrot* like a toy boat, almost flat on her larboard side. In an instant of heart-thumping dread that made him sick and giddy with fright, he realised the danger they were in: this was no squall to be weathered in an hour or two of frantic effort, but a mighty hurricane - a tempest that might take a week to blow itself out. Or worse, if he lost his nerve, or for a moment failed in his duty, sink, and drown them all. A disaster Lemmy, watching with Tom and Polly from the safety of his day cabin, his face pressed to the transom window, groaned could happen again and without the least bit of land in sight.

Throughout the night and early Friday morning, Billy struggled to keep his little brig afloat in winds the like of which he had never experienced before and in a sea, that battered and pounded her like a twig on a racing mill pond and so many times flattened her side rails almost to the sea, it was a wonder she didn't turn turtle and sink. And with the wind screaming like a banshee[241] in the rigging came the rain, a rain that fell in a breathtaking, face stinging, deluge to soak everyone aboard in a never-ending cascade of icy cold water that soon flowed like a river across her slanted decks to spill from the scuppers in a never-ending waterfall.

Without sleep and tired beyond endurance the *Parrot's*, frightened crew clung to every hand hold they could find to keep them safe. Shrouds, masts, yards, nets and rails and greeted the new day in a daze of apprehension that hoped the storm would soon blow itself out. All of them bearing the cuts and bruises and aching pains of wrenched and twisted muscles, stubbed and grated toes, chaffed and scorched hands and torn and bleeding shins from a night of trial and exertion they never thought to live through.

Others were less lucky, Midshipman Anstruther was badly concussed when a swinging block[242] caught him a glancing blow on the back of his head to leave him dazed. Two others, forecastle boys, fractured a wrist and sprained ankle between them when they slipped and fell on the almost vertically arching deck. Which Trucky, acting the part of surgeon he dearly wanted to be better than the sailor he was, fixed the best he could. Which, was very good, indeed and made all the better by the pint of Blackstrap rum and tincture of laudanum he gave them all. Which helped them to a dreamlike sleep that instantly forgot their pain and fear of death now so close upon them.

During this awful time of dread and despair Tom and Polly and every *idler* aboard the *Parrot - a mild term of abuse given to boys whose duties did not involve sailing her, tradesmen, store men, servants, and the like,* including Sergeant Finch's Marines, took their turn at manning the water pumps and every sort of rope, pulley, or line used to fix, move, or sway her yards and sails. Braces, buntlines, guy's, downhauls, halyards, and sheets, all of which they dragged, hauled, heaved, or otherwise manhandled on the treacherously sloping, surging, foaming, slippery wet deck at Duffy's command. A deck that each time they did, threatened to spill them into a sea they would never get out.

Down below in the rudder locker and unbeknown to anyone, but Tom and Polly, Lemmy and Pilchard, did what they could to steady the rudder as only they knew how and by doing so greatly eased the aching burden felt by Duffy, Archie Sparrow, Dancer, and Nipper as they struggled to control the *Parrot's* wheel and give what direction they could to her heart stopping flight through seas, sixty feet higher than their heads

By midday, the wind began to moderate to little more than a fierce blow and a fleeting glimpse of the sun breaking through the billowing clouds, allowed Billy and Sam to take a measure of their position, which, if they were right, and they were sure they were, saw them driven more than two hundred miles south west of where they wanted to be. A distance they could make good by late Saturday evening, they both agreed. A day late for their first rendezvous that night with the fugitives, but with two nights left to contact them, time yet to complete their mission, if nothing else went amiss, which sadly it soon did.

It happened as the *Parrot* ploughed through calmer seas and much kinder winds later that afternoon, when the fore topgallant mast suddenly broke in two as they turned on a very graceful larboard tack and lurched over the side into the sea in an ear-splitting, splintering crash of broken yards and hopelessly tangled stays and rigging, which fortunately didn't kill or injure anyone, but brought her to a jarring stop. A disaster everyone aboard knew would put precious hours on a journey now fast running out of time.

Later that evening Duffy reported to Billy the repairs he had done, but to his dismay, told him the damage to the fore topgallant mast was far worse than anyone could have known and could not bear the weight of any more sail until a better repair could be made.

'Is there nothing you can do Duffy?' Asked Billy, visibly crushed by this bad news, but still hopeful something, anything, might be done to salvage their vitally important mission, which now seemed perilously close to ruin. 'Surely we could make a jury rig[243] from one of the spars of wood we have in our stores?'

'We've nothing that would do, Captain, least ways that's what the carpenter says and he should know him being apprenticed in the trade these last two years aboard the *Duke*,' answered Duffy, turning his head to greet Sam as he knocked and entered Billy's day cabin.

'Bad news I'm afraid, Sam,' said Billy, trying not

to sound too disappointed as he fixed the point of his brass dividers into the chart he had spread out on his table. 'The fore topgallant mast is sprung[244] beyond repair and Duffy says we've nothing suitable to jury rig a replacement.'

'Yes.' Answered Sam, knowing they would never make their rendezvous now. Not tomorrow night nor even on Sunday night and realising they must limp their return to England for the repairs they desperately needed. A crushing disappointment, but nobody's fault.

For a long moment, Billy studied his precious charts, double-checking the course and distance he had earlier plotted. 'Are the boys fed and rested?' He asked, distractedly, as he sipped a mouthful of cold coffee. 'They must be exhausted, every one of them?'

'Yes,' answered Sam, with a smile, 'and grateful too, by all the noise they're making, you would think we had just rounded the Horn[245] and not the coast of Ushant, though a great distance from where we ought to be.

'They did well. Very well, indeed,' said Duffy, proudly. 'We couldn't have asked more of them if we had wanted to, them being so young and inexperienced and young Tom and Polly worked as hard as any of us and placed themselves in the greatest danger.'

'I know,' sighed Billy, 'but I fear we must ask more of them. Look,' he said, pointing to the chart with his brass divider. 'This is our present position and the course and distance we must travel if we are to make our rendezvous by late Sunday night or early Monday morning, the last opportunity we have to rescue our émigrés, who I fear, may be captured or gone by then.'

'It's a good distance Captain, but with luck and a fair wind we might just make it, though I fear it will be a close-run thing if we do,' said Sam with a confidence Billy smiled to hear, but no more believed than he knew he did. For it truly would be a close-run thing.

But the fair wind they hoped to find never came and throughout that Friday night and well into Saturday morning they chased what little breeze there was. A puff here, a gust there, a hard blow somewhere else, but never enough to take them more than fifty miles closer to where they wanted to be. A spit of land, almost an island, really, barely seven miles long surrounded by the Revolutionary French navy and with cannon enough to sink a fleet of warships if ever they wanted, too. It was a truly arduous struggle and one even Lord Spencer would think worthy of the meagre pay rise he had promised the mutineers, a week ago, but now cautioned he shouldn't by the King. But as the

Parrot's weary crew went to their mid-day meal wondering when their trials would end, Billy, Sam and Duffy sat down to a council of war.

'We cannot possibly make our rendezvous to-night, gentlemen nor even Monday morning if this wind continues to make fools of us, but we can do something that may yet save the day. It's risky. Very risky, indeed, but with a bit of luck we might just pull it off,' said Billy, his confidence grown by the plan he had only lately hatched. 'What I intend is this. You Sam and you Duffy and some of our prime hands will take one of our three boats, the new pinnace I think, and sail for the Quiberon this very instant. You will make better head way than we can and barring any unforeseen mishap, you will arrive in good time to rescue our *friends,* who must fear and wonder where we are with every hour they spend on that lonely shore.*'*

'God, give you joy, Captain, I'll do it and no mistake,' beamed Sam, almost jumping from his stool in excitement. Knowing, as every junior officer in the King's navy did, that this was the sort of thumping, dangerous adventure that would, if he carried it off successfully, and he felt sure he could, bring him to the attention of Lord Bridport and the Admiralty. Attention that might, if he was truly lucky and with Billy's good reference, confirm his appointment as Lieutenant.

'Thank you, Captain,' said Duffy, with a smile of pleasure, little caring there were many dangers, they and their crew must soon face in an open boat, far out at sea.

'You deserve it, Sam and you too, Mister Duff. You both do. More than anyone else aboard,' blurted Billy, wishing it could be him, but knowing his place was with the *Parrot.* Captains being discouraged by Admiralty orders from such bold adventures when others, sadly more expendable than he, could take his place.

Without more ado, he laid out his plan, which would have them pretend to be French fishermen seeking shelter in the calm waters of Quiberon Bay to repair their battered sails and nets after the terrible storm. Avoiding at all costs the mighty Citadel Vauban with its heavy battery of guns on Belle-île,[246] the island fortress six miles south of the southern tip of the Quiberon Peninsula and, equally importantly, any enemy ships that might be anchored there. And if they could, and he was certain they could, sail deep into the bay and wait throughout Sunday until signaled by the fugitives that night. Who would show they waited their escape with a flashing, white light at midnight and every half hour after that, until dawn broke.

'When you see the signal, you will land the pinnace just north of the village of St. Pierre,

472

Quiberon, he pointed to the chart and carry them off without the least delay to meet with us as soon as you possibly can. We will be waiting for you four miles south of the Point de L'Échelle,' here he pointed again at the chart. 'The promontory that marks the southern tip of Belle-île. We will be there early on Monday morning and will wait for you until you come, unless the French navy chase us off. But if they do we will come back when we can and signal our position with a blue and white light hung in our mainmast top, which you will answer with a red and green light. Is that understood?'

'Yes,' answered Sam.

'Yes,' answered Duffy.

'Good, now are there any last questions before you go?'

'No sir,' answered Sam, his tired face beaming a smile that said he was the happiest boy in the King's navy.

'You Duffy?'

'No Captain. You can count on us. We won't let you down. We'll carry them off just as you have planned and without those Frenchies ever knowing we have.'

'I know you will, but there is something else you must know.' Drawing them closer, their faces lit by the candle on the table between them, he whispered the password, Lieutenant Galbraith had given him he said must be exchanged with the fugitives to show *he* was a friend sent by him and no other. But not, he was careful to avoid, the second password the mysterious Lieutenant, whose face he had never seen, except in shadow, had given him on that foggy night in Wish Street and said, with such a ponderous gravity it chilled him to the bone, must be his and his alone to keep.

A silly rigmarole of questions and answers that made no sense to him at all, no matter how often he turned them over in his head, Lieutenant Galbraith said would reveal a secret of the very greatest importance to the British Government and one, which would make him and his crew hostage to the orders one of the fugitives would give him. Orders he must obey without question and to make it certain he did, he gave him an Admiralty Letter signed by Lord Spencer and Mister Evan Nepean. Which gave him full authority to act as he saw fit and to ask what help he needed from any King's officer, even if he was the highest born Admiral or General there was. A letter sealed in waterproof canvas that had never left his pocket. 'You have it fixed clear in your head Sam, Duffy?'

'Yes, Captain, I do. 'When we meet them they will introduce themselves with the words, *'Marquis de la Rouërie* and we will answer, *vive L'ancien Régime,* repeated Sam, in poor, but near passable French. 'But I fear my French, what little I have, is not as good as it should be.'

'It is good enough for what we want Sam, but say no more than that or we will never see you or Mister Duff again. Except when this war is ended and that might be a long while yet.' And with a laugh that urged them both to the door and an adventure that was to begin within the half hour, he said goodbye, little knowing they were already betrayed by an unseen, ruthless enemy, the traitor, Pascal, whoever he was.

As they left, a crouched and cramped figure, hiding in a cupboard beneath his cabin, who had heard every word, including the passwords, smiled a wicked smile. *He would*, he thought, as he found the door and cautiously peeped into the dark and empty passageway, *be the first to volunteer his services to Lieutenant Robinson and Mister Duff on their perilous and certain to be disastrous venture. He would see to that. Oh, yes, indeed, he would make very certain of that.*

29

Malarkey Postelthwaite Poses A Problem, One Ethan, Isaac And Indie Had Too Long Ignored

3.26pm Saturday 21 January, present day

'NO! We shouldn't Facebook her just yet, Indie, we should think this through, first? We can't be sure ....'

'Can't be sure of what?' Interrupted Indie, eagerly turning from her computer screen, already showing her Facebook page, to look at him, her face a gently frowning scold that dared him to say why they shouldn't.

'Malarkey,' he answered, in a chill, unsettling voice, as he sat on the window seat beside her and stared at the leaden sky over the snowcapped roof scape of Kips Bay,[247] which far better than the CBS lunchtime news said heavier snow was on its way that gloomy, Saturday afternoon and perhaps much more of it tomorrow.

'Malarkey?' She gulped, barely able to speak his name, so mad was she with the crazy boy whose life had become so impossibly entwined with their own; a boy born so long ago he must be two-hundred-year dead by now.

'Of course, Malarkey still has your iPhone, Indie' gasped Isaac, his smiling face, a puckered scrunch of concern.

'Yes,' she glowered, 'but what does Malarkey Postelthwaite and my stolen iPhone have to do with us contacting, Adriana, right now?' She asked, the words barely out of her mouth before a sudden trepidation wiped the smile from her face. The thought of that rascal stealing her precious mobile with her Apps and music, still a hurt she couldn't bear, but worse by far her mother everyday asking where it was and growing more suspicious he had stolen it. Which of course he had! A boy she thought was an Albanian actor come to America to play the part of Captain Hook in an Off-Broadway production of Peter Pan. The story they had concocted to explain the flamboyant, cherry red tricorn hat, coat and breeches he wore and the clay pipe he smoked. A boy as gay as Christmas with all the lights and trimmings, she heard her father say, though not unkindly, but as a statement of fact.

'Everything,' answered Ethan reading her mind, 'because Malarkey's vanity, troublesome nature and selfish obstinacy go hand in hand and if Kiya's magic worked half as well as we know it can that last day we saw her in Trinity Church yard, all those months ago, when she sent him back to where he came from, Monday the 5 of June 1797 to be precise, then home he most definitely went, but with your iPhone in his pocket.'

'But why should that be a problem, it can't work there,' said Indie

'Because if we know anything about Malarkey Postelthwaite its three things; first he couldn't keep a secret to save his life, not even to save Captain Kepple's life, who he claimed to like better than anyone he ever knew. Second, he didn't want to go back home to 1797, much preferring stay here with us stretched out on our living room floor everyday eating *Lay's* potato chips and watching the TV or listening to Avril Lavigne, who he adored like no one else, even trying to escape when Kiya said he must, though he never had a chance. And third, I'm absolutely sure the very first thing he did when he walked into the crowded Moorshead Tavern on Broadway, where he said he worked as a pastry chef, the best there was since the great Sylvain Bailly or even Avice, his noble apprentice,' he sniggered, they had heard him say that a hundred times, 'was to tell everyone who cared to listen where he'd been that *afternoon* and what he'd done and seen. Not that anyone would believe him, I'm sure, but might?' He exclaimed, 'if he showed them your Apple iPhone, which might have battery enough to play a tune or two, even there, in 1797. And if they did, it would cause a sensation enough for Montard to hear about it and when he had bribe or force the truth from him, which he easily would.'

'Oh, no,' she sighed.

'Oh, yes,' said Ethan.

'But what would he do then, Montard, I mean?' She asked.

'Come looking for us,' he answered.

'Oh,' she gulped, the thought he might never crossing her mind, until then, might already be here watching them.

'Maybe,' said Isaac, 'but it's more likely he will hack into your Apple Account first and then into your Facebook Account and, if he already has, he could be monitoring both, even as we speak. Hopeful he might hear something that would lead him to the final piece of the Rebus of Akhenaten, the dancing girl. Remember Tom said he, I mean *she,* saw he had eight parts of it assembled when she and Bibi escaped from Eden.[248] So, at some point in the past, our present or future, he has found or stolen every piece of the Rebus she and Billy had, but one, of course. And that *one* may be Elizabeth Caetano's? So, there is no way we should contact Adriana through your Facebook. Nor ours. Or mums or dads for that matter'

'*No,*' said Ethan, peering out of the window to see a man in a dark coat staring up at him, the turned-up collar and woolly hat he wore hiding his face. A coincidence, perhaps, but maybe not, he grimaced, as he hurried on his way, the snow falling in a flurry all about him, his shadow stretched across the lighted street.

'But maybe he hasn't hacked into my accounts, Isaac, not yet anyway, we're only supposing he *might* have.'

'That's right and anyway he wouldn't know how on his own, so he would have to come here, to this present time and pay someone to do it for him and even then, he might not be successful against their security systems, which are near impossible to hack into anyway. So yes, he might not know anything about you, me, Isaac, Apple, or Facebook, but even if he doesn't we must be really careful not to lead a trail he might follow.'

'So, what do we do?' Asked Indie, utterly exasperated, her finger hanging over the key pad of her computer.

'We use Rudy's Facebook, upstairs, but send a coded message only she can understand,' said a gleeful Isaac.

To Be Continued

Brief Historical Notes

The Pharaoh Akhenaten

The Pharaoh Akhenaten (Amenhotep IV) reigned over ancient Egypt for sixteen years, from approximately 1352-1336BCE (Before the Christian Era). From the beginning of his reign Akhenaten made himself the enemy of the Priests of Amun-Ra, whose worship of the many ancient gods and goddesses of Egypt, but mostly their own supreme god, Amun-Ra, he opposed. Believing there was just one God, Aten, the creator, and giver of all life.

In earlier times the god Amun - the hidden one, the local god of Thebes and Ra - the creator sun god, were thought to be separate gods, but under the influence of the priests of Thebes, came in time to be thought of as one and the same, god. A combination that gave them immense power, wealth, and influence over the people of Egypt and the pharaohs who were their kings.

By denying Amun and making Ra, now renamed, Aten, supreme over all other gods, Akhenaten took power for himself. But why did he do this? Why did he attempt to destroy a religion already

481

many thousands of years old? Did he truly believe in the *one* God he named Aten? Many think he did and have even gone so far as to wrongly claim he was, or later became, the biblical prophet Moses? Or was it simply a lust for power and wealth greater than he already had, as is the want of all powerful men and women? Or was he insane? Or was it something else that drove him to war with the priests? Scholars are divided on this issue because after Akhenaten's sudden and yet unexplained *disappearance* in 1336BCE the priests of Amu-Ra with the help of his wife, Nefertiti, and his daughter, Meritaten, did all they could to remove all trace of him and his astonishing reign from the historical record. Not even his burial chamber, if there ever was a burial chamber, has ever been found, and every possible search has been made to find it. So, there is little or no information to guide them in their inquiry.

What is known, though, is that he was married to the beautiful Nefertiti[249] - and she truly was an incomparable beauty, had six daughters the eldest of whom was called, Meritaten and one son, Tutankhaten/Tutankhamun by his second and some say, favourite wife, Kiya. Who also disappeared along with her younger sister, Tefnut soon after his *reported* death, a death that never found a body or any hint of one.

After his disappearance, his son Tutankhaten/Tutankhamun became Pharaoh when aged just eight, but he too disappeared in mysterious circumstances in the midsummer of 1327BCE. Though not before Nefertiti, his hated step-mother died and Meritaten his half-sister was banished from Egypt forever.

History would have it that Tutankhamun's (as we will now call him) mummy was famously and most remarkably found by Howard Carter and Lord Carnarvon in 1922 after a long and difficult search, and in a place, no one suspected it would be, so unlikely was its location. But was it Tutankhamun? The astonishing funeral treasure they found in *his* tomb would certainly suggest it was *him,* but the tomb was almost certainly meant for another; a high-born person of some distinction, but not a Pharaoh. Is the tomb a fake?

What is certain is that during Akhenaten's short and very turbulent reign and certainly for many years after he disappeared, Egypt fell into a state of near anarchy and turmoil bordering on its complete military collapse. But why? Was this just the usual politics of family power and greed? Or is there a greater mystery yet to be unearthed? A mystery, perhaps that gave an ancient, but highly organized, sophisticated, cultured and artistic people the *power* to cut, shape, build and move

483

stones we would find difficult to cut, shape, build and move even today, even with the engines and machines we have at our disposal and could not have done so, even a hundred years ago. Not least the building of the three great pyramids at Giza, which appear to have no purpose other than to point to the sky.

A power that after Akhenaten's disappearance Egypt lost forever, for no work of that great magnitude was ever undertaken again and Egypt's preeminent position in the world was lost forever. It was as if a science and technology, an ancient knowledge, long ago brought to the world by an unknown race of people and known only to an elite, priestly cast for tens of thousands of years, simply vanished overnight, an ancient knowledge that if it were known today would bring the light of peace or the dark of chaos to the world.

The French Revolution, 1789

The cause of the French revolution is too complex for these few notes (though the success of the American Revolution/Rebellion of 1775-1783 was certainly at the heart of it), but one factor amongst many ignited the grumbling discontent of her people: France was bankrupt after years of war with Britain, in Europe and in North America. So-much-so, on Tuesday 14 July 1789, barely six years after the Americans kicked their British 'cousins' - the people of their beginning, out of North America, an enraged Paris mob, thinking they might do the same with their own tyrannical government, stormed the then near empty Bastille prison and began what was soon to be the end of *L'ancien regime.* The ancient regime of King Louise XVI and his court of pompous, self-regarding, greedy, over privileged and all too powerful for their own good, church and aristocracy.

It was a time of revenge, cruelty and truly horrible murder that sent France's European neighbours, not least Britain, who still smarted from her American defeat, into a spasm of fear the like of which would not be felt again on Continental Europe for over a hundred years.[250]

French Revolutionary War, 1792-1802 and Napoleonic War, 1803-1815

It was the execution of Louis XVI on Monday, 21 January, 1793 that signaled in earnest the start of this last war Britain was ever to fight with her longtime adversary, France, though it began in a small way in 1792 when France declared war on Prussia and Austria. Interestingly, it was a belligerent and spoiling for a fight, France who declared war on Britain on the morning of Friday, 1 February 1793 and not the other way around, as is often believed.

The first action between these two great powers took place on Wednesday, 13 March 1793 when HMS *Scourge,* captained by Commander George Brissac, attacked, and captured the very much larger French privateer, *Sans Culottes* off the Scilly Isles with the loss of just one man killed and one man wounded. The first casualties in a war that was to last a long and truly arduous, twenty-two years. Though a short lived if capricious, not to say, nervous truce was signed in 1802[251] that gave back more to France than she deserved.

Given the proximity of France to England – just twenty-one miles separates their nearest ports, Dover, and Calais, it is little wonder that throughout the war scores of French spies, many of them pretending to be royalist sympathizers, émigrés, as they were popularly known, crossed the English Channel in search of news that would bring them victory. Often with smugglers who daily crossed the Channel with their contraband, their criminal activity overlooked by an overburdened navy too busy to stop them. Most, though not all, finding refuge in the many ports and villages on the south coast, not least in Portsmouth – England's busiest naval base throughout the war, and nearby, Lymington, where a regiment of French royalist soldiers and several hundred émigrés made their home.[252]

But not all French spies and rabble rousers crossed the Channel to England, many went to Ireland, where they did all they could to support the Irish to a revolution they hoped would end the years of English, Protestant occupation of their Catholic country.[253]

Indeed, such was France's support for the Irish now, though it very soon fizzled out, they even agreed to invade Ireland in the late December 1796. And would have succeeded had it not been for the dreadful winter storm that battered the shores of Bantry Bay for the best part of a week, sending her army of fifteen thousand highly trained and well-equipped soldiers under the command of General Lazare Hoche, back home to France. An army the British would have been hard pressed to defeat, so hot were the Irish for rebellion back then. A rebellion actively supported by America, which did all she could to connive at a British defeat and continued to do so for the next two hundred years. Not least, allowing, without noticeable dissent, and possible encouragement, many of her citizens to enlist in the French Revolutionary cause, one of whom, Colonel William Tate, an Irishman by birth, but an American by proxy, led the last invasion of Britain on Wednesday, 22 February 1797.[254]

It was a long and truly dreadful war, one that saw hardship and suffering on all sides, but one that also saw the rise of two matchless Generals and one peerless Admiral. The brilliant Duke of Wellington, whose, hard fought campaigns finally brought France to defeat on the battlefield of a rain soaked Waterloo, on Friday 18 June 1815, and General Napoleon Bonaparte. A short limbed, incorrigible brave, bad tempered, Corsican Frenchman with a lust for power and a genius for war. Who, at one time or another, bested most of the European powers with the finest army France has ever known – if not the best navy, which the British had by a mile. A navy that boasted many fine officers and men, but none better than Rear Admiral Lord Nelson, whose astonishing defeat of the French at the Battle of Trafalgar on Monday 21 October 1805 destroyed the French fleet and made Britain's navy master of the seas for the next hundred years. A navy the Americans did much to dismantle after the 1914-1918 war, as they did the Empire she controlled.

But it was a navy quite unlike the navy we know today, a navy in which the Captain of even the smallest vessel afloat was a god-like figure with the power of life and death over his crew. A man set so high above his men he could not be spoken too without first giving his permission, and then, only in the most respectful and demeaning manner. A man who could order his men and boys flogged and caned a dozen times or more - very much more, for the least infraction.

Little wonder throughout the war the navy was so dreadfully short of men and boys it began to kidnap them against their wishes. A vile business known as the *press,* which saw a gang of trusted sailors, known as the *press-gang,* sent ashore by their Captain to kidnap by force any likely man or boy they could find for service that might last for years without end. Though they were never men and boys of rank or profession!

Life in Nelson's Navy

Every ships company was divided into two distinct groups: the quarterdeck officers and the lower deck seamen and they were as different as chalk and cheese. The officers were educated gentlemen from good families, the seamen were *not.*

The lowest rank of officer was a Midshipman and boys as young as eight, though most often aged between twelve and fifteen, could be found aboard a King's ship and would serve a minimum of six years in that rank before sitting their Lieutenant's qualifying exam at eighteen. If they passed this stiff oral exam in front of three Post

Captains they could reasonably hope, but not always expect, to be promoted to the rank of Lieutenant. Many were not and remained Midshipmen for the rest of their lives and hated they did.

But if they were promoted to Lieutenant, and a good many were before they were eighteen - one at least is known to have been promoted when he was just thirteen, the next most important promotion was that of Post Captain a rank equivalent to a full Colonel in the army. Which once achieved ensured he became an Admiral because every Admiral in the navy was selected from the list of Post Captains in the date order they entered the list no matter how incompetent they were. Admiral Nelson for instance, because his uncle was Comptroller of the Navy, was promoted *Post* as it was referred, too at twenty and in turn promoted his adopted son, Josiah Nisbet *Post* at eighteen. This practice was called *jobbing* or *jobbery;* the giving of the best promotions and ships to family and friends.

In contrast, most seamen could never hope to be a commissioned officer, rather the best they could hope for was promotion to Warrant Officer, or Petty Officer, the backbone of any King's ship - as it is to this day. The most senior of these non-commissioned officers was the Master, who was responsible to the Captain for navigation and pilotage of the ship. Next in order of rank was the Boat-swain who was responsible for the sails, rigging, cables, anchors, boats, seamanship, and discipline. Who was followed by the Gunner, who, not surprisingly was responsible for the ships guns, gunpowder, and many muskets. As well as these exemplary seamen, there were a variety of other trades and professions which found employment at sea: pursers, carpenters; shipwrights, sailmakers, armorers, cooks, chaplains, schoolmasters, and surgeons.

Unlike their officers, and save for pursers - who were for the most part, self-employed, penny-pinching rogues of the worst stamp, and cooks, who mostly couldn't cook, these men were promoted on merit, often having served long apprenticeships, though merit without their Captain's patronage wasn't much use to anyone.

As common as it was to see Midshipmen as young as twelve on the quarterdeck, it was equally common to see boys, and sometimes girls, as young as four or five on the lowerdeck, though most were very much older than this and already quite skillful in the work they did. They were for the most part desperately poor, illiterate, orphaned boys, glad of a warm bed and all the food they could eat – and food was plentiful in a King's ship, if so truly awful it was chokingly hard to swallow.

The youngest boys and girls did little more than fetch and carry - nippers and powder-monkey as they were called, but the older boys worked alongside the seaman at their various tasks until they were rated 'Able'. The luckier boys might find work in one of the trades until they were rated carpenter's mate, or sailmakers mate, or armorers mate. Some worked as officers' servants or were recruited into the Marines, which most every ship had, to guard the officers from the men they treated so badly. But none of them ever earned more than four pounds a year. Though all of them worked harder than it is possible to imagine and with a knotted rope, or rattan cane – *starters,* as the Boatswain and his mates, called them, laid across their backs to better see them do it.

The Spithead Mutiny 1797

One of the most startling events to happen during the French Revolutionary War was the Spithead Mutiny of April, 1797. Not the first mutiny the navy had ever known, one of the most famous being the mutiny on the *Bounty* in 1787 when Fletcher Christian a grumbling, self-regarding Manxman of doubtful ability stole Captain William Bligh's ship from under his feet, but very definitely the longest and most serious. So, called because it began at Spithead Roads, the famous fleet anchorage between Portsmouth and the Isle of Wight.

The mutiny officially began on the morning of Sunday 16 April 1797, though it had been simmering for months, when sailors on the eight ships commanded by Admiral Sir Alan Gardner refused his order to weigh anchor and sail the two miles to the second fleet anchorage at Portsmouth, St Helen's Roads, which lies just off the north-east corner of the Isle of Wight. Before the day was done the mutiny had spread to all the other ships in Admiral Lord Bridport's Channel fleet.

The mutiny was for the most part peaceful, but so amazing was it, it brought Lord Spencer (the late princess Diana's great-something grandfather), the First Lord of the Admiralty, and a man noted for his good sense and intelligence, all the way from London to sort it out, which he pretty much did, though it took many a week to persuade the King and Parliament he had.

During this time, hardly a ship left Portsmouth harbor, but Admiral Sir Peter Parker, her Port Admiral, noted in his private journal, seeing a small, 10-gun brig of war, HMS *Parrot* leave the Roads on Saturday, 22 April, sometime in the afternoon. Manned, he claimed, with the good humor he was noted for, by the oddest collection of *midgets* he had ever seen. Bound for goodness knows where, because, he huffed, *no one bothered to tell him what they were doing.*

End Notes

1 The ancient Egyptian calendar divided the year into twelve,
thirty day months (360 days) with an additional five days
of celebration at the end of the year, midsummer eve,
or June 20 as we would know it today, a celebration that
probably ended on June 24. A practice that is perhaps
the reason why many cultures, taking their lead from the
Egyptians, even to this day, celebrate midsummer on
June 24 the end of celebration rather than the beginning.
This of course accounts for 365 days of the year, but not
the extra quarter day it takes for the earth to circle the
sun, which the Egyptians probably allowed for in their cel-
ebrations, periodically adjusting the day it began and the
day it ended, thereby ensuring their three, four months,
seasons; The Season of Flood (June to September), the
Season of Sowing (October to January) and the Season
of Harvest (February to May) were fixed, as their farmers
insisted they were.

2 An immensely powerful priestly cast who were the jealous
guardians of Egypt's ancient wisdom, mystery and magic,
a knowledge they alone knew and fiercely guarded, which
reached back to the very beginning of human history. And
so long forgotten, we little know when it began, but ab-
surdly guess it was between seventy thousand years ago
(when the human brain apparently grew in size and in-
tellectual capacity - though why it did, is unknown, a sort
of genetic fluke it is supposed) and two hundred and fifty
thousand years ago, a guess that cannot be true, though
there is no evidence to prove it is not?

3 Modern day Luxor, which is situated on the east bank of the
River Nile four hundred and fifteen miles from the Mediterranean Sea and three hundred and fifty miles south of

the Giza pyramid and temple complex, which is situated
on the west bank of the Nile near modern day Cairo.
Which was little more than a village in 1336BCE.

4 His name translates to the Living Image of Aten, the one and
only God his father worshipped.

5 Under the influence of the Priests of Amun-Ra his name was
changed to the Living Image of Amun an insult intended
to shame his father whose name was now banished from
the kingdom.

6 An open ended, often heavy necklace made of twisted, rope-
like strands of gold, silver, bronze or iron, known to have
been in use for at least fourteen thousand years. The
ends of the torque were often of an ornate design that
spoke of the status of the wearer or the magic he or she
claimed it possessed.

7 Fifty miles south of Thebes and four hundred miles south
of Giza, as Akhenaten intended she would when he attacked the priests, safe from harm with the hundred loyal
soldiers he left to guard her.

8 It is a matter of historical record that in 1946-1947, Muhammed edh-Dhib and his cousin, Jum'a Muhammed,
both Palestinians, discovered the first of the hidden caves
at Qumran. A plateau and ancient Iron-Age settlement
on the north-west bank of the Dead Sea and found inside, what are now called the Dead Sea Scrolls. A trea-
sure-trove of biblical and historical writings dating from at
least 150BCE-70AD. By 1955 ten more caves had been
found, some large and some small and in one, cave 3, in
1952, a Copper Scroll written in an ancient Hebrew dia-
lect was found, which was substantially different from all
the rest. Not least, because it was thought by scholars to
be a *hard* copy of a now lost papyrus written in 1350BCE.
Though this is an approximation and it may have been

496

written (seems likely it was) after 1336BCE when the Pharaoh Akhenaten disappeared. A papyrus, which, intriguingly gave cryptic directions to sixty-three treasure sites where apparently, many tons of gold, silver and jewels were hidden, none of which have yet been found - perhaps was never intended to be found. Importantly the first word written on the Copper Scroll spells the name Akhenaten, whilst much of the rest is worn with age and corrosion. Given these facts it is not unreasonable to suppose the Templars (but most particularly Serjeant Guyard Montard - who claimed he owned it, an ancestor of the Count de Montard) had in their possession in 1128 a papyrus found in cave 3 or some other cave on or near the Qumran site. The so called, *lost* papyrus, a map or text describing where of the Rebus of Akhenaten was hidden, if not its secret? An added level of ancient security.

9 A small, two masted vessel with sails that are square rigged (side to side) on both her fore and mainmasts, she has no mizzenmast (rear most), but does have a fore-and-aft rigged trysail on her lower mainmast. Her masts and sails describing the type of vessel she is, as they did all sailing vessels of the day, as they do to this present time.

10 Henry Adams was born in 1713 and died aged 92 in 1805.

11 It is not accurate to call all sailing vessels, *ships*, a term that describes sailings vessels with three or more, square rigged masts, though other sails may be rigged, including trysails. It takes an experienced seaman to know the difference, but for convenience vessels/boats of every description are often called, ships.

12 In nautical terms the beam refers to the width at widest part of the vessel and as a rule the wider the beam the more stable in the water she is.

13 The bow is the front end of the vessel and the stern the

497

rear end.

14 A large triangular (or trapezoid-like) sail, rigged fore-and-aft
    (front-to-back), from the mainmast, it's swinging wooden
    boom reaching over the quarterdeck and poopdeck, al-
    most to the stern rails.

15 An ocean going sailing vessel in 1796 was by any standard
    a small miracle of complex engineering, as complex to
    build as any car or airplane is today and with very few,
    basic tools to do it.

16 There were (as there are today) four grades of Admiral in
    the navy of 1796 in the ascending order, Rear Admiral,
    Vice Admiral, Admiral and Admiral of the Fleet. Each
    rank, except Admiral of the Fleet, was then further divided
    by one of three colours know as flag colours in the as-
    cending order Blue, White and Red. So, a Rear Admiral
    of the Red out ranks a Rear Admiral of the White and so
    on. Admiral Crookhampton was a very senior Vice Admi-
    ral of the Red.

17 The great men of the day who ran the navy from their Lon-
    don headquarters in White Hall, it is still there today and
    much as it was.

18 1775-1783.

19 The English were apt to call themselves English at this time
    rather than British, which they mostly still do!

20 Once an Indian footpath, The Bowery or Bowry Lane,
    begins (as it does today) at the southernmost tip of Man-
    hattan Island and meanders to the northern end of the
    island - as it once was, a distance of just twelve and a
    half miles and thereafter, all the way to Canada. It is the
    oldest path/road in modern day New York City. The name
    derives from the Dutch word for farm or farmland (farm
    path), which, in 1797 Manhattan Island mostly was. With

very little habitation beyond New York City, except for farms and cottages, it occupied the southernmost corner of the island barely half a mile wide and perhaps a mile and a half long.

21 New York was occupied by British forces until the end of the war in 1783 and endured frequent attacks by the American Revolutionary forces. This attack was just one of many against the British and loyal Americans and there were as many loyal Americans as there were American's at this time, hence, the not unnatural supposition the war was both a rebellion and a civil war.

22 A Dukedom is the highest rank in the English peerage below the monarch.

23 In 1797 Manhattan Island was an Island bounded on the west by the mighty Hudson River, on the north by the Spuyten Duyvil (Spitting Devil) Creek, a narrow torrent of water now piped underground and no longer visible, on the north east by the Harlem River and on the south east by the East River.

24 At its widest part Manhattan Island is two and a half miles wide and from a high vantage its four connecting rivers were easily visible.

25 A frigate was a fast, three masted, square rigged ship carrying more than twenty-eight guns, but less than forty-four guns on one or possibly two decks. Admiral Nelson called them 'the eyes of the fleet' and every Captain worth his salt longed to command one, such was their speed and agility.

26 Equal in rank to a Warrant Officer, though a self-employed civilian, the Purser oversaw the ship's money (if the Captain allowed it) and supplies, much of which, he himself bought and then sold to the crew in a private, money

making enterprise and always at a very high profit. Pursers were much disliked by everyone and many were rogues of the very worst sort.

27 In 1788 a guinea was a single gold coin worth at least twenty shillings or one pound, but the changing price of gold at this time saw its value rise to as much as thirty shillings or one pound ten shillings in old, pre-1971 decimal money. In 1816, its value was fixed at twenty-one shillings. The term is still used and has a value equal to one pound and five pence.

28 A rank one higher than a Captain, but lower than a Rear Admiral.

29 Much smaller than a Fleet of Ships a squadron would comprise of five, but less than ten ships and would be commanded by a senior Captain, Commodore or Rear Admiral.

30 Diarrhoea.

31 A small single masted vessel rigged fore and aft/front to back like a modern yacht.

32 A natural limestone arch on the Dorset Coast, near Lulworth Cove, a beautiful place to spend the day and little remembered now, if at all, for the bloody skirmish that was fought on the shingle beach and the rolling fields above the village in the autumn of 1796, between the local Militia, the Revenue (Customs) men and the greatly outnumbered, Langstone Owlers. Who, to everyone's surprise mostly got away in their distinctive, red straked schooner, the *Seahorse - an escape that spoke of the connivance of powerful men, who wanted only a few of her crew captured, her captain most of all. W*hich was later sold to Titus Dimple and Captain Bully Drier for a tenth of her price and with no objection from the Crown author-

ities they did, grateful for the information they had given them. Which led to the capture and conviction of her captain, Albert Grub, and his eldest son Clary, who were later hanged for the smugglers they were.

33 It was not an uncommon practice at this time for Admirals to promote their sons and nephews to the rank of Post Captain at a very early age, a rank equivalent to a full army colonel and a rank once got, never taken away.

34 A tall, perhaps one hundred and twenty or fifty feet tall, four sided, narrowly tapering stone monument, pointed at the top like a pyramid. Egyptian obelisks were monolithic structures made from a single piece of quarried stone often weighing many hundreds of tons, so large, modern engineering is unable to explain with any certainty how the ancient Egyptians erected them, except to say they used a wooden pulley or crane of some fantastic size and many tens of thousands of men who had little else to do with their time except erect them. Always cut with hieroglyphs, the ancient writing system of Egypt, they were usually placed in pairs beside the gates of a temple complex or some other notable building structure; a palace, a treasury, or a monument.

35 This sort of visual illusion is called a movement after effect and is very common. To see one stare at a moving object for a little while, a black and white spinning spiral has a very powerful effect, and then quickly turn your eye to look at a blank, neutral surface and you will see it again for some seconds after that.

36 The optical illusion Tom experienced when she looked at the pyramid of Khufu through the Eastern Gate, is thought by many Egyptologists to be the real purpose of the pyramids. To guide the eye of the worshipper towards the full moon, which the Egyptians believed was the left Eye of Horus (his right eye being the sun), the god of light

(and time). The Eye of Horus, Wedjat was thought to be a powerful protection against evil; most particularly the evil of Seth the god of chaos and destruction. Optical illusions (or so it is believed) are now well understood by science to be the distortion of immediate sense perception caused by the brains faulty interpretation of the limited or contradictory visual information it receives. Simply speaking the brain makes a best guess of what little sensory information it has at its disposal. Or, rather more worryingly/ intriguingly, provides only the information it does, reality being a projection of the brain and not the perception of something out there! Not so far-fetched because cognitive science acknowledges our brains/minds contribute to the reality of our perceptions. No one perceives the world exactly like anyone else and the reality we share is a compromise that ignores the difference.

37 An Egyptian hieroglyph shaped like a key with a loop above the T bar, the symbol for eternal life.

38 The invasion of France's Quiberon Peninsula on Brittany's Atlantic coast by French émigrés began on the 23 June 1795 and ended in massacre on the 21 July the same year. It was a tragic mistake and brought great suffering to the people living there.

39 This is probably the Anubis, the god of mummification and the afterlife, who was the protector of the dead.

40 The story of Gabe, his younger sister, Bibi, and brother Raphie and the extraordinary Nanochromes begins in Book Five: The Totem of Tarhuhiawaku, but far from ends there as you will later read in Book Six: The Masters of Time, *the last book in the series.*

41 So named because the evolutionary pressures imposed on their survival after the cataclysmic climate change of 2084 and the axial tilt that followed, produced features

in their *human* bodies that resembled those animals, but though they did, they were still human. Or were they? Read Book Six: The Masters of Time *to find out.*

42 The fossil record suggests, Homo Sapiens (wise man), modern man, first appeared about 200000/250000 years ago and were distinct from apes and other human species at this time. Including Homo Neanderthalensis - Neanderthals as they are commonly called, Homo Erectus, Homo Denisova, Homo Ergaster and Homo Rudolfensis, all of whom became extinct, though the genetic evidence suggests some bred with Homo Sapiens before they did. Their descendants being alive in all of us today.

43 Nanotechnology is the technology/engineering of the infinitely small.

44 Modern day Lebanon, Israel, Syria, and Jordan, but sometimes including parts of southern Turkey and Iraq, a place and people who have forever have been at the very heart of human civilization.

45 Sadly, no longer in print, though a copy might be found. Ceridwen is one of the most beautiful and fascinating women in Welsh legend, a sorceress who had the gift of poetic inspiration (second sight as, indeed, Polly/Tefnut has), whose words spoke of the invisible that everywhere surrounds us from her home beside Llyn Tegid (Bala Lake) in North Wales. See the portrait of her by Christopher Williams in the Glynn Vivian Art Gallery, Swansea.

46 We see things (visible light) because they either absorb or reflect electromagnetic radiation within a narrow portion of the electromagnetic spectrum. For humans, it is a window of 400-700 nanometers, in a spectrum that includes much lower and much higher frequencies of electromagnetic radiation, including X-rays and radio waves. Snakes, for instance can see infra-red light and birds can

see ultra violet light, portions of the electromagnetic spectrum respectively above and below our own visual experience. If a material allows light to pass directly through it - is transparent in the way that glass or water are, or exists, as it were, beyond our visual spectrum, it is said to be invisible to us - there, but unseen. Tom's *magic* light absorbing suit, though science fiction in the present-day, may not be in fifty or a hundred years from now - a possibility already hinted at.

47 Founded in 1127 the Templar Knights were a holy order of crusading knights famed for their fierce courage in battle and known to their enemies by the distinctive white mantle (sleeveless garment) emblazoned with a Red Cross they wore over their armour. The Sword and Shield of Aten - Akhenaten's once famed bodyguard, was reformed anew from the bravest of their numbers just days before the order was almost destroyed in 1307, their sole purpose to protect and serve the Rebus of Akhenaten, the gold plate the Templars had found on the Temple Mount in Jerusalem in 1128. It is the most secret society of the Templars, so secret, few, if any modern-day Templars or scholars know of its existence, its organization and structure or, more importantly, what its oath sworn duty is. A duty revealed in Book Two: The Secret of the Château Tollendal and the authors authorized web site: www. TheSwordAndShieldOfAten.com.

48 A group of Neolithic stones, many thousands of years old, situated in Brittany France, north of Carnac and the Quiberon Peninsula.

49 Read, Book Three: The Battle of the Stones to know more about this minor skirmish, despite Sal thought it was a battle, but one that preceded the Battle at the Château Tollendal, several hours later. A battle the like of which the modern world has never known before, but not the last

battle this valiant group of new found friends would fight
against their hated enemy the Drummers. A battle more
than any other in those violent years of revolution and
war that proved the extraordinary courage and gallantry
of the French soldier, but a battle the French so little talk
about today, least of all the courage of Captain Bauda,
Sergeant Dusere, Gile and Lieutenant of Marine, Robert
Camus whose memory deserve so much more than their
empty silence.

50 Three upright (Neolithic) stones supporting a table like
stone, thought to be a burial chamber.

51 The pharaoh Khafre was the son of Khufu and Menkaure
was possibly his son. The three of them reigned over
Egypt between 2589 – 2503BCE. Some Egyptologist believe the pyramids of Khufu and Khafre were built many
thousands of years before they began their reign and that
they merely named these ancient structures/monuments
for themselves. If this is true who built them and why? A
question answered in Book Six, The Masters of Time.

52 Hurst Castle, three miles west of Lymington on the Bour-
nemouth Road.

53 It is hard to be sure, but it is possible the lights Tom observed were/are 'hot spots' in the earth's electromagnetic/
geomagnetic field, a physical phenomenon generated
by the movement of molten iron alloys at its core. Which,
though entirely invisible to the naked eye, surge many
hundreds of thousands of miles into outer space, where it
interacts with the solar winds, the charged particles ema-
nating from the sun, in ways science little understands. A
field of powerful magnetic energy that constitute the magnetic north pole we are so familiar with. It is also possible
the prismatic effect of the dust and sand on the outside
of her visor, combined with the damp of her warm breath
on the inside, is the reason she saw what she saw. That it

was an illusion!

54 It is noteworthy that the earth's geomagnetic field has changed dramatically over time and is certainly not the same now as it was in 1335BCE, nor sixty million before then when dinosaurs roamed the earth. A physical phenomenon that if lost or significantly changed, for whatever reason, would destroy the earth's atmosphere and all life within it completely. As the loss of Mar's once powerful electromagnetic field destroyed its once, *fertile,* life giving atmosphere. Something the ancient Egyptians perhaps knew, as it seems likely they did, as did many ancient people around the world - their kinsmen, as many believe they are. In Britain, France, North America, and South America, to name, but four of the many places their descendants came and built their impossible to believe megalithic, stone-age structure with their primitive tools and apparently primitive knowledge of physics. At Stonehenge, Carnac, Manhattan Island and at Nheengatu in the Amazon Jungle. Many of which circle the earth in a hard to measure, but discernable pattern, often in the line of sight of significant stars and formations.

55 In Book Five: The Totem of Tarhuhiawaku, this highly complex process is described in simple, but staggering detail.

56 A coarse, hard wearing country cloth made of cotton and linen.

57 David Collumbell was a famous London gunsmith at this time and his pistols can still be bought.

58 This amazing seven feet tall, withered stump of a time polished, two branched tree turned to petrified stone was once an everyday feature of Pennington Marshes and stood beside the salt pans until it was lost in a storm in 1838. The last visible remnants of the tropical forest that once grew there and so much did it look like

a scarecrow it was called the Scarecrow Tree by all who knew it. A sight many to this day claim to see when the moon is bright on the Marsh. A ghost tree that speaks of hard times to come to those who do, but hard times to be avoided if they do a good turn to the first person they meet on their way home. Man, woman, or child and with the words, three times repeated: *thanks, be to you we met this ghostly nigh by Pennington Marsh.*

59 Pennington was famous then for its donkeys, which roamed the marsh, beach, common and fields often coming into the town.

60 Amongst other things the Court of Chancery dealt with claims and disputes involving money and property and was notorious for its painfully slow, deliberation and exorbitant costs, which could swallow a disputed property whole, leaving nothing for anyone. Better not to go to court than have the lawyers take all your money and lose anyway, something Titus only too well knew and Mrs Dimple feared would surely happen.

61 A schooner is a fast and highly maneuverable vessel perfect for smuggling and piracy in the English Channel and might have two or three masts. Generally, her fore, main, and mizzen sails are always rigged fore-and-aft and her fore topmasts are square- rigged, for maneuverability and stability. To be precise this would be called a topsail schooner, allowing other variants of sail pattern to apply as in a Fore-and-aft schooner or a Staysail schooner.

62 Strakes are the horizontal planks fixed to the outside frame of the hull of a vessel from the keel up and from bow to stern and are either fixed end to end (carvel built), which gives the hull a smooth appearance, or are overlapping from top to bottom (clinker built). In the case of the *Seahorse*, her top strake is painted red.

63 The bowsprit is the round wooden spar that projects from a ships prow to give anchoring stability to the foremast stays, the standing rigging that prevents the foremast from falling backwards and with the added benefit other (jib and stay) sails may be fixed.

64 A yard is the horizontal or diagonal wooden spar(s) on a mast from which the sails are fixed.

65 A fore and aft, triangular sail, which is set at an angle to the mast, sometimes called a Latin sail because it has been popular since Roman times.

66 Thwarts are wooden seats fixed across the two sides of a small boat her rowers, paddlers or sailors sit upon, wooden plank-like structures that also provide an added side to side support.

67 British military cannon of the day used Colonel Albert Borgard's 1716 ordinance system of describing a cannons size by the weight of the cannon ball it fired. A four pounder being the smallest cannon in service with a barrel diameter of just 3.05 inches, which was just big enough to fit a cannon ball the size of cricket ball in and certainly not big enough to dent the sides of the *Potosi, but big enough to kill a score of men and more if loaded with grape shot.* The largest cannon in service were forty-two pounders with barrels 6.68 inches in diameter, big enough to knock the *Potosi* to a splintered ruin if the pirates had them.

68 Mouth of the cannon.

69 The side to side, inward narrowing of the beam of the topside of a ship's hull and upper decks relative to the maximum beam of the hull.

70 The left (or port) side of a vessel.

71 The taut ropes like tapering ladders, which fix the mainmast, the topmast, and the topgallant mast - the three
   main parts of the mast to the sides.

72 The upper deck forward of the foremast often called the
   fo'c'sle.

73 A mass of small round iron balls packed tight into a canvas
   bag and fired from a cannon with terrible effect on the
   timber and men it hit, much like a giant shotgun which
   spreads its pellet in an arc.

74 The raised deck at the stern of the *Cherub,* which, like the
   Parrot forms the roof the Captain's day and night cabins
   below. The ideal place to jump unseen onto the *Potosi,*
   where the fighting was probably less fierce and with easy
   access to the cabins below.

75 A ship's Purser was a private position which required an
   investment of several hundred pounds to buy the stores
   and supplies he would later sell at an inflated profit to the
   sailors, who were often long in his debt.

76 A deliberately rough patterned silk.

77 A small wig much like the wigs a modern-day barrister
   would wear, with three rolled curls above each ear to say
   how expensive it was.

78 Singapore as it is known today.

79 Speaking as a young lady born in 1785 it's not surprising,
   Tom talks of her waking, sleeping and dreaming mind,
   when perhaps she means her conscious and unconscious mind, which since Sigmund Freud (1856-1939),
   the famous psychoanalyst, has come to play such an
   important part in the understanding of *mind,* a still as yet
   largely unexplained phenomena of brain activity.

80 The feast day of Saint Michael, Gabriel and Raphael, the
    Archangels, which is celebrated on the 29 of September,
    a Holy Day of Obligation in the Catholic Church back in
    the Middle Ages, which was why Montard was obliged
    to have a bath. In many public schools and universities,
    even today, the Christmas term beginning in September
    is called the Michaelmas Term.

81 The word sarcophagus (plural sarcophagi) comes from the
    Greek word 'sarx' meaning flesh and 'phagein' meaning
    eating. It is a stone coffin stored above ground the meta-
    phorically eats the flesh of a corpse - a flesh eating stone
    recepatacle.

82 A ceiling supported by an arch or, more usually, by several
    arches of complex design, with a keystone at the apex
    holding it in place.

83 Chartres Cathedral was built between 1193 and 1250 and
    is situated in the town of the same name, fifty miles south
    west of Paris. Like all great churches, Chartres exerts
    an emotional force on those who visit and worship there,
    little wonder those with a darker purpose make use of this
    same force for their own evil ends.

84 The last mass of the day in the Catholic Church and be-
    cause it was, it was near midnight when Montard climbed
    down those secret stairs to find his evil destiny.

85 This fabulous stone paved labyrinth was finished in 1205
    and is well worth a visit.

86 Many churches at this time were built on ancient sites of
    pagan worship.

87 The First Crusade began in 1096 and finished in 1099, this
    was followed by the Second Crusade in 1147-1149, the
    Third Crusade, 1189-1192, the Fourth Crusade, 1202-
    1204 and so on until at least the Ninth Crusade, 1271-

1272, though many historians list a great many others.

88 A five pointed star, usually symmetrical in shape, but some-
    times not, as when one of the points is extended beyond
    the others.

89 A pentagram surrounded by a circle or circles.

90 A Typhonic Beast in ancient Egyptian culture is part man
    and part animal, usually depicted with an animal head
    and man's body. The head of Seth or Set has a long curv-
    ing snout like an anteater and has flattened horns like a
    giraffe and a body, often seated, that may be a dog or
    fox, but in truth resembles no known animal.

91 An enneagon or nonagon is a nine sided, regular polygon,
    in which all the angles are equal (140 degrees) and all
    sides are equal.

92 Denbigh is a beautiful market town in Denbighshire, North
    Wales, but in 1307 this small fortress town on a hill was
    in the hands of the English and would be known by the
    French as an English holding.

93 The destruction of the Templar Knights by King Philip IV of
    France is widely believed to have begun on Friday 13,
    1307.

94 Blood stones are naturally occurring, notably hard silica,
    shot through with a variety of coloured minerals, which
    give them a speckled pattern/appearance - red, orange,
    white and black being quite common. The natural or pol-
    ished shape and patterning of a stone will raise or reduc-
    es its value, the more meaningful or unusual the pattern
    the more valuable it is to the wearer, who will pride its
    beauty and its magic power. The stone given to Montard
    by Sahura is a particularly unique spelling as it does the
    name of Seth in hieroglyph and is a type of blood stone
    called a heliotrope, a green, translucent stone with blood

like inclusions, which are both startling and lovely to see.

95 It was indeed the custom of the navy of the day to auction the belongings of a sailor or Marine killed in battle, or who died at sea and send the money made home to their wives and families.

96 St James Park.

97 Once adjacent to Downing Street, but now long gone and built upon by the Foreign & Commonwealth Office.

98 A Benedictine monastery founded in 1590, which overlooks the harbour from its hilltop position.

99 Perhaps the oldest cafe in France and still there to this day.

100 France's oldest theatre company.

101 Molière (1622-1673) is one of France's most revered dramatists.

102 *The Imaginary Invalid* is a satire on Paris doctors.

103 A popular and very simple method of making a quilt pattern look far more complex than it is, which sews nine equal squares of patterned, floral, striped or plain fabric into one big square, which is then quartered and rearranged, to form a new pattern - the disappearing nine patch, so to speak. This process is then repeated several times over to make the size of the quilt required.

104 Candid Camera was a hit American TV series that began in 1947 and finished in 2004, which played practical jokes on unsuspecting people, whilst they were filmed by a hidden camera and was much copied and shown around the world.

105 She is referring to the Cottingley Fairies a series of five photographs first published in *The Strand Magazine* in

1920, but taken in 1917 by Elsie Wright and Frances Griffiths. In 1997, it was the subject of a film called, Fairy Tale: A True Story. If they were pictorial cut outs from a magazine or book, as they appeared to be, they were never recognised, as such and fooled a great many experts!

106 A relatively small two masted sailing vessel with main and mizzen masts which are rigged with sails fore and aft and with a jib sail, fore staysail, and a mizzen topsail to give her a turn of speed.

107 A flat roofed, funeral house made of mud bricks or stone.

108 An intensely blue, extremely valuable, semi-precious stone which has been worn as jewelry since Neolithic times, the earliest pieces, which have found in burials being twelve thousand years old.

109 The exact location of the Land of Punt, is not known with any degree of accuracy, but is thought to be to the south east of Egypt on the coast of the Red Sea in what is modern day Sudan, Eritrea, Ethiopia, Djibouti, Somalia, the Horn of Africa and even the southern Arabian Peninsula. Places steeped in ancient mystery, lore, and wisdom the world has chosen to forget.

110 A two-cornered hat fashioned front and back to form a half-round, fan shape.

111 The rag bag of second hand clothes every ship of the day clothed its sailors in.

112 Baggy shorts that were made from very hard wearing and uncomfortable sail or duck-canvas, usually the hem fell to just below the knee.

113 Very hard wearing cotton originally made in Nanking, China.

114 Pinchbeck is an alloy of copper and zinc that gives the appearance of being silver.

115 A wide, deep brimmed straw hat often painted by sailors with tar.

116 The senior officer who made sure every ship was manned and provisioned ready for sea.

117 The Transport Office was situated in the Naval dockyard and is still there to this day, but long before the royal navy had an intelligence service to boast about, the house in Wish Street was the secret headquarters of a group of naval officers dedicated to the overthrow of the French Revolutionary government. Many of them active in their secret inquiries in Paris where Britain had many highly-placed agents until the war ended. Intriguingly, many, including Lieutenant Galbraith, were also member of The Sword and Shield of Aten, a membership that is open to this day to those with a brave, good, and honest heart.

118 Very strong ale, beer, or barley wine, in this case a strong barley wine.

119 Water leaked or drained into the bottom of a vessel, which becomes very smelly over time.

120 The raised deck just behind the mainmast and forward and beneath the poopdeck always considered the Captains private space.

121 Any hole in the side of a ship which allows the passage of a cable/hawse, sometimes called a cat-hole.

122 The mainmast is the tallest by ten feet of the *Parrot's* two masts and is positioned forward of the quarterdeck. The side to side moving boom of the trysail passing over the quarterdeck and the poopdeck and with a two feet clearance above the wheelhouse.

123 The foremast is forward of the mainmast and between these are two large, foot high, black wooden grill covered hatchways, which allow the entry of her stores and just forward of these, is her capstan. The machine, which lowers and raises her anchors. Above the hatches and capstan, fixed in a square wooden frame are stored the *Parrot's* two small sailing/rowing boats.

124 A ships rowing boat, though it might be rigged with mast and sail.

125 A cheap, if very effective, standard issue, naval sword most often worn by lower-deck seamen.

126 An affectionate though sometimes derogatory term/name for a Midshipman, the most junior ships officer and in Nelson's navy often a very young boy of twelve, though many incompetent or passed over for promotion. Midshipman were as old as fifty or sixty!

127 From the bows to stern the *Parrot* had four upper decks; the poopdeck, the highest of all her decks at the stern, beneath which was Billy's day cabin. This was accessed by two, six step wooden ladders one on either side of the quarterdeck, which was also a raised deck and on which stood a small, canvas covered wheelhouse. Billy would enter his cabin from the quarterdeck. The quarterdeck is the most important deck on any ship and sailors on duty there are always well turned out in their uniform and respectful of its status. Below the quarterdeck, where Billy now stood, came the maindeck, which was flush to the forecastle deck at the bow. A three-step ladder, two on each side of the maindeck gave access to the quarterdeck and the forecastle respectively. The two hatchways led down to the *Parrot's* lower decks.

128 Bags and personal belongings often tied up in a canvas sack.

129 The second largest class of battle ship the navy possessed at that time.

130 The term Admirals', Captains' or some other officers' duty conveys they were sent under orders that must be obeyed.

131 A nautical mile is 2026.66 yards and is longer than a standard mile, which measures 1760 yards. A cable length is one tenth of a nautical mile or 206.66 yards.

132 Bow to stern.

133 Behind, towards, or nearer the stern.

134 Fifty yards.

135 Ratlines are ropes fastened horizontally between the shrouds to give them their ladder-like appearance.

136 A three quarter, double-breasted, navy blue, worsted jacket.

137 Royal Marines.

138 Euclid (323-283BCE) was a Greek mathematician whose book, Elements, a book of mathematics/geometry, is one of the most important books ever written and as such taught to this day. Any educated young man of the time would have known this work well.

139 Plato (424-348BCE) is thought by many scholars to be the greatest philosopher ever to have lived, but perhaps Socrates (469-399BCE) his teacher and friend deserves the same accolade, he was certainly more interesting than his pupil. Again, the teaching of Socrates and Plato alongside many other Greek philosophers would have been a standard for privileged boys of the day, like Midshipman Anstruther and should be taught today.

140 A violin made by the incomparable Stradivari family some-time between 1680 and 1725, thought to be the finest violins ever made. In 1797, this was perhaps a not too expensive violin to own, but in 2012 it would be a fabulously expensive violin to own, worth many millions of pounds.

141 The Master, a senior Warrant Officer, was responsible, after the Captain, for the ships navigation.

142 The Fountain Inn was by tradition the haunt of Admirals and Post Captains and certainly not Midshipman like Kettle, despite his dead uncle was a very senior Admiral.

143 Essentially, someone who has emigrated, but in the context of the French Revolution, a political refugee.

144 A three cornered hat, with the back and two sides rolled to a curve to form a triangular shape.

145 A word thought to mean a person, no longer of any consequence, from the French, 'ne compte plus.'

146 Diorite is an extremely hard igneous stone, which is impossible to carve into complex shapes - as the ancient Egyptian's so often did, without the tools and machinery to do so. Minimally, turning lathes, saws and drills, Egyptologists have yet to discover anywhere in Egypt or the ancient world. But even more intriguing than their intricate carving was the ability of the ancient Egyptians to produce a satin smooth finish that in modern times can only be achieved by the application of precise, laser-like heat or powerful ultrasound?

147 Small statues carved in the shape of people and animals the deceased person knew in life, family members and pets, but more often servants and officials who would care for them in the afterlife.

148 This hymn/poem can still be seen today inscribed on the

west wall of the rock cut tomb of the courtier Ay at Amarna, Egypt.

149 Wedjat, the Eye of Horus, spoken and/or displayed is the only a guard against the power of Seth, or so the ancient Egyptians believed it was, as many people still do. There are several spellings of this word in common usage and none appear better than another.

150 Various names for the god Horus whose help she called.

151 Dashing young men of wealth and fashion, poor Lauder would never be.

152 A very old fashioned in 1797, Colonial, tricorn hat with a jug-like spout at the front.

153 Once a village on the outskirts of London where soldiers were shot and men, women and sometimes children hanged, it is very near Marble Arch.

154 Oliver Cromwell (1599-1658) was the General who led the Parliamentary forces - the Roundheads in the English Civil War (1642-1651). A man of fierce, unbending reputation, much like Admiral Kettle's dog.

155 London's first professional police force which began life in 1749 and finished its duty one hundred years later in 1849, though it caught only known or named criminals and never investigated crime as the police do today.

156 Full to overflowing.

157 The Greek goddess of retribution, who strikes down all those whose vanity speaks ill against the gods.

158 An old term of abuse that describes a man betrayed by his wife for another woman, as the cuckoo betrays the bird whose nest it lays its egg in.

159 The guarded entrance to a naval or military establishment, in this instance the steps to a small boat berth, but not much guarded by anyone in 1797.

160 The Warrant Officer responsible for the maintenance of everything fixed and/or moving onboard the *Parrot*, including her stores, anchors, cordage (ropes), sails, rigging and, most importantly, working aloft in all kinds of weather.

161 Now a very expensive residential and commercial development, including bars, cinemas, and leisure entertainment facilities, so grand, neither Billy nor any of Nelson's men would recognise it.

162 Now Kings Road, Southsea and the house that was the home to both the naval secret service and The Sword and Shield of Aten is still there, though greatly changed and ignored by all who pass it.

163 An old naval term meaning a seaman has deserted his post.

164 The daughter of Ra and goddess of harmony, truth, justice and morality.

165 The war fought between the major European powers, though primarily Britain and France, from 1756 to1763, which became entwined with the French Indian War in North America from 1754 to 1763. Read Book Four: The Children of the Ankh, particularly the Historical Notes, to learn more about this making of modern day America.

166 Wainscot is the insulating/decorative wood paneling used to cover a wall. In the Fountain Inn in 1797 and for a century before, the wainscot paneled the vestibule entrance to the high ceiling, as it did the several spacious rooms inside. A gleaming polished oak that was very attractive to the naval officer's eye. By the late eighteenth century, the

style was changing and it was the fashion to panel walls in wood to the mid-point, and never more than three and a half feet high, where a circling Dado rail would separate it from the painted or papered wall above.

167 The heavyweight boxing champion of the fleet and first heavyweight champion of the world, in 1810 – though he cheated

168 Toilets used every day by eight hundred men.

169 A stout wooden pin, twelve to eighteen inches long and an inch to an inch and a half thick used by seamen to secure ropes or lines to the sides of a vessel. Heavy, rounded and shaped with a handle and a shank it could be a deadly weapon in a fight and was often used as a cudgel.

170 A quarter of an old, pre-decimal penny, there is no coin that is its equivalent today.

171 Bedlam or the Bethlem Hospital was the first mad house (as it was called then) to be opened in London, England. A priory in 1247 that was well known in later years for allowing Sunday visitors to purchase a ticket to see and laugh at the mad men and women who were incarcerated in chains and filth there.

172 Customs officers who rode the coast roads looking for Owlers/smugglers.

173 The bottom of the sea and a euphemism for drowning and the grave it becomes for those who do.

174 A thin mattress, so called because it was generally stuffed with straw and the French word for straw is paille.

175 As with many sailing vessels of the day, but most particularly because Mister Adams made the *Parrot* from the sunken wreck of the *Wasp*, it had both a small night cabin

for Captain Kepple to sleep in and a very much larger, full width day cabin behind it where he could work during and with the luxury of a glazed transom window that overlooked the stern. A cabin, which extended beyond the stern post (the upright post that rises from her keel that is the *Parrot's* true structural end and on which her ton of rudder is bolted) by ten feet making it bigger by far than any other cabin. Bigger than the officer's wardroom forward of it with its six, kennel-like cabins and living space of fitted cupboards, benches, and wooden dining table.

176 To this day every day at sea begins at 12pm and is thereafter divided into five, four hour watches and two, two hour watches - the so-called dog watches from 16.00-18.00 and 18.00 – 20.00, the ships bell, usually hung on the quarterdeck sounding every half hour, night, and day.

177 A mixture of rum and water.

178 By which he meant they would demote or dismiss him from the navy.

179 A sea anchorage in the upper Thames estuary, just north of the Isle of Sheppey

180 Shorten or reduce the area of sail exposed to the wind.

181 Shoes, like Dutch clogs.

182 Napoleon Bonaparte (1769-1821), perhaps the Greatest French General who ever lived and Emperor of the French from 1804 until 1815, when he was defeated, but only just, at the Battle of Waterloo.

183 Thomas Tompion was born in 1639 in Northill Bedfordshire and died in 1713 and made the best watches and clocks then, brilliantly engineered timepieces that were the envy of the world and so very expensive, Billy could not have hoped to buy one until he was a very senior

officer.

184 The three Fates are Clotho, Lachesis and Atropos, the
     daughters of Zeus and Themis the goddess of divine
     order, law, justice and custom. Life is woven by Clotho,
     measured in its length by Lachesis and cut to shape
     (ended) by Atropos, who decides the manner of our
     death. It is the belief of many even in this day the Fates
     preordain all our lives and that there is no escaping the
     life they have chosen for us, we have perhaps chosen
     with them, but must make it better by the good we do to
     others. That despite who we are, or who we think we are,
     to do good to others is a choice we can all make at no
     cost to ourselves - our happiness, our health, our dignity,
     or our wealth. But the best good of all is to do good to our
     children, our own most particularly, but others, too, who
     deserve our every care, concern and sacrifice and whose
     better life leads to the betterment of us all, but most im-
     portantly to the betterment of our reincarnated immortal
     and divine soul, which is our Fate. Read Book Five: The
     Totem of Tarhuhiawaku and Gabe's description of how
     the development of the Nanochromes, as an advanced
     part machine, human species revealed a truth long de-
     nied by modern man/woman; the soul is the essence of
     our humanity. Our reason for being!

185 It was many months later that Britain learned that Colo-
     nel Tate was acting under the direct orders of General
     Hoche, his landing at Fishguard in South Wales with
     weapons and uniforms he had captured at the Battle of
     the Quiberon in 1795, being a clever diversion that hoped
     his attack on Ireland would be ignored long enough for
     him to find and arm the Irish rebels he had come to help.

186 Kiya's accidental discovery of the wand in the cylinder
     of her sceptre is truly amazing, as you will later read it
     is. Because, her finding it there, at that precise moment

522

in 1335BCE, a year after her husband, the Pharaoh
Akhenaten gave it to her, was, not only the beginning
of her *physical* journey into the future, a journey she
wasn't supposed to make without her sister Tefnut's,
second wand to help and guide her to her husband, but
an impossible conundrum. One that begs the question,
can a thing (the wand in this instance) be in one of two,
three or more places at one and the same time - as it
seems likely it was? Was both in the cylinder and not in
the cylinder, when, Tom *returned* it from the Land of Nogoback, where Kiya, in a fit of jealous temper, left it - as
you will later read she does? A conundrum reminiscent
of the thought experiment done by a famous physicist
in 1935 called Schrödinger (1887-1961), who tried to
make sense of what is called the *measurement problem*
in quantum physics, which suggests that at the infinitely
tiny, subatomic level, things (particles) are only observed
when someone tries to measure them. Call them to their
conscious *mind, as it were,* and are literally in a state of
being and not being, until they are. Which implies subatomic space is a space quite different from the physical,
Newtonian universe we know, though the two must be
intimately connected in some yet unknown way, the one
giving birth to the other. In Book Two: The Secret of The
Château Tollendal and Book Four: The Children of the
Ankh, Ethan, Isaac, and Indie discuss the problem of time
travel, particularly the problem of temporal paradox, the
problem of people or things returning to some past time
to meet themselves/itself, something that can't logically
happen, if they share the same linear time-dimensional
space. But perhaps can happen if space and time are not
what we think they are, but something else; something
imagined? Note, Kiya several times dreams the future
before she physically enters it, hinting her unconscious,
dreaming mind experiences time - past, present and
future, as her conscious, apparently rational mind, does

not. Are unconsciousness and subatomic space one and the same thing and our physical being, no more than a transient wisp, an ethereal present?

187 The Apis bull was the most sacred animal in Egypt and was believed to protect both the living and the dead from harm.

188 An upright spitting cobra fashioned in gold the mark of an Egyptian royal.

189 There are a total of six cataracts in the Nile, areas of shallow water, rocky inlets, small waterfalls, and white water rapid that impede the flow of the Nile from north to south for all but the smallest boats. The sixth, an area of shallows and rapids, is just north of modern day Khartoum in Sudan, where the Blue Nile and the White Nile converge from the north and south to form the Nile.

190 Isis, purest of all women, friend of the downtrodden who restored her husband and brother Osiris, god of the underworld to life after he was killed and mutilated by his evil, older brother, Seth.

191 Floating shops often owned and sailed by women.

192 Larger than the gig and other small rowing boat the *Parrot* stowed in a cradle on her maindeck a pinnace could carry ten or twelve boys in a rough sea and with a mast and sail to speed her along.

193 A nasty disease caused by not having enough vitamin C in your diet.

194 The distinguished family of Staffordshire potters whose brand is probably one of the most distinctive in the world as beautiful today as Josiah Wedgwood II made them in 1797.

195 Thirty-two pints or eight quarts of milk in the old Imperial Measure.

196 Two hundred and twenty-four pounds or one tenth of a ton (2240lbs) in the old Imperial Measure.

197 A small, semicircular platform of wood or iron built on the trestle-trees at the head of the lower mast and gives spread to the topmast rigging and forms a handy work place.

198 The highest order of chivalry or knighthood given by the Queen, founded in 1348, it is, after a peerage, the Victoria Cross and the George Cross, the pinnacle of Britain's honor system.

199 The navy wouldn't have proper uniform for another sixty years.

200 The poor in 1797 were five inches smaller than the middle and upper classes and this remained so until the 1950's, when universal welfare began to exert its effect. So, malnourished and lacking in vitamins and minerals were they, their health was poor and their life expectancy greatly reduced and their lack of vitamin D caused Rickets, a disease of the bone that bowed their legs.

201 The ancestral home of the Spencer family since the 1500's in Northamptonshire.

202 A low bed mounted on trucks or wheels, which could be rolled under another bed to save space.

203 Hampshire.

204 A Shaman is a priest, magician, soothsayer, medicine man and sometime Chief of an aboriginal tribe. A very powerful man or woman, whose claim is to communicate with the spirit world asking the help of the souls of their

ancestors departed and the gods who reside there, in times of need. It is a powerful and ancient system of belief that stretches back to the dawn of time that absolutely *knows* the world we live in, the physical world we know, is merely a human world, one that is, but a heartbeat away from the spirit world we must all one-day return, too.

205 Lief Ericson, navigator, explorer, and heroic Viking Chief was probably born in Iceland around 970 and is thought to have travelled to North America sometime between 1000 and 1004, the first European and the first Christian ever to do so, landing it is now believed in present-day Canada, either in Newfoundland or at some other place on the St Lawrence River. There is no firm evidence he ever travelled further into America than this, but there is anecdotal evidence he did and left a vast treasure in the Adirondack Mountains, a treasure horde that was the spoils of a lifetime of pillage in Europe and North Africa, as far as the River Nile, which he supposedly sailed as far as Thebes. A treasure he left under the guard of Tostig and his spearmen until his return. But return he never did and the men he left behind were either killed or became part of the great Iroquois Nation of Indians. Perhaps the greatest Indian Nation ever to live in North America, friends of the British in war and in peace, but never the French or the Americans who defeated them and stole their sacred lands, which is most of New York State.

206 A mullion is a vertical support that divides several windows from each other, whilst also giving support to the lintel or frame above it, very popular from Elizabethan times (Elizabeth I, 1533-1603) when great quantities of expensive glass were used in very large window systems.

207 A suspended seat at the back of a horse drawn carriage or coach on which a servant or footman sat, or at the front where the driver sat, also called a rumble seat.

208 A naturally occurring chemical element with a great many legitimate uses, which, in past times was used both as a medicine and a poison and one quite hard to detect until modern times.

209 One of London's famous Inns of Court, the professional association for barristers throughout England and Wales, the other three, which occupy the same substantial London site are: The Middle Temple, The Inner Temple and Gray's Inn. A fabulous place for a visit, you hardly believe you are in London.

210 A small island at the south-western end of the English Channel, which marks the north-westerly tip of France, a landmark every sailor knows almost as well as England's, Lizard Peninsula, which is its opposite shore, 150 miles away.

211 Factory ships.

212 A term used to describe all those boys not employed in sailing duties; cooks, sail makers, carpenters, Marines, etc.

213 The *Parrot* could hoist eighteen sails, five of which were on each of her two masts in the bottom to top order: foresail/forecourse and mainsail/maincourse, fore lower topsail, and main lower topsail, fore upper topsail, and main upper top sail, fore topgallant, and main topgallant, fore royal, and main royal.

214 To suddenly lose the wind from your sails and come to an abrupt, often violent stop.

215 The Lizard Peninsula in Cornwall, England a truly beautiful and evocative place.

216 Billy's use of the term fishing smack is not altogether proper if he believes these quite small, cutter-rigged

coastal fishing vessels were off to the Grand Banks of Newfoundland. An Atlantic crossing too far for them to sail with so little room for water and stores. But he perhaps uses the term as a catch-all for fishing vessels in general, many of which did fish the Grand Banks for cod or the Atlantic bluefin tuna

217 A flat board of inch thick, wood shaped on one side to a quarter circle, six inches in radius and held by a line at each corner. The shape of the log and the lead weight attached to its bottom acted as a drag, holding it partially submerged and stationary as the vessel sailed on.

218 The lowest deck on the *Parrot* where her wet anchor cables are stored.

219 Bones, teeth and tusks of whales and walruses etched into complex patterns and drawings and much prized by sailors as amulets and talisman they wore about their necks, as Montard wore his.

220 Sphagnum moss, which he no doubt picked from the Great Morass, last Thursday, which is a mild antiseptic, something his dear old dad probably told him, because few doctors used it back then.

221 A block of soft sandstone about the size of a house brick used for cleaning the wooden decks.

222 The *Parrot's* two masts, her fore and mainmasts were made of three parts - imagine three pencils tied in an overlapping, step-like way near their ends to give the finished structure great strength. The lowermast, which passes through her decks to rest on her mighty keel being the thickest, strongest, and most secure of the three, the topmast above this and the topgallant mast above this middle part, being slightly smaller. Each mast is fixed to the one above with iron hoops strong enough to with-

stand the enormous pull of her sails in the wildest wind.

223 Built in 1717 this famous school (now part of Chester University) is still there to this day standing next to the canal, the Northgate Bridge, and the city walls, which provide an excellent view of its architecture and back yard, where Billy and his many school friends played.

224 Euclid was so renowned his work is still a powerful influence today, but it is a two-dimensional mathematics of straight lines in a multidimensional universe, bent out of shape and as such perhaps, too much influences the mathematics we use to understand it?

225 The first jigsaw puzzle was invented by John Spilsbury, a London map maker and engraver in 1760. Called dissections they were sold as an aid to children's education. With the invention of the treadle-saw and later the jigsaw they took on their familiar shape and quite naturally, became known as jigsaw puzzles.

226 St Werburgh's Street as it is today.

227 Hinge bolts, which allow the rudder to turn, left and right. The pintles or massive pins are firmly attached to the rudder, which then fit through the metal gudgeons, attached to the stern post.

228 Flotsam is the floating wreckage of a ship or its cargo.

229 Jetsam is a part of a ship or its cargo *deliberately* put into the sea; jettisoned, as it were.

230 The abolition of slavery in the British Empire came into law in 1833, but was only applied to all her territories in 1843 and not in the United States of America until 1865. It is claimed by some there are more slaves in the world today than ever before – surely the worst indignity a man, woman or child could ever endure!

231 Pemba Island is one of the largest in the Zanzibar Archipelago, often referred to as the Spice Islands.

232 Doctor's or surgeon's assistant.

233 An upright wooden wall or partition built abeam (side-to-side/right angle to her keel) to prevent the *Parrot* flooding from bow to stern if she was holed beneath the waterline.

234 The language of poets, bards and saints as any Welshman/woman would tell him, but he was an English boy born and knew no better than to mock what he couldn't understand!

235 The royals and skysails are hoisted above the fore and mainmast topgallant sails in that order, though it is odd he called for skysails which are rarely used and tricky to hoist with a crew so inexperienced.

236 A top-hat with a curved brim and a distinctive red and white plume at the side.

237 The coercion, trickery, and kidnap of people into slavery.

238 The Salem Witch trials of 1692, which killed several people, but not one boiled in an iron pot.

239 A large bin-like lockers, usually stored in the hold where its weight will add to the stability of the vessel, where the several tons of cannon balls, musket and pistol shot she will need in a fight are safely kept.

240 Underwear with long sleeves and legs, once very fashionable.

241 A fairy spirit of Irish mythology, who wails when someone is about to die, perhaps deriving in part from the Fates of Greek legend.

242 A wooden pulley, much used aboard sailing ships.

243 A temporary mast.

244 Broken.

245 Cape Horn is the southernmost tip of South America, a fearfully dangerous sea.

246 In English, Beautiful Island.

247 The Ratzer map of 1766-67 and the Thomas Kitchin map of 1778 show that Kips Bay in modern day New York was once called Kep's Bay, perhaps a misspelling. It is now the upmarket, densely populated medical district on Manhattan's, East Side, but was once acres of rolling farm land, ponds, dykes, ditches, and streams. But in ancient times the low hill above Kips Bay was the site of an ancient stone circle in design much like Stonehenge in Wiltshire. Which connected in a chain of stone circles across North America, from New York city to the present site of Los Angeles.

248 Read Book Five: The Totem of Tarhuhiawaku to know more about this extraordinary discovery, news Tom is desperate to tell Billy in the hope he might somehow prevent what has already happened.

249 A bust of Nefertiti can be seen in the Altes Museum in Berlin, though photographs of her have been endlessly reproduced.

250 A reference to the Great War of 1914-1918, perhaps the cruelest and most cynical war ever fought.

251 The Treaty of Amiens was signed on Thursday, 25 March 1802 and was formally ended by the British fourteen months later, on Wednesday, 18 May 1803, much to Napoleon Bonaparte's pleasure.

252 Many of these soldiers and émigrés died during the hero-

ic, but ill-fated English invasion of the Quiberon Peninsula in July 1795. See the short Historical Notes in The Rebus and the *Parrot,* Book Three: The Battle of the Stones, for a little more detail of this tragic, ill judged, mistake on the part of the British.

253 Paradoxically, whilst many Irish men and women hated Britain and supported the French throughout the war, thousands served with courage and distinction in her army and navy, as they would for many more years to come.

254 Much is made of the modern day Anglo American alliance, but in truth, France and Spain are America's oldest allies.

Made in United States
Orlando, FL
09 October 2023

37727966R10293